DECEPTION AT THE DIAMOND D RANCH

Greg "G.R." Stahl

— A Cade Rigens Mystery —

DECEPTION AT THE DIAMOND D RANCH

G.R. Stahl

coffeetownpress

Kenmore, WA

coffeetownpress

A Coffeetown Press book published by Epicenter Press

Epicenter Press
6524 NE 181st St.
Suite 2
Kenmore, WA 98028

For more information go to:
www.Camelpress.com
www.Coffeetownpress.com
www.Epicenterpress.com
www.grstahl.com

Cover design by Scott Book
Design by Melissa Vail Coffman

ISBN: 978-1-94207-850-0 (Trade Paper)
ISBN: 978-1-94207-851-7 (eBook)

Printed in the United States of America

For Wendy,
I'll go to the Grand Canyon with you anytime.

— PART I —

*"There are beginnings and endings in the mountains, where folds
layer one upon another, concealing mysteries tucked inside. Each
crease is a beginning, and each crease is an end. They're dawns and
dusks, and they're folds within us as much as without, places where
questions and answers mingle as one."*

—Miles Fourney's journal

ONE

*Boise, Idaho
Tuesday, July 28, 2015*

CADE RIGENS WASN'T SURE WHEN HE LOST HIS FAITH. Now he wore a bullet-proof vest and crouched behind a dumpster where it smelled like urine.

The man next to him was draped in a black tactical uniform with knee pads, vest, harness and helmet. A side arm was strapped to his leg. The man raised into a crouch and looked up and down the alley, then talked into a hand-held radio.

"Get into position and go on my mark."

Cade thought back through his decades of circuitous self-discovery. Sometimes he wondered if he'd ever had faith at all. Then again, he wasn't even sure he knew how to define the term. Science was a kind of faith, after all, and he believed in that. He believed in photosynthesis, plate tectonics and erosion, all complicated concepts that explained near-invisible processes. Wasn't it the same with God, he thought.

The police officer patted Cade on the shoulder. "Just stay out of the way."

Cade nodded, and the man waved to a team of five more officers across the alley. They crouched together, Cade the only one not dressed in a police uniform, instead wearing jeans and a light-blue button-up beneath his vest.

"There are three militants," the man explained. "The other team will enter from the front and go to the ground floor. We'll go in the back and head for the fronton in the basement. We do not know their positions or intent."

He lifted the radio to his lips.

"On my mark. Three, two, one . . ."

When he said go, there was a flurry of shuffling boots as the team barged through the alley door. Their weapons drawn, they descended a short flight of steps to a high-ceilinged room with hardwood floors, red-painted lines on the walls and large glass panes. It was a sporting surface that looked similar to a racquetball court, but the room was full of chairs lined in a grid and facing a stage and podium on one end. Behind the podium, high on the wall, were two flags: one American, the other the red background and crisscrossed green and white stripes of the Basque flag. A banner near the floor read, "2015 Jaialdi Pilota Invitational, Boise, Idaho."

"Clear!" said one of the officers, loud enough to hear but soft enough not to carry throughout the building. The others followed suit.

The lead officer motioned for two of his teammates to move toward a doorway in the back of the room. "We've got to clear the whole level," he said.

Cade stood back as the officers moved in unison to cover each other and shuffle through the doorway. Cade followed, but the final officer held up his hand, the motion for the entire team to still. Cade heard a door click somewhere within the building's labyrinth of halls and offices. The team went through a door labeled GIZONEZKOEN KOMUNA. Cade didn't know how to read or speak the Basque language, but he knew it was the men's locker room. He followed and found the officers crouched behind a tile knee-wall, making motions to one another in an apparent effort to develop a plan without producing sounds. Cade lifted his head to peer further into the room. On the other side near a line of white porcelain vanity sinks was a woman in blue jeans, long-sleeve shirt and sunglasses crouched and fiddling with wires on a small box—exactly as he'd asked her to do. He felt his pulse quicken. The only way they could succeed was if everyone walked out alive. He reached for the lead officer's shoulder, but the man had already stood, his sidearm drawn and aimed at the woman.

"Put your hands behind your back and lay flat on the floor. Do not test us!"

The woman paused, her head cocked their direction, then slid her arms behind her back as instructed. For a moment it seemed like the confrontation would be over before it began. Then, instead of laying down, she sprang with the dexterity and muscle memory of a sprinter. She disappeared at the end of the room through another door.

The lead officer cursed, and all four of the men in uniform gave pursuit. Cade began to follow, but before he could get to the closing door heard the sharp cracks of firing weapons.

He pushed the door open and passed into a long hallway with a concrete floor and cinderblock walls, an enclosed space illuminated by the harsh flicker of emergency lighting.

"Clear the building. Go, go." The officers ran the length of the hallway and disappeared around a corner, leaving a prone body on the concrete. Cade heard their footsteps ebb further into the building. He was alone, his eyes cinched with frustration. She'd done exactly as he'd asked. The problem was, they weren't supposed to shoot her. Above all, they were supposed to avoid casualties. He went to the prone figure.

"You can get up," he said.

A moment passed, and he heard her breathe deep before rolling over to reveal red and yellow blotches on her chest, stains left by the police team's paintball guns.

"That shit hurts," she sighed.

"I only want to guess about that."

"You can take my word for it. It hurts."

"Thanks for playing the role," he said. "You did a good job."

"I'd say you're welcome, but I wouldn't mean it."

Cade motioned for her to join him, and they went to the ground level where two more bodies were sprawled across the floor.

"That's it, exercise off!" Cade said, his voice edgy and elevated. "You're the cops here, so don't let me tell you how to do your jobs, but there are to be no casualties. Is that clear? No casualties!"

The two men who'd been laying on the ground rolled over. Like the woman from the lower level, they were covered in colorful stains from the police team's training weapons.

Cade went to the officer in charge, the man who'd asked him to stay out of the way in the alley. "We need a debrief," he said. "Right now. Everyone in the basement in fifteen minutes."

The fronton smelled antiseptic like a school gymnasium, but it wasn't an educational institution. It was a place where three generations of Basque Americans played a game dating to the sixteenth century. They'd brought the game, pelota, with them when they immigrated to the American West around the turn of the twentieth century, and at one time the fronton on which they now gathered was thought to be the largest indoor sporting surface in the Pacific Northwest. It was also a large open area suitable for a variety of gatherings.

Cade went to the front of the room and cleared his throat. The din from the gathered police ebbed a little, and he cleared his throat again. The room fell silent.

"Thanks for the exercise today," he said. "You did a good job, but I think we're still mismanaging the threat. It's been a year since the last visible public land standoff, and things are escalating across the West. These political actors may have faded from public view, but the movement that spawned them is boiling. Government and law enforcement officials need to understand what motivates these people because we haven't seen the last of seemingly average folks demonstrating antigovernment rage with violence. If something goes wrong here this week, we don't want to reproduce the events of Waco or Ruby Ridge. I'm afraid that's where things were leading this afternoon."

Cade scanned the room to confirm he had their attention.

"I'm not a police officer, just a bureaucrat whose job it is to put together a public hearing this Saturday as safely and effectively as possible. But in case any of you have forgotten, this fringe movement has been festering for three decades and has experienced recent growth. It was born out of the Sagebrush Rebellion and county supremacy movements of the '80s. Its sympathizers embrace theories about a nefarious New World Order, a socialist, gun-grabbing federal government and the evils of law enforcement. In the last couple years, the number of antigovernment Patriot groups swelled from about a hundred and fifty to more than a thousand. They've been emboldened for a bunch of reasons, but make no mistake: when the Bureau of Land Management backed off at gunpoint last year, these men and women experienced an injection of self-righteousness. I know you'll do what needs to be done, but if you injure or kill anyone, you'll make a Martyr of them. I'll stand aside in a minute and let the real police take it from here. First, though, are there any questions?"

An officer seated near the middle of the room raised his hand. Cade pointed and nodded.

"We're planning a security detail for a government public hearing. Why would a patriot attack a federal proceeding?"

Cade took a breath, realizing how far they were from a solid understanding of what could happen in a worst-case scenario.

"Look, you can get online and read about it in your spare time, but these guys view themselves in some sort of Hamiltonian light—liberating the people from an oppressive homeland—or, in this case, an oppressive Washington, D.C. Let me be clear: these are highly-militarized groups with ideological motivations that often result in illegal actions. This kind of domestic extremism is like a religious war for some of these people, and it threatens to tear the fabric of our nation apart. There's solid intelligence that groups sympathetic to their cause may take action leading up to or during our public hearing this Saturday. We need to be ready. Any more questions?"

Nobody moved.

"Thanks for your attention. I'll turn it over to your commander, who'll run through more scenarios and plan for tomorrow's exercises."

Cade stepped aside, and the lead officer took his place. Cade had requested that local police handle the security, but now he wondered if that was a mistake. Federal law enforcement, as bad as they'd been at managing the rural uprising in the West, had more experience dealing with the nuanced threat. The commander at the podium began his lecture by talking about the dangers of close-quarter combat and snap shooting.

Cade made his way to the side of the room where Amaia Ibarra, the paintball-stained cop he'd talked with in the hallway, leaned on one foot, the other tucked under her butt and pressed to the wall.

"You think the tension about this park is that serious?" Ibarra asked. "You don't think you're overblowing things just a bit?"

"I don't know," Cade replied. "Federal officials still don't know what to do about these guys. Too much of a heavy hand risks tragedy, but allowing them to flout the law at gunpoint isn't the answer, either."

"Training police is only part of it."

Cade lifted a brow.

"They've been emboldened by politicians and pundits trolling for votes and ratings. Some of the politicians treat these guys like heroes. That's only gonna bring out more people like them. A big part of the solution—maybe most of it—is political. Maybe there's no need for anybody to be shot with paintballs."

It was a clear jab, and Cade felt it. Before he could open his mouth to argue or apologize, she turned and went up the stairs.

Cade sighed, folded his arms across his chest and listened. The police commander introduced the next scenario they'd use to prepare, this time focusing on the public hearing's outdoor venue. The sporting surface where they were now gathered would only be used in case of bad weather.

"We'll get together for the next exercise tomorrow morning," he concluded. "Before we adjourn, though, I want to take a moment to bow our heads in prayer."

He looked at Cade. "Would you do the honors?"

There were no mirrors in the room, but Cade was sure his disgust showed plain. Prayer wouldn't help these wet-behind-the-ears local police. It wouldn't make them better shots, give them better judgement or endow them with an understanding of the tensions between the new and old West. What they needed was determination and perseverance, not trumped-up hope in some on-again, off-again divine power.

"Do what you need to make yourselves comfortable," Cade said and turned into the stairway to go.

TWO

Americans and Basque flags drooped from streetlight poles that lined a concrete sidewalk embossed with symbols, words and poems from a different continent. The poles were interspersed with honey locust trees that would turn gold in another month, transforming Boise's Basque Block into a kaleidoscope of color and culture. The street's buildings were one and two stories tall, at least half of them made of brick, and they housed a variety of epicurean eateries with culturally-rich fare.

Cade walked the shady side of the street, watching the embossed symbols and poems pass beneath his shoes. A song portrayed in the old Basque language, Euskara, caught his eye. The artistic rendering included a musical staff and notes, and below it was an English translation:

"The tree of Guernica is blessed. It is much-loved among Basque people. Blossom and spread your fruit to the world. We honor you, sacred tree."

Not far away, in front of a well-preserved brick house, was a medium-sized oak, a descendant from a tree planted in the Basque town of Guernica in the fourteenth century. The tree of old was a sacred place where Basques from throughout Northern Spain gathered for town meetings. Each time it died, it was replaced with one of its own descendants. One of those had survived the 1937 bombing that claimed as many as thirteen hundred civilians during the Spanish Civil War, an event famously portrayed in one of Pablo Picasso's most well-known works. Now here it was, a branch on that lineage firmly rooted in the middle of an isolated city in the Western United States. Like the Guernica Tree of old, Boise's oak was a focal point for community events and gatherings. If the weather cooperated, it's where they'd hold the public hearing about the new national park in a few days, an event that had been carefully choreographed to occur in the midst of an international Basque celebration that was held only twice a decade.

Cade heard a hollow thump and followed the noise to the white picket fence that divided the street from the historic property. He discovered Officer Ibarra beneath the Guernica tree's deep shade. Her back toward him, she was erect and tense. With a flutter of her feet, she raised her right arm in a backward sweep, allowed it to drop and release a small wooden ball. Cade heard the familiar thump again when the ball knocked into a wooden backstop at the end of the dirt court.

She didn't acknowledge Cade as he entered the yard and stood in the shade alongside her. She grabbed another ball, took a running start and swung her arm again. The ball rolled fast, knocking one wooden pin into another.

"I didn't understand much about my heritage when I was a girl," Ibarra began without looking, but confirming she'd seen Cade arrive. "My dad built a bola jokoa court like this in the back yard of our house across town. We used to play when he got home from work. It was just part of growing up. It's weird now, watching this process to designate a national park. Being Basque is just who I am. It never occurred to me to seek recognition for it, but I really want the park to succeed, to help my ancestors get some credit for their contributions across the West. I don't understand why anybody would be against that."

Cade squinted toward the city's central buildings where a sky crane was silhouetted against the blue. New commercial buildings were sprouting like cheatgrass in the spring, and the city was gentrifying fast.

"I don't think anybody's against Basques," Cade said. "It's the U.S. government they're upset with. In the American West, the agencies that manage public land are visible targets. It's an old fight that doesn't have much to do with you, me or the Basque people."

She walked the dirt strip between two parallel concrete walls and erected the three pins, then returned with the wooden balls she'd tossed. The activity was a form of bowling, another game Basques brought with them when they immigrated to the West.

"Do you think the government deserves some of the heat they're getting?" she asked.

"Not really," Cade said, a little more abruptly than he'd intended. "We're just trying to protect the natural resources that make this part of the world unique. It's too bad that rubs some people wrong."

"Cause and effect," she said. "For every action there's an equal and opposite reaction. According to Sir Isaac Newton that's a scientific law. I'd say the government probably deserves some credit for making the situation what it is."

Cade folded his arms across his chest. "You're right about one thing. We're dealing with people who don't respect laws."

She squared her shoulders and looked straight at him.

"That's my point. You represent the government and express the kind of black-and-white attitude that starts fights."

Cade cinched his arms tighter, then shook his head to let it go, but she pressed.

"You're a bull in a china shop, Cade. You think you can just say, 'that's the law, and that's how it is, and all these people are off their rockers?' I hope Miles Fourney didn't take your attitude with him into the mountains."

"You're crossing the line," he said.

"Am I? You think you can send a kid into a divided rural America wearing a Park Service uniform and expect the region's conflicts to part like the Red Sea before Moses?"

"It wasn't like that, and you know it."

"All I know is the kid's gone, the case is closed, and you seem to be getting on with your life just fine."

Cade felt his teeth grind, and his hands balled into fists.

"Listen here, Amaia. I was jumping out of planes into smoke-filled forests when you were nothing but a twinkle in your mother's eye. I've saved dozens of homes from burning into ash, and probably a few lives, too. I've seen attitudes about our national forests and national parks go from pride to disdain and back again. You may not lecture me about right and wrong, and you sure as hell can't tell me Miles Fourney's disappearance was my fault. That kid knew the stakes when he took the job."

Ibarra put her hands in the air and backed away.

"Why don't I give you a few minutes," she said and stepped toward the front gate. "We still on for lunch?"

He waved a dismissive arm and went toward the back of the property where a small brick building housed his office on the first floor and a small apartment on the second.

The screen door slapped against its frame, and Cade entered a dimly-lit room where half a dozen maps were thumbtacked to wavy lathe-and-plaster walls. They showed the geography and topography of southern Idaho and northern Nevada. Across the top of each were the words "Legends of the Basques National Park."

Once comfortable in his office chair in the back room, he took a breath and tried to let it go. He wouldn't have said it aloud, but Ibarra wasn't wrong. There was a new edge to him, a sharpness that worked in certainties rather than understanding. Where once he saw the nuance of a sunset, he now saw night or day. Why hadn't he just gone with the flow and offered some superficial prayer when the police commander had asked him to? It didn't matter who he prayed to. He could offer his whims to the Universe, the Governor, or the God-damned feral cats in the alley if he wanted. But he couldn't let go of that part of himself that only embraced what could be proved or disproved. He ran his fingers through his silvering hair and breathed deep, allowing his thoughts for just a moment to drift back to the way things used to be.

He fumbled at the top drawer of his desk and took out a yellowing envelope. When he turned it on end, two items slid onto his palm: a small picture and a piece of jewelry. He held the photo near his lap, far from his eyes as if restraining something that could jump up and bite, but angled it so he could see the story it told. It showed a wildland fire fighting crew dressed in green and yellow fire retardant gear standing in front of a plane. He was near the center, his arms around two of them. She was on the far end, jaw clenched with determination, his little girl all grown up and ready to jump out of planes like her old man. He sighed hard and returned the photo to its envelope.

The other item was a gold chain with a pendant shaped like a Pulaski, the axe-like tool firefighters wield to chop down trees and dig fire breaks. He rarely wore it anymore, but it was a keepsake that grounded him when he did. He fastened the clasp and tucked it inside his shirt.

THREE

THE FOG OF HIS DARK-OF-NIGHT DREAMS evaporated in tatters and tears as Cade heard sounds coming from the office on the first floor below— the squeak of an antique doorknob turning, heels clicking on hardwood floors, an old wood step creaking as it bowed under load.

Either unwilling or unable to tell dream from reality, he rolled back into the warm cocoon of his blankets.

Another floorboard creaked, pulling him abruptly and completely into the cold darkness. He sat stiffly upright and strained his ears without looking. The city's soft glow fell through two skylights onto the hardwood floor. The ceiling angled down to low vertical walls with wavy-paned windows that allowed a little more of the city's scattered light to creep across the floor's hundred-and-twenty-year-old wood grain. Shadows concealed the room's dark corners and the top of the stairs only twenty feet away.

He heard it again—the creak from another old board succumbing to the weight of a planted foot—the soft in-and-out hush of light breaths working through the home's ringing silence.

An incredible swell coursed his veins. He sprang with a guttural tone toward the top of the stairs where he slung a battery of profanity into the darkness, unaware of the nature or severity of the threat. He had only instinct to work with, and that supplied him with almost complete aggression.

"Hold it," came a voice from the shadows.

He stood dumbfounded, his blind charge broken. The door at the bottom of the stairs creaked open. He retreated behind the wall that divided his bedroom from the stairway. It sounded like something a police officer would say; had he heard it right? Someone telling him to "hold it," or did he miss something? "Hold it or I'll shoot?" Why would the police be there unannounced? It wasn't Amaia; he'd have recognized her voice, and she wouldn't let herself into Cade's apartment like that. Maybe it was something more dangerous. Were the local Basques angry about the park?

He looked around for anything he might use to defend himself—just shelves of books and a chair in the corner next to a lamp. Slung over the back of the chair were the green slacks and gray shirt of his Park Service uniform, the gold background and black lettering of his name badge glistening in the skylights' orange glow.

He didn't have anywhere to go, and the notion of retreat didn't occur to him. Keeping his body away from the open air near the top of the stairs, he reached an arm inside the stairwell and flipped a switch. The hot glare from an uncovered bulb bent around the corner and blinded him, but it would blind the intruder as well.

He peeked into the stairs and saw with only a glance a wiry figure whose face was concealed by the brim of a big cowboy hat. One of the man's hands gripped the railing, the other dangled empty by his side. If he had a gun he wasn't ready to use it.

The ranger's instinctive raw aggression resumed, and he launched into a barrage of jugular verbal assaults and advanced into the stairway. The intruder, seeming strangely confused, stepped backward.

The ranger sized up his opponent as he advanced. The man didn't seem to have a gun, nor did he look strong or particularly motivated—all of which were peculiar qualities for someone who'd just broken into a downtown office and apartment. The ranger's sense of danger ebbed slightly, but he maintained pressure as the intruder backed down the stairs into the kitchen, through the open front entryway and, finally, out the front door. Cade flipped the lock on the doorknob and pulled the door shut, making sure that whatever happened from that point forward his visitor wouldn't be able to get back in the house.

Streetlights lit the scene. The carriage house where Cade's office and apartment were located was made of brick and sandstone. It was situated behind the larger brick home with the Guernica oak out front. Along with neighboring buildings that hemmed the place in, they were completely walled off from the city and hidden from view.

Cade eyed the intruder, whose head was tilted forward, his face concealed by the cowboy hat brim. He noticed the man seemed shorter than he'd surmised.

"Give me a good reason I shouldn't use the sidewalk to shave the stubble off your face," Cade growled. "What are you doing in my office so late?"

The figure picked up his head to reveal two big, brown eyes bordered by long eyelashes atop high cheekbones and smooth, olive-colored skin.

"Cause I don't have any stubble to shave," the woman spat as she pushed the hat higher on her forehead. The ranger recognized her almost immediately: a rancher from the plateau who'd been working sunup to sundown to make sure his own work failed, a woman who'd been leaving him badgering phone messages all week. He also suddenly realized with a frown that his adrenaline-charged response to the stranger in his home had totally absorbed him. He was buck naked, locked outside, standing face-to-face with a woman with whom he'd been dueling politically for months.

"You've been a pain in my ass for a long time," he said. "I should have you arrested."

"Let's get to the naked truth of it."

He felt his face flush at her taunt.

"I'm going to find the police." He turned to march into the city, then realized he'd need to go inside for clothes or to use the phone. He kept a key hidden on the front porch but didn't want to reveal its location or that he hid a key at all. He was stuck. "What do you want?"

"I barely know you, you self-important son of a bitch. I didn't come here so late to break into your apartment or see your bare ass. I don't have the time, and you didn't answer the door—or any of my phone messages for that matter. I just let myself in to leave a note. Like I said in those messages, I'm trying to help."

Help with what, the ranger thought. This woman had done nothing but subvert his efforts to help designate Idaho's first national park. She'd organized anti-park petitions and rallies, and attended every blasted public meeting there was to deliver some soliloquy on how ranching as a way of life was more endangered than any species. Cade suspected she was involved in more nefarious activities, too. In June someone had tossed boxes of nails around a Park Service truck in a remote part of the plateau. The truck got two flat tires, and the ranger who'd been doing cultural surveys on pottery shards in the canyons had to walk twenty-two miles to the nearest ranch just to make a phone call for help. He even wondered sometimes if she had something to do with the kid's disappearance that spring. She and other locals had been questioned by police, but the Elko County sheriff was just as pissed off about the new park as anyone. Cade didn't trust him or other local officials to do their jobs right.

"You help me?" he asked. "You've done nothing but try to make me fail."

"I found something. You should see for yourself. I think it has to do with that Fourney kid's disappearance. You'd know better than me."

Cade couldn't tell if he was angry or annoyed, but the overwhelming rush of adrenaline he'd experienced upon waking had drained him almost complete. He wanted to be rid of his visitor. He wanted clothes. He wanted to go back to sleep. He didn't want people to taunt him anymore with his shortcomings regarding the missing kid. He must have been staring blankly into space because she continued.

"I think I found the kid's backpack."

Cade didn't believe her. And, the fact was, he'd finally started letting it go. It was his fault the kid was out there. It was his fault the kid had been swallowed by the mountains without a trace.

"I'll be camped in Sheep Creek canyon tomorrow night," she continued. "You want to know more about your missing kid? You can meet me there."

"Miles Fourney went missing in the Jarbidge Mountains," Cade said. "I'm not sure where Sheep Creek is, but that doesn't sound right. I can't leave Boise, anyway. I'm hosting two members of Congress and a delegation from the White House this week."

She stepped back and took measure of him.

"You're different than I thought," she said.

"You probably imagined me with clothes."

"No, you seem broke somehow. Or maybe crunched or splintered or something—like broke wasn't good enough for you."

"Please go."

"I've got to go out Sheep Creek to check on the cows one way or another. I'll be there tomorrow whether you're coming or not. You need directions? I'll be at the confluence with a small side creek called . . ."

"I can figure out where your allotments are," he interrupted, but the truth was he didn't care. He'd spent all summer feeling guilty about Miles Fourney's disappearance. He had work to do. It was time to move on.

She pivoted on her cowboy boot heels and walked away, clunking beneath the covered wood porch of the Big House toward the front street.

Cade stood naked in the glare from a security light where moths and flies swarmed. For just a moment he felt the blissful still quiet of the night. There was a longing there for a piece of himself he'd locked away. He felt it in a flash in the pit of his stomach: the full engrossing expanse of the Milky Way, the harmonious chorus of thousands of nighttime crickets rolling across the desert, the imposing strength of snow-capped peaks and the humbling reality of being in the food chain in grizzly country. Just as quickly then, that piece of himself—which was once almost all of who he was or wanted to be—was gone.

He returned to the front of the carriage house and pried at a paperclip protruding from a crack in the windowsill. Attached to it was a key, which he put in the lock and turned to open the door.

He'd forgotten to ask how she got in, but he must have forgotten to lock the door when he went to bed. His home in the city was a kind of Purgatory he'd sought, and the door to Purgatory had been unlocked. The lady had walked right in.

Then he considered the irony: she'd just as easily drawn him back out.

FOUR

CADE LEANED AGAINST A TIMBER COLUMN beneath a porch roof yanked askew by a hundred years of gravity. The steam from his coffee rose in the slanted sun as he squinted into the courtyard where he'd had the confrontation with the rancher. A group of wide-eyed tourists filtered past on a sidewalk that threaded the space between the porch where he stood and the property's bigger home, which had been converted into a small museum.

He'd lived some interesting places during his thirty years with the Park Service, but his arrangement at the historic Basque boarding house with an archaeological dig in the front yard was probably the most unusual.

Historians weren't exactly sure why the carriage house had been built, but it might have been used to store wagons at one time. It had almost certainly been a whiskey distillery during prohibition, and had later been converted into an apartment. It was a little far afield from the new national park's geographical boundaries, but it was a fitting place for a headquarters. Field offices would handle on-the-ground work; the Boise property would be the showpiece.

The tourists' eyes were bright with curiosity as they examined the corner of the house where old timers once stood to smoke cigarettes, lighting matches by striking them on the bricks. The white scratch marks they left were still plain, having weathered a hundred years of shifting winds and rain.

Cade watched another group emerge from the property's bigger house. As they went through a screen door the volunteer guide explained that the structure was built in 1864 by one of Boise's first mayors. Later, in the early-1900s, it was bought by a Basque family and converted into a boarding house. Hundreds of Basque sheep herders had lived there. In fact, the strength of Boise's Basque community owed its existence in part to the familial atmosphere, warm hospitality and homeland traditions that people of Basque heritage found at the boarding house. The property changed hands a few times over the years, but had recently been placed on the National Register of Historic Places and then was bought by the United States Park Service.

The guide turned his group to the archaeological dig where the earth was divided into one-meter squares using stakes and string. He told the tourists that the Park Service had centered the dig at the location of an old outhouse, which had been positioned over a stream that swept waste south to the Boise River. Outhouses usually collected an array of interesting artifacts, and the operation so far had turned up an assortment of clay marbles, glass bottles and an odd sphere of concrete or stone whose purpose and origin hadn't yet been determined.

One of the people in the group pointed into the dig and asked something about genuine artifacts. Cade couldn't quite make it out from across the yard.

The guide craned over the pit, reached down and retrieved a small booklet.

"Definitely not an artifact," he said, and glanced at Cade, who strode across the courtyard to examine the find. It was a pocket-sized copy of the United States Constitution with a picture of George Washington on the cover. There was a blue sticker on the cover proclaiming "No LBNP," which Cade knew was the rally cry of those opposing the new national park. It stood for, "No Legends of the Basques National Park." There was only one person who could have left it, but why had she been snooping in the dig?

"Folks, excuse us for a moment," Cade said. "I need to steal a moment of your guide's time."

He looked at the guide. "Any idea how long that's been there?"

The man shook his head. "I'm guessing we'd have seen it if it was there yesterday."

"That's kind of what I think. Go ahead and finish up your tour."

Cade returned to the porch, sat in a chair and opened the booklet as the group went around the corner near the bola jokoa court. It had been read and re-read hundreds of times, with dog-eared, finger-stained pages; passages underlined in blue ink; and notes scribbled in the margins. He read one of the underlined introductory passages.

"Only a virtuous people are capable of freedom," it read. "As nations become more corrupt and vicious, they have more need of masters." The words "virtuous people" were underlined twice.

He let the rest of the pages flip under his thumb and saw more under-lines drawing attention to passages about "God's people," "virtuous peo-ple," "providence," "tyranny," "debauchery" and "debt." The selected words read alone had the distinct effect of framing the founding document in the context of good and evil alone. He arrived after a while at a series of hand-scrawled notes that seemed unrelated. He read them aloud, working to pronounce syllables that had never before crossed his tongue: "Tartaro" and "Heben Nuk."

His spine tingled at the weirdness of it all. There was certainly noth-ing odd about a portable copy of the United States Constitution, but the underlined passages, incomprehensible notes, protest sticker, and middle-of-the-night break-in were all mixed in the same stew, and it was start-ing to taste a little rancid. He'd been bracing for problems, but he hadn't expected things to be so difficult to understand.

He reached for his cell phone and dialed Officer Ibarra, who agreed to meet him right away.

AN OVERHEAD DOOR CHIME RANG as Cade nudged his way into a small Basque Block cafe. The walls were stacked with hundreds of imported wines, and a woman stood behind a countertop cooler that displayed cheeses and chorizos with labels written in Spanish and French. It was a contradictory mix of musky and fresh, an epicurean anomaly in a city that boasted a lot of pretty ordinary fare. Cade found Ibarra sitting at a table wearing a set of neatly-pressed police blues. He pulled out a chair and sat across from her.

"You want coffee?" he asked, and she shook her head no.

"I'm good," she said. "Been up since six."

He nodded, waved to the woman behind the counter, and she brought him a small cup on a saucer. He raised it to his lips and looked out the window where a maintenance crew used a boom lift and ladder to string lights and banners from streetlight poles in preparation for the five-day celebration. It would all kick off in a few hours.

Cade knew he owed Ibarra an apology for his tone the day before, but he couldn't bring himself to do it right away. While she looked over a menu, he kept gazing out the window.

A half-dozen cranes poked skyward, revealing the construction sites for five or six whole-block commercial buildings. He hadn't lived in Boise long, but it sure seemed like it was bursting at its seams. There was debate about how to manage everything from traffic to zoning codes, and tensions were building in proportion to the bricks and mortar.

He turned back to Ibarra, who put her menu on the table. She was in her mid-twenties, but the police uniform added ten years. He'd never told her, but she reminded him somewhat of his daughter: the same sort of spit and fire, but also some kind of kid-down-the-block innocence and vulnerability. It's one of the reasons he'd taken her under his wing when she'd volunteered to review and compile materials for the new park. It was an opportunity for her to pad her grad school application; he got to relive a cut-short life.

"Thanks for playing the bad guy yesterday," he started. "I know it's not the kind of work you signed up for when you joined the force."

"It's okay, I'm not always gonna be a cop, anyway."

He knew her dream was to earn a PhD in Basque Studies. The police force was a vehicle to save money for school, but it didn't make her a bad cop. In fact, the opposite was true. She was conscientious, thorough and smart—the kind of qualities Cade thought the department could use. If she stayed with the force, he found it easy to imagine her climbing the ranks.

"I'm also sorry I snapped," Cade continued. "I don't appreciate what you were implying about Miles Fourney's disappearance, but I have no excuse for losing my temper."

He reached for his coffee. That the apology was difficult was a symptom of their complicated friendship. When his intern vanished in the mountains that spring, they'd become acquainted when Ibarra interviewed him as part of the investigation. Her volunteer work helping with the park had grown out of that introduction.

"Thanks for your apology," she eventually said. "I guess I'm sorry, too. I didn't mean to push like that. I'm just really invested in this park. It gets me fired up to see anything threaten it."

"Maybe you're not the right person to MC this weekend. It's a public hearing. It's supposed to be a neutral forum."

"My sergeant said I'm too green to help with security, and my career goals align with the role you've asked me to play. It'll make my dad proud if I can stand up and talk about Basque culture a bit. Nothing about that has to be partisan."

She grabbed her menu.

"We good here?" she asked.

He nodded.

"Mind if I eat?"

"Of course not. I'll pick up the tab."

She went to the counter and returned with a small piece of sourdough topped with half a hard-boiled egg, bacon crumbles and red sauce, something Basques called a pintxo. In the Basque country of Spain and France, pintxos were bread topped with fish or lamb, along with cheese and garnishes. The cafe's menu was limited but included an array of pintxos and several kinds of paella.

"I'm glad we got apologies out of the way," she said, "but I'm guessing that's not why you asked me over here. What's up?"

"I'm getting worried about security. We had a break-in at the offices last night. I don't think anything's missing."

"When exactly?"

"Late. It was dark."

"With you there?"

He nodded.

"Did you see who it was?"

Cade paused. Amaia had been uncommonly invested in the Miles Fourney investigation. He didn't want to pass along information that would get her hopes up unless he confirmed it. It would be easier to skip identifying the rancher lady than to explain what she'd said about finding Miles Fourney's backpack.

"No," he lied.

"You have anything at all?"

Cade handed her the pocket-sized Constitution from the dig.

"Whoever it was left this."

She flipped it over so the blue No LBNP sticker faced up.

"Where'd they drop it?"

"In the dig off the front porch."

"Not in the office?"

"Correct."

"So you don't actually know it belonged to the person who broke in."

"I guess that's right."

She ran her thumb along the booklet's ragged-edged pages.

"Did you look inside?" she asked.

"That thing's well loved."

She opened it and scanned.

"I might know these words," she said and held a page up so Cade could see. "At least I might know where to look them up." She'd found the page where Heben Nuk and Tartaro were scribbled.

She turned the page.

"You know what this is?"

She pointed to more handwritten notes, a nonsensical grouping of characters: 4—N 58E—.

He shook his head no.

She flipped the booklet closed and waved it in the air, revealing a Lauburu tattooed on her forearm.

"You mind if I keep the book?"

"Be my guest. I just want the police to be aware the tension we've been talking about is real. With the Jaialdi festivities starting in a few hours, maybe additional security is in order."

"Duly noted," she said. "They'll probably want you to file a report, but for now I'll just pass it up the chain of command."

She put the pocket Constitution in her briefcase.

"The Lauburu," he said with a nod at her arm. "I don't think I ever asked why you got it. Or, really, why it means enough to you to have it tattooed on your arm."

She turned her hand palm-up to show him the ink-work more carefully.

"I'll tell you the story about my grandma another time, but the Lauburu is a pretty obvious choice for anyone with Basque heritage. It would be like a Southwest Indian getting a Zia. It's about embracing your heritage."

"The grandma story is what I meant."

"You know what the Lauburu means?"

"It's the Basque culture's symbol," he said.

"That's what it is, not what it means."

Cade nodded.

"There are different interpretations, but one of the most common is that the four heads represent the forces of nature: earth, fire, wind and water. The vertical heads represent sunset and are associated with water and fire. The horizontal heads represent sunrise and are made up of earth and air. Some say the Lauburu is synonymous with the sun. If you don't remember anything else, just remember that the Lauburu symbolizes vitality and life, and Basques are damn proud of it. When Roman troops arrived in the Basque country in 17 BC, the Lauburu was used as a war banner to defend the territory, so it's older than recorded history."

She threw a five-dollar bill on the table.

"Tip," she said. "I need to get to work. Is there anything else?"

"That's it for now," he said.

Cade followed her out the door. She turned left toward the police station, and he went across the street beneath the lines of dangling Basque and American flags, beneath the Guernica oak, around the old brick house and into the first-floor office where he spent most of his work days. He sat at his desk and saw a blinking red light indicating he had a voicemail. He pushed the Play button and sat stiffly upright as a woman's voice percolated through the phone's black speaker grill.

"Mr. Rigens, this is Fey Dunham. This is my last message, so I hope you'll stop ignoring me. Like I said last night, I think you'll want to see this. Call me back or meet me out there."

She left a phone number that began with 775, the area code for most of Nevada. Dunham lived near an isolated border town called Jarbidge, one of half a dozen towns that would be directly impacted by the new park. Cade had learned to tune the woman out, but now she was using the kid's disappearance to get his attention.

He grunted into his hands, but on some level he was barely willing to acknowledge, Cade knew the emotion was because he hadn't been there when the kid went missing. While his team worked with local authorities to comb the mountains, Cade redoubled his work in the office. He didn't really care whether the new park succeeded or failed, but with successful designation he'd been promised a shot at director of the agency's Pacific West Region. After that it would be an easy jump to the deputy director or director's offices in Washington. Besides, the local search and rescue crews knew the country, and he'd only have put himself in harm's way.

His cell phone dinged with a notification, and the starched blue collar of his shirt felt suddenly tight. He had ten minutes to make it across town for a meeting, and he looked forward to the walk. In fact, he'd need the fresh air and brisk pace to calm himself before sitting at a table with one of his least favorite people in the state capital's power structure: the governor's chief of staff, a woman named Rachel Simplex.

FIVE

CADE'S FEET CLICKED BRISKLY ACROSS THE FIRST-FLOOR rotunda of the Idaho state Capitol. He paused in the center of an inlaid marble rosette that pointed north, south, east and west and gazed up at two enormous flags—one the Stars and Stripes, the other the navy-blue silks of the Idaho state colors. Beyond the flags some two-hundred feet was the apex of the Capitol dome where a small ring of bulbs surrounded a blue sphere that gazed down like an iris. He couldn't see them all, but he knew the oculus over his head had forty-three small stars signifying Idaho was the forty-third state to join the union alongside thirteen larger stars that honored the country's original colonies.

While it was beautiful, the building was mostly empty the majority of the year. The Idaho Legislature—consistently one of the United States' most conservative political bodies—met only during winter. Even when lawmakers couldn't agree on a year's spending blueprint, they always wrapped up by April when headgates were opened, irrigation ditches filled and fields planted. Agriculture had slipped to the state's second largest industry behind the tech sector, but many of the state's elected officials were farmers and ranchers, and that's where political leverage lived.

Cade craned his neck, noticing a tight spiral staircase that wound in a knot near the dome's top. He wondered how you got there and who had permission. He didn't get outside much anymore but still liked to explore and made a mental note to ask around.

He went north across the rotunda and climbed a set of marble steps, then continued among the dome's five-foot-wide Corinthian columns toward the second floor where he was certain his meeting was already underway. When he walked into one of the governor's west-wing conference rooms he found the participants quietly fidgeting with pens and paper and poking at cell phones. He wasn't late at all. He took a seat among the eight people with whom he'd been working for the previous two years to solve some of the state's biggest land-use riddles, which tended to center on the abundance of public land and tension about how to use it or protect it—or both.

A spindly spider plant hung in the window and obscured some of the view. It cast shadows on the conference table where the group, including Cade and the Governor's chief of staff, Rachel Simplex, was seated. A man Cade had never met sat silent in the corner. He wore a pressed suit and wire-rim glasses—a lobbyist, Cade thought.

Ebullient chatter rolled among the room's beige-painted walls where photographs of central Idaho's rugged wilderness hung. One showed the folded meanders of the Middle Fork of the Salmon River. At the center of a hundred-thousand-acre wilderness area, it was perhaps the most remote major river in the lower forty-eight. Another showed a mountain tarn beneath a tapestry of granite peaks, possibly the state's famed Sawtooth Mountains, protected by Congress as wilderness in the 1970s. A third showed the sharply incised canyons of the state's desert southwest, the landscape the group now worked to celebrate. The photos were windows into a side of Idaho that seemed far away from the city's tight networks of concrete, steel and glass.

Cade picked up a pen and crossed his legs as the chief of staff took charge.

"Thanks for coming," started Simplex, whose amber hair was tied into a professional, asexual bun. She sat tall and erect and made commanding eye contact with each of her visitors. "Before we start, I want to introduce Stan Hubbard with Hardrock Holdings, a member of the Nevada Mining Association. He'll be participating as an observer today."

A few of those seated at the table turned and welcomed Stan. Others smiled and nodded.

"I know it's early," she continued, "but this is a big week for us, a week when we establish a clear path toward designation of Idaho's first national park and deals that make all of you, and the constituents you represent, happy. So I want to congratulate everyone for rolling up your sleeves and doing the hard work that's made getting this far possible."

"Here here," said a woman who represented the Idaho Water Users Association and its hundred-and-seventy-five-member irrigation districts that kept water flowing on fields of lentils, potatoes, wheat, alfalfa and other cash crops.

"We've still got a ways to go," said a man representing the Nevada Mining Association. "I hope we don't let this happy atmosphere distract us. At least three of my members are mad as hell, and I don't see any way to ease the tension."

"Thanks for that," Simplex said. "That actually brings me to an important point for today's meeting that we didn't discuss when we planned it."

"What could be more important than figuring out logistics for picking up the Interior Secretary and members of Congress at the airport?" asked the woman representing the irrigators.

"It's not just public hearing logistics," Simplex said, "but the hearing's purpose. I don't want this to be too much of a shock, but we might not be as far away as we thought from finishing this thing."

She reached into a gray soft-cover briefcase and withdrew a manila folder. From that she took out a set of papers and squared them on the table in front of her.

"We're on the cusp of making history," she said and looked around the table at each of them. "This is the week. You've all put in the time and done your jobs really well. You put in the hard work and now, at the public hearing on Saturday, we're going to announce finalization of the park."

She looked to see if she'd gotten their attention. She had. They looked back in collective stunned silence.

"As you know Idaho's senior senator has promised to deliver our finished work to Congress. What you don't know is that she's been quietly working on Capitol Hill to get the votes. I talked with her people yesterday. She's adding the park to a must-pass omnibus package that's moving during an emergency session Friday afternoon. It should be on the President's desk Monday morning. Ladies and gentlemen, instead of a public hearing on Saturday, we're going to announce designation of Legends of the Basques National Park."

Cade cupped his hands over his face and took a deep breath. He was working to help make the park happen, but this was too much, too fast.

The backlash would be strong and swift. Simplex knew that. He marveled at the brash move, which he assumed she orchestrated. He sat back to allow the coalition participants time to react—and braced for their revolt.

Seated around the table were representatives from The Sierra Club, Idaho Water Users, Shoshone-Paiute Indian Tribes, Nevada Mining Association, Idaho Cattle Association, Basque Museum & Cultural Center, and Cade, who represented the National Park Service. There were far more people involved with this historic effort to strike a chord of compromise, but these had been the seven key negotiators and architects of the deal. They'd all gone into the discussions grudgingly. Two years later they'd emerged with at least some appreciation for each others' points of view.

Cade looked across the table at The Sierra Club representative, Jack Jerrys, whose alabaster beard seemed somehow dignified despite his insistence on wearing sandals and Hawaiian shirts on almost all occasions. Cade then looked at Sean Webber of the Cattle Association. Webber had disheveled black hair, three-day stubble and pressed Wrangler jeans. Cade remembered the day he watched the two men from totally different universes find common ground. All they'd needed was a night under the stars and a bottle of booze. It was during a coalition camping trip they held for the exact reason of getting to know each other better, and the two of them stayed up till dawn reaching a new understanding about each others' positions and backgrounds. Webber believed his cattle made the range healthier; Jerrys was convinced they did longstanding damage. On the issues they were irrevocably divided, but what they figured out was that they both loved the land. With that thread of authenticity between them they'd found enough mutual respect and trust to forge solutions that might work for them both. Or, to use Webber's words, "give us both heartburn, but at least we both got it."

With the hard work of building consensus out of the way, the group had transitioned to collecting feedback and working to gently mold public opinion in favor of the park. For the six months leading up to public hearings in Elko, Boise, Twin Falls and other strategically-selected cities, they'd waged a media campaign to build support. Cade was surprised at the amount of energy his coalition partners—and particularly the governor's staff—put into scripting and re-scripting the message. There were meetings about meetings to prepare for additional meetings and long conversations about how to talk about things they were going to talk about weeks in advance. He understood the need to be strategic, but it was the first time in his life he felt like he couldn't always speak his mind for fear of upsetting someone whose fundamental goals he shared.

None of his peers spoke following the chief of staff's surprise announcement, so after a few minutes it was Cade who broke the silence.

"I'm an advocate here, but don't we owe it to the people to let them speak? Saturday is supposed to be an opportunity to air grievances or offer support, a chance for the people to take ownership of this proposal and make it their own. Am I the only one who remembers the public hearing in Elko? People had a lot to say. I don't think the people of Idaho and Nevada are going to take it well if we suddenly tell them the park's a done deal. It's gonna look like it was pre-ordained."

"You know that's not true," Simplex shot back. "You've been sitting at this table for two years. This has been hard work. Am I wrong?"

"I'm just saying, why rush? We've done everything right so far."

"You strike when the iron's hot," Simplex continued. "What happens in Washington, D.C. isn't necessarily connected with what happens out here. The iron of the Washington, D.C. political machine is hot right now. Maybe more important, the public hearing on Saturday is going to be different. There'll be some protestors, sure, but there'll be thousands of Basques from all over the world here this week. We're going to announce designation of a park that celebrates their culture. I think it's going to be different than it was in Elko."

"What about the land deals?" Cade pressed.

Simplex didn't answer right away. Webber from the Cattle Association joined in.

"He's right. We haven't resolved negotiations around a few of the key private property rights."

"Like what?" Simplex asked. "I understand we lost ground when Miles Fourney and his field work went missing. But near as I can tell we've negotiated with key ranchers concerning grazing allotments and a few other private landowners who are willing sellers. We can work out old mine claims after designation and add to the park as they come in. Look, after the years of hard work you all just invested, I thought you'd be excited. We've got guaranteed new water rights for farmers drawing off the Snake River; we've got a new Native American cultural center; we're buying out the most controversial grazing rights at top dollar, money that will go directly to struggling ranch families; we're setting aside 750,000 acres of the West as a national park. What's not to like here?"

Cade bit his tongue. He'd said his piece, and he wouldn't fight publicly with Rachel, who was a master at subtly coercing people to share her opinion. Over the years he'd seen how she planted ideas and allowed or encouraged people to take them to the collective as their own. Cade had come to think of her more like a puppeteer holding the strings of a marionette than a lone political operative. In this way he also considered her dangerous. In a sense she was more than one person; she could bring the force of dozens of people to bear on a given situation. Cade watched as she nudged and massaged the atmosphere until, one by one, the stakeholders acquiesced to the sudden victory they'd been working toward for years. The whole thing made Cade scratch his head. That the big push circumventing public input was coming from a conservative governor going against the wishes of his base constituency didn't make sense. Either Simplex was confident she could mold public opinion by standing her boss up in public, or there was something else at play.

Cade didn't have much of a chance to mull it because Rachel succeeded at getting the group to celebrate. The participants' initial resistance transformed. Where at first their faces were grimaced with furrowed brows and frowns, arms folded across their chests, a ripple of excitement rolled across the room. Cade watched as Rachel conducted the symphony of their attitudes into a final movement. They discussed roles each would play before and during the public hearing. The woman from the Basque Museum would pick up the Interior Secretary at the airport. Amaia Ibarra would MC and talk about Basque history and traditions. Cade would pick up the members of Congress and present about the National Park Service's history and mission. Simplex's boss, Governor McGown, would cap the proceedings with an announcement about the new park's official designation.

The spider plant's shadow crawled most of the way toward the window, indicating a climbing sun and ebbing hour. Simplex glanced at her face-up phone and announced it was almost noon.

"Keep these developments to yourselves," she said. "We need to control the conversation, and if news leaks early someone else has control. We've been working on this for years. We'll dictate when it starts and how it goes."

The participants nodded as they rose and their idle chatter mounted as the meeting concluded. Cade remained seated, his eyes focused on Rachel, who looked strong back at him. She stayed put while the others shuffled into the hallway, the white noise of their chatter ebbing with them.

"This is reckless," Cade said when the prattle was gone.

"I hoped you'd stick around," she replied. "You have a minute?"

Cade nodded.

"Great, let's go upstairs to talk."

Simplex walked to the door, held it open and offered an artificial smile. Cade smelled the woman's perfume and offered a half-hearted smile in return.

"Down the hall to the elevator," she said.

Their clicking feet echoed in the silence of the state's dormant lawmaking halls.

Cade had never enjoyed an especially chatty or warm relationship with Simplex, who frequently attended the park coalition's collaborative discussions despite not being an official part of them. They'd tried back when the collaborative was new, but Cade couldn't sense in Simplex any kind of higher calling or the humanity that comes with one. She was smart and likable in a completely superficial sense, and despite hundreds of hours spent working in the same room Cade found he didn't know the first thing about who Rachel Simplex was. He didn't know if she was married, had kids, where she lived or if she'd played any sports in college. She was eager to take charge and motivated by people's attention. Beyond that she didn't seem to offer much aside from the power of her position, which was plenty to earn her a high level of social standing among the state's political elite.

Over time Cade and Simplex learned to exchange formalities and move on when they arrived at coalition meetings. Cade became friends with one or two of the participants while Simplex's superficial warmth and quick wit seemed to win over everyone except Cade.

They arrived at the elevator, and Simplex pushed the button for the fourth floor. Once there, they went between two statues to a room with a straight-south view of the Boise Train Depot where immigrants once climbed off of Union Pacific trains ready to roll up their sleeves and start new lives. On the west side of the room was a door with a keycard lock and glass window. Behind it were more stairs that went further into the dome.

Cade turned to face her, unsure why she'd asked for a private meeting. He wanted to set the tone but didn't have anything to say. He watched as she pushed the sliding doors shut.

"I need you to check your tone before you address me in front of the group," she started.

Cade rolled his eyes.

"Don't give me a dismissive look, Cade. We have a deal. You help me get this park through; I'll nudge your career along."

"Fine," he said, "but I don't suppose you asked me up here to offer a motherly talk about tone."

She nodded and looked out the window into the heart of the city.

"You were right about the land deals," she said. "With park designation coming in three days, we need to get those deals wrapped up. You've got the maps and legal descriptions. I need those indexed and on my desk today."

"Some of those are sensitive negotiations. Some are unlikely to go through."

"Leave the politics to me. I know your team's been working on these for months. I want those documents on my desk by two."

Cade silently fumed. Of all the pieces and parts of the park he'd worked on, the land deals were most sensitive. They had potential to pit neighbors against each other and otherwise seal ill will toward key federal land managers for generations. Simplex had known what she was doing when she asked for this conversation in private. There's no way the other collaborative participants would endorse rushing the land deals.

He thought back to his musing about her as a puppeteer and felt the invisible threads of his own marionette strings.

"Papers will be on your desk in two hours," he said. "Are we done here?"

"I love it when you see things my way."

SIX

CADE WALKED WITH SLOW PURPOSE, his eyes barely noticing the sidewalk cracks that passed with hypnotic cadence, his mind working inward and backward, probing the experiences that made him who he was.

He'd been eleven when he started to let go of his trust in people. He and his brother were playing a game where one would wear a blindfold while the other gave instructions about how to walk without seeing. They'd been at the pool about a mile from their house, and Cade wrapped his towel around his head. He knew the way from dozens of walks, but at some point grew disoriented. Still, he followed, unable to see but trusting the one who could.

At one point, when Cade was most lost, his brother told him to take ten steps forward, turn right and take a few more steps. Cade was puzzled but did as instructed. He walked forward, noticing a subtle incline, turned right and then felt his stomach flutter as he tipped into space. His forehead made contact first. When he pulled the towel from around his eyes, he saw he'd been walked off a tractor trailer loading dock. He squinted at his brother, who began to back away—and then as Cade regained his feet, ran.

It was the first time Cade knew he couldn't trust something if he couldn't see it. All these years later he had that familiar pang. He couldn't see what Rachel Simplex saw on the political chess board and it gave him that disorienting sensation of falling.

When he returned to central Boise's Basque district he found it transformed. The street was barricaded, artisans and vendors under pop-up tents, and fifty or so people milling about. The area was filled with an overwhelming smell unlike anything Cade had inhaled before. An upbeat sound slipped from the open back door of a social hall: the wheezy sounds of an accordion accompanying a chorus of voices that sang in a language he couldn't understand.

Living in the culturally-rich area came with almost-daily lessons about food, history and sense of place. They were lessons that satiated Cade's curiosity, but they also made him uncomfortable about how little he actually knew about the world beyond his home.

The unfolding five-day Jaialdi—a word that literally meant "festival" in Euskara—would be a fresh opportunity to learn. It was a huge festival founded a couple decades before to showcase Idaho's Basque heritage. Now a mature tradition held in the sweltering heat of July, organizers expected up to forty thousand people from communities around the globe. The ensuing days promised traditional dances, songs and competitions sandwiched inside a five-day party. The whole thing would culminate Saturday afternoon with the public hearing Cade was organizing, a gathering Rachel Simplex had suddenly transformed from a community dialogue into a political lecture.

Cade looked again at the Guernica oak, a tree that symbolized discourse, dialogue and self-governance. It had seemed such a fitting place to host the hearing, but with the park's outcome now preordained, the location seemed like a cheap stunt.

The mid-morning crowd was beginning to swell. He turned and saw a vendor preparing paella in a six-foot pan. Realizing he hadn't put anything in his stomach but coffee, he approached and discovered an assortment of traditional cheeses and croissants in a case next to the frying mass of vegetables, rice, pork and fish.

"Un cafe con leche, por favor," he said, "y . . . y . . . Oh, shoot. Can I just get some cheese and a coffee with milk?"

The man behind the frying pan looked at Cade with squinted eyes and head askew. "I understand Spanish," he said, "but being Basque and being Spanish are different things."

"Right," Cade said. "I know that, sorry."

"English is my first language; Euskara is my second. After that is Spanish and a little bit of French."

Cade knew better. He'd lived on the block more than a year and was working to help designate a park that would celebrate Basque culture in America. Interested in breaking the awkward moment, he told a self-deprecating joke.

"You know what you call someone who speaks three languages?"

The man looked back with questioning eyes.

"Trilingual."

Cade paused to confirm he'd set the hook.

"You know what you call someone who speaks two languages?"

"Bilingual," the man said.

"And you know what you call someone who speaks one language?"

The man remained silent, aware he'd arrived at the punchline.

"American. I'm American through and through, and not always as smart as I think. Sorry if I offended."

"You'd have to work harder than that to offend me," the man said and handed Cade his coffee and cheese. "I'm American, too, and proud of it."

Cade thanked him and turned back toward the house. He raised the paper-cup coffee to his lips but stopped short before taking a sip. A rickety-looking man in a cowboy hat had just let himself through the gate and proceeded to stutter-step around the house toward Cade's office. Cade recognized the man, a half-tethered old timer who'd poked around the property often enough to have drawn some attention.

Cade put the coffee down and hustled to the courtyard behind the main house where he found the man squatting amidst the fresh dirt and squared-off strings of the archaeological dig, his head turned down in examination.

"Can I help you with something?" Cade called.

The man's head tilted up to reveal light-blue eyes that oozed like liquid from a pair of weathered sockets. He stood tall, dusted off a pair of faded Wranglers, and stepped onto the sidewalk. He wore a big white cowboy hat, and a gleaming belt buckle shone from his waist like a dinner plate. A handlebar mustache curled above his lips.

He looked at Cade with suspicious eyes, and a long silence crept between them before the cowboy answered a question nobody had asked: "Not too good," he said in long, semi-high-pitched Western drawl.

Cade took a closer look. Gray stubble protruded from a mole at the corner of the man's jaw like tiny barbs from a prickly pear cactus. There was a package of Drum tobacco sticking from his shirt pocket. White crusted sweat stains ringed his armpits.

"What's not good?" Cade asked. "I asked what you're doing here."

The cowboy continued as if Cade hadn't already asked two direct questions.

"When I was nine I inherited a mining company. I never saw it, but they say it came with a bunch of bullion. I forgot about it over the years, but I came up here to take a look and found it was all gone. The bullion's gone, and I can't find it."

Cade sighed. It was time to usher the man back through the front gate as quickly as possible.

The cowboy took a hand out of his pocket and used his fingers to add emphasis as he counted back two generations on his family tree.

"You see my great grandfather had a mining company. I came up here to look for my inheritance, and I can't find it. It's all gone."

"Do you know where your great grandfather got his gold?"

"Of course, he was a miner," the cowboy grumbled. "I'm just looking for the mine."

"Was it a mine or a mining company? You've said both of those things."

"It was lots of mines, all patented claims. I inherited a mining company, not a mine."

Cade's eyes narrowed. The man was high, crazy, or worse—perhaps deranged by too many lonely days in the hot sun running cattle. The cowboy continued with a gush.

"My dad was a horrible drunk. He was always drinking. You could say he didn't want to stop, or maybe he couldn't, but either way he didn't. I just remembered about the bullion and came up here to see what happened. My name's Andy Jim the third, and my dad was a horrible drunk."

Cade took a deep breath. The man had just gone off the rails.

"Where were you before you were looking for your inheritance?" Andy Jim the third looked to be in his fifties, about the same age as Cade.

"I was working. I got stung real good. Life dealt me a few tough blows. I forgot about the bullion and came up here to see what happened."

Cade didn't know what to do with the conversation or whether he should continue to engage the man at all. He'd thought he might confront him about snooping on Park Service property, but found him benignly nuts. Cade just wanted to get on with his day.

"Sir, I have work to do, but I still have a question. Why are you here, in this yard? You've disturbed a sensitive archaeological site, and that's not exactly okay. What's this place have to do with your missing inheritance?"

The man put his hands in the pockets of his Wranglers.

"I just followed the kid," he said. "He stole my papers, and I followed him. He figured it out, I think."

"What kid?"

"The kid who worked for the Park Service in the mountains."

Cade felt moths flutter in his gut. Miles Fourney was commanding too much of his attention even after vanishing. He felt like his next question was simultaneously inevitable and avoidable, so when it came out it emerged low and almost meek.

"What did he figure out?"

"He nearly talked me to death about my inheritance and the Lost Sheepherder Mine. He stole my papers, so I followed him."

"He was hired to track down mines we need to plug for safety reasons, and this was his office. Your mining inheritance was the kind of story he was supposed to document."

"Well, he stole my papers," said Andy Jim. "Didn't ask, stole."

Cade held his breath and studied the man. They were about the same height, but Andy Jim's cowboy hat made him appear an easy eight inches taller.

"Do you know anything about that?" Cade finally asked. "About what happened to the kid?"

"I don't aim to tell you I've got much respect for him after he stole my papers, but I'm no murderer if that's what you mean."

"It's not," Cade lied, his mind weighing the possibility that the lady from the night before might not have been outright lying about finding the kid's backpack. "I just wondered if you knew anything."

"I know I can't find the bullion."

Despite the man's incriminating connection with the missing Miles Fourney, there was something about his sincerity that tugged at Cade. The guy was unhinged, but he didn't seem to be lying or manipulative, a contrast with the morning meeting he'd had with Rachel Simplex whose intentions were almost impossible to divine.

"Andy Jim, I need to get on with my day, but I'd like to escort you off the property."

"This here's publicly owned land, ain't it?"

"Well, yes, but I'm in charge around here, and it's time to go. You can sign up for one of the tours like the rest of the public. The dig here is part of those tours, and you'll get a full explanation."

The man's aquamarine eyes twitched back and forth as Cade walked with him and held the front gate open.

"Maybe we'll see you later," Cade said.

"I don't reckon you will."

Cade stood in the open gate and watched as the man disappeared in the sea of moving bodies, unaware in a conscious way that he'd already begun to reprioritize his day.

SEVEN

H IS MIND SPINNING WITH THE IDEA that Miles Fourney might have
been followed by the crazy old cowboy, Cade went to the front porch
and sat on a wood bench with peeling green paint to ponder the reports
he'd read and search parties he'd spoken with.

The kid had made a few critical errors, but his story was a riddle nobody
had unraveled. He'd left the town of Jarbidge around sunrise on his way to
the summit of Jarbidge Peak. It was a long but straightforward climb, and
the kid had signed the summit register, presumably pretty early in the day.
Then he'd vanished like a cloud sifting through the high desert twilight.

Two county sheriffs' forces, a search and rescue team, and agents from
the U.S. Forest Service and National Park Service had combed the mountain
for more than a month. Nobody found anything. Not a shirt, not a backpack, not a shoelace or a body—nothing. The leading theory was that he'd
gotten lost during his descent, strayed off route and fell down the cliffs on
the mountain's northeast ridge, but there wasn't a trace of him anywhere.

The search had ended, but Cade couldn't stop thinking about it. The
kid was his employee, his responsibility. That Miles Fourney had traveled
to the remote part of the West in the first place was because of work Cade
assigned him. The kid was supposed to take photographs and log GPS
coordinates of old mines, nothing more, nothing less.

Now, three months after Miles Fourney disappeared in one of the most
remote mountain ranges in America—and two months after the search
had been called off—Cade had something new to ponder. An unexpected

swell of excitement surged in his chest. After all the time he'd spent sitting in an office chair waiting for someone else to figure it out, he had a small chance to set things straight.

He stood and went for his office.

He first went to the shelves full of three-ring binders, pulled down pertinent property files and called Rachel Simplex, inviting her to pick them up. Then he climbed the stairs to his second-floor apartment and went to the closet where he rounded up a backpack, sleeping bag, water bottles and warm layers, all of it dusty from six years of neglect.

The process of rounding up gear took longer than expected, so when he finally returned to the first floor office, Simplex was there, her lips drawn taught and the multi-colored binders filling her arms.

"I'm heading to the plateau," he said. "I'll be overnight."

"Overnight?"

"There's something I need to see."

"What are you talking about?"

Cade ushered her into his office.

Among the maps depicting park boundaries, properties to be purchased and mines to be reclaimed was a Mercator-style rendering near Cade's desk that didn't match the others. It showed a large portion of the same topography but was speckled with red, green and orange push-pins and a dozen hand-written notes. It was a map Cade compiled during the search for Miles Fourney. It showed a month's worth of dead ends.

"They were looking in the wrong spot. I need to go to a place called Sheep Creek."

"You're going out there to look for Miles Fourney? He's been missing all summer, and the public hearing's in three days. We're hosting two members of Congress and a delegation from the White House, and you're in charge of most of it. We can't afford to lose you for fifteen minutes."

"That's flattering, but you know I'm not that important."

"Your regional managers won't allow it."

"I'm not asking. I'll be back tomorrow. I'll help with everything."

"You're a month behind as it is."

"This isn't a negotiation." Cade looked at his watch. It was a little after two. He'd need to get there before dark. "I'll be back tomorrow."

"You could lose your job if you don't get back here on time, let alone be up for that promotion we discussed."

Cade nodded.

"The kid's been missing for months. He's probably not alive."

"I know."

"When's the last time you went for a hike? When's the last time you went camping?" She nodded at the dust-covered gear scattered at his ankles. "Do you even know what you're doing in the wilderness anymore?"

Cade put a hand on her shoulder, a motion he intended as condescending.

"It's been a while," he said, then picked up his bags and went for the door.

EIGHT

An hour's drive south of Boise, Cade exited the interstate and aimed his white government issue pickup south toward the new park's geographical core: a complex of isolated desert canyons that cut through seventeen-million-year-old volcanic rock.

He fumbled for his cell phone and poked at the screen as he drove, attempting to call some of the ranchers he'd negotiated with during the preceding couple of years. Some were subsidiaries of large corporations, but others were family operations that made hardscrabble livings. What they had in common was their dependence on public land grazing leases to fatten and feed their stock in the summer. As part of the national park deal, some $300 million would be appropriated to permanently retire nearly all of them. The confounding part was, some of the ranchers didn't want the money. It turned out ranchers liked to ranch more than they fancied retirement.

Cade threw his phone across the cab as all three calls went to voicemail, then drifted to the side of the road. He considered calling Sean Webber of the Cattle Association. Sean could easily contact all of the ranchers at once, but he'd probably confront Simplex and trigger a dust-up that would jeopardize the whole park. Cade had to handle things himself, and that meant making this unplanned sojourn an efficient trip.

He leaned into the seat, pushed his truck door ajar, and propped his feet in the open window. His fingers drummed across the steering wheel as he pondered what to do, his eyes probing the big empty to the south, his nerves mounting as he considered what might be out there, the chance there could be answers about what happened to Miles.

The problem was bigger than the woman who'd invited him. He hadn't so much as driven a dirt road in years, let alone lace up a pair of boots or don a backpack. Sweat beaded around his neck, and he felt his pulse quicken.

One step at a time, he thought. The only way he'd get through it was to move slow, and the first thing was to figure out where, exactly, he was going.

He reached for his phone and dialed Officer Ibarra.

"We're talking a lot these days," she answered.

"Amaia, I might have a fresh lead on Miles Fourney. Sorry I didn't tell you. It took most of the day for me to come around to the idea myself."

"That's my case, Cade."

"I know, I already apologized."

"This better be good."

"Did anybody ever search an area called Sheep Creek?"

"I'm not even sure where that is offhand."

"Me neither. You have a map handy?"

"Where are you?"

"On the road, a little south of the interstate."

"Just a minute."

Desert heat blew through the cab. Cade's breaths were short, his nerves twitchy.

"This isn't precise, but you need to go to Bruneau and follow some dirt roads from there. Google Maps isn't too helpful. As you know there's a lot of open space down there."

"I'll stop in Bruneau and ask."

"So, what happened? Why now?"

"The rancher who's been dogging the park—she reached out, says she found Miles' backpack."

"Cade, you realize you're probably being set up."

"I've thought about it. At this point I intend to see it through."

"Let me know what you find out. You already know how that case got under my skin. Miles knew what he was doing too well to have just fallen off the mountain."

He turned the phone off and put it in the glove compartment, then steered back onto the highway. The first hint of the snow-streaked Jarbidge

Mountains rose from the horizon before he dropped into a flat-bottom canyon and a farming town called Bruneau. A sign at the edge of town announced: "You Have Entered the Impact Area of the Bruneau Hot Spring snail." As he passed he craned his neck to see the other side where an angry local had scrawled: "Would the last person to leave take the goddamned snails with you." The people of Bruneau didn't care for wildlife protection laws any more than they cared for gun control.

He coasted in front of a one-story bait and tackle shop next to a pickup with oversize tires and mule deer antlers bolted to the bumper. The antlers framed the red, white and blue of an Idaho license plate. He went into the store and found a heavyset lady behind the counter scratching at a Bear Assets Bingo lottery ticket.

"Howdy," she said without looking.

"How you doing?"

"Well, with any luck I'll win a million bucks so I can get the hell out of this place. What can I do for you?"

"I'm looking for Sheep Creek," he said, "but to be honest I forget if it's a tributary of the Bruneau or the West Fork."

"It flows into the Bruneau," she said and pivoted in her chair to reference a stack of maps, pulling one out labeled Sheep Creek.

"Sheep Creek," she said, "has its own quadrangle."

"What you looking in Sheep Creek for?" came a voice from the other side of one of store's isles, and a man in Carhart coveralls and a John Deere ball cap appeared.

"I'm looking for a friend."

"Your friend all right?"

"Long story."

"Anyway," said the lady who'd spread the Sheep Creek quadrangle on the countertop, "you want to head out Highway 51 toward Elko, then hang a left after the airstrip in Grasmere."

"This is Highway 51, right?" Cade pointed to the road outside the shop.

"Yep, it splits just outside town, but there's a sign that makes it easy. Where you going in Sheep Creek?"

"There's probably a few places to look first."

He studied the map. There were three locations where dirt roads worked close to the bunched-together contours that signified Sheep Creek's steep canyon walls. One was within a few miles of a backcountry airstrip. He pulled a pen from his pocket and circled the three locations, adding emphasis to the road near the airstrip.

"Is the canyon very deep in these places?"

"Oh, it's a big canyon," she said. "A thousand feet. You can't get in there except a few spots. Tough country."

"This friend of yours," said the man in the coveralls. "He's up there already?"

"I don't really know."

"You have water?"

"Some."

"You have food?"

"Not yet."

"You realize you're headed to the middle of nowhere, right? People die out there."

"I aim to buy provisions before I leave." He scanned the shelves where a limited selection of canned goods were stacked. "How much daylight you figure is left?"

"The sun is setting about nine-thirty give or take, so there's a few more hours," the lady said.

Cade went to the shelves and pulled down cans of pear halves, pineapple chunks and Chef Boyardee ravioli; a loaf of bread; jar of peanut butter; carton of raisins; and gallon of water. He returned to the counter where the man and woman talked about what they'd do with the million dollars the lady wasn't going to win.

"The government takes half of it, you know that?" said the man. "They take thirty percent off the top, and then you have to file it on your taxes, too."

"Don't forget to subtract the hundred thousand you'll blow on some crazy party," Cade said.

The man in the John Deere ball cap gave a dismissive smile.

"A glass of iced tea and a sunset," he said. "That's my kind of party."

The lady rung him up and asked for thirty-nine dollars and change. The ranger considered questioning how she arrived at that number for such a mediocre array of provisions and then dismissed the thought. She'd been helpful enough, and there wasn't time to squabble over five or ten bucks. The sun would set in two hours. He had to keep moving. It was time to find out what happened to the kid.

AN EMPTY STRIP OF ASPHALT slipped beneath Cade's tires as the engine of his Park Service pickup labored south. The road crested a basalt escarpment to a plateau where the sea of sagebrush was awash in late-day light.

He pulled to the side of the road in the ghost town of Grasmere and pried his truck door ajar. The desert wind was hot in his silvering hair, and his six-foot frame cast a long shadow into the desert. He looked past the shuttered windows of an old gas station and café to an expanse of sagebrush broken in the distance by a meandering dark slash, the canyon that Sheep Creek had carved from such uncompromising land. To the south was a gravelly airstrip where a small white and red airplane was parked. Beyond that Cade saw a narrow dirt road running straight as an arrow into the desert. He referenced the map he bought in Bruneau, then returned to the steering wheel and turned onto the dirt road, a plume of dust rising in the desert calm behind him.

At a small tributary marked Mary's Creek on the map, Cade pulled onto the road's sunbaked shoulder and went to his tailgate where he stuffed gear into his sun-bleached backpack. He shoved his sleeping bag in first, then loaded water bottles and food, an extra layer of clothes. He stowed the map in his pocket and locked the truck, then paused. He hadn't been at the end of a dirt road in years. The moment seemed to call for some kind of ceremony or reflection, but he simply took a first step, then a second and without formality was underway.

He scrambled along small basalt ledges working east along the south canyon rim. A few grazing cattle turned their heads and watched as he stepped among boulders and dust-dry cow patties, and he fell into a comfortable, contemplative rhythm.

Cade was once a man forged by sunrises and starlight, rocky canyons and meandering rivers. He never intended to succumb to the haze of city lights or the suffocation of thousands of neighbors. He'd once detested walls of steel and windows, and city blocks full of offices and clutter. At one point he thought the Park Service offices at Mammoth Hot Springs in Yellowstone were as much civilization as he could bear. He'd visited the ocean in his thirties and found its unrelenting horizontality frightening. He was most at home in more vertical landscapes—places that invented and reinvented him, natural marvels that could move him to tears.

When he was a boy, Cade and his dad had traveled across the West on a return trip to Pennsylvania from Seattle. It was June, and the spring wildflowers painted mountain meadows with shades of gold, purple, white and crimson. When they'd drifted through the shadow of the granite-spired Tetons in eastern Idaho, Cade's jaw had dropped. "This is where I'm going to live," he'd declared. It didn't happen right away. He'd gone to Alaska and worked on a fire crew. Then he'd bounced into Boise where he landed a job at the National Interagency Fire Center. That led to more summers on the fire line and then smokejumper school. He was eventually selected for the smokejumper crew based in West Yellowstone, a stone's throw from the Tetons where his boyhood dream had taken root.

All the while, he kept the land close. He'd loved his wife and daughter, too, but the land proved more constant, more forgiving. The land was always there for him. His family wasn't anymore.

After about two miles, Cade stopped and sat on a flat slab of basalt where he sipped some water and drank in the view. The canyon had grown into a deep crevice topped with cliff walls. Beyond the canyon the Jarbidge Mountains jutted from the horizon and collected the sun's final rays. Jarbidge Peak where Miles Fourney left his last known mark on the world was most prominent, but it was the first in an impressive chain of mountains stretching south into Nevada. The mountains were little more than small humps on the horizon, but their presence was a steadying force for Cade.

He returned the plastic water bottle to his pack and resumed his march as the shadows caught him from behind. In another hour the sky would be black, and he'd need to be at Sheep Creek by then. He could navigate by headlamp if he needed, but working into new country under artificial light was an adventure he hoped to avoid. He quickened his steps and relished the advancing cool of twilight.

When he arrived at a cliff above the confluence of Mary's Creek and Sheep Creek the sky had faded into purple-black, and the land was visible in soft shades of gray. At the end of a long slope of sagebrush was a small delta of sand at the confluence of the two creeks. As if on cue, he saw the fast flash of a match or camp stove and knew he'd arrived at the right place. He located a notch in the canyon's upper cliff and descended toward the willows where a tidy, well-kept camp gradually came into view. The spark he'd seen from the canyon rim was gone, and the willows were full of ink. He slowed and probed the space for watchful eyes, the sound of his heartbeat rising in the stillness.

"Are you Cade?"

A feminine voice came from the darkness where the slender silhouettes of willow stems were all he could make out.

"Yeah, Cade Rigens from the Park Service. I think you're expecting me."

He stood motionless for twenty seconds or more. He'd stand like that as long as it took. In Boise she'd been on his turf and he'd felt strong and confident, but he had the distinct notion that she now had the upper hand.

There was finally a rustling of brush, and a woman emerged with a rifle in her hands, its stock loose in her grip, its barrel drooping toward the sand.

"Go set up while there's some light left, then we can get to talking."

NINE

CADE LAID HIS SLEEPING PAD IN THE OPEN AIR of the fading twilight, fluffed his bag on top of it and returned to his host by the willows. He sat on the sand and watched as she unwrapped a prepackaged burrito, looked at him briefly, and stuffed it, uncooked, into her mouth. She gazed into the canyon as she chewed and after a slow swallow looked back at Cade.

"You ever seen a Mormon cricket?" she asked.

Recognizing her strange question as an opportunity to get comfortable, he played along. "I've heard of them, but no, I've never seen one."

"Well if you've seen one, you've probably seen a bunch." She took another bite of her burrito.

"Then I guess I've never seen a bunch, either."

"Mormon crickets," she began with her mouth full and then swallowed. "Mormon crickets form up in big swarms during a drought, so many they turn the desert black with their bodies. You can't drive down a road without squashing thousands of them. They just crackle and pop under your truck tires. Makes a god-awful smell, all those dead crickets baking in the sun."

"Sounds like something to see," he said. "When's the last time you saw Mormon crickets in this country?"

She continued as if he hadn't said anything.

"We've been on this land a long time, Mr. Rigens. I'm fourth generation out here. You and your park, this Legends of the Basques business, you're gonna bring people to this country like Mormon crickets. Only there'll be no way to squash 'em with truck tires."

Cade had mixed feelings about what the new park meant for traditional ways of life on the plateau, but he didn't think it was his job to quell her concern. It wasn't black or white, and maybe nobody knew how to piece it together just right. He offered enough, he hoped, to stay on good terms.

"There are lots of ways to use this land," he said. "I understand your concern about the people and whether or not you'll be able to keep running cattle."

"Park Service," she said with venom in her mouth. "We've got the Bureau of Land Management, the Forest Service, the Fish and Wildlife Service—all of 'em on our backs out here. And now the god damned Park Service. None of you know this land like we do. We take care of it every day. We have to. It's how we make a living."

He knew this wasn't a debate he could win, nor did he want to try. Cows were hard on the desert, but ranching was a way of life that was as integral to the American West as knights in shining armor were to medieval Europe. The allure of the independent, hard-working, pull-yourself-up-by-the-bootstraps story was ingrained in the West's identity, both in reality and the public's imagination. Not knowing what to say without angering her further, Cade reclined against a rock while she finished the final bites of her dinner. When she was done, she leaned forward with fresh purpose.

"You're probably wondering why I asked you the whole way out here."

"They've been looking for that kid all summer, but I don't think anybody's been out here in the canyons, just in the mountains where he disappeared."

"You've got to remember this conversation's between you and me. I've got friends who would hog-tie and brand my ass if they knew I was talking with the Park Service. But this isn't about your park; it's about the kid. I've got to do the right thing, and that's tell someone what I saw. But you've got to understand I don't like what you stand for, you and your government running around like you own this land."

"It's between you and me," Cade agreed.

She looked uncomfortably into the shadows, then returned her gaze to Cade.

"I've got an uncle, loony as a cartoon. He runs all around the place looking for his lost family inheritance. He got out of the crazy house down in Blackfoot a few years ago and started back on his treasure hunt. Last summer I was on my way south from Jarbidge to check on some cows. I saw the Park Service kid talking with my uncle along the road. I'm guessing that was before he went missing, but I don't know for sure. It wasn't but a few days later all those search and rescue folks showed up and started hiking the mountains all day looking for him."

"You think your uncle had something to do with the kid's disappearance?"

"He's pretty wacky, but he's harmless. I'm wondering if the kid caught a bit of Uncle Andy's gold fever, though. Last I saw him, the kid was coming out of the Jarbidge Community Hall with his fancy backpack and boots. And this is one of the things I'm aiming to tell you. There was a group of local folks, people pissed off as a bull with its nuts in a knot about your national park. They followed him. He probably never knew it, but they followed him into the mountains that day for sure."

Cade felt his face cinch taught.

"Was this in May, the same day he went missing?"

She nodded slow.

"You mean people saw him leave Jarbidge on his way into the mountains? Why the hell hasn't anybody said anything?"

"I already answered your question about that. We don't like you or trust you and your Legends of the Basques nonsense."

"He's just a kid!" Cade seethed. "He doesn't have anything to do with the park."

Her face was calm. "But he did. He was here to do work for you and your park."

"It's not my park," Cade said. "It's not even a done deal, and even if it was it's been vetted in a process conducted by a half dozen groups representing tens of thousands of people, some of them from all around the country. The park is for the people, a way to preserve their heritage and the nature around them."

She spat in the dirt.

"The heritage is alive and well, man. I'm living breathing proof of that. This land might not have too many people, but it's alive with history."

Cade leaned his head back to calm himself. He didn't come here to argue about what the West was and what it was becoming. He wasn't even sure about the answers to those questions. The clear sky was moonless and speckled with stars impossible to count. The big glowing smudge of the Milky Way was slung across the heavens like a banner declaring the insignificance of a single, lonely life on a hunk of rock orbiting a star in some random corner of such vast space.

"Who were they?" he eventually asked, his temper calmed. "Who were the people following Miles Fourney into the mountains?"

"You can't ever mention my name in association with any of this."

"Between you and me."

"There were about a half dozen, and I didn't know 'em all. I think a few were militiamen from Elko. But my ex-husband was in the group. He used to be a rancher, now mostly deals in old guns. I never asked, and he's never told. I just know they followed the kid into the mountains before he went missing, and it's the right thing to do to tell somebody."

Cade had given up hope that Miles Fourney was alive, and he sensed on some level the burden the woman carried. With that came a pang of compassion. He knew how hard it was to earn a living running cattle in the desert—one of the last places on Earth they belonged. Now here she was, broken by a failed marriage, broken by a difficult way of life and maybe about to be broken even more by the park they were trying to designate. He knew it was true. Cattle and national parks didn't mix. Her cows would be removed from the land.

"There's something more," she went on. "The real reason I asked you all the way out here." She stood and led him through the willows to the dry riverbed where soft sand had accumulated among river-smoothed rocks. "You got a light?"

Cade pulled a headlamp from his pocket, and the riverbed glowed under its hot glare.

She knelt and swept some grains of sand aside. "I pulled it out a bit when I found it, enough to see what I think it is. I decided to leave it and get in touch with you. That was about a week ago, same day I first called."

Cade knelt by her side and pulled an orange backpack shoulder strap from the sand. There was a tribal depiction of a bird on the strap—the Osprey brand logo.

"If I remember from when I saw him leave Jarbidge, the kid was wearing an orange backpack," she said. "Seems like more than a coincidence."

She was right. Miles had owned an orange Osprey backpack. Cade began to scoop sand from the riverbed with his bare fingers, certain he was digging toward Miles Fourney's skeletal remains entombed in the canyon's timeless cycles of raging snowmelt, parched summer skies and frozen winter winds. He dug around the edges of the pack enough to be sure it was buried with its straps toward the sky, and not wrapped around the shoulders of a decomposed body. He pulled the pack from the sand, tossed it aside and continued to dig. He scooped through the sand and into the rocks. His knuckles bled as he clawed into the riverbed and tossed boulders into the night. His hole wasn't more than three feet deep when Fey stopped him.

"He wouldn't be buried down in the rocks," she said. "You can't dig up the whole canyon."

He knew she was right. He aimed his headlamp around the dry riverbed. There could be more; there had to be more, but only rocks and sand passed through the white glare of his light. Using small stones, he set up cairns near the riverbank and organized the stream bed into a grid. He walked from bank to bank, systematically combing the area for further signs that Miles Fourney had been there, or perhaps been washed there by the river. After thirty or forty passes, he'd found only a faded red bottle top. He returned to where his political adversary sat by the unearthed pack.

"You sure it's his?" she asked.

"Pretty sure. You're right. He had an orange backpack."

He pulled it between his legs and shook it free of sand. One of the chest straps was torn and the material faded, but except for that it was in good condition. He pulled the zipper open. Off the top, he removed a coil of rope and climbing hardware, then took out two water bottles, one empty and one half-filled, a backpacking stove and small fuel canister, a fleece jacket coated with sand, a Snickers bar still sealed in its wrapper and a small satchel filled with a first aid kit, roll of cord, duct tape, waterproof match container, knife, iodine tablets and a roll of toilet paper in a zip-lock bag.

He reached further into the pack and located a handheld GPS unit, clearly no longer working, and another plastic zip-lock laid flat with documents. Cade opened the plastic bag and slid out two pages, the first a copy of a USGS topographic map of the Jarbidge Mountains. It included hand-written numbers near the sites of old mines, the job Cade had sent Miles to do that spring. He scanned the map and found seventeen entries along four dirt roads and one near the headwaters of Gorge Gulch Creek on the southwest ridge of Jarbidge Peak.

He turned to the second page, a photocopy of a hand-drawn map of the same place. It was labeled with the town of Jarbidge, the Jarbidge River, the Jarbidge Jail and a hand-written list that read like incomplete notes from a college lecture:

> *Born - ?*
> *December 5, 1916 - murder*
> *Dec. 12 - mail in creek*
> *Arrest: Dec 12-13?*
> *Jarbidge jail - transfered to Elko*
> *September 1917: Elko trial*
> *Conviction - January 1918*
> *Prison: 1918-1943, Carson C.*
> *Death: 1945, California (Sacramento?)*

In the lower right corner, near the summit of Jarbidge Peak was the label Heben Nuk and a small drawing of a Basque Lauburu with an eye in its center.

"What's this?" he asked.

"I've lived out here my whole life and never heard of a place called Heben Nuk.

"These maps don't even include the canyon we're in," Cade said. "How did Miles end up out here? You say your ex was one of the people who followed him into the mountains?"

"He'll be back in a few days. I don't usually keep track, but I think he went to Boise to get ready for the public hearings they've got scheduled for Saturday."

Cade had half a mind to pack up, hike out and head for Boise right away. She saw the look in his eyes.

"It can wait 'til tomorrow," she said. "That's where you're heading anyway, right? But hear this if you haven't heard anything else. My ex-husband was a son of a bitch and a limp-dick lousy lover, but he doesn't have any funny business in him. Just another ornery cowpoke trying to make a living out here. He might know something, but he's got no devious blood. And he's not gonna like what you stand for any more than I do."

Cade understood her guilt. He also knew he'd interrogate the son of a bitch as soon as he had the chance.

"It's late," he said. "I need to get on the road early to help set up that meeting you just mentioned, but thanks for your help. I'll call a federal law enforcement team and have a crew give this place a closer look tomorrow."

Weary from the day's adventure, Cade crawled into his sleeping bag and welcomed the smooth nylon that caressed his skin. The cool bite of the night nibbled on his nose as he breathed air scented thick with the sweet smell of sage. The stars swirled overhead, and he drifted into a series of fitful dreams. The visions came slow at first, but they were well-worn neural circuits carved deep into his unconscious. He heard his little girl's gleeful scream as he encouraged her to ride a bike. He saw her high-cheeked smile when she graduated from smoke jumper school. He felt the intensity of her determined expression when they took off into the Wyoming clouds that day. Then it was all chaos: raging wind, blinding smoke, frantic yelling, her wide-open eyes, then nothing. Just the big hole torn in their lives when none of them came home.

Cade's eyes ripped open to behold the unfathomable beauty of the night sky. He sat upright, reared back his head and peered into the heavens, inhaling deep and allowing his clammy skin to dry and warm. He'd learned to control his daytime thoughts, but his mind worked on its own when he slept. He took another breath and turned to lay back down when he noticed Fey leaning against a boulder, watching him.

"There's another thing," she said. It was as if she'd been waiting for him to wake. He gave a groggy nod in the starlight, ashamed she might have seen his restless sleep.

"How long have you been sitting there?" he asked.

She didn't answer, but continued.

"I didn't tell you because it doesn't make sense, but here it is: The Lost Sheepherder Mine. It's a legend in these parts, but some folks think it's true . . ."

Before she could explain and before Cade could ask, the canyon was filled with an ear-splitting crack followed by a whistle that hissed through the silence. Fey dove to her belly and crawled to her rifle while Cade, still cocooned in his sleeping bag, rolled helplessly into the willows.

"What was that?" he called across the sand in an agitated whisper as he worked to free his arms.

"I told you folks don't like you out here," she hissed. "Did you drive a Park Service vehicle out here?"

Cade shrugged in the dark.

"I told you they'd hog tie and brand my ass."

She pulled back the bolt on her rifle and let a bullet slide into the chamber, then placed the weapon against her shoulder. She aimed toward the rimrock where Cade had arrived under a twilight sky. Another crack echoed among the canyon walls, followed by a whistle that hissed over their heads and exploded in the rocks. With that, Fey's rifle let loose a deafening roar.

And then the canyon returned to stillness.

TEN

CADE LAID ON HIS CHEST and let his ears search the long slope above camp. He thought he heard the rustling of boots working through sage. He wiggled out of the cocoon of his sleeping bag, and crawled to Fey's side.

"What do they want?" he whispered.

"You tell me, ranger man. I knew it was dumb trying to help you."

She lay on her stomach, her rifle still aimed up the slope.

"Who did you tell?" he asked. "Who'd you tell you were coming out here?"

"Nobody," she spat. "I told you once, and I'm not telling you again: We don't like you. You're the one who drove a Park Service truck into country where they hate the government."

Cade wore a pair of long underwear bottoms, his chest smeared in the sand, his city-soft back speckled with goose bumps.

"From the sound of their legs in the brush, there's more than one," he said.

"One," she replied with a nod into the darkness. "And getting close. What I can't tell is if there's more up top."

Cade looked but couldn't see anything but the canyon rim's silhouette. Either her eyes or ears were way better than his. Maybe both.

"We've gotta go up-canyon or down-canyon," she said. "We can't defend ourselves here. Up-canyon, we cross that open space. Down-canyon is rough, deep and narrow. There's no easy way in or out."

"Down then."

"We could get trapped."

"I'd rather be trapped than killed."

He crawled to his sleeping bag and slid into his pants and fleece sweater, then picked up Miles Fourney's backpack and threaded his arms through the straps, leaving his own gear scattered in the sand. He returned to Fey, who was packed and waiting.

"He's most of the way here," she said. "Whatever direction we go, we need to leave now."

"Are your eyes really so good you can see in the dark?"

She nodded.

"Then you lead."

Fey slipped to the riverbed where they'd dug the backpack from the sand. The rifle over her shoulder, she turned downstream and climbed over a shadowy boulder. Another crack split the silence followed by a whistle and rain of stones. Cade jumped into the riverbed and tripped as he struggled to keep up with Fey. He heard their pursuer's feet hit the stones and felt a surge of panic that quickened his pace as they rushed into the canyon's depths.

Towering cliffs shot abruptly skyward, and only a narrow strip of starlight penetrated the bottom. Hoodoos jutted from the rim like Gothic pillars supporting the sky. The scuffing of their boots was the only sound, and it echoed among the river-carved ramparts.

When they'd traveled what seemed like a couple miles Fey finally slowed, and Cade caught up. They crouched in the shadows and listened, silence confirming they'd left their pursuers behind, at least for a while.

They were at a distinct bend in the creek, which Fey whispered was the beginning of an area called Bighorn Country, where a tributary fed from the west, the way they needed to go to get back to the highway. She suggested they climb into the side canyon to bivy, then hike out in the morning when they could see, and Cade agreed. He climbed from the riverbed and pulled her up by her extended hand. Resigned to the work ahead, they began to climb.

Fey hiked in silence, and Cade appreciated her calm. She was comfortable outside, even under pressure. It was a small glimpse into the steely determination she'd displayed protesting the park the previous couple of years.

After climbing a few hundred feet, they arrived at a vertical cliff wall, which they followed looking for a break that would offer passage to the secluded safety of the upper canyon. The farther they hiked, though, the more formidable the fortress of rock became. The wall was as impenetrable as the night was dark. They had to go up.

Cade stopped at a distinct deep crack in the cliff and encouraged her to drink some water while he dug into Miles' pack. He took out the coils of rope and climbing hardware.

"You ever climbed?"

"Like hell," she whispered.

He ignored her opposition and fashioned a climbing harness from a piece of webbing by tying it into a loop. Then he gave her a cursory lesson in the art of climbing a sheer rock wall. It had been years since he climbed, but he knew the technical part well enough. It was strength he'd miss.

He reviewed the plan with her. He'd climb without a headlamp to avoid drawing attention; he wouldn't talk for the same reason; so, it was imperative she understood how the system of ropes and hardware worked. She'd belay, which meant she'd dole out rope as he climbed and catch him if he fell. It would be his life in her hands.

He slipped into the harness and fastened the waist belt, then swung a sling of carabineers, cams and chocks over his shoulder, doing his best to keep the gear from clanking in the canyon's stark silence.

"You ready?" he asked, and she shook her head no. He turned his back to her and surveyed the rock. The crack that split the wall would be his route to the top. He'd use it like a ladder, jamming his fists and feet in to work his way up. The fissure went into the dark and out of sight. With some luck it would go to the top. Cade reached a hand up and made a fist inside the crack, creating purchase between his skin and the rock. Then he pulled and jammed a foot below his fist.

He'd climbed the basalt crags of southern Idaho a few times, but he'd never taken his gear to the remote canyons of the Owyhee Plateau. The plateau's canyons were rarely climbed by anyone. That meant the rock, in addition to being loose, would be covered in dirt and guano. Frequently-climbed crags became less dangerous the way a well-used trail becomes worn and smooth. He also knew there were fifty-fifty odds she'd catch him if he fell, so he had to make conservative decisions.

He worked his feet up inside the crack and reached another hand above his head. He stepped his feet up again and repeated the process. In this repetitive fashion he climbed thirty or forty feet, straining muscles he hadn't used in years. He turned to look at Fey, but all he could make out was the rope dangling into the canyon's star-lit shadows. He placed a small metal chock into the crack, clipped the rope to it using a carabiner and continued to climb.

Confronting fear had once been a familiar sensation for Cade, something he did over and again for reasons he didn't entirely understand. He'd pursued a career fighting fires for exactly that reason. There was something liberating that happened deep within him when he jumped from a plane into a tinder-dry forest with an inferno bearing down. His senses became tuned, his heart went into tasks and failures became learning experiences. Now on the rock for the first time in years, he tasted some small part of that again. The exposure helped him become entirely present.

Cade had long held that the laws of physics people harnessed in outdoor pursuits translated to fundamental truths in various corners of their lives, and climbers had to focus entirely on success. It was kind of a function of faith that success was within his grasp. The more he was willing to push through and past scary circumstances, the more belief and conviction coursed the various veins and arteries of his life.

The question was: when had he lost it? His whole belief system had shifted. He suddenly believed in career advancement more than advancing up the side of a mountain. He believed in late nights in the office more than nights under the stars. Now here he was again, reigniting neural patterns that hadn't fired in years.

He couldn't tell how high the cliff was, and based on what he'd seen during the day it could be a hundred feet higher. The rope was plenty long, but the wall was a mystery unfolding with each strain of his overextended muscles.

When he'd climbed what seemed to be fifty or sixty feet, the crack began to narrow. And then, without ceremony, it dwindled to a finger's width and after a few more strenuous pulls it vanished altogether. He brushed his palm against the stone-hard surface and felt nothing but smooth desert basalt. He placed a small chock, clipped the rope to it and then froze. The sound of boots crunching on rocks came from the top of the cliff somewhere above his head. With his fingers cinched tight and the muscles of his back straining, he didn't have much time. He had to move—up or down—and, because of Fey's inexperience, down wasn't really an option.

He looked into the starlight and saw that the cliff climbed about ten feet higher to a sizable ledge. Above that was more vertical stone going thirty or forty feet higher to the plateau. He'd have to go up, and go up as quickly and quietly as he could.

He brushed his palms across the smooth rock again and located a dime-sized protrusion that he cinched with the fingertips of his left hand. He pinched down on it and felt his forearm flare in protest. He wedged his toes into the crack and heaved upward, locating a larger ledge with his right hand. When his fingers curled around the ledge, the weight of his body shifted. He all but flew off the cliff but cinched his fingers as he felt the toes of his boots skid.

He resisted the urge to call down to Fey, and with a strain he felt might dislodge an intestine, muscled his feet back onto the wall and pulled himself up to discover another large hand-hold. Once again somewhat secure—and worried he'd created enough noise to draw attention—he inched his way higher until his head was even with the ledge. He looked to the upper canyon rim about forty feet higher and saw a man wearing a headlamp. The light on his forehead created a silhouette of his frame, and it was easy to see he carried a rifle. He wasn't even fifty feet away, but he was on a different level of the cliff wall and walked away from where Cade clung.

Cade remained still as stone until the man disappeared. It was long enough for his forearms and back to throb with the effort, his calves knotted tight. Once again alone, he hauled his body over the precipice and turned to give the rope three big tugs—the sign he'd told Fey would signal he was at the top—and then he waited.

For a long time, nothing happened, but Cade knew they were exposed by the cliff edge, so he began to pull on the rope, which he'd tied to her harness before starting the climb. After twenty feet of coils were looped at his feet, the rope pulled taught, which was good: he knew she was still tied to the other end.

He pulled some more until he could feel the full weight of her. Then he put his back into the task, hauling her up by towing the rope one hand over the other until her angry eyes appeared at the top of the cliff.

"Who do you think you are?" she said.

"Shh," he panted. "There's somebody here."

"You bastard, I didn't even have my gun," she spat. "I wasn't ready."

"That's why I pulled you up. We need to get somewhere safe."

He coiled the rope and stashed it near a rock, then took stock of their location. It was a ledge mid-way up the canyon wall.

"I'm not climbing anymore," she said. "This ends now; we're stopping."

Her resistance clear, Cade knew they'd traveled as far as they could. He also knew their mid-cliff perch was about as safe a spot as any as long as they kept their lights off. He went away from the precipice to the ascending cliff wall and crouched in the sage.

"You roll a lot when you sleep?" he asked.

"I sleep like a stone," she said, and sat with her back against the rock, her knees drawn to her chest, her chin resting on her knees. Cade took off his fleece sweater and draped it over her shoulders. She pulled it tight around her neck.

"Thanks," she said.

"I'm sorry I pulled you up the cliff."

She stared into the darkness.

"I'm sorry I asked you to come out here," she said. "Not because this is a lousy experience—which it is—but because, well, you seem like a decent man."

She sat up from her crouched position and looked at Cade. They'd arrived at an understanding. For the moment, anyway, they had each other, and that's all they had.

She leaned her head on his shoulder. He wrapped his arm around her, and she nuzzled close, the smell of her somehow comforting Cade in a way he hadn't known in years.

ELEVEN

FIFTEEN MILES SOUTH OF GRASMERE NEAR the edge of the gaping black abyss that was the West Fork of the Bruneau River canyon, Paul Dunham's pickup truck headlights knifed through the desert. They arced across a sagebrush hillside as he rounded the sharp curve of his driveway, then shone on his trailer, a mobile home he and Fey had hauled to the clearing to keep better watch over their cows. They'd used it as a working ranch house more than a vacation home, but it had been a place for weekend getaways, too. In the divorce, she'd gotten her family's ranch near Jarbidge and most of the cattle; he got the mobile home.

Paul parked in the dirt beside the trailer and stepped into the night. Turning away from the dashboard lights was like stepping off a busy city street; he was suddenly able to see the place for what it was. The stars of the desert were so vivid and bright, the only source of light and plenty to see by once his eyes adjusted. He made out the tack shed where he used to store his leathers and shoe the horses, the empty stable, fences that fell into the brush and the locked shed where he stored his guns. Since the divorce he made a living buying and selling old guns, which he stored in a well-protected shed at the corner of the property.

Paul usually lingered in the grandeur of the nighttime plateau at the end of a day, scratching his back against the door jamb and drinking a few gulps of desert air perfumed with sagebrush. He'd roll a joint and let his mind bend the reality of it all so the sky seemed three-dimensional and he a mere speck floating through the abyss. But this wasn't a night for celestial whimsy. He'd been on his feet more than twenty hours and wanted sleep, needed sleep, needed to let it all go for a while.

He went into the trailer and took off his boots, leaving them in a corner where he also leaned his rifle. He fed his cat, which purred against his legs, but didn't bother to feed himself, take off his clothes or brush his teeth. He lay on the couch, pulled a knitted blanket over his shoulders and let the day's anxieties tumble in his mind.

He rolled and grunted, finding it difficult to let go of the things he learned and did, knowing his actions were justified even if they'd crossed lines he didn't imagine possible when the day started. It was confusing, and his sleep was unsettled. He rolled onto his side, then back to his stomach and through several restless fits of tossing arrived at that mysterious place between sleep and awake. Then he rolled once more, his feet twitched, and the deadly silence took him.

Three times he was pulled from the depths of repose. Three times he woke with separate but related dreams to consider.

In the first he was making love with Fey, her skin melting into his, her legs wrapped around his waist, her breaths heavy and mingling with his own. "I love you," she whispered. "I love you." He felt her friendship like he had so long before: real, comfortable, tangible. It was immediate and omnipresent, a gratification of having achieved an improbable level of intimacy and all the promise and hope that comes with it.

When he woke he was compelled to call her name, to reach for her hand. But the trailer's silence was his only companion. He was aroused at the intensity of the fantasy, but his throbbing libido faded as he stared into the quiet. He rolled over and fell back into his heavy hypnosis.

In the second dream he was in a small room with Fey, and they were trying to sort something out. They were interrupted by a knocking, and she went to the door to greet a handsome man of about six feet with a full head of silvering hair. Paul withdrew from the room as if the scene had become a movie. He watched as the man removed her shirt and pinched her erect nipples. They slipped off each other's clothes. She arched her back revealing the soft curve connecting her ribs to her hips, and he drew a pair of faded baby-blue panties down her slender legs. The man nestled his head between her thighs, and she sighed, her eyes closed with consumption of the moment. His head moved slowly up her stomach, stopping briefly at each breast, and then their waists met. Her arms reached around his back, and she groaned.

Paul woke once more to the silence. Again, he was aroused, but he loathed his arousal at having watched the only woman he ever loved enraptured in the arms of a man she barely knew.

In the third dream he was on the porch of his trailer talking with his brother. They talked about Fey, and Paul told his brother it wasn't all lost, that anything was possible, that sometimes unlikely things come to pass. His brother looked at him with purpose.

"If she walked back into your life right now would you fuck her?"

Paul's answer was quick.

"Of course I'd fuck her."

"Then I'm afraid you've got a ways to go."

For the third time he woke, only morning was breaking, the space among the trailer's low ceiling glowing gray with the first diffused light of the high-desert day.

The cumulative effect of the three visions was immediate, and he sat amidst the silence of his trailer in the sagebrush near the canyon rim. He looked to the corner where his rifle was propped, its barrel leaning against cracked wood paneling, its stock on the toe of his dusty cowboy boot.

He sat upright and swiveled his feet to the floor, folded his arms across his chest and took a breath. He'd set a course, and now he'd see it through.

He grabbed his gun and boots from the corner and a box of Snickers bars from the kitchen counter, then left the front door swaying in the breeze as he climbed into his truck and fired the engine to life.

THE DAY'S FIRST SUN SLANTED THROUGH the passenger side of the windshield, and a dust plume rose in the still air behind him. For a while it was like any other morning driving to town for groceries or gas. When he arrived at Mary's Creek, though, the sight of the Park Service truck reminded him that things had changed. He'd set it afire with a clear enough head, but the sight of its smashed windows and soot-stained paint were a fast reminder that his life wasn't the same as it was a morning before. He'd been consumed with jealousy—that was part of it—but he also hoped to make it clear that the new national park was a declaration of war for the people of the plateau. He was confident that between burning the truck and scaring the hat off the ranger with gunfire he'd made a clear statement. With a little more luck he'd find the ranger with his Fey and break the bastard's fingers one by one.

Paul continued another mile south to the Grasmere airstrip and the dilapidated old store and gas station that used to be the only place you could buy fuel or food for seventy-five miles. The store and its half-dozen sheds and garages were the only structures that offered cover from the wind, sun or watchful eyes.

He walked around the old buildings until he found three dry-rotted two-by-fours nailed to the sides of a garage door, which faced east toward the canyons. He clawed at the boards until they tumbled to the ground with a spray of dry sand. Then Paul Dunham backed his truck into the garage and shut the door.

And he waited.

TWELVE

F EY DUNHAM SHIVERED IN THE DAWN CHILL. She was tucked tight against a chocolate-brown escarpment of rock, the dirt beneath her back hard as stone, her hands tucked into her sleeves to keep her fingers warm, the sweater the ranger gave her bunched beneath her head as a pillow.

It would have been nice if they'd had time to grab their sleeping bags, but she'd never been shot at before and, ashamed as she was to admit it, had lost some of her wits. She grew up around guns, had a collection of rifles she used to shoot coyotes and rodents, but she'd never shot at a person. She'd heard lots of brash talk over the years from men oozing with spirit-drenched testosterone, but she'd never seen a person actually shoot at another person—let alone at her.

She looked across the canyon and saw the first faint hint of dawn cracking the horizon above the cliffs. Ten feet over her shoulder, also tucked tight against the wall, the Park Service ranger tossed in his sleep. The man had demons that made him sleep real light, that was for sure. A chorus of chirping crickets flooded the canyon. The morning was still, their predicament strange.

Government people were just people like anyone else; she supposed that was plain. But there weren't many who actually grew up on the land. It seemed like most were from big-city places and colleges, and she'd suffered from their endless reams of rules: regulations to keep cows out of the water, laws to protect the damned snails, rules to make sure the sage grouse could screw without human interference. The government had a rule written down for anything a person could do or want to do in the desert, and it didn't make sense. The land was big, and there was plenty of it to go around. Plenty for cows, sheep, Indians, ranchers and all the critters, too.

Fey knew the Owyhee Plateau of southern Idaho. She knew it lifetimes better than some Cade Rigens from Boise. When she was sixteen, she'd spent the first of two summers building Highway 51 with her grandpa's construction company. She'd worked on the dynamite crew with her uncle who'd been shot down in Korea and spent most of the war in a prison camp. He was short on work ethic and long on stories, and his blood was red, white and blue, too. After long days blasting the roadbed across the plateau, they'd recline by a campfire and listen to Uncle Andy spin yarns about the war. They often ended with the same old moral: "We're damned lucky to be bred and born in America," he'd say. "We've earned our right to live as we see fit, and by God we'll fight to keep it that way." She just didn't ever imagine they'd be fighting against the same government Uncle Andy had fought for in the war. That's what it felt like, anyway, like they were fighting an all-out campaign against the Park Service for their way of life on the plateau.

During her days on the road crew with Uncle Andy, Fey would get raging nitro headaches from handling too much dynamite, but the head-aches usually let up by late afternoon when she'd hike into the canyon to fish for cutthroats. She loved the thrill of landing a big fish, the subtle jerk of the rod, the wiz of line, the waist-deep fight to bring the fish home. She'd known the plateau her whole life, but during those hot summer eve-nings alone among vertical cliff walls and trickling waters that sounded like wind chimes in the willows she grew to love the place. The plateau was as much a part of her as she was part of it.

The ranger snorted over her shoulder, and she looked to see his eyes slowly un-crease, his irises poking into the clear gray of dawn.

"You got dreams, mister," she said, "stuff you can't let go of." He turned his head to the east where the stars were receding. "We should get moving. We've got places to be, and—well, with all the bullets from last night."

He mumbled in the stillness. Fey couldn't make out what he said. Not a morning person, she guessed.

He stood and peered east, then looked up and down the canyon, brushed some of the dirt off his pants.

"You know a way out of here?" he mumbled.

"Up-canyon the cliffs get a little lower, same as I told you last night before you decided to be a hero and climb a damn cliff wall. We can find a way to the plateau up there, then we can hike back to Mary's Creek and find your truck."

"We could go back the way we came," he said. "Follow the canyon back upstream."

"Not sure we should."

He nodded his agreement, swung the missing kid's pack across his shoulders and started rustling through the sagebrush along the base of the upper cliff wall where they'd nested for the night. She shouldered her pack and quickly caught up.

"Any idea who'd want to shoot at you out here?" the ranger asked.

"Not at me, but I can think of lots of folks who'd want to shoot you."

"I've been living around places like this for thirty years," he said. "I've come across lots of folks who didn't like me because of my uniform, but I've never been shot at."

"Makes two of us," she said.

She looped her thumbs through the shoulder straps of her backpack and let her mind drift as the miles mounted, the hike giving her time to ponder the ranger from angles that weren't at first natural. She hated that his job was to regulate the land, but she didn't altogether hate him. He seemed to appreciate things not everybody did. It was subtle the way he paused to hear the sound a bee made when it flew past or turned his face toward the warm sun for a quiet moment of God-given reflection. He was doughy and out of shape, but obviously comfortable on the land. He seemed to fit as well as anybody she knew even if he didn't know the first thing about branding Herefords or shooting coyotes. He seemed like he could survive in the wild just fine, might even prefer it to the city if he had the chance. But his presence on the plateau was a nagging thorn in her chaps.

They'd walked a half-hour when they finally found a notch where the rock crumbled and a slope of steep scree angled down. They clawed on all fours up to the plateau and were confronted with the immediacy of the new perspective. Where there had been vertical rock moments before, there was an endless flat plain. Only the Jarbidge Mountains to the south gave any indication there was any variety at all. The canyon and conversations from which they emerged were invisible. The view was almost all sky.

Fey suddenly felt freed from their ordeals but maintained her uneasiness about the ranger. While she didn't trust him to regulate her cattle, she believed he'd tell the truth as he saw it. He seemed like a man of good character, and that made her uncomfortable. She wanted a better understanding of someone she'd long considered an enemy.

"How do you figure you feel about the land out here?" she asked, her curls dangling from beneath her white cowboy hat.

He didn't answer right away, but seemed to roll the question between his fingers like a plug of tobacco he was about to stick in his cheek.

"The same as I feel about lots of beautiful places," he said. "I love it."

His response grabbed her attention. It's the exact thing that had been tugging at the back of her mind all morning.

"Love's a big word," she said.

He slowed. "I'm serious. I think about the land like I think about my wife. Any relationship has to be reciprocal. We take from the land incessantly, but we rarely give back. We're obligated to give back."

Her temples pulsed. She understood his declaration as a challenge of her integrity.

"You don't think I give back? What do you think I do out here all damn day? My way of life, my business, they depend on the land's health."

The ranger didn't answer at first. Maybe she'd taken him off guard.

"I appreciate that you earn a hard living," he said. "But running cattle in the desert's hard on the land and hard on the critters that depend on it. You ever seen pictures of cattle country before and after the cows? The streams get eroded, the plants gnawed down, the water's cloudy and sour. It's not natural."

She stopped and turned her full attention on him.

"What isn't natural is all the rules and regulations you government people use to have your so-called reciprocal relationship. Why don't you try giving your wife a two-inch-thick rulebook and tell me how it goes. You should spend some time out here under this big sky on the back of a seventeen-hand bay rounding up cows. That's natural. That's a relationship. You can't have a relationship with a place you've never been."

She saw a thought crawl into the ranger's mouth, but it didn't come out. He bit his lip, and she knew, at least for the moment, that she'd had the last word.

They climbed over a chocolate brown boulder pockmarked with air bubbles, a sign of its volcanic origin, and a crow landed amidst the sagebrush nearby. Fey looked to discover a dozen or so crows soaring against the sky, their big black wings hissing in the morning's blue breeze. The morning wind whipped her curls as she had an uncanny memory from a long-ago night after the nitro headache was gone and she was camped beneath the stars of the plateau feeling the satisfaction of a hard day's work with her uncle.

"You know what they call a group of bears?" Uncle Andy had asked, the firelight dancing in his eyes.

She'd shaken her head no.

"A sleuth. It's called a sleuth of bears," he'd said.

"You know what they call a group of crows?" he'd asked, a wry smile crawling onto his lips.

A flock, she'd answered.

"No," Uncle Andy had replied. "It's called a murder. A murder of crows."

THIRTEEN

THERE WERE NO ROADS OR TRAILS connecting Sheep Creek's Bighorn Country with the ghost town of Grasmere, but Fey proved her knowledge of the area's rugged cracks and crevices. She easily oriented them west and then southwest and initiated a rugged six-mile hike through boulders and waist-deep sagebrush to within a few hundred yards of the dirt road Cade drove to get to the canyon the night before.

She crouched next to him as they scoured the plain for any sign of the people who'd ambushed them in the dark. The horizons empty, they walked fast until Cade's white truck came into view across the scrub. As they marched closer, Cade saw something wasn't right. At first his truck looked unusually dirty, like a dust storm had consumed it and left it camouflaged.

"Something off with your truck," Fey said, and Cade nodded, his eyes squinting against the vehicle's apparent disfigurement.

As they got closer it became apparent that its windows were smashed and white paint stained with soot. The words "RESIST! No LBNP!" were scratched across the driver's side doors.

"I told you people were angry about the park," Fey said.

Cade was tired of her condescending tone about culture gaps and didn't respond. The air was stained with the scent of burned rubber and singed synthetic upholstery. The smell stung his eyes and burned his nostrils. The truck's paint had bubbled, the metal showing from beneath a thick coat of soot. The front had borne the brunt of the flames. Both front tires were gone, the hood and cab contorted and askew. He looked in the broken driver's side window where it appeared the fire had been started on the seat. It had burned so hot it couldn't even be called a seat anymore.

"This is a felony," Cade said.

Fey stood a few feet behind him, surveying the totality of the destruction.

"I imagine shooting at a Park Service ranger is, too," she said.

"Someone around here is going to jail."

He tugged at the truck door and was surprised it creaked open. Fragments of broken glass dropped to the ground by his boots. The steering wheel had melted through at the bottom, and the dashboard was a mangled mess of contorted black plastic. He reached across the cab to where a CB receiver had been the day before. Its soot-stained metal case was there, but the wires and hand-held microphone were melted into a single glob.

"We're not safe," he said. "We need to keep moving."

His attention moved to the steering column where his fingers found the metal ignition slot. It was an absurd notion to think it could work, but it might be worth a try. He pulled the truck's key from his pocket and inserted it, then turned. The engine coughed, its starter somehow not traumatized too severely by the flames, the battery somehow still intact and connected.

"Get in," he said. "We've got a ride."

Fey stood in the road incredulous.

"Are you kidding me? It's four miles to Grasmere. Let's start walking."

"We're out of time," Cade returned.

"You get that thing started, and I'll think about getting in."

Cade climbed the whole way into the cab and sat on a lump of melted black plastic and metal. He had to clench his stomach muscles to stay upright, the back of the driver's seat completely gone. He cranked hard on the key.

The starter churned slow, grinding against forces it wasn't designed to harness. For ten seconds or more he cranked, then pushed the metal gas pedal, its rubber coating burned away, to prime the engine—if that was even possible. Then he tried again, torquing on the key as if the harder he pushed the better the chance of resuscitating the vehicle.

To his surprise, the engine wobbled to life. It didn't sound good. It sounded like a sick child hovering over a porcelain toilet, but it ran.

He shrugged at Fey, who stood speechless. Then she went around the truck and climbed in, crouching on her toes where the passenger seat should have been.

"You're not gonna make it far in this bucket of charcoal," she said.

"Maybe not, but we're about to find out."

FOURTEEN

FOURTEEN

THE TRUCK ROLLED SLOW ON ITS rims and knifed into the dirt, leaving parallel-running rills like a farmer had tilled the surface to be planted in rows of wheat or corn.

While their progress was slow it was faster than walking, and when they arrived at the airstrip in Grasmere, they found it quiet and untended, exactly as it had been the day before.

"They must have left," Cade said. "Whoever it was is gone."

The only movement came from gently drifting tumbleweeds and a few light puffs from an orange windsock at the west end of the airstrip. His watch read 9:05. Under normal circumstances, he'd be in Boise in two hours, and hardly anybody would notice he'd been gone. Assuming they tried to keep driving the burned truck, it would take forever to drive to the nearest town. Hitchhiking might take even longer along the desolate strip of desert highway.

"How are we getting back to Boise?" he asked.

She pointed northwest where the dilapidated store and gas station stood sentinel. It was the only structure visible anywhere on the horizon.

"What do you mean?"

"I'm not pointing at the store," she said, and Cade understood. She was pointing at the red and white plane he'd noticed when he arrived the day before.

"Oh no," he said. "I'm not getting in that thing."

"I only have enough fuel to make it to my ranch, but we can get you home from there."

"Jarbidge is a hundred miles the wrong direction. I'll lose my job. At the very least I'll lose my promotion."

She looked at him with slotted eyes.

"Promotion? What kind of priorities do you have? I'm offering you a way out of here."

"I'd rather hitchhike."

"According to the maps we found in the orange backpack, the answers about what happened to Miles Fourney might be in the Jarbidge Mountains."

"I can come back after the meeting on Saturday."

"Suit yourself, but I'm going home." She rested her hand on his forearm. "I'll see you in Boise in a few days. Don't expect me to go easy on you."

He nodded, and then failed to find any words that conveyed the mixture of emotions he felt. After all the months they'd spent as political adversaries fighting about the park, the notion that things would go back to the way they'd been seemed inevitable—and ridiculous.

She sprung from the truck and trudged through the sagebrush toward her plane. Cade sat motionless, his mind swirling.

Like hiking and camping, backcountry flying was something he never did anymore. Two summers earlier he'd declined an order from his boss to join wildlife officials in planes equipped with radio telemetry equipment mounted to their wings, equipment used to fly the central Yellowstone caldera doing a population census of radio-collared grizzly bears. He'd been reprimanded that same year for refusing to join the National Resources Conservation Service to fly into the backcountry to repair remote snow monitoring stations that had been damaged during a powerful spring storm.

He was firm in his decision but looked down to find his hands wringing the straps of Miles' orange backpack. He unzipped it and took out the plastic bag with the maps. The kid had gone out there for Cade. He'd done Cade's work. He might have died for it.

Cade studied the photocopied map of the Jarbidge Peaks, the words Heben Nuk scrawled across their southwest flank. His finger moved mindlessly over the small diagram of a Basque Lauburu with an eye in its center. Questions piled up in his mind like fall leaves blowing against a fence.

He moved impulsively, climbing from the charcoal truck and running toward the plane where she'd already climbed atop the wing and was tugging at the cabin door.

"GET YOUR HEADSET ON; there's a checklist under your seat," Fey said from the pilot's seat. "Grab it and read it off."

The plane was a small aircraft, a red and white Piper PA-28 Warrior, a model popular at civilian flight schools because it was affordable and pretty easy to handle. She'd told him she used it to commute from Jarbidge the twenty or so miles to her grazing allotments near Sheep Creek.

Cade frowned at her request for a checklist. Wasn't this a situation where she should just turn the thing on and take off? It's not like there was a control tower to police things. Besides, he had a litany of reservations about backcountry flying. Good pilots went down in small planes flying over the West's rugged mountains. A simple pocket of unexpected wind, a stalled engine or encroaching weather could knock a Cessna out of thin mountain air like a hand swatting an insect. One of the men he'd flown with over Yellowstone had more than thirty years of experience, but even he had nosed into a mountain trying to fly home in an unexpected spring storm. Cade had been part of the rescue party, and there'd been no body to recover, just scraps of fuselage scattered among the Beartooth Mountain scree. Fey had the air of a new pilot, and the back of his neck tingled with the number of things that could go wrong. Backcountry planes had little engines and relied on thermal currents for lift. There was no tarmac, no lights, no control tower, just rocks and little tufts of grass poking from the airstrip. His posture was stiff. She asked if he was okay.

"I haven't seen a written checklist for years," he said.

"Complacency kills," she said. "Buck up. We're gonna do it right, or we're not leaving the ground."

Cade found her response reassuring, even if he knew a veteran pilot didn't need an actual checklist in the middle of nowhere. He reached beneath his seat and located the document, a laminated piece of paper with typed black print.

She pushed the starter to turn the plane over, and it coughed like an old car for eight or nine seconds before coming alive. They put their headphones on and adjusted the microphones so they were less than an inch from their lips.

"Testing," she said.

"Got it," he replied and began to read the list. "Auxiliary fuel pump off."

She looked at a gauge on the dash. "Check," she said.

"Flight controls."

"Check."

"Instruments and radios."

"Got it," she said.

The list went on: Landing gear position lights, altimeter, directional gyro, fuel gauges, trim, propeller, engine idle, flaps, seat belts, parking brake, fuel mixture, engine instruments.

"Doors and windows," he said, arriving at the last item on the list.

"That one's you. Lock the door we climbed in through," she said and pointed to the lever by his head.

Cade cranked it into the locked position.

"Check," he said.

"Good. Now if we go down, that's your way out. Only one entry and only one exit. If it's jammed, kick as hard as you can; it'll give. Let's get this bucket of bolts in the air."

Cade looked out the window to the west where the grass ended at the highway. Tumbleweeds rolled toward them and accumulated in the sage. He also saw the wind sock beginning to puff with the day's mounting breeze, a steady west wind, which would mean they'd need to taxi the length of the airstrip in order to take off.

While Fey worked at the controls, Cade looked toward the highway and old ghost town where some odd movement caught his eye. A truck drove along the back side of the gas station and then turned their direction. He followed its progress—even considering for a moment that he might be able to ask for a ride. When it reached the end of the airstrip, the truck turned toward them and promptly ran over the pole where the wind sock had puffed moments before. Then it stopped, its door opened, and a man emerged with a rifle in his hands. Cade estimated he was a hundred to a hundred-and-forty feet away.

"Something's up," he said, and Fey glanced, then looked hard at the man advancing with the gun.

"That motherfucker," she whispered, her eyes alight with angry recognition, "has lost his mind."

Cade looked at her.

"Cade, meet my ex-husband, Paul."

"I thought you said he didn't have any funny business in him."

She stared straight ahead and ignored Cade.

"Yeah, I'm pretty sure that's what you said. You said he was a limp-dick lousy lover and didn't have any funny business. That's nearly a quote."

"We don't have time for this shit," she said. "Brace yourself. We're getting out of here."

"What if he shoots the plane?"

"He won't."

Cade heard the crack of a rifle and looked to see the man holding the weapon's stock to his shoulder.

"I think he disagrees."

"Just warning shots. He won't try to hit us."

The plane reverberated with a tink. Cade looked down to see a small round hole allowing light through the fuselage below his legs.

"Those aren't warning shots," he said.

She was positioned perpendicular to the runway and throttled the plane, which jumped to life. She turned east toward the canyons, and their heads tossed left and right as they taxied. Using the west wind to take off posed two problems. First, it put them on the ground longer. Second, and more importantly, they'd have to head back toward the angry ex-husband. Fey explained this to Cade in fast, short syllables as they bumped across the rocks.

Cade turned and saw that, for the moment, the bullets had stopped. Fey's ex-husband had returned to his truck. The Piper rumbled to the end of the airstrip where she turned to face west. Cade looked through the windshield where two movements were apparent: rolling tumbleweeds and a big Chevy pickup barreling down the airstrip directly in the path they needed for takeoff. Without a word Fey adjusted the prop angle, checked the flaps, squinted and then throttled the Piper's 160 horsepower engine.

"Fey," Cade said as the plane began to move and bump over the airstrip's stony surface.

She looked silently and sternly ahead.

"Fey," Cade said again as the plane picked up speed, and the pickup grew larger in the windshield. His fingers tightened around the edge of his seat.

"Fey!" he shouted, but nobody was listening. He'd become a life-on-the-line bystander to a game of hate-your-ex airplane chicken.

He gnashed his teeth as the truck's brakes locked, and the plane barely scraped over its roof, finding lift in the morning's breeze. They climbed a short distance, and banked counterclockwise. Cade was barely able to make out the crack of a rifle three more times. No more mysterious round holes appeared beneath his legs, and his pulse slowed, if only slightly.

Then there was only the thrum of the prop knifing through the desert air, the soft g-forces from the plane banking to the left. Cade was on the high side of the turn, and the ground was visible through Fey's window. They were over Mary's Creek where he'd hiked into the canyon with the promise of discovery the night before.

"You think it was all your husband?" Cade asked. "The bullets last night, the backpack, the truck. I mean, what's going on? You think he could have killed Miles Fourney?"

"I don't know," she said. "That's not the same man I married. I don't know."

Cade saw plainly that she wasn't sharing everything, but he felt safe again and for the moment that was enough. The thrum of the plane's engine rumbled through his bones, reminding him that he'd relented to a mechanical force larger than he was and so much smaller than the natural forces it sought to harness—a place he'd promised himself never to go again.

The land fell away as the plane arced into the mid-morning sky. Cade peered through the window as Mary's Creek merged into the deep black gash of Sheep Creek where they'd fled into the darkness. She turned east, and Cade saw the shadowy slash of the considerably larger Bruneau and Jarbidge river canyons cutting out of the Jarbidge Mountains, which loomed ever-larger on the horizon.

Once again he took out the pages Miles left in his pack, the words Heben Nuk rolling over and again in his head. Somewhere up in the mountains was a place called Heben Nuk, and one of the last things Miles Fourney ever did was scrawl its location on a map.

FIFTEEN

THE SUN OVER DOWNTOWN BOISE CRAWLED toward late-morning, and Officer Amaia Ibarra found herself unable to concentrate, the day's unfinished reports and meeting schedule distracting from what was actually gnawing at the back of her mind.

Her hand drifted to the small copy of the United States Constitution sitting on the corner of her desk. She flipped the cover and scanned the pages that had been dog-eared and passages underlined in blue ink.

"Only a virtuous people are capable of freedom," read one. "As nations become more corrupt and vicious, they have more need of masters." The words "virtuous people" were underlined twice.

Nobody at the police training exercises had ever mentioned the Constitution as a key to understanding the threat they might face at the public hearing on Saturday, but now Amaia began to ponder the idea.

She got up from her squad room desk and went to the lounge where she found Jim Gustafson, a department sergeant and her direct supervisor, reading a Consumer Reports magazine focusing on RV trailer reviews. With three kids under the age of ten, Gustafson wanted to buy something comfortable for the whole family but tough enough to drag up rutted dirt roads to hunt elk in the fall. He'd been researching trailers all summer, enlisting opinions from his colleagues, but still hadn't committed to anything.

"Hunting season's going to come and go by the time you pick one," Amaia said while pouring hot water into a mug and adding a tea bag.

"One more season in the wall tent," he agreed. "Maybe I'll find a sale this winter."

Amaia cleared her throat to change the subject. He looked up, aware something was on her mind.

"Remember the kid who vanished down in Nevada this spring?"

"It's no concern of ours anymore. It was always pretty far outside our jurisdiction and, bloody hell, that case is colder than an iceberg. That kid was coyote food months ago."

"What do you make of this?"

She slid the copy of the pocket Constitution onto the table. Gustafson picked it up and leafed through, then turned back to the title page.

"There's nothing odd about our Constitution, of course. This particular one, though—there's a whole organization built up around these, called the Center for Constitutional Conduct or something. Some guy annotated the whole thing to establish its divine inspiration, among other things. From what I understand they print millions and distribute all over the country."

"How do the annotations work?"

He flipped to the front and held the booklet open with one hand while making air quotes with his other.

"'Our Constitution was made only for a moral and religious people. It is wholly inadequate to the government of any other.' That's a quote from Founding Father John Adams, but it's an annotation that came from somewhere else. The Constitution is here, sure, but there's an overriding message that wasn't in the original document. The gist is that the Founding Fathers, directly influenced by the work of Moses mind you, intended the U.S. to be totally beholden to a Christian God and never intended the government to have any power at all. It's a line of thinking embraced by the state's rights folks who want to transfer federal land to the states and corporations."

"Why do you know about it?"

"Friends from church. There's some kind of connection between some people of Mormon faith and this type of thinking. They tried to convert me, so to speak, so I did some homework and decided to stick with the uninterpreted version of our Constitution. Make no mistake, though: millions of these little documents have been distributed all over the country and have found footing among anti-government conservatives who support what they call 'original intent.' That's the idea that the Constitution, like an owner's manual, is a set of precise instructions that shows how to operate a republic."

"So you'd say this anti-park sticker fits?" She pointed to the blue NO LBNP sticker affixed to the booklet's cover.

"Oh, yeah it fits. I'd expect someone reading this document ragged like it is to be against federal land management in general, and a new national park in particular. You're associated with that, right?"

"Just a volunteer helping with Basque cultural stuff, which got me the opportunity to MC on Saturday." She took a sip of tea. "Along these lines, what would you say is the difference between a person who's patriotic and someone who's labeled an alt-right patriot?"

"I don't know, Amaia. On some level it's just words." He pushed his chair away from the table and leaned back, extending his feet while he organized his thoughts. "Now that you ask, I guess I have some ideas. Some of these guys are just misguided by propaganda like the annotations in that constitution you have there. But in others it's more insidious, and the militias that are popping up are patriotic in name or identity alone. They're really what I'd call anarchists who want to overthrow the system while wrapping themselves in our flag.

"For a lot of people in Idaho and across parts of the rural West, I'd say they fall somewhere in between. I guess you'd call them Constitutional originalists or something—the state's rights advocates we were just talking about. Some are peaceful protesters, some affiliated with militias. What they seem to have in common is that they don't like government telling them what they can and can't do. That leads down a variety of rabbit holes. Most Americans, myself and you and most of the people we're talking about, I hope, are patriotic."

Amaia nodded. "So a Constitutional originalist doesn't like the rule of law?"

"It's not that simple, but if you have to boil it down I guess you could say they don't like laws enacted since the Constitution was ratified."

"That's basically all laws."

"You can see why I didn't join my friends from church."

"I can't believe you know all of this from Sunday school."

She smiled, pulled the booklet across the table, pushed her chair in and turned to leave.

"Real quick," Jim said, and she turned. "You asked about the missing kid and then turned the conversation toward that copy of the Constitution like they were connected."

"I haven't put it together, but I'm mulling something."

"Just remember you've got real work to do. That case is closed, and I don't want to hear about you digging around in it again."

She was about to tell him okay, but a curly-haired head belonging to one of the front desk clerks popped though the open doorway.

"Amaia, you have a call from the Owyhee County Sheriff's Office. Want me to send it to voicemail?"

"No, I've got it," she said and nodded at Gustafson on her way out the door.

It took a minute to navigate the corridor of cubicles leading to her desk. She plopped in her swiveling chair, picked up the receiver and pushed a button with a flashing red light.

"Officer Ibarra."

"Amaia, this is Sheriff Cam Acee of the Owyhee County Sheriff's Office in Murphy. How you been?"

"It's been a while, everything okay?"

Acee was a middle-aged no-nonsense cop who grew up on the range and ran for sheriff after a stint in the Marines. In Amaia's experience he was short on tact but had a big soft spot for the vulnerable and downtrodden. They'd gotten along pretty well during the initial search for Miles Fourney.

"One of my deputies just radioed from a Highway 51 patrol. I'm letting you know right away because of our work together. He's got a Park Service truck that could pass for a piece of charcoal. Found it along Rowland Route Road near Grasmere. You know anything about that?"

"Was anyone in the truck?"

"Empty and, like I said, burned real good. Sure as shit, it looks like someone drove it like that, too. It's hard saying what happened, but there aren't any people nearby. He says it looks like someone drove it from Mary's Creek to Grasmere. That's got to be three or four miles."

"Sheriff, I believe Cade Rigens, the lead Park Service ranger from Boise—he drove out there yesterday. If something's happened, there's only one possible suspect: a woman who's been dogging the National Park effort for months. He went out there to see her."

"You got a name?"

"I think it was Fawn or Fern. No, Fey. Fey Dunham. I'd suggest an APB on a Nevada resident named Fey Dunham."

"So you don't know what he was up to or why he went to see her?"

"Actually, he was dusting off that missing persons case you and I worked on this spring."

"What in God's name for? Mr. Rigens isn't even an officer of the law, but that case is so cold it's got ice sickles dangling on it."

"The lady told him she found the kid's backpack in the desert. He went to check it out."

There was silence on the other end of the line.

"Sheriff?"

"Sorry, I just got to wondering. Maybe I'll send my deputy to look around some more. Not sure what he'd be looking for, though."

"I'll see if I can call the ranger."

"Don't bother. We found a piece of plastic that used to be a cell phone in the truck. Not that it would work in that part of the world anyway. At this point we'll file an official report and make a reference to this conversation. As long as that's okay with you."

"Of course. Let me know if anything turns up."

Amaia put the receiver in its cradle with one hand and simultaneously picked up her cell phone with the other. She dialed Cade, and the call went directly to voicemail.

She put the phone back down and stared out the window toward the collection of mountains on the horizon. Somewhere out there Cade had gotten in trouble, and now questions were piling up faster than anyone could dig.

— PART II —

"This is where ideas are supposed to be congruous, but instead I look out on mutinous mountains standing in disorderly formation, defying any notion as simple as order or rank. A mosquito settles on my ankle where the evening already nips. It gorges and leaves behind a welt: itchy and real, raw in the evening cool."

—Miles Fourney's journal

SIXTEEN

THEY'D BEEN IN THE AIR THIRTY MINUTES on a south by southeast heading. The hot brown of the desert gave way to valleys creased with cool green stripes of timber. The Jarbidge foothills gathered beneath them, and Cade felt shaken and shattered, sweat covering his palms and beading around his eyes. He couldn't see himself, but he knew he was ash-white with fear.

Fey turned the plane east as they approached the mountains. The prop made a buzzing sound that vibrated the whole of the plane. It was a lawn-mower of an engine, far too small to keep a couple thousand pounds of metal and flesh in the thin mountain air.

"We'll cross the Jarbidge River in a minute," she said. "You'll be able to see into the canyon and get a glimpse of town as we pass."

She looked directly at him. "You okay?"

He nodded yes while his insides screamed no.

"There's a plastic bag if you gotta throw up."

"I'll be fine," Cade said, and he would. He'd logged thousands of hours in the air. His stomach wasn't the problem.

"Suit yourself," she shrugged and continued explaining the country that passed beneath. "Over here on my side you can see north into the Diamond Desert, kind of a triangle-shaped peninsula between the big river canyons. It's some of the hardest-to-get-to country in the United States. That's where we're headed, into the top end of it where my family's had a ranch for four generations."

Cade looked down and saw a small collection of buildings deep in the valley's shadows. Roads weaved up the mountainsides, and rust-colored tailings that had been hauled out of mines were plain.

"Where are you landing?" he asked, hoping his voice didn't reveal his mounting nerves. The canyon was tight and the mountains steep.

"We're doing a big counterclockwise circle and putting down on a strip near my ranch. We flew right over it a while back. Don't let it stress you out when we pass an obvious airstrip on the flats. We're heading closer to the mountains. It's a little exciting, but the wind let up. We'll be fine."

They came around 180 degrees to face northwest, back the direction they'd come, and Cade saw a large, grass airstrip come into view. She was too high to land, so he understood it was the spot she'd described. He wished for handles to grasp.

They continued counterclockwise, passing again over the Jarbidge River canyon, this time lower and facing south toward the mountains, which stood tall in the windshield. Fey leveled the plane a few hundred feet over the west canyon rim and cruised toward the peaks. Cade's grip tightened like a vice on his knees. They maintained altitude, but the ground rose up to meet them. Cade still couldn't figure out where another airstrip might be.

"Just another minute," Fey said. Her grip on the controls was tight, her eyes focused ahead. He recognized the look and knew the mood. When a pilot's body language was keen and tense it meant everything wasn't okay. When you flew in the mountains, there was a point when turning back was no longer an option. When a valley's walls were too tight or the air too cold, you maintained course until you found terrain wide enough to bank or a pocket of warm air that would offer loft. If you didn't find either you careened into the side of a mountain or chopped through a stand of timber. Fey's body language said they were in trouble.

A side canyon flashed beneath the plane, which was now only fifty or sixty feet above the ground. Sagebrush, rocks and earth passed in a blur so smooth Cade couldn't bring any of it into focus. It looked like a tree top could reach up and snatch them from the air, turning the plane into scraps of weathered metal rusting beneath the changing seasons, their bones bleaching under the hot desert sun.

Outside his window a dirt road appeared from a small canyon and climbed onto a plateau that gathered beneath them. The road straightened as they maintained a steady south heading. With practiced precision, Fey adjusted the flaps, throttled down and allowed the plane to drop.

They touched down with the harsh rattle of wheels rolling on uneven ground and ran fast on the dirt of an ordinary desert road. Had he misread her body language? Were his instincts that far gone? Fey had executed a near-perfect landing—on a dirt road.

"That was thirty miles as the crow flies," she said, speaking into her headset mic. "We took a round-about route, just over a hundred miles in about forty-five minutes. It would take all day to drive. It's the only way it makes any sense for me to run cows over there."

Cade didn't hear her. He was still trying to relax his clenched knuckles from around the hard curve of his knees.

She slowed and nearly stopped, pausing to pop her window open, then throttled the engine back up and turned in the direction from which they'd landed. They drove on the road like a car, heading toward the grade Cade saw from the air moments earlier.

"Welcome to Nevada," she said.

"What if there was someone driving up here?" he asked.

"Nobody drives up here."

"You own the road?"

"It's a public road, but nobody drives up here except me. I have permits from the FAA and BLM. Relax man."

Cade was exhausted and didn't have the energy to argue.

The plane's wing tips barely cleared the slope on the right as the road titled into the canyon, and the center of Fey's universe came into view.

"Welcome to the Diamond D Ranch. We're at the confluence of a couple creeks where I get my water." She pronounced creeks with a soft i sound: "cricks." Cade hadn't heard it like that since his rural Pennsylvania youth.

The road flattened near the canyon's bottom, and they emerged from between basalt buttresses that had been hiding most of the canyon from view. Cade saw where the creeks came together to form an oasis of fertile land. The valley was flat and green, surrounded by thirty-foot cliffs that blocked most of the view in every direction except south, where the mountains poked their craggy tops above the cliffs. They were still in the desert but on its edge now. Somewhere nearby the land tilted upward toward those peaks.

"We're about ten miles from town," Fey said. "Back past the way we came is Deer Creek Grade—drops a thousand feet to the river. Technically it's closed, but you can pass with a good four-wheel-drive. From the bottom of the grade it's just a few miles along the river to Jarbidge."

The plane's cabin rumbled as they crossed a cattle guard and entered the core of the ranch. On the right, tucked against one of the canyon's ribbons of cliff, were two houses and a cabin, all three structures two stories tall. Two huge cottonwood trees grew in front of the larger home and offered shade from the August sun. Across the road the creeks flowed through a series of corrals. There was an assortment of structures scattered across the canyon, too. One was a huge drum suspended on cross-braced metal stilts ten feet above the ground, probably a fuel tank. The plane's hangar would be nearby, but all Cade saw were huge metal doors mounted flush in a cliff wall.

Fey positioned the plane beside the drum and pivoted a hundred and eighty degrees so the tail faced the doors, then let the engine sputter and cough to a stop. Cade removed his headset and popped the cabin's door open. It was still morning, but the desert heat had built. The scent of sagebrush mixed with cow manure rushed in to meet them, and he heard the gentle sounds of the stream bubbling across the corrals. He climbed onto the wing and jumped to the ground, where he was greeted by a tail-high border collie.

"That's Sherman," she said, pointing to the dog. "Like the tank, not the General." Cade knelt to pet the dog, but his ears went flat and tail quit wagging. "Nothing personal, but he usually doesn't like men 'til he gets to know them."

Cade returned to his feet while Fey unspooled a hose from the fuel drum and started filling the first of the plane's two twenty-five-gallon tanks, one on each wing.

She gazed across the ranch while she worked and took in the scene like she was drinking a glass of cold water.

"How long you had this place?"

"I've been out here my whole life. Did you know the Shoshone Indians had something like eight different words for home? For me the only two that ever mattered were Diamond and D."

She coiled the fuel hose and hung it from the stilts beneath the drum, then went to the two big sliding doors mounted flush in the cliff face. She pushed them aside to reveal a cavern dug from within the stone bulwark. She pointed to the port-side wing.

"They're calling for afternoon storms the rest of the week. I don't want this baby out in the weather. Lay a shoulder into that wing, would you?"

They leaned into the task together, and the plane easily rolled backward into the shelter.

"As to the question you're about to ask," Fey said, her legs pumping like pistons in the dirt, "I don't know what it's for. Maybe dad dug it out before I was old enough to remember. Either way, I had these doors installed, and I'm making good use of it."

"It's huge."

"Big enough for a plane," she agreed.

Cade gazed at the shelter's formidable granite roof while she placed chocks around the plane's tires. Given the importance of the shelter for her plane, he found it odd to see an almost-perfect circular hole in the ceiling. Below that was a small pile of rock and an empty plastic bottle labeled Dasani.

Fey motioned for Cade to join her and pushed the doors shut, locking them together with a Masterlock padlock. He followed her along a small walkway to the largest of the houses. Cottonwood trees towered over the path, their leaves shuffling in the day's mounting heat. She climbed a small set of steps and held a screen door open.

His eyes were slow to adjust, but the room smelled like soap and peeling linoleum. As the shadows came into focus, he recognized the contours of the home's kitchen. She went to a cupboard and pulled down two glasses, filling them from the tap. She held one out, and Cade was overcome with the idea that water sliding down his throat might be the one simple pleasure he most desperately wanted. He tipped the glass up, swallowed once to open his throat and let the rest slide freely into his gut where he felt it cool him from the inside. As his eyes continued to adjust, he made out more of the room. White-painted cupboards were built around a brick fireplace that had a hearth big and tall enough to sit on. Brick stairs spiraled toward a second floor.

Cade asked for another glass of water, and she stepped away from the sink to show he was welcome to fill it himself, which he did. He took a gulp and put the glass back down. She watched him intently.

"Park Service in my house," she said. "Never would have guessed it when I called you last week."

"Park Service in your house and dirty as hell."

He surveyed his clothes, padding the thighs of his pants and producing a billow of dust.

She looked toward a doorway leading further into the house. "You'll probably want to use a phone."

She was right; he'd thought a lot about it. What he wanted most, though, was to keep looking for Miles Fourney. Having police descend on the Diamond D Ranch to ask questions and comb the countryside wouldn't help. Spending a couple hours filling out police reports didn't interest him at all. Time was a limited resource

"Can I start with a shower? I need to think about the phone call, who to call, what to say. Do you know anybody who might know where Heben Nuk is?"

"I'll take you to town and drop you at a place where you can get food and a room. Maybe someone down there knows about this Heben Nuk place. From there you can call the police, call for a ride to Boise or set out for the mountains if that's what you've got to do. We should get you on your way as soon as possible."

"What about your husband?"

"You mean my ex-husband."

"I'll need to report what happened."

"He deserves whatever he has coming, I guess. I feel for him. He was a good man before . . ."

"You think he'll come here?"

"It would take him all day. Wouldn't get here 'til late."

"Will you be safe?"

"He's mad as hell at me, but he wouldn't touch a hair on my head. You understand, right? He thinks he's still in love with me."

Cade looked down at his pants, torn across the thigh from jamming his leg in the cliff the night before. Fey was filthy, too, her palms black, clothes caked with dust and sand. Despite the dirt that covered nearly all of her, Fey's eyes twinkled through the kitchen shadows, her skin soft, her breasts rising and falling with her breaths. Cade probably understood better than she realized. Fey's ex-husband had let a beautiful woman slip through his grasp.

"I guess that makes sense," Cade replied.

"I can handle him," she reiterated. "And I understand you'll do what you have to. Maybe just think on it before you do. Now, let's get cleaned up before we go to town. You'll need clothes. Wait here a minute."

She disappeared up the spiral of bricks that went to the second floor and returned a few minutes later with a white towel, small navy-blue washcloth and a stack of neatly-folded clothes.

"Paul left these, and he's not getting 'em back. There's a pair of boots by the bathroom door, size ten or so and yours if they fit."

She opened a drawer and pulled out a plastic grocery bag for his befouled clothing, then pointed toward the front of the house where he found a door leading into a small bathroom with a claw-foot bathtub, pedestal sink and wall-hung toilet with its flush handle on a three-foot chain. Suspended above the bathtub was a halo of chrome draped with a plastic shower curtain.

Alone, he wadded his clothes into a ball and crammed them into the plastic bag before stepping into the full force of the shower and drawing the curtain closed around him. It was the first time in a day he paused to consider how worn out he felt. He leaned his forehead against the shower's pipes and let hot water stream over his shoulders. Stripes of brown swirled into the drain between his feet.

He'd barely begun to scrub clean when the water turned lukewarm. He scrambled to lather and rinse the rest of his body and wasn't sure he'd cleaned as thoroughly as he could. After toweling dry and slipping into the clothes Fey gave him, he turned to face a full-length mirror on the back of the bathroom door. The reflection he saw was him but at the same time someone different than he expected. In some ways, wearing Wranglers and a red button-up shirt made him look like a rancher, but that's not what caught him off guard. His eyes were puffy, their sockets dark recesses.

Six years before he'd been muscled and lean from miles in the back-country. Since moving to Boise his midsection had become doughy, his chin soft. He maintained God-given strength, but city life had changed him: restaurants instead of stove tops, wine instead of water, politics instead of the mountains. Until making the career move, his whole life had been engineered around where he wanted to live. Now with a different kind of star at the center of his universe, he found other activities in its orbit, and he'd become a product of his surroundings. Within the context of Fey's ranch and his first trip into the wilderness in half a decade, he saw himself plain and felt a pang of shame.

He pulled the door open and went into the living room. Out a big front window he saw Fey on the other side of the road, freshly showered, wearing faded Wranglers and a tight t-shirt, working with an axe to split logs. To her left was an unruly pile of sawed logs, to her right a tidy stack of split firewood. She worked with machine-like cadence: unrelenting, regular and precise. Her wet hair was down, her curls dangling on her cheeks. She lifted the axe and let it fall in a smooth, strong, coordinated swing that split a log almost perfectly in half.

He turned and looked around the room. She had an apparent taste for metal artwork. Hanging on the walls were mountain scenes and sunsets made from cuts of some kind of scrap metal. She had a slate-gray couch that was more modern than he'd have guessed for a ranch house in one of America's most isolated strips of land. Like Fey herself the room was austere and homey, tough with a girly touch.

Cade went to a waist-high table where a sealed envelope awaited opening. He took a look. It was addressed to Paul and Fey Dunham and was marked with a return address from the Department of the Interior. Curious, he held it up to the window but was unable to see what was inside.

He shifted his attention to a bookshelf next to the table. The top two shelves were stacked with an assortment of paperback and hard-cover titles. He scanned them and found works by C.S. Lewis, J.R.R. Tolkien and Pulitzer-winner Wallace Stegner—not what he expected at all.

On the bottom was a collection of pottery vases, but the shelf in between is what captured his attention longest. It had a collection of photographs in small wooden frames propped upright using easel-back hinges. All of them pictured a small boy, no more than two or three. One showed Fey holding the boy on her hip. The meaning seemed plain, but if she had a son he wasn't home. Cade looked closer at the picture. There was no indication the child was hers except that she radiated an inner beauty difficult to describe. He simply understood it to be the radiance of motherhood.

The screen door slammed, and he looked to see Fey in the doorway with narrowed eyes and slumped shoulders, a posture he couldn't immediately place.

"You always go snooping as soon as you get to someone's house?"

"I didn't mean to . . ."

"Well you did."

The home's silence took over, and small sounds came into focus: the buzz of flies flinging against the screen door, wind rustling through the cottonwood branches. He felt the heavy everywhere-scent of sage drifting in and out of his lungs, but the house was otherworldly quiet, and he didn't know what to say or do. He'd struck a raw nerve with his curiosity.

"I didn't know," he said.

"Of course, you didn't, just thinking about yourself."

The silence resumed. Cade didn't know what to do, so he decided to probe.

"What happened?"

"Wouldn't you like to know."

"Give me a break, Fey. What's the boys' name?"

The tension was palpable, something more tangible than land-use issues or cultural divides. They looked away from each other, furtive glances around a room full of everything but the obvious conversation they'd already started. After a long, quiet minute her features finally softened, and she looked back at him.

"Tanner," she finally said. "His name was Tanner. He's been gone a year and a half, and nothing's been the same since he left."

Cade sat at the table and listened as Fey relayed the pain of her only son's passing.

"It was spring calving season. Paul and I were rounding up the pregnant cows near Sanovia Creek. We had our backs to him a few minutes, but that was enough. When we turned around he was gone. Found him tangled in some branches in the creek. It was too late for Tanner. We didn't know it then, but it was too late for us, too."

Sorry didn't seem like enough, but it's what came out. At the same time, her story sunk like a fist in the soft of Cade's stomach. He looked away to hide his glistening eyes. Outside the window he pondered the wood pile she'd been working on. One log at a time, she'd placed, chopped and tossed the wood in a stack. Eventually the entire pile of sawed logs would be split and stacked. Like climbing a mountain, any enormous task could be broken into one small step at a time.

"That was right out here?" he asked, pointing to the creek beyond the wood pile.

She nodded yes. "A little farther upstream."

"Why would you still live here?"

"It's my home; why would I leave?"

"I couldn't bear it. To stay, that is."

She looked at him the way a teacher looks at a troubled student.

"God knows I've tried to get my head around that point of view. Paul couldn't bear it either. A lot went wrong with us, but his leaving the ranch didn't help."

"Why'd you stay?"

"This is my home since I was a little girl. It was my father's home and his father's home. I'm not leaving that. Besides, you've got to take your knocks head-on."

Cade shook his head no.

"Why are you just now interested in finding out what happened to the missing kid?" she asked. "What was his name again? Miles? He's been gone for months. Why didn't you look for him back in May or June?"

"You might find this hard to believe, but I don't visit the wilds anymore. Can you imagine a Park Service ranger who doesn't go outside? Yesterday was my first time leaving a paved road in years."

He looked far away, back into years passed. They came back fuzzy, just shadows of experiences he'd had and a man he'd once been.

"There's a place in the Central Yellowstone Caldera called Fairyland Basin. It's a remote valley that takes three days off-trail travel each way and a static-line rappel into the canyon. Once you're there, so far from everything, there are these six-foot stone hoodoos that gave the place its name. They stand around like ancient people, forever frozen in time. It's like a bunch of people suffered the fate of Lot's wife, frozen into pillars of salt, fleeing the destruction of Sodom and Gomorrah. I used to love arriving there. I'd recline against a tree and watch the moonlight overtake Fairyland Basin, the soft hush of the wind caressing the hoodoos. I used to love how my pulse slowed and my vision cleared. It's been a long while since I felt like that."

She looked at him carefully, her wrinkled forehead showing she wasn't sure how to bring him back—or if she should.

"I thought it was the missing kid. Not to diminish that, but whatever happened to you seems bigger."

Cade didn't realize at first, but he nodded absentmindedly, confirming at least a little that she'd probed into the truth. She drew her lips tight, closed her eyes and lifted her head toward the ceiling, breathing deep through her nose and exhaling through her lips.

"Is it the same thing? Did you lose someone? You reek of it. Haven't come to terms with it. Maybe haven't even tried. No more determined to deal with it than Paul was."

Cade's slow nodding continued.

"And that's why you're suddenly hell-bent on finding out what happened to the kid. You were too much of a coward, but now you think you can come out here and find yourself or something."

Cade shook his head no while she nodded yes.

"If you pass a national fucking park out here because you're too much of a coward to face the reality of your life, I'm gonna blow a gasket."

"It's not like that," he said.

He stared out the window at the wood pile. It was five feet high and twenty feet across. It would take weeks or maybe even months of hard work to split and stack it all.

"I'm sorry to hear about your son," Cade said.

"I imagine you are."

SEVENTEEN

A PLUME OF DUST ROSE UP behind Fey's 1971 International Scout. Its light blue paint was rust-stained in spots, but it ran smooth and strong, able to tow a horse trailer against the desert's steep grades. Its top was off, its windshield folded flat on the hood. They drove all of twenty-five miles per hour, but she could feel her curls whipping around her head in a tangled, unhurried frenzy.

The Jarbidge peaks loomed in the windshield. The high peaks were green, the sagebrush austere, the sky perfect blue. Below the dramatic alpine backdrop was the deep crevice of Jarbidge Canyon, which seemed to grow in depth and breadth as they neared.

The road split at the canyon rim, and Fey turned toward its edge where they tipped onto two big switchbacks that crossed spotty stands of juniper and slopes of volcanic scree. At the bottom of the grade was a one-lane bridge that spanned the Jarbidge River, which burbled August-slow.

The canyon's main road was marked "one-lane" on a yellow diamond-shaped hazard sign. It snaked beside the river, which weaved among willows and cottonwood trees. About forty-five minutes after leaving the ranch, the canyon yawned to reveal more sky. The walls were mostly covered in sagebrush, but there were stands of pine, too. It was difficult to tell where the desert ended and the mountains began.

Fey noticed how the ranger gazed across the river at the canyon wall where a cluster of hoodoos were silhouetted against the blue. She found herself staring at them, too, but took her eyes off the road long enough to barrel headlong over a patch of rough rock.

The Scout's decades-old suspension sucked up some of the bumps, but the jolt was enough to toss both of their heads back. She heard a sudden hiss and knew she'd hit one of the road's thousands of angular rocks too hard. The hissing lasted all of forty-five seconds, and she rolled to a stop. The pulsing chorus from thousands of chirping crickets overtook them.

"Welcome to Jarbidge," she said. "This here's like a rite of passage."

"How many plies are you running?"

"That's not the problem. It's not the thickness of my tires."

"What is it then?"

"It's the sharp rocks, Einstein. I get a few flats a year. Eight, by the way."

"Eight flats?"

"No, eight-ply tires. Help me swap out the spare. Jack's in the back, tire's on the tailgate."

She went to the tire and began loosening lug nuts while the ranger lay in the dirt to position the jack. He stopped moving, though, and seemed to be staring at the west canyon rim.

"What's the problem?" she asked. "You having trouble finding the axle?"

"What's the story with those rocks up there?" he returned, pointing to the hoodoos as he stood and brushed dust off his legs.

Fey followed his gaze to the canyon wall where the columnar forms were silhouetted against the hillside.

"Beautiful," he said. "If you use your imagination, you can see their bodies at attention, heads alert, watching. It's like they're waiting for something."

"The Indians say those rocks are monsters that guard the valley," she said, her hands continuing to work at the spare tire. "One of those monsters was called Tsawhawbitts. They say he roamed the canyon with a giant basket, picking people up, putting them in his basket and eating them later. Northern Nevada, southern Idaho—it's Indian country, but not Jarbidge. They say the Indians avoided this place because of that legend. Nobody lived here until they struck gold, and those are the idiots who couldn't pronounce Tsawhabitts. Came out Jarbidge."

"That's supposed to be the monster up there in the rocks?"

"Depends who you ask."

"Like Soddom and Gammorah," he said.

"Huh?"

"Nothing. Hey, I gotta use the facilities. Hope you don't mind if I jump down to the stream bank for a minute."

She waved her hand with disinterest, and he disappeared into a thicket of willows by the river.

Convenient timing, she thought, then heard the rumble of another vehicle heading up-canyon.

She turned and saw a plume of dust rising from the dirt that connected northern Nevada with Idaho and not much else. The dust rose in a diagonal column above the riverside willows in the gathering afternoon breeze. As it neared she recognized the yellow four-door pickup. It had a carpenter's rack over its open bed and a yellow Don't Tread on Me sticker on its front bumper. It belonged to her brother-in-law, a dime-store cowboy from Nampa, one of the farm towns outside Boise that had rapidly transformed into an industrialized suburb. Her dad had said the guy was "all hat and no cows," which gave an idea what he'd thought of his son-in-law's older brother. The man was family, though, and he fancied himself savvy at business. He owned a used car dealership specializing in American pickup trucks, and he tinkered with tractor engines for cash on the side. He also owned a small cabin in Jarbidge.

The rocks popped and crunched under the truck's tires as it pulled alongside the Scout. Morgan Dunham climbed out under the shade of a Band of Indians baseball cap.

"Fey," he said with a nod.

"Morgan," she returned. He was gruff but handsome with a full beard and strands of silver at his sideburns. He had a middle-age pot belly, but otherwise was tall and broad with thick forearms. He wore a snap-up cowboy shirt with blue piping around the collar. "You're a long way from home. What are you doing out here the middle of the week?"

"Poking around." He looked at Fey's truck. "Things not going well for you?"

"Nothing I can't handle."

"Can I help?"

"I've got it. I've got help, anyway. My friend's taking a piss by the river."

"Friend?"

She'd told him all she would. Morgan Dunham was family, but Fey didn't like him.

"We've got it sorted," she said.

He held a hand up as if to say he surrendered, then changed the subject. "Have you thought any more about my proposal?"

She exhaled at the mention of it. She'd thought about selling him her ranch, but the more she pondered the notion the more conflicted she was. She knew change was coming and wasn't sure how long she could hang on. Even if she could she wasn't sure it would survive the new national park and the people who would come with it.

"A little," she said. "I'll have to think some more."

"Don't think too long. I know things out here are hard, but I don't want you to miss the opportunity. Let's keep the ranch in the family. It's ours to defend."

Fey's mind drifted. What if she hadn't helped build the highway near Sheep Creek when she was a teen? Would people have stayed away? Would she be thinking about selling the ranch to her ex brother-in-law then?

"It's complicated out here, Morgan. Things are probably harder than you think. The market's tough, but the park might bury us."

"That won't happen. When your great grand pappy's horse took a sip of water and ate a blade of grass, that was beneficial use. That's how private property's made. It's a natural law. It's the order of things. It's about protecting our liberty and property."

Fey snapped back hard. Had he really just said "ours" to defend as if he owned the place? She thought back to the conversation she'd had with the ranger near Sheep Creek that morning.

"Let me ask you a question, Morgan. How do you figure you feel about the land out here?" She waved her arm west toward the canyon-rim hoodoos and upper reaches of her ranch.

"That's easy," he said. "It's your birthright. Like I just said, it's about beneficial use. Your great grandpappy made beneficial use of it, and it's yours. That's a pact between you and God."

She looked at him with narrowing eyes. "You didn't answer the question. I asked how you feel about it."

He looked away to gather his thoughts, which gave her a chance to study him. She couldn't say exactly why, but he seemed trapped in the shell of himself. He was there in the desert but somehow walled off from it. She knew he kept an annotated pocket Constitution in his shirt pocket, could drone on for an hour about how the founding document was divinely inspired and that the federal government took the land away from the states. But there was nothing about him that made her think he actually understood the land. Her thoughts swirled, but maybe what she was trying to figure out more than anything was that there was no indication Morgan Dunham belonged to the land the same way he proposed it belonged to him. Her dad and uncle had had their problems with the federal government, but she wouldn't have described them the same way. They were of the land, and the land was of them.

"A birthright," she said eventually. "Like air or water."

"That's the idea."

The sun shone hard on the road, and Fey realized she'd becoming queasy with thirst.

"You have anything to drink?" she asked, relieved for an opportunity to change the subject.

"Yeah, of course." He went to his truck and opened the rear driver's side door. "Bottled water okay?"

She nodded yes. As he approached she noticed a rifle laying across the rear bench seat. He rummaged through a small cooler and held out a twenty-ounce bottle of Dasani.

"You hunting?" she asked.

"You know how it is. Wanna be ready for the coyotes."

She knew his explanation was likely—in fact most everyone in Jarbidge carried a gun of some sort—but the hair on the back of her neck tingled. She turned to go back to the Scout and was surprised to see the ranger standing there, finally finished with his business in the willows. He was about thirty feet away, and Morgan was still wrestling with the cooler inside the open back door.

"You have two of those waters?" Cade called. He must have seen Morgan hand one to Fey.

Fey walked toward him fast with her water extended. "You can share mine," she said. She heard the thunk of the truck door closing over her shoulder.

"Na, it's okay," Morgan called. "He can have one, too."

She turned and saw Morgan extending another bottle in one hand, the other pushing the truck door closed. He took a confident step forward, and then made a series of half-steps, his eyebrows curled in an expression of confusion.

"Do I know you?" he asked.

"Don't think so," said Cade.

Morgan looked him up and down.

"I do. I think I know you. Aren't you that Park Service guy. I saw you at the meeting in Elko."

Morgan glanced at Fey, who crossed her arms defensively.

"What are you doing with this guy?" Morgan looked Cade up and down, then threw the bottle on the ground near his feet. "Since I'm giving you some water, I'd like you to give me something back. Why don't you show me how you have title to this here land."

Fey was furious.

"This isn't your fight, Morgan. These are my cows out here, my ranch, my livelihood."

She'd known the ranger all of eighteen hours, but it's the first time she saw him shrink back and seem smaller than he was. She knew he had strong answers to Morgan's question; she'd been debating the same points with him. But his tongue was suddenly tied, and the silence lasted ten or twenty seconds—and seemed like a minute.

"I asked you a question?" Morgan steamed. "How do you figure the government owns this land?"

Fey jumped in.

"It's not like that. Open your mind to another point of view. The government doesn't own the land. You and me and all of us do. He's just doing his job. He's not even all that different. Just another son of a bitch who fell in love with the desert."

"Since when have you been on the side of the federal government?" Morgan asked, reaching to his shirt pocket where Fey knew he kept his annotated pocket Constitution.

She cut him off.

"We don't want to hear your interpretation about state's rights or the divine inspiration of the Constitution. Leave the lawyering to the lawyers. And for God's sake, fall in love again, Morgan. Fall in love with the land or your wife or your brother. Just fall in love with something that matters. Stop being a victim."

Fey wasn't sure when it happened, but sometime during their conversation Morgan's face had turned red. He looked uneasy, unsettled. He actually looked dangerous.

"I saw Paul the other day," Morgan said, looking at Fey with a smug expression. He continued to address her but shifted his big, unblinking pupils to Cade. "We talked about going up to Boise for the national park hearing on Saturday. Whipping some sense into those bastards trying to take over our land. You should come."

"I'll be there," she said. "But Paul and I aren't talking. You already know that, though, right? What are you getting at?"

"Remember when that goddamned Forest Circus came and closed the South Canyon Road? Remember how we handled 'em then? This national park's gonna suffer the same thing. We'll bulldoze it back open, that's what we'll do."

Fey remembered it well. The Forest Service had closed a road to protect trout in the Jarbidge River. Hundreds of protesters descended on Jarbidge that July and, using little more than their bare hands and common spades, reclaimed the roadbed. Newspapers across the nation showed photos of protest signs and banners, a movement coined the Jarbidge Shovel Brigade. People had showed up with "DON'T TREAD ON ME" Gadsen flags featuring a curled-up, ready-to-strike rattlesnake.

"An Enemy Hath Done this to the South Canyon Road," Morgan said, reciting a picket sign he'd carried during the heart of the effort to reopen the road. The event had had the undertones of a religious war.

"I was there," Fey replied. "I pulled out rocks and lifted dirt with my own shovel till my hands blistered. But you're wrong about one thing. Nobody's gonna reclaim anything out here because that park isn't going to happen. Things are staying the way they are. We'll stop it, and that's why I've been working my ass off to organize the people and why I'm going to Boise just like I went to the hearing in Elko last week. Just in case it isn't clear, though, I'm not getting in any car with my ex-husband—or your sorry ass, either. End of conversation."

The whole time Fey and Morgan talked Morgan kept his eyes on Cade. Fey knew the conversation was meant for his ears, not hers. She suspected Cade knew that, too.

"Does Paul know you're running around with another man?" Morgan asked.

"What I do in my free time isn't any of your business."

The man continued looking at Cade, his eyes unblinking, untrusting. "Paul's my little brother," Morgan said. "It sure as hell is my business."

With deft movement that didn't seem possible from such a large frame, Morgan pushed Cade against the truck, his forearm to Cade's throat. Cade already seemed out of sorts. Now he was completely on his heels, his breath short, his face reddening. With no blood flowing to his head it would only take another minute until he passed out. There was no way he'd match the strength of a man who wrenched on tractor engines every day. She reached under the Scout's front seat and took out a revolver, pulled back the hammer and held it beneath Morgan's chin.

"Get your sorry ass away from here," she said.

Morgan blinked and inched away. Cade's breaths came back in rasps, and he slumped forward.

"Get away from here now," she said again, the gun still under his chin.

Morgan wiped his beard with his palm and stepped backward, his eyes locked on Cade.

"You screw over my brother, you screw over me," he said, then yanked open the door of his truck and climbed in.

With the realization that the rifle in the back seat was within arm's reach, Fey's pulse quickened until the truck was in gear and pulling away with a skid of stones and cloud of dust.

With his breathing nearly back to normal, Cade doubled over and snatched the bottle of water Morgan had thrown at his feet. He twisted off the cap and took a sip.

"Does that guy always drink Dasani?" he asked.

"I don't know, why?"

"I found an empty bottle of this stuff in your hangar this morning."

EIGHTEEN

THE DESERT DIRT POURED FORTH before the tires of Paul Dunham's white Chevy pickup as he headed south on a network of dirt roads he knew from the time he was a teen. He drove as fast as he could, which varied between fifteen and fifty. When the road opened up, he stomped on the accelerator, and the truck's tires hovered over the dirt more than dig into it. When the road was curvy or bumpy, his progress slowed, and his head bobbed side to side with the vehicle's jostling. It was in those moments when the truck was being tossed and he was forced to slow down that he was lulled into reflection.

He wasn't sure why he'd shot at the plane. He might have hit a fuel line or a wheel or, worse, actually hit Fey. He'd watched from the airstrip in Grasmere as the plane banked toward the Jarbidge Mountains. He'd watched for ten minutes as its buzzing engine ebbed into the huge of the desert quiet. Eventually it was just another invisible speck in an expanse of perfect blue sky. Then he'd knelt on the airstrip with his head in his hands.

He knew he'd seen it when the ranger got out of the burned truck and ran to the plane: an orange backpack strapped to his shoulders. That backpack was supposed to be gone. He should have burned it.

So much had changed since Tanner died. He knew there was nothing either of them could have done, but he'd blamed himself anyway. So had Fey. What sort of man could weather that kind of storm? And now this, the backpack unearthed and the remaining ragged threads of his life threatening to unravel.

He saw Scott Table, a distinctive mesa rising from the desert out ahead and knew the Idaho-Nevada border was close. He'd soon drop into the headwaters canyons of the West Fork of the Bruneau River, then travel a slow network of roads across the top of the Diamond Desert.

The back roads of the Owyhee Plateau were a complicated maze of interconnected paths. A few were maintained and signed by the Bureau of Land Management; most weren't, and a bunch of things could go wrong. Getting lost was one of the easiest to think of, but most of the roads were little more than four-wheeler trails that weaved through the sagebrush and dropped over dramatic ledges of rhyolite or basalt. A four-by-four pickup could handle a lot of them, but not all. And none of the desert's roads were reliable in the winter, especially if there was any hint of moisture. When it rained the silty two-tracks quickly turned to deep tire-gumming mud. Even well-prepared groups—people who had jerry cans of gas, high-lift jacks, and full-size spares—got stuck. The best way to avoid trouble was knowing the roads, and even though Paul knew them the way a teenager knows the nape of his girlfriend's neck, he didn't know them all.

At a fence that stretched across the desert, seeming to divide one patch of sagebrush from the next, the truck's suspension groaned as it compressed across a metal cattle guard. Then the dirt continued to pass beneath his old white Chevy, a vehicle that had been with him since he'd graduated Elko High, proud home of the fearsome Fighting Indians. He'd used the cash his grandparents gave him as a graduation gift to buy the truck, and now fifteen years on it had taken him on hundreds of adventures. It had 260,000 miles, and the engine purred to life even on the coldest high-desert morning. Its rear leaf springs and struts were shot from bumpy desert driving, but Paul didn't much care. It was a constant in his life, one of the few things that helped him feel grounded since his brother shipped overseas for a tour in Iraq and his dad was killed by an asleep-at-the-wheel asshole in the northern Nevada desert. In a flash he'd been alone.

He'd been a decent student and played trumpet in the marching band, which they called the "Band of Indians" at Elko High. Paul always wondered why they did that, kicked the Indians onto reservations and gave all the white kids the name. Anyway, when his dad died he tossed the trumpet aside and returned to the work he knew. He was hired at a cattle ranch in eastern Oregon and then later in south Idaho.

It was during the south Idaho stint that he met Fey at one of the Twin Falls Livestock Commission's Wednesday sales. It was an auction for bulls they'd use to breed new Herefords. The auction was set up with bleacher-style seats in a semi-circle around a small corral where the animals milled, and an auctioneer stuttered through the paces of procuring high bids. Paul had been in the back waiting for a particular strong bull he'd scoped in the corrals when he noticed her on the other side of the semicircle, in the front row where padded seats were positioned near some cable fencing. Her chestnut curls fell from beneath her white cowboy hat, her bare shoulders revealed by a red tank top, her arms covered in dust and dirt from a morning's work on the range. He was immediately smitten and found himself looking and looking away like a schoolboy with an adolescent's crush.

When his bull was led into the ring, and he finally joined the bidding, there'd been only one other person with whom to compete, and it was Fey. She'd bid him up a grand more than he was prepared to spend. He'd gotten into the spirit of the battle, thinking himself savvy for finding a way to flirt with the beautiful woman whose name he didn't even know. Then she'd simply stopped and left him holding his hand in the air. Paul achieved the winning bid, obligated to pay six-thousand dollars for a five-thousand-dollar bull.

He was at the same time angry and fascinated. When he'd told her how much of his money she'd wasted, she simply smiled and said she'd consider paying him back. He already knew she wasn't a traditional woman, but then she proposed to take him to dinner. He'd accepted, of course, but had no intention of letting her pay. Her company would be payment enough, but he'd lost that time, too. They ended up splitting the cost, but it had been the beginning of their time together, and he'd eventually go on to win her heart.

The Chevy groaned across another cattle guard as Paul arrived at a T intersection in an area called RD Gulch where a small creek shimmered like glass as it flowed across its basalt-ledge bed. He turned left and sped to another T intersection, the desert dust suspended among the canyon walls in his wake.

It had been ten years since their romance sparked to life at the Stock Commission in Twin Falls, since they'd worked the range together, since Tanner had made an indelible stamp on their lives. Those worlds were gone now, and Paul was alone again, scratching at his vision of what life should have been and grasping at the tattered threads of a love affair that unraveled right before his bloodshot eyes.

The desert dirt continued to slip away beneath his determined tires. It was an all-day drive, but he'd make it. He'd square things with the park ranger before another day was through, and he'd make things right with Fey.

NINETEEN

CADE WIPED A WAD OF AXLE GREASE on the thigh of his borrowed pants. With him working the tire iron and Fey handling the tires, they swapped the flat for its spare in less than ten minutes.

"Great company you keep," he said with a nod in the direction her ex brother-in-law drove off. "First your husband, now your in-laws. I can't wait to meet your brother."

"I don't have a brother," she said. "And you'd do well to think before you speak." She smiled as she patted the revolver, now tucked in the waistline of her pants.

They returned to the road and rounded a half-dozen curves before an assortment of houses came abruptly into view. Cade blinked back the transition. A sign near the side of the road declared "Welcome to Jarbidge." Tied between two four-by-four posts beneath the sign was a banner declaring "No LBNP!"

Like the road they traveled to get there, the town's streets were dirt, and only a few crisscrossed the canyon floor. They led to small cottages interspersed with a handful of modest vacation homes. Nearby hills were littered with detritus from old mines: scrap metal and wood timbers scattered among tailings that hadn't been touched in sixty or seventy years. Jarbidge was a lot of things, but first and foremost it was a boom town that, like all mining towns that didn't find a way to reinvent themselves, went bust. It collected tourists during the summer and hunters in the fall, but there were little more than twenty full-time residents to keep the lights on in the winter. The mountains now rose around them instead of sitting idly on the horizon.

"It's weird to be here," Cade said, thinking aloud about his experiences. "I feel like people look at me different in small towns like this."

"You ever visit the Bronx or Brooklyn?" she asked.

"No, but if you're talking about rough city neighborhoods I've been to the south side of Chicago."

"How do you think they look at a woman in a cowboy hat in those places? I've got the same problem. It's about community. It's not these people's problem that you've never visited."

"At least I appreciate what the government's done for me out here," he replied and regretted it as soon as he did.

They crossed the Jarbidge River on a one-lane bridge. Without warning Fey pulled to the side of the road. "Get out."

He looked at her, confused. Her expression was unflinching.

"Seriously," he said. "I don't mean to be a jerk. I just don't understand how you and your brother-in-law can dump all over federal law as if it's the law of a different country. Last I checked those are the same laws that give you freedom of speech, the right to bear arms, the right to an attorney and all sorts of birthrights that make your life in this country what it is. I don't get why people close to the land would detest the system of rules that works to preserve and protect it."

"Get out," she said again. "Go on, we gotta talk."

She ushered him back to the bridge where they gazed down at the passing water. It collected and swirled behind a rock where willow stems vibrated with the water's unrelenting thrum.

"You shouldn't have provoked Morgan," she said.

"I shouldn't have provoked him? I'm pretty sure you mean that the other way around."

"No, he attacked because you gave him the opportunity. It's not about what you did; it's what you didn't do."

A red-tailed hawk swooped through the breeze above their heads and rested on a nearby cottonwood limb. From their perch on the bridge, the raptor's unblinking eyes were plain and watching.

"That's not on me," Cade said. "That man's upset for a lot of reasons, but one of them's because you broke his brother's heart. I'm a bystander here."

"Listen, his brother's broken heart gave him a reason to act out on something he already felt about you. If he didn't feel it, he'd have ignored the other stuff, which really just amounts to an excuse."

"I'm pretty sure he'd have been less happy with a Park Service ranger than whatever I look like in your husband's clothes."

"It's not what you're wearing; it's how you carry yourself, how you feel, what you believe, whether or not you believe in yourself. People can smell that stuff. You smell like self-doubt and fear. You're strong, Cade, but you've lost track of yourself."

"Just fucking great. A lecture from a cowgirl about how things used to be, back when a gallon of gas was twenty-four cents and bacon and tomato soup was half a dollar, and integrity meant something and your fucking cows didn't do any damage to the land."

"Cowboys are heroes because they stand for something, man. Courage, optimism, hard work. The cowboy way of life is about a code of conduct. It inspires people to do better and be better. It means little by little, bit by bit, even in the smallest ways, you believe you can change things for the better."

Cade rolled his eyes.

"You know this Miles Fourney kid, he isn't your problem or your solution. Nothing's gonna solve your issues except you. You know that, right?"

Cade folded his arms and stared at the swirling current.

"Did you notice the picture above the shelf at my house?"

He stared at the creek. The water sounded like wind chimes, a delicate demeanor that belied a power that could erode granite, move a beach, take a life away or build it up.

"What's your purpose," Fey pushed. "What's it really? You lost your purpose, Cade. People can smell it. Morgan did."

Cade's eyes stayed fixed on the passing water while Fey dug into the front pocket of her jeans and took out a white handkerchief. She laid it flat on the stones and smoothed it with her palms, movement that recaptured Cade's attention. The handkerchief was wrinkled, but didn't look like it had been used for much of anything. It was embroidered with navy blue thread spelling out a numbered list.

"I've been carrying this every day for a couple years, since Tanner died. I'll never be over it for good, but you need it more than I do."

Cade read the words. They formed a list of suggestions that, taken together, formed something of a creed.

1. Live each day with courage.
2. Take pride in your work.
3. Finish what you start.
4. Do what has to be done.
5. Be tough, but fair.
6. Keep your promises.
7. Ride for the brand.
8. Talk less and say more.
9. Remember some things aren't for sale.
10. Know where to draw the line.

"I've got half a mind to teach you how to handle a gun, so you can defend yourself proper, but this'll serve you better in the end. This list started back when there weren't any laws on the range. It goes by different names—Code of the West, Cowboy Commandments, Cowboy Way."

She looked downstream where the hawk lit from the branch with several sweeps of its giant wings.

"The list varies depending who you talk to, but none of that matters. The point's always the same. It has to do with fair play, loyalty, respect for the land. People out here aren't upset with the government for nothing. They want a trickle-up philosophy where people have voices, where hard work, loyalty, courage and intention add up to something that makes sense. They want to live in a world where The Cowboy Way matters. You can't come in with an easy solution like finding a missing kid to make yourself feel better. You've got to do the work. You've got to have the courage to dig up your demons and stare them in the eye. You've got to take pride in the work of finding yourself and being a better man. You've got to finish it and do it because it needs to be done. Be tough enough on yourself to do it and fair enough to take a break every now and then. This is a promise you make to yourself, so that's between you and God."

Cade stared at the stream. The guilt was something he'd learned to live with. It was as much a part of him as his hands and feet, and it influenced the way he worked in the world just as much. He'd never even considered it was something he might eventually get rid of or move past.

"So why are you helping me look for the kid?" he asked. "Why help if you think I'm doing it for the wrong reasons?"

"I probably get it better than you know. Given what you've been through, it's just something you have to do, and at this point you can't get it done without me. More important, it's the right thing. That boy's got parents, too. I'm sure they need closure the same as you."

They returned to the truck and drove south on Main Street where a wall of cottonwood trees stood between the road and the river, and modest houses crept close to the road. Several properties had rows of shovels stuck in the ground handle-first, proud totems at having reopened the Forest Service road fifteen years before. The anti-federal sentiment was clear in more obvious ways, too. Protest signs decrying the national park hung from trees and stood proudly in front yards. "NO PARK," "Don't take MORE of our land away!" "Don't keep us out!" "No LBNP!" "This Land is our Livelihood" "We the people that live and love here say NO!"

Cade still had the handkerchief Fey gave him wadded in his fist. He flattened and read it through. Take pride in your work, finish what you start, live each day with courage, be tough but fair, ride for the brand.

It's the last one, ride for the brand, that stopped him short. It was a near-perfect list about how to live more fully, fairly and with grace. No matter how you got your head around it, though, there was no mistaking that riding for different brands meant working for different outfits. It meant being on different teams. No matter how things worked out, he and Fey rode for different brands.

He looked her direction. Her chestnut curls flapped happily against her forehead. Her body relaxed, she seemed at peace in the high desert. She noticed his gaze and looked back, smiling. He felt a fresh pang of shame.

If he followed The Cowboy Way, there would be a new national park. If she did, there wouldn't. He appreciated her unexpected help and nurturing attitude, but he knew confrontation was inevitable.

TWENTY

COMFORTABLE WITH HIS BOOT PROPPED in the Scout's open door frame, Cade studied the town of Jarbidge as they neared its main intersection. He saw more rows of blade-in-the-air spades along front-yard fences and a huge boulder in a city park that he assumed was the same stone removed by an angry mob in 2000. Most obvious was a twenty-foot-tall sculpture of a shovel, its blade in the dirt, the words "No More Roadless" painted in black on a red background next to, "Jarbidge Shovel Brigade."

The community's anti-federal pride seemed almost entirely aimed at the land managers who administered the hundreds of thousands of acres that encircled it. It was ironic that those same federal agencies had facilitated the mining and ranching that made the town possible to begin with. Fey's brother-in-law had made his opinions about that clear, Cade supposed: property ownership was a birthright, not something that could be arbitrated by any government.

They arrived at an intersection where the road widened and blended with dirt parking lots. To their right was a red-painted building shaped like a barn and built from logs. The sign hanging across its facade read Jarbidge Community Hall. To their left was a bar or restaurant with a covered front porch and wagon wheel railing.

Stones crunched beneath the Scout's tires as Fey stopped on the wrong side of the road in front of the restaurant. The sign hanging over their heads declared "OUTDOOR INN: BOOZE, GRUB, ROOMS."

Looking down at his borrowed belt buckle, Cade hesitated before stepping into the street. After the confrontation with Morgan he felt like he stood out in some way. Another sign near the front door announced, "No Guns Allowed." It was an old-West place in most any way Cade could think. Instead of horses tethered to the railing there were a half-dozen mud-spattered four-wheelers. Except for the motorized transportation, it felt like they'd stepped five decades into the past.

"Let me do the talking," Fey said. "I don't want you messing things up."

He followed her inside.

Over the bar was a sign that read, "We don't have a town drunk, we just all take our turn." The walls and ceiling were white but scrawled with thousands of loops of handwriting in black magic marker. A sign above the bathroom door read "Outhouse," and about two dozen aluminum hunting arrows protruded from the drywall above the sign. A group of men in cowboy hats sipped from coffee mugs in the corner. A gray-muzzled border collie lay on a small throw quietly licking its paws.

"Morning Fey, table or stool?" a woman behind the bar beamed.

"Neither, I'm looking for Fredi. Need to visit the museum."

The woman behind the bar eyed Cade.

"Ma'am," he said, trying to squeeze his syllables into his clothes.

She nodded and turned back to Fey.

"Fredi's out back emptying the slop bucket. She'll be a minute. Why don't you sit while you wait."

They took a pair of stools near a man smoking a cigarette over a plate of French fries. The woman who'd greeted them was behind the counter, and two other women were hunched over an open spiral notebook discussing the procedures you had to go through to open and close the restaurant.

"How are the cows?" the man with the cigarette asked Fey, a smug grin on his face.

"Checked on the Sheep Creek herd yesterday," she replied without acknowledging his sarcastic expression, which Cade assumed meant he thought it was funny for a woman to run cattle. "I'll bring 'em in come October. We've got another herd in upper Buck Creek. We'll work 'em down to the Diamond D in September."

The man didn't ask another question. She'd been direct enough to shut him up. He looked at Cade.

"Who are you?"

Cade extended his hand.

"Visiting from out of town," he said.

The man nodded but didn't reciprocate the handshake. Cade let his hand return to the bar surface, its wood grain polished from decades of leaning elbows and scooting mugs. Cade looked at Fey, and she understood his unstated request.

"He's my cousin," she joined. "That okay with you, Jim?"

The man nodded again and didn't ask anything else, instead focusing on his French fries, looking up only when a ruckus of rattling pans came from the kitchen. A black-haired woman with pale skin sprang from a door tying a white apron around her waist. Her eyes came alive when she saw Fey.

"It's been too damn long," she said and walked around the bar, wrapping Fey in a hug so tight it untucked her shirt.

"Time's going too fast," Fey said. "Feel like I haven't seen you in ten months. On top of that, sorry to do this to you, Fredi, but I've got a favor to ask. I'm on a timetable and need some help."

Fredi's spine stiffened, her warm demeanor not gone but an air of seriousness there at the same time.

"Can you let me and my friend here into the museum?" She waved at Cade. "Happy to tell you more on the way."

The woman took her apron off and pulled a set of keys from her pocket.

"No questions asked," she said. "Come with me."

They followed Fredi past the line of four-wheelers and went toward the Jarbidge Community Hall, the red building on the other side of the street. Fredi slipped a key into the doorknob and pushed the place open. She held an arm out, encouraging them to enter.

"I'll need a phone, copier and fax machine," Cade blurted.

"Excuse me," the woman said. "Any friend of Fey's is a friend of mine, but we haven't even met yet."

Cade felt his face flush, mostly with frustration but also a dose of embarrassment.

"I work for the Park Service. I'm not on the job, but I'm looking for a kid who went missing earlier this summer. We found something interesting last night, and I need to make some calls, maybe send a fax. Name's Cade Rigens."

Fredi looked at Fey.

"You helping this guy?"

"It's the right thing to do," Fey shrugged.

"The same way his park's gonna put you out of business and run this town over with tourists?"

"We can talk about that later," Fey said. "Finding the kid's the right thing to do; you know that."

Fredi took a deep breath and looked at Cade from beneath her jet-black mop of hair.

"I know who you are. That doesn't change that we never met before, so I'd appreciate if you minded your manners. Copier, phone and fax are by the bookshelf in the back." She pointed to a doorway that led to another room. "They're in the open, so I hope you don't need privacy."

The room smelled like dust and aging wood. The walls were draped with maps of the surrounding mountains and canyons. A map of the proposed park was hung using knives someone had stuck through the corners directly into the old logs.

Cade heard the women talking in hushed tones over his shoulder as he clunked across hardwood floors into the back room. He assumed they were talking about him, but he was too focused on what he might learn to worry about it.

He picked up the phone and dialed a number he'd practiced a dozen or more times in the weeks leading up to the public hearing. The voice on the other end was forced, but pleasant.

"Boise Police Department, how can I direct your call?"

"Officer Ibarra please"

"Officer Ibarra is away from her desk; can I transfer you to voicemail?"

"Can you tell her it's important? Tell her it's Cade."

"Hold one moment."

Cade drummed his fingers, wondering if he could remember her cell phone number if she didn't pick up at work. He heard a click.

"BPD, Ibarra speaking."

"Amaia, it's Cade. I have a . . ."

She cut him off, her tone clipped.

"Where are you? The Owyhee County Sheriff found a burned-up piece of charcoal they say belongs to the National Park Service. What happened to your truck?"

"I'm okay. I'll file a report. Look, I'm short on time and called for a favor."

"What do you want me to tell the sheriff? What about the park? Aren't you supposed to be finalizing preparations for the public hearing on Saturday? What could be more important than that in your universe right now?"

"It's the kid, Amaia. She was right. The rancher lady found Miles Fourney's backpack. I'm following a lead to see where it goes, and I'll get back to Boise as soon as I can. I don't have much time, so I don't need a bunch of police making this official. Can you help me?"

Silence, then: "I'll do what I can."

Cade looked over his shoulder to make sure he was alone.

"Can you run a couple of names through NCIC? John and Paul Dunham?."

"Isn't Dunham the name of the woman you went to see? You should probably know that I gave the Owyhee County Sheriff her name. They're probably looking for her."

"If that's true, they're looking for the wrong person. Like I said, I don't have time to go into it right now. Can you help?"

"Hold on a sec."

Cade heard fingers clattering at a keyboard and shifted his focus to the wall in front of him while he waited. The phone sat on a shelf suspended by crooked L-shaped brackets that had been screwed into the logs using stainless steel lags. Beside the phone was a line of old paperbacks with genres ranging from Anne Rice to Ayn Rand, but a few titles seemed to focus on local history and lore. He dragged a finger across the protruding spines, accumulating a wad of dust as he went. When his finger reached the title,"Jarbidge Outlaws," he pulled the book from the shelf. The pages flipped past his thumb until he discovered a rough-drawn map that looked remarkably similar to the one in Miles Fourney's backpack. The entry was titled "Too-Cool Kuhl." He stuffed the book into the backpack as the receiver crackled back to life.

"Okay, yeah. Not much on this Paul Dunham guy, just a few speeding tickets, a DUI from a while back. The other guy, though. Let's see, he's got an OTH from the Army (that's an other than honorable discharge; doesn't say why) after a tour in Iraq and, oh . . ."

"Oh what?"

"He's on a watch list of possible domestic terrorists for involvement in a citizen militia called Common Sense, apparently named after the Thomas Paine book. It looks like these guys were orphaned, raised by the grandparents, now also deceased. Their juvey files are sealed, but the older brother in particular has been getting into trouble since he got back from the Middle East. Cade, if these guys are suspects in the incident with your truck you need to let me know."

"I actually don't know who burned my truck, and that's the truth, so I'll have to think about it. Like I said, I'm just trying to look into some fresh clues about Miles and get back as fast as possible. Which brings me to the second favor I have to ask. Can you look at something for me? I think it's Basque."

"How am I going to look at something?"

"I'm at a fax machine. In Jarbidge."

"Nevada? How did you get to Nevada when your truck was found a hundred miles north of there?"

"I wouldn't be here if it wasn't important. Give me the number, and I'll send a fax with some drawings: symbols and stuff. Amaia, it includes a Lauburu, but it's more than that, some words I don't understand."

"A Lauburu in the kid's pack? I don't think he was Basque, was he?"

"I don't think so. There's a map, too. I'm heading up to check the coordinates. You ever hear of a place called Heben Nuk?" He spelled it out.

"Actually, you may recall those words from the pocket Constitution you found in the yard here."

"I knew I saw those somewhere. Any idea what it means? I think you said you might know where to look."

"I might, I'll get on it after we talk."

"There's no cell coverage out here, so you'll have to wait for me to call again."

"Cade, I'm not sure why you're asking about members of a militia in conjunction with all this, but I do know that if they have any involvement you need to be careful."

"If I'm not mistaken, it was me who told you that same thing just a few days ago, but thanks."

He hung up, went to the copy machine and lay Miles Fourney's map face down. He pushed a green button and winced as a white light flashed from left to right. The copier spit out an eight-and-a-half by eleven-inch page with the map on it. He slipped that into the fax machine, typed the number Amaia gave him and pushed SEND. The page slid through the machine with a smooth hum.

Finished, he turned and saw the two women waiting for him to stop fussing with the equipment. He was immediately worried Fey might have heard him relay her ex-husband's name over the phone, but Fredi's body language spoke loudest, her eyes stern and hands on her hips.

"Were you going to put that book back?" she said.

Cade was embarrassed but felt a stitch of relief.

"Did you just steal a book from this little low-budget community operation?" Fredi pressed.

"Sorry, I wasn't thinking, just saw something and wanted to look at it later."

She held her hand out. He unzipped the pack, retrieved the small paperback and handed it to her.

She thumbed through and stopped at the entry titled "Too-Cool Kuhl."

"Don't suppose this was the page that got your attention?"

His surprise must have been plain because both women looked at him with question marks for eyes.

"How would you know that?" he asked.

"It's the same thing the kid asked about when he came in here last spring. The story's about a man who's famous for all the wrong reasons. That man also happens to be Fey's great, great grandfather."

TWENTY-ONE

AMAIA PUT THE PHONE ON ITS CRADLE and stared south across the city, thinking through dozens of family stories she'd heard. Heben Nuk seemed familiar and at the same time a piece of trivia that was barely out of reach.

The fax machine beside her hummed to life. She grabbed the page and took a look. The reproduction quality was poor, but the map was clearly labeled with the words Heben Nuk, just like Cade said.

In the lower right corner was an out-of-place sketch of a Lauburu within a circle with an eye at its center. She knew immediately what it was: an old Basque tombstone. The question was, why? Why did the kid have a drawing of an old-world Basque tombstone in his pack when it was his job to look for mines?

She reached for a manila folder near the corner of her desk and pulled out the pocket Constitution, flipping to the page where the words Heben Nuk and Tartaro were scrawled in messy blue ink.

The words certainly looked like an old Basque dialect, and based on entomologies she guessed it was from somewhere other than Bizkaia, the southernmost of the seven Basque provinces and the place most of Boise's Basques came from. It was easy to pick out because the Basque language was so unique on a global scale.

From about the sixth century BC, Europeans wiped out all of the pre-European languages in Europe except the Basque language, Euskara. Scholars attempted to link it with others, like the Berbers of North Africa,

the Mayans, and Old Sanscrit, but it never worked. The language was
unlike any other in the world.

There was an old story she'd heard from her grandma about the devil
spending seven years among the Basques to learn their language, but he
only managed three words. When he crossed a bridge to leave the land of
the Basques, he forgot them.

Basques call themselves Euskaldunak, literally meaning "those who
have Euskara," or "those who have Basque language." The whole culture
was built on that foundation, which made it possible for Basques through
history to govern themselves as a civil society.

Why had the kid marked a place on a map using what looked like an
old Basque dialect? And what was the connection between Miles Fourney
and this heavily-used copy of the Constitution?

Amaia sat stiffly upright. She'd been planning to ask her father, but she
realized she knew another place she could look first.

She compiled the materials into an over-the-shoulder briefcase and
headed for the back stairway, which led to a double door that hinged onto
Boise's Main Street. A hot August wind puffed against her cheeks, and she
heard the white noise of a crowd punctuated by the percussive sounds of
acoustic music. The festival was a block away, and its sounds easily carried.

She threaded her way among cars backed up at a red light and passed a
cluster of two-story buildings built in the false-front style of the old West,
festival smells and noises flooding her nose and ears. She went to the edge
of a corner patio, and the full scale of the celebration came into view. The
street that usually passed for a quiet art district was barricaded at both
ends and mobbed like a Friday night county fair. People were lined up at
tents where kegs foamed into plastic cups; cooks slung paella and blood
sausage across tables on paper plates. A woman played an accordion on the
sidewalk by the white picket fence, and a full band prepared to step onto
a flat-bed trailer that had been parked in front of the Guernica oak across
the street. Amaia shouldered her way through the scrum, went around
the trailer and let herself in through the white picket gate that divided the
street from the historic house that once housed two generations of her
ancestors. She didn't entirely mind that the Park Service had acquired the
property, but it wasn't a seamless fit, either. The houses deserved to be in
the careful hands of Basques who appreciated their history on a personal
level, not the ham-handed grasp of the United States bureaucracy.

That wasn't why she was there, though. She'd seen the words Heben Nuk somewhere before; she was pretty sure she knew where. She went beneath the Guernica oak, past the bola jokoa bowling court and used the key Cade gave her to let herself in to the Park Service office. She retrieved a ten-inch-thick stack of typed white paper from a shelf and returned to the courtyard where she dragged a chair into the shade. Crowd noises flowed around the front house from the unfurling Jaildi as Amaia took a deep breath and got to work. She first divided the stack into ten piles and placed them in a semicircle on the ground around her. Starting on the left, she picked up a stack, put it on her lap and began to read.

Each page contained a legend, each legend an origin more than three thousand years and an ocean away. She was surrounded by words older than recorded history itself, and as she read she slipped into the world of her ancestors where genies, giants, gods and goddesses were real. There were stories about Mari, the Earth goddess who made the weather; Akerbeitz o Aker, a genie who took the shape of a goat; and Basajaun, a huge hairy figure who taught people skills like farming and ironwork. They were mythic characters from the old country, but they were helpful telling the story of the American West, too. They were the stories of Amaia's upbringing as an Idaho Basque, the cultural threads that knitted her people together so far from their ancestral home.

In the morning light of the courtyard Amaia's finger mindlessly traced the outstretched lobes of the Basque Lauburu tattooed on the underside of her forearm. She'd been fifteen when she got it to commemorate her homecoming and honor her grandmother, the family matriarch and master storyteller. As a small girl Amaia would sit on the floor while her grandmother became one with the gentle back and forth of a rocking chair and spin yarns Amaia couldn't have imagined.

Like the lore and legends encircling her now, many of her grandmother's stories were myths from the old country. It took Amaia years to understand how unique it all was, that nobody she knew had ever heard tales about the giant race called the Jentilak, the Christmas messenger named Olentzero or the god Sugaar who met with the goddess Mari every Friday to plan the week's weather.

It was her grandmother's passing that had shaken Amaia to her bones and prompted her to have the ancient Basque symbol tattooed on her arm. It was her grandmother's love of storytelling that gave Amaia's career aspirations a calculated trajectory that went beyond the police force. She had her sights set firmly on a PhD that would honor her roots, and there was little that would deter her in that quest.

In the meantime, her volunteer work on Legends of the Basques National Park would help her get into grad school, which her police work would fund.

She pulled a ruled yellow notebook from her briefcase and jotted a few notes about the first legend. She put it back in its place and picked up the next stack of paper when she heard stutter-step footsteps clunking around the porch of the front house. She looked up to see a wobbly man in a cowboy hat. He had a handlebar mustache and a stubble-peppered mole near the edge of his jaw.

He stopped outside her white-page semicircle of ancient Basque legends.

"You're not the man I'm looking for," he said.

"I'm not a man at all. Can I help you?"

"Is Cade here?"

"He's not."

"But you work here?"

Amaia didn't answer, but was captured by the man's eyes. They were the most amazing shade of light blue she'd ever seen.

"S, s, sorry to bother you, but the man named Cade said I could have the pamphlet back."

"What pamphlet?"

"I dropped it in the yard yesterday."

Amaia's gears worked. Could he be the guy who broke into the Park Service office two nights before?

"I don't mean to be rude, but I don't know you or what you discussed with Cade."

"I'm Andy Jim the third. Cade told me . . ."

Amaia cut him off.

"I don't work here, and I don't know what you're talking about. I do know Cade, so when I see him I'll ask about it. For now, as you can see, I've got a lot of work to do."

"I'm s-sorry to take up your t-t-time," the man said with a small bow that looked curiously close to a courtesy. He turned and stutter-stepped beneath the covered porch toward the street.

Amaia took a breath and looked again to make sure the man was gone, then reached inside her briefcase and took out the small copy of the United States Constitution she'd gotten from Cade. She thumbed through it again, watching the dozens of underlined words and dog-eared pages slip by. She stopped at the page with the scrappy handwriting and read the words again: Heben Nuk and Tartaro. Below them a grouping of characters that didn't make any more sense now than when she first saw them: 4—N 58E—.

Tired from concentrating on clues that didn't add up, she allowed her eyes to drop to the stack of paper in her lap, and her mouth fell open. The stack was titled Legends of the Tartaro.

She flipped the cover aside and began to skim stories she'd first heard as a child. It was a collection of four legends, each a version of a story about a man-eating giant.

TWENTY-TWO

SMALL SQUARE WINDOWS ALLOWED DIFFUSED SUNLIGHT to filter across the old wood floor of the Jarbidge Community Hall. There was an American flag on a staff in the corner, a wood stove along the south wall, and a weathered pew positioned near a central table where it looked like community leaders might meet to conduct official business.

Cade followed his hosts to the east side of the room where a desk was buried in paper. It was an antique clearly used for storage rather than any kind of work.

Fredi shoved the mound aside and sat, nudging a folding chair out at Fey with the heel of her boot. Cade dragged a chair from across the room.

Fredi opened the book and skimmed.

"You want to explain why you took this?"

"You seem to have it figured out," Cade returned. "You tell me."

"I don't actually know," she said. "It seems pretty coincidental that both you and the missing kid wanted to look at the same thing. It's also a little strange you seem to be drawn to a story about Fey's great-great-grandpa."

It was weird but he'd had no idea about the family connection. He reached inside Miles' pack and took out the map he'd faxed to Amaia.

"May I?" He extended his hand, and Fredi returned the book.

He flipped to the chapter titled "Too-Cool Kuhl" and pressed it on the desk next to Miles' map. They weren't identical, but Miles' version had clearly started as a photocopy from the book. The list of notes, foreign words and Basque symbols had all been added later.

"That explains why I took it," Cade said. "What's the story? What was Miles looking for when he came here?"

"Maybe it'll help if I tell you about Fey's great-great-grandpa." She looked at Fey as if seeking approval.

"Nobody in my family ever mentions his name," Fey shrugged. "No skin off my back."

"Ben Kuhl was the last man in the Old West to rob a horse-drawn mail stage, and kill a man in the process. He was also the first person in history to be convicted of a crime using a fingerprint. The story goes that he was after four-thousand dollars in payroll. It doesn't seem like much, but when you adjust for inflation it's more than fifty-thousand dollars today. He was arrested and convicted pretty quick because of a bloody palm print on an envelope that he left by the river. The money he stole—that was never recovered, and he spent the rest of his life in prison."

Cade looked again, and harder, at Miles' version of the map. The notes made a little more sense now that he imagined Ben Kuhl's name at the top like a title.

> *Born - ?*
> *Dec. 5, 1916 - murder*
> *Dec. 12 - mail by creek*
> *Arrest: Dec 12-13?*
> *Jarbidge jail - transferred to Elko*
> *September 1917: Elko trial*
> *Conviction - January 1918*
> *Prison: 1918-1943, Carson C.*
> *Death: 1945, California (Sacramento?)*

"It looks like Miles was retracing Kuhl's movements based on information he got from this book," Cade said.

Cade dragged his finger from one location to the next on the map: the murder site on the main road, the recovered mail by the cemetery, the jail on the north side of town, and then the roads that led south toward Elko.

"What do you think he was looking for?"

"The kid spent hours in here over a period of weeks going through files and reading old claims back in April and May. You know, doing his job."

Cade scanned the room and tried to imagine Miles Fourney sitting by one of the small square windows reading about one of the old-West's last outlaws. He tried to imagine how Miles' work might lead him to such an unrelated topic. He was supposed to be looking for mines, not retracing the events of an old robbery.

"Fredi, do you remember what day Miles Fourney wanted to know more about this outlaw?"

"I remember it specifically because the next day was when he supposedly went missing."

Both women looked at him again, waiting.

"I used to be convinced Miles fell off a cliff and died of exposure or something. I'm starting to wonder, though, do you think this little freelance investigation might have gotten him in trouble?"

Fredi shook her head.

"The kid seemed sure of himself. Specific, too. He wanted information about Ben Kuhl and his arrest. If he was worried about anything, he didn't show it."

"Did he talk about going to the mountains? We now have multiple maps pointing to a spot above town labeled Heben Nuk. We know he gathered this timeline about Ben Kuhl the day before vanishing. We know a group of men, including Fey's ex-husband, followed him up there the day he vanished. Fredi, do you know what's at the spot marked Heben Nuk?"

She flattened the maps on the desk and studied them.

"It's not exact. The GPS coordinates and words aren't precise, but they point above the old Success and Bluster mines. They're two of the originals. Bluster was struck in 1910. Used to go by the name Winkler. It followed a gold vein that went pretty deep into the west ridge. Someone said both claims were sold about 1980, but I don't know much about it. There's seventeen miles of tunnels carved out of those mountains and no saying what links up to what. Just to make sure it's clear, there's no way in hell it's safe in there."

She handed the map back to Cade, who folded and returned it to the backpack.

"You all are burning daylight if you're actually heading up there today. The sun doesn't set 'til nine or ten, but time's a wasting."

Cade folded his arms across his chest.

"We haven't answered the other big question," he said and looked at Fey. "How's the family connection work? How did a man in prison produce a lineage that includes you?"

Fey stood and prepared to leave.

"Kuhl had a son before he went to prison," she said as she walked away. "He got married and had kids, and they got married and had kids, and so-on. You get how that works, right?"

Fey always seemed composed, so her condescending tone caught Cade off guard. She turned to face him and changed the subject.

"Fredi's right that you'll run out of daylight. You should wait 'til morning."

She looked away for a moment before looking back to meet his eyes: "I can put you up for a night if you want."

Cade kept his arms folded, unsure what to make of the invitation.

"I thought you were trying to get rid of me."

"And I thought you were trying to move on. You going to accept or not?"

She extended a hand.

He looked across the room at the map of Legends of the Basques National Park speared to the wall using knives. With each step he sensed the answers closing in.

He took her hand, and she pulled him to his feet.

"Let's get back to the ranch," she said. "We've got an expedition to plan."

JARBIDGE WAS DUSTY AND QUIET, the town still except for a wind that rushed through the pines and fluttered through aspen trees, noises you had to listen for to hear.

Stapled to the logs on the front of the Community Hall was a weathered poster with a picture of Miles. "MISSING," it declared. "Miles Richard Fourney, Last seen May 11, 2015. 5'10", 165 pounds. Wearing shorts, boots and orange backpack. Call with information about whereabouts." The picture showed a young man with sandy-blonde hair, hiking staff in hand and smiling from a mountain summit with patchy snowfields in the background.

Cade pulled the poster down and studied it, thinking through the months and possibilities that had passed. The mountains were dangerous, but it seemed less and less likely that Miles vanished because of a back-country screw-up.

The rumble of an approaching truck grabbed his attention. A large white pickup with dormant emergency lighting on its roof approached. Green stripes along the side panels made its purpose plain: a Bureau of Land Management law enforcement patrol—and a chance to return to the life he'd been neglecting.

Cade instinctively held his arm in the air, and the truck drifted to the side of the road where he stood with Fey, Fredi having already returned to work. The driver's-side window slid down smooth. Inside were two men in pressed khaki-uniforms, both with black utility belts equipped with hand-guns, handcuffs and other tools of the trade.

"Howdy folks," said the driver. "Staying cool?"

He looked at the flyer in Cade's hand.

"Don't hold your breath waiting for that one to come back. The kid had the right to be stupid, but he abused the privilege."

Cade felt his pulse quicken.

"What do you mean?" he asked.

"Just that he was dumb as a box of rocks. It's tough country, and he wasn't ready for it. If stupidity was painful, he'd have suffered an awful lot."

Both men chuckled. Cade scrunched his hands into fists, but didn't let his anger boil over.

"Did you know him?"

"No, I'm just stating the obvious. Maybe it's not his fault. The people who sent him into the mountains don't get many IQ points on him. Anyway, what can we do for you?"

Cade didn't respond. He'd forgotten momentarily that it was he who'd held his hand up to flag the truck.

"You alright, mister?" the driver said.

Fey jumped in. "He's had a long day. The heat's starting to get to us."

She talked with the rangers while Cade slipped into an unplanned introspection. The BLM officer had struck his raw nerve of guilt, but it was the underlying reason Mile Fourney had been sent to Jarbidge that made him think hardest. Cade looked to the side of the road where another picket sign protested the park. He looked at Fey's slight figure standing next to the imposing presence of the government truck. He looked at his own western clothing and felt some degree of kinship with her—a sort of return to the steel center of who he was, a core tempered by hundreds of hours and thousands of miles under the West's wild skies.

What would the Park Service do for this place, really? Sure, it would protect the land and bring people and money, but at what cost? He gazed down the dusty main drag and tried to imagine it paved over with macadam and dozens of RVs lined up waiting for an open spot at a gas pump, huckleberry jam and carved black bear figurines stacked on shelves at the Outdoor Inn. He tried to imagine people speaking French and Japanese while taking pictures of the canyon with their iPads. The visions were among the easiest to dismiss he'd ever considered. Those things in Jarbidge would be like a pentagram in his grandfather's central Pennsylvania church.

He came abruptly back.

"You boys are a little out of your jurisdiction," he interrupted. "It's Forest Service country up here, isn't it?"

"We'll determine jurisdiction," the driver said. "You keep track of your cows."

Cade's face reddened. There's no doubt he was the man's superior in the federal pecking order, but he hadn't yet decided whether to pull rank, ask for help or send the guys on their way.

"Are you boys heading to town?"

The driver nodded. "Back to the field office in Twin Falls if that's what you mean by town. We were supposed to be off today, but patrols are stepped up. A government truck was burned last night, and there's a missing Park Service ranger. We're on the lookout for a woman from these parts. She's supposed to be the key suspect. I guess they call 'em a 'person of interest' these days."

Cade's pulse ramped up. They needed to get away from the truck. He turned the flyer in his hand so he could see the photocopied picture of Miles Fourney smiling from atop a mountain peak. He took a deep breath and spat in the dirt between himself and the truck.

"Thanks for stopping. You boys have a good afternoon." He patted the open window frame.

The driver squinted at Cade, then adjusted his gaze to Fey. The man in the passenger seat slipped the sunglasses down his nose. Maybe he'd tried to usher them down the road a little too abruptly. He patted the opening again and stepped backward.

The engine coughed to life, and the vehicle drifted north toward Idaho and the sinewy sagebrush canyons that converged on one another before folding into civilization beyond.

Cade looked at Fey, whose expression asked the question plain.

"I forgot to mention," he said. "They think you burned the truck."

TWENTY-THREE

THE WHEEZY NOTES FROM AN ACCORDION sounded tinny in the court-yard where Amaia skimmed the four old legends about a mythical beast called the Tartaro. Much like the cyclops from the ancient-world stories by Ovid and Homer, the Tartaro was a one-eyed sheep herder who ate people. Also like those stories, the beast captured a man who blinded the Tartaro with a hot iron and donned a sheep-skin disguise to escape. Amaia scanned all four versions of the old legend and wondered if her memory was failing because none included the words Heben Nuk.

Frustrated, she stuffed the Legends of the Tartaro in her briefcase and returned the rest of the Basque lore to the shelf in the Park Service office. She'd have to ask her dad after all.

She returned to the street where a colorful sea of bodies overflowed onto sidewalks and restaurant patios. She looked across the crowd and saw a cowboy hat protruding above the surrounding heads. Curious, she went to the front of the flatbed where a triangle of steel converged on a two-inch hitch. She climbed atop the hitch and used the added height to get a clear view. To her right the musicians were about to start another set and the accordion player flicked the switch on her mic, producing an amplified screech. Hundreds of heads jerked toward the stage, and Amaia instantly felt their probing eyes.

Her quarry, though, was indifferent and stuck out from the crowd's coordinated movement. His stutter-step gait was clear from afar, and the longer she looked the more certain she was that he also had a handlebar mustache. He walked away from the stage beside another man who wore a pressed navy-blue suit and wire-rim glasses. Amaia swooped from the flatbed and shouldered her way into the mob, following as discreetly as she could.

The crowd thinned at the west end of the block, so Amaia turned to face a boisterous group of Basque men speaking Spanish or Euskara—possibly both. She smiled and greeted them in Euskara while pointing to the wobbly old cowboy and navy-blue-suit man just thirty feet away. They smiled in understanding and carried on with their conversation.

Amaia watched as the unlikely pair went to a black SUV parked by the traffic barricades. The well-pressed man opened the back door, leaned in and cradled a cardboard box, then heaved it into the cowboy's arms. Without formality, the cowboy turned and stutter-stepped in the direction they'd come while the other man drove away.

Amaia turned and followed the old man, watching as he pulled pocket-sized Constitutions from the box and distributed them to anyone willing to accept. Amaia went to a young woman still holding one of the booklets.

"Mind if I have a peek?"

"Get your own," the woman spat.

Amaia rolled her eyes.

"You can have it; I just want a quick look."

The woman relented, and Amaia thumbed through enough pages to see that it was identical to the document she carried in her briefcase, only new. If the old cowboy had access to boxes of pocket constitutions, why had he asked Amaia about the one in her possession? It was time to ask him a few questions.

The crowd began to sway as the band leaned into a minor-key folk song about lost love, and Amaia shoved her way out ahead of the cowboy, making her way almost directly in front of the stage. The swaying bodies parted when the old man arrived at her location, and he recognized her with a skeptical sideways glance.

"You know you need a permit to distribute those things," Amaia started.

"This here's a free country," he said, his voice as loud as seemed possible to compete with the amplified music. "P-p-people have the right to read their Constitution."

"Didn't you say you lost one of those?"

The man shrugged.

"What do you know about the Tartaro and a place called Heben Nuk?"

Andy Jim looked like he'd been smacked in the temple and took a step back.

"I've been looking for that."

"For Heben Nuk?"

"For my Constitution."

"What do you know about Heben Nuk?"

"I don't know where it is."

"Who's the man that gave you that box?"

The cowboy humped the box from one thigh to the other.

"I help him, he helps me."

"Who is he?"

"I have rights. I d-don't have to answer your questions."

"I enforce the laws, and you're breaking one right now passing out booklets without a permit."

Amaia wasn't sure if the city's laws backed her up. Vendors needed to register, but people giving things away might not. Either way, she didn't think the old man would be versed in municipal code.

"You have something that belongs to me," the man returned. "I'd like it back."

"Sir, you may not realize this, but you've implicated yourself in a missing persons case."

"Who, the kid that disappeared in May? I already told the Park Service ranger: that kid stole my papers, and now you stole my book. I'm the victim here."

"What do you know about the kid?"

"He was a crook, and he vanished looking for Heben Nuk."

"If he stole from you, that would give you a motive."

"A motive for what?"

Amaia studied his body language. He was casual and calm—not defensive at all. Maybe he was telling the truth.

"Are you sure Heben Nuk is a place?"

For the first time in their interaction his body language changed. He looked not at their surroundings, but through them. The festival buzzed, but he was stone-still for a minute.

"What would it be if it wasn't a place?" he asked.

She decided to test the waters they were both wading further.

"Did you know the Tartaro is a mythical creature? I think I remember the words Heben Nuk from the story, but I haven't been able to figure it out."

The man didn't say anything, his far-off gaze taking him to another place or time—or both. When he spoke again his words no longer fit the conversation.

"My dad was a horrible drunk. He either didn't want to stop or he couldn't. Either way, he didn't."

Amaia was beginning to understand the man wasn't tethered to the same reality she was. There was a lost-in-space sheen behind his beautiful blue eyes that made her uneasy.

"The other notes you wrote in the booklet, do you know what they mean? The numbers and letters?"

"It's what I got off the papers the kid stole. The kid stole 'em!"

The conversation got weirder with each beat of the band's ethereal song, which surged in building harmonies she remembered from the time she was a girl.

"Sir, I'm going to have to take that box before I can let you move on."

"Like hell."

"I'm not negotiating."

The man muttered under his breath and pushed the box at Amaia. She put her arms beneath it and felt the weight of hundreds of small booklets meant to get the attention of people attending the festival that week.

"I'll get my pamphlet back," the man returned.

She looked and saw his liquid-blue expression had changed from lost and unhinged to something else. He'd looked untethered, but gentle; now his eyes revealed a hint of unmitigated anger."

"I'd be happy to give you one of these," she said.

He looked at her the way a parent considers a misbehaving child, and then the corners of his mouth angled into a disheveled, out-of-place grin. He tilted toward her in a mock bow, then slipped backward into the mass of moving bodies, his cowboy hat bobbing up and down in time with the music as he went.

She turned to nudge her way through the throng, slipping between a food cart and a t-shirt vendor and aimed for Sixth Street where her car was parked along the curb outside the police station. She went through the barricades that closed the Basque Block to traffic and walked until she located the royal blue Subaru wagon she inherited from her dad. She pushed the button on her keychain and unlocked the door, chucked the box of Constitutions in the passenger seat and sat stiffly inside, instinctively reaching for her radio to report the bizarre interactions she'd just had with the old man named Andy Jim the third.

Then she paused.

The investigation into Miles Fourney's disappearance had always been a stretch for BPD. She'd been assigned a supporting role that included interviewing Park Service employees and the kid's family, and then passing her findings on to the Elko County Sheriff in Nevada. She'd worked on it long after she was told to move on, though, and when they found out, she'd been instructed in no uncertain terms to let it go.

She lowered the radio, turned the key in its ignition and eased into the traffic, driving two blocks until she was stopped at a red light. With a moment to reflect, she felt her shoulders relax and broke into a broad grin, laughing at the nerves she'd experienced confronting the old codger. After a spring and summer of failure, after they'd ordered her to let the Miles Fourney case go, here she was working like a vigilante to uncover just one more clue.

She looked in the front seat at the box full of booklets she'd confiscated and noticed a pair of words on the outside of the box: Hardrock Holdings. She didn't know what it was, but made a mental note to check when she had the chance.

She leaned into the rear-view mirror to check her laugh lines, but her smile quickly vanished. She wasn't sure, but a couple cars back she thought she'd gotten a glimpse of a pickup with faded beige paint, a cowboy hat visible through the windshield.

She felt perspiration spread across her shoulders and soak through her blues. She turned to get a better look and felt her tension grow. The vehicle stuffed up close to her tailgate was a shiny black SUV, its windshield tinted so dark she couldn't see inside.

She cinched her fingers tight, stomped on the gas and abruptly merged with oncoming traffic. A horn blared and tires chirped as cars swerved and slowed around her. She sped to the next light and turned again, glancing in the mirror and finding no pickup truck or SUV there at all. She shook her shoulders and took a deep breath.

Had she imagined it? Maybe the day's uncanny events were starting to get to her.

She traveled main roads for another mile, went through a light and turned into a restaurant parking lot next to a thicket of riverside cottonwoods.

She didn't know if she was being paranoid, but she refused to park outside her dad's condo. She looked around and took another deep breath. There was no one there, but she'd stay in the parking lot a while just to make sure.

TWENTY-FOUR

SLATE-GRAY CLOUDS SUFFOCATED THE HIGH PEAKS, and a sharp wind whipped the plateau as Fey and Cade made their way toward her ranch. They'd left town a half-hour before and clawed up the raw bumps of the Elk Creek grade. Now they were atop the plateau in the full force of an advancing storm. The desert dust that whipped up behind the Scout peeled sideways and swirled into the canyon. Cade's shirt flapped like a flag, and Fey's curls lashed at her cheeks.

It was tough to tell without the sun as a reference, but Cade guessed it was a little after four in the afternoon. They descended the final grade into the Diamond D Ranch where ribbons of black basalt encircled the ranch. Tumbleweeds wheeled across the road and collected in drifts against the cliffs.

Fey pulled beneath one of the cottonwoods outside the house and let the truck's engine cough and sputter to a stop. The tree's branches thrashed back and forth, and a few raindrops spattered their cheeks.

"The ranch isn't ready for a storm," Fey shouted against the wind.

Cade looked around. The screen door at the back of the house flapped open and closed. A blue tarp that had covered a pile of manure was puffed up like a sail. Across the road in one of the corrals a freaked-out filly spun against the wind.

"Help me pin this place down."

Cade leaned toward her with his head cocked sideways, unable to hear.

"Help me pin this place down," she shouted again, and he nodded his understanding. He opened the truck door as a heavy branch crashed to the ground only twenty feet from where she'd parked.

He followed her to the blue tarp, and they struggled against the wind to pull it over the manure and fasten it to the ground with cord and rebar stakes. She pointed toward a stable where heavy wood shutters were open wide, and Cade understood her meaning. He went to the stable, pushed the shutters closed and latched them tight. He turned and saw Fey heading toward the corrals from the house where she'd latched the door that had been slapping against its frame. He met her by the fence as the storm let loose its fury. One of the small trees growing atop a nearby cliff was fully exposed. It bowed to the canyon, and then cracked violently in half. Visibility dropped to a hundred feet or less as a downpour saturated the desert in seconds.

They stood at the fence and watched as the filly ran, bucked and spun. She pawed at the ground and swung her hindquarters side to side.

Fey grabbed a halter that was draped over the fence.

"Stay here," she shouted.

She climbed the fence and went into the corral with her hand extended. Cade saw that she was talking, but couldn't hear what she said.

With a soft touch to the filly's withers, the horse spun, and Fey backed away, the horse gulping in erratic breaths. A flash of lightning lit the scene, followed by an ear-splitting crack. The horse spun again, wild with fear. Fey stood about ten feet away, but she'd miscalculated. With a half revolution, the young horse moved closer and kicked, catching Fey on the shoulder and knocking her to the ground.

Cade jumped up on the fence, but paused, remembering Fey's admonishment. This was her ranch, and she could handle herself. The filly's spinning didn't stop, though. She bucked like a helicopter toward the spot where Fey was only just sitting up and starting to get her bearings.

"To hell with instructions," he muttered and jumped into the corral. He ran to Fey and coaxed her into a crouch. As the filly spun closer, Cade grabbed her under her armpits and dragged her to the fence, where he propped her against a dripping-wet post.

"Jesus, don't you understand instructions?" she said. "I told you to stay put."

Cade shrugged, rain soaking him through.

"Let's get back to the house," she continued. "That young lady will have to fend for herself tonight."

Cade pulled her right arm over his shoulder and helped hoist her feet over the fence. Once safely out of the corral, they crossed the road and paused only when they were under the cover of the front porch. Fey hunched over, her breaths heavy, her left hand on her knee, her right held close to her shoulder, a pool of water forming around her feet.

"Sorry I snapped," she said. "Thanks for your help out there."

Cade pivoted to say you're welcome, but she wasn't paying him any further attention. Instead she stared into the wild white crush of the storm. Her features glowed soft, her eyes hard as nails as she surveyed the valley where black basalt cliffs were totally hidden from view. There was a dramatic flash followed fast by a furious crack of thunder that rolled through the downpour's white noise and across the desert beyond.

TWENTY-FIVE

THE ENGINE OF PAUL DUNHAM'S CHEVY PICKUP roared as its tires spun in the mud and sprayed the truck's sides with a heavy coat of dripping desert silt. Paul kept the gas pedal mashed to the floorboard and worked the steering wheel back and forth as the vehicle weaved wildly. He was going too fast to keep total control, but if he let up he'd be stuck in the desert for at least a day and probably two or three while he waited for things to dry. This was the exact reason people got in trouble in the Diamond Desert. If rain or snow caught them by surprise, no one would ever hear from them again or, if they did, it was because they'd been found by search and rescue crews a week later.

The sky was angry, the rain heavy, and Paul's windshield wipers flapped back and forth fast but barely enough to keep the road visible in his headlights. The hot-white flash of a lightning bolt split the sky out ahead.

Paul maintained his high RPMs for another fifteen or twenty seconds until he started to feel the tires gain purchase on firm ground. The truck's suspension buckled with the passing of large rocks. He stomped on the brake to stop while the truck was still on solid footing. He'd gone as far as he could, at least without adapting his approach. He couldn't see the landmarks he typically used to gauge distance, but he estimated he was somewhere near Bearpaw Mountain, a sagebrush-covered dome that would put him fifteen or twenty miles away. Whatever he did, he needed to do it fast before the desert mud got even deeper.

Storm-driven wind and spray assaulted him when he opened the truck door, but he jumped into the fray with purpose and used the brim of his cowboy hat to protect his eyes from the worst of the gale. He reached into the truck's bed and pulled out a heavy set of linked metal chains and carried them to the front left where he knelt and laid them flat beside the tire. In the two minutes it took to clear mud out of the wheel well, arrange the chains and drape them over the tire, he was wet the whole way through. He worked with determination at the three other sets, then climbed back into the cab and paused to catch his breath.

He felt cold rainwater drip down the small of his back, his shirt glued to his shoulders and arms, his jeans soggy and uncomfortable. If going back to the warmth of his home and purrs of his affectionate cat on the West Fork of the Bruneau occurred to him it was fleeting. He pulled open the ash tray and took out a small photograph of a smiling young family under a sagebrush sunset. He saw Fey, Tanner and himself, a family in its gravy days: smiling, happy and mired in the hard work of life on the range. That the ranger was with his Fey was more painful than he could have guessed, but they had the backpack, too. He'd been certain when he threw it in the river that the canyon would swallow it forever. He'd set the ranger straight easy enough, but he needed to get his hands on the backpack, too.

He returned the photograph to the ash tray, threw the truck in reverse and crept backward a couple feet. He embraced the full force of his fury and went once more into the storm, fastened the chains, returning to the truck five minutes later, thoroughly wet and freshly determined.

If he was right about his location it was fifteen miles to the Diamond D Ranch and twenty to town. It would take some time in this weather, but he was confident he'd make it. He slammed the transmission back into gear and gave the truck some gas. His chained tires achieved new purchase in the mud as he skidded haphazardly into the storm.

TWENTY-SIX

THE BOISE RIVER SWIRLED WITH ICY CURRENTS through the city's urban heart. The river was completely surrounded by city streets and sidewalks but had been preserved as a forested oasis amidst miles of concrete and asphalt.

Amaia walked into the cottonwood cathedral that leaned over a riot of streambank vegetation. She followed a paved bicycle path a quarter mile to a row of modern condos. Their styling was crisp, their grounds well-kept, but with their tan paint and shaker roofs they might as well have been erected anywhere in the country. They were a contradiction for anyone with a colorful history of cultural significance—especially someone like her dad.

Amaia grew up in a modest bungalow with a big back yard on the other side of town, but when her mom died her dad thought it would be smart to get away from house maintenance and lawn care. Amaia had protested, but her opinion on the matter barely registered. He'd traded-in the house with the bola jokoa court and basement wine cellar for a Kimberly One Condo. The condo's only redeeming quality was that it had a patio perched above the Boise River greenbelt and a roof-top deck above its third story.

Amaia climbed onto the riverside porch, pulled a keychain from her pocket and let herself in through the back door. She was immediately greeted by stacked cardboard boxes and piles of jackets coated in a light layer of dust. The unintelligible banter from a television news program worked down a set of stairs. She let the door click shut behind her and took a breath. It smelled like bed sores and antiseptic.

She climbed the steps to a large room where she found an elderly man on a gurney in front of the fast blue flashes of a television set. An intravenous pole with an IV bag stood next to him, and a needle protruded from his left arm.

She lay a hand on his shoulder, and he looked up.

"Hi Dad," she said and leaned over to pull his head into the soft of her neck. He reached for a remote that lay on the bedding and clicked the power button. The blue flashes and droning voices vanished in exchange for soft orange light and silence.

"You're sweating," he said. "You okay?"

"I'm fine. It's hot."

She scanned the room. The furniture hadn't changed since her mom died. Along the far wall was a gas fireplace framed by a river rock mantle and hearth. On the mantle were little pictures of smiling people alongside a small Basque flag that jutted from a vase. On a wall near the kitchen entrance was a metal rendering of a Lauburu. The condo was captured in time, preserved first by his loneliness, but also now by his sickness.

"You should have let me move in with you," she said. "I hate that you have strangers taking care of you."

"You have a life; I want you to live it. Plus, you're—what—just a few miles away. It's nice having you around."

"Have you heard from the people managing the donor list?"

"Still two spots back. It may not happen. You have to be okay with that. It's out of our control."

Tears welled at the corners of her eyes. He reached up and wiped one away with his thumb.

For eleven months Amaia's dad had been waiting for a new liver. For eleven months she'd watched as his health deteriorated. At sixty-five, he wasn't old by any measure, and he was the only family she had. It was painful watching her once-proud father slip so far from the big-eyed, never-stop-moving caricature she'd known.

"Tell me about the park," he said. "I'm proud you're helping with that."

"It's getting closer, I guess. They only have a few more hurdles. I'd love for you to see that. There's a public hearing on Saturday, and I've been asked to give a presentation about Basques in Idaho to kick it all off. I'd love if you could come."

"It's not easy for me to get around," he sighed and pulled her hand into his. "I'm so proud of you. Keep your chin up, kid. I'm not out of this fight yet."

A smile crawled across his face like a ray of sun poking through clouds. She felt herself smiling back. Love had a funny way of shining up a shadowy room.

"Dad, do you have the energy to think through a few stories? It's sort of related to the park. I have a couple questions about Euskara and some old symbols that look like they're Basque."

The old man fingered a button on his gurney, and it pushed into a sitting position. She knew he'd do anything for her as long as he could summon the strength.

"What is it?" he said and put a pair of glasses on his nose.

"You sure you're strong enough?"

"Don't be ridiculous. Using my brain isn't going to kill me. What's got you worked up enough to come over here?"

She pulled the materials from her briefcase and slipped out the map Cade faxed. She pointed first to the words, Heben Nuk.

"These words, I can't figure out what they mean, and I'm hoping you'll know."

His eyes glazed over.

"Dad?"

"Sorry, I was thinking. I haven't seen them in a while."

"But you know them."

"My mom used to tell a story, and I know you know it. It's from the old legend of the Tartaro, the one-eyed giant. You remember the story my mom used to tell?"

"Actually, I have a few versions in my briefcase, but I can't find the words."

"Then you probably have the wrong versions. Why don't you go to the file cabinet over there. I have some oral histories and other documents from mom. You need to know where they are, anyway."

Amaia crossed the room to a black two-drawer file cabinet positioned like an end table with a lamp on top. She clicked the lamp on and opened the top drawer."

"It's in alphabetical order. Look for Ayala, your grandma's last name. Then look for Euskadi. The interviews are organized by topic, and I think we were talking about the Basque Country that day."

Amaia felt the stiff file edges flip beneath her finger until she found a set of typed white pages labeled Euskadi, the name for the autonomous Basque country. She took the papers to her father, who leafed through and hummed when he found what he was looking for.

"Most people are familiar with the story about Odysseus blinding a giant with a hot poker and hiding in a sheepskin to escape," he said. "It depends who you ask, but some think the Greeks might have stolen that story from the Basques. There's not much indication the cultures interacted, but in the Basque tradition the giant is called the Tartalo, Tartaro or Torto. Your grandma knew the story from her dad, the first Basque in our family to arrive in the West. He ran sheep in northern Nevada and made note of it all because the Indians had a similar legend about a man-eating giant who guarded the valley near Jarbidge."

She helped steady the page as he read aloud.

> *"The Tartaro was a giant beast with a single eye in the center of his forehead. He was a shepherd and a hunter, but he also hunted men. He ate sheep every day and then after taking a nap ate people who crossed his path."*

The story unfolded exactly as Amaia had reviewed—and how she remembered from her courses in the classics. Instead of Odysseus there was a boy, and instead of a cave the creature lived in a barn. When the boy was captured by the Tartaro, he heated an iron rod in a fire and plunged it into the giant's eye, then used a sheepskin to disguise himself and escape. That's where the similarity ended.

> *"The Tartaro's mother lived nearby and met the boy and exclaimed how lucky he was. She gave him a ring as a gift. He put it on his finger, and the ring immediately began to cry out, 'Heben nuk! Heben nuk!' The Tartaro chased the boy who, crazy with fear and unable to pry the ring off his finger, took out a knife and cut his finger off. That's how the boy escaped the mad pursuit of the terrible Tartaro."*

"So, it's a ring," he said. "And I guess the ring can talk: 'Heben nuk! Heben nuk!'

Amaia leaned back, her eyes aimed into his angled high ceiling.

"But what does Heben nuk mean?" she said. "It looks like it could be a Basque dialect, but I can only guess based on context."

"You're right; a Basque from Bizkaia would never write it that way. They'd write Emen nago or maybe even Emen nau. Heben nuk might be from the north side of the Pyrenees."

She shrugged.

"You're overthinking it, Amaia. It's probably just an ancient way of saying Hemen nago, which as you know means 'I'm here' in modern Euskara."

Amaia looked at the map Cade found in Miles Fourney's backpack, the words Heben Nuk positioned in the high peaks above the town of Jarbidge. She leaned into her chair, her mind grinding. Even if she knew what the words might mean, most of the questions remained. Why had someone marked a map with the words, "I'm here" in an old Basque dialect that nobody even knew anymore?

She looked at her father, already less alert than he'd been a minute before, and her heart sank. She hadn't gotten around to asking about the symbol in the corner, but that was okay. He'd solved the hardest-to-crack part of the riddle.

"I knew you could help," she said and kissed his forehead. "You mind if I stay a few hours? I'll need to go home and feed Izie, but it'd be nice to stay."

"Always," he replied.

He pushed the button and returned the gurney to its horizontal position.

She took the glasses from the bridge of his nose and put them on the table, then sat with his hand in hers as his breaths became soft and his chest moved gently up and down.

TWENTY-SEVEN

THE WINDOWPANES VIBRATED WITH A ROLL OF THUNDER, and then all
Cade could hear was the white noise of rain falling sideways into the
side of the house. He watched through the big bay window as twilight
swallowed the storm.

"Sit down," he heard and turned to see Fey carrying a plate stacked with
omelets.

"You sure I can't help?" he asked, taking a seat as instructed. "Especially
with your shoulder."

"I'm fine, and I don't mind serving up some food. Especially since Paul
left, I hate eating alone. Sometimes I have all the ranch hands over at once,
but I didn't want to overwhelm you. I'm no traditional housewife, but I
don't mind cooking for friends."

She sat at the end of the table, looked at him briefly and bowed her
head. He copied her body language, but didn't pray. Instead, he pondered
all the years that had gone by since he'd last prayed for any reason other
than when he felt helpless, alone or scared.

Fey lifted her head and put a cloth napkin in her lap. He did the same.
"Don't stare too long, it'll get cold. My mom called these sheep wagon
omelets. They only take a few minutes of prep."

The sound of the storm became background noise to the soft taps and
clicks of their fork prongs and knife edges. Hungrier than he expected,
Cade quickly finished an omelet and helped himself to a second, finally
slowing enough to consider the food: eggs, onion, green pepper, parsley.

The meat, though, was unique.

"These are good," he said. "Thanks for the meal. Why'd your mom name them after a sheep wagon?"

"You tell me."

"Is it lamb?"

"Not lamb, lamb fries. Wanna guess what part of the lamb they're from?"

"You're making me nervous."

"That's right, they're little strips from a castrated ram. Basques— American Basques—use 'em as part of a few different recipes."

Cade poked at the rest of his omelet, prying out a small piece of meat and studying it.

"Fried in olive oil and garlic," she continued. "It's good meat, a lamb from the ranch here. I mostly run cattle these days but keep a few sheep around. My dad was truer to tradition. He ran this place as a pure sheep ranch, but I found better profit in beef."

"What do you mean tradition?"

"Basque tradition," she said. "That old murderer isn't my only great-grandpa."

Cade stared, surprised at himself for labeling her entire existence based on a single ancestor.

"Why didn't you mention you're Basque?"

"Because I'm American. What are you, Cade? German? Austrian? English?"

"German, I guess, among other things. My grandfather spoke some kind of German dialect, but I get your point. I'm American, too. How'd your Basque ancestors end up in Jarbidge?"

"Like most Basques around here, they showed up at Ellis Island and came out to run sheep and work the mines. That old Ben Kuhl might have homesteaded this place, but I'm lucky my Basque ancestors passed it down the way it is."

"You're lucky to have such a prized piece of land," Cade agreed and took another bite of his eggs, thinking back a few days to another moment when she'd talked about sheep.

He'd been groggy in the middle of the night, and then bullets had flown over their heads, but she'd said something about a sheep mine, sheep herder or something.

"It's just legend," she chuckled. "I got it stuck in my head that night because my uncle was so wrapped around the axle looking for it. I was wondering about the kid. It was his job to look for mines, right? Since he'd been talking to Uncle Andy, who knows?"

Cade wiped the corner of his mouth with his napkin and put it back in his lap.

"How's it go?"

"The short version's that, about twenty years before the Jarbidge gold rush, some prospector named Ross made a strike in the mountains. Ross showed it to a sheepherder, a guy named Ishman, and the sheepherder told his boss, a man named John Pence. Then this Ross character and the sheepherder both died before they could pass along the location, and John Pence couldn't find it. If you ask me, Ishman killed Ross, and Pence killed Ishman before keeping the gold for himself. But it's all just stories from a colorful time in Jarbidge. I got to thinking there's a chance this Miles Fourney was looking for the same thing as my Uncle Andy. Now that I've told you, I don't see how it helps. I personally think my uncle lost a lot of his marbles over it."

Cade took a breath in thought.

"What if Heben Nuk is the same thing as this Lost Sheep Herder Mine?"

"If that's the case, then it's already mined. You heard Fredi. Heben Nuk on the map is the same as the Success and Bluster mines, so assuming the legend was real there's nothing left. Are you still set on following the kid's trail into the mountains? You sure you have the time?"

Cade didn't answer right away. He knew it's what he wanted, and he knew he didn't have time. He nodded.

"I'll take you," she continued. "We'll want to get up early to gather gear and get up there before the storms. It's hell to be stuck up high in bad weather."

"Have you been up there lately."

"Not in a decade, and I've never hiked into the area marked on that map. It'll be rough country, and, Cade, there's no guarantee there's anything there at all. You know that, right?"

"After the past couple days, I'm willing to go back empty-handed, but I can't go back without looking."

She sliced her omelet with her fork and changed the subject.

"Is all your family from Pennsylvania?"

He was relieved for a change of topic.

"One of my ancestors was a minister who started a church in a town called Hollsopple; another was a coal miner in the same town. My grand-dad, the son of the minister, he worked his whole life in a steel mill. My dad was the first in the family to go to college."

"You're descended from miners?"

"Farmers, too. I've got a lot of respect for the livings people make off the land and in the factories. Real, hands-on work you can see at the end of a day. My job's different. I guess it has potential to be big, but day-to-day you can't see that what you did accomplished anything. Just some hair you lost sitting at a desk reading emails."

The conversation stretched for an hour or more, and Cade felt his hard edges soften as he learned about Fey and revealed a bit more about himself.

He marveled at how people of any background or political persuasion were able to come together and share their basic humanity over a meal. Sometimes it took conscious effort, but when people put ideology and labels aside, they almost always found they had more in common than they had different.

He stood eventually and rounded up their dishes, carrying the stack to the kitchen. Fey arrived a moment later with the serving plate and glasses. He washed while she dried, and after a few minutes she gave the final glass a shine and put it in a cupboard, then hung her towel from a hook over the sink.

"You as tired as me?" she asked.

"I could sleep through an earthquake."

"You'll find my guest house wasn't built on a fault. Grab your pack and come with me."

"A quick question," he returned. "Do you have a phone?"

Up to that point he still hadn't seen one and wasn't sure.

"Of course I have a phone," she laughed. "This isn't a third-world country."

Cade glanced away in embarrassment.

"Mind if I make a call?" he managed. "I'd like to see if my friend figured anything out about the map."

She led him to a door that, up to that point, had remained closed. She pushed it aside and showed Cade into a small room with a desk, laptop, fax machine, telephone and a charged-up cell phone with a blinking LED.

"The cell phone's useless out here, but the rest of this is my lifeline to the markets. I've got to buy and sell cows, hire and fire cowboys, keep my grazing leases up to date. It doesn't pay great, but it's a full-fledged modern-day business. Have at the phone and let me know when you're done so I can show you the guest house."

He felt silly at his continued inclination to stereotype her. If he'd thought about it, he knew she needed an office and the wits to use everything in it. He picked up the phone and dialed Officer Ibarra.

"This is Amaia." Her voice was groggy.

"Sorry, did I wake you?"

"Cade?"

There was an awkward pause. She seemed out of it.

"You haven't explained why you're still out there or what happened to your truck."

"You okay?"

"You've never asked me that in all the time we've known each other."

"Well, are you?"

"Yeah, fine. I stopped at dad's a few hours ago. You just woke me. Since you asked, though, it's been a weird day. I had a couple run-ins with a man who's been looking for you. Remember a crusty old codger from the Basque Block named Andy Jim? He's got it bad for that little pocket Constitution you found, said you offered to return it. That true?"

Cade thought backward. It seemed like such a long time ago.

"He was kind of nuts, so I didn't think much of it. Now that you mention it, he said Miles Fourney stole something from him. That was one of the reasons I came out here."

"Did he say what was stolen?"

"Papers. I didn't ask, and he didn't say. Just papers. Could've been anything."

"Where are you now?"

"On a ranch near Jarbidge."

"Whose ranch?"

"I'm safe, if that's what you mean."

"It's not," Amaia returned.

"Did you figure anything out about the page I faxed?"

"Hold on, let me go to the back porch so I don't wake dad." Cade heard the padding of feet on wood stairs, then the opening and closing of a door.

"My dad was pretty helpful, actually. The words Heben Nuk break a few rules of the Basque language as I know it. They basically mean 'I'm here.' They seem to come from a story about a one-eyed giant."

"Like the Cyclopes?"

"Exactly. I've found a few different versions, but in the old story my dad had on file here the Cyclopes' mother gives the young man who escapes a ring. When he puts it on his finger, the ring cries out 'Heben nuk! Heben nuk!' so the giant can find him. The boy cuts off his finger to get away. Taken alone, those words on the map simply say 'I'm here,' but only an old-world Basque, and probably only a Basque from a particular region, would recognize it."

"What would it mark?"

"How should I know? None of this stuff makes sense. I'm just telling you what the words mean."

There was a pause.

"You know, Cade, there's another detail that comes straight from my family stories. I can't imagine it's related, but it's interesting. The oral history my dad pulled comes from a second-generation Basque who heard the story from her dad, a sheepherder from northern Nevada. She said her dad was captivated by the similarity between the Tartaro legend and some story the Indians told about a man-eating giant. It might be nothing, but I guess he's buried in a cemetery near there."

"He have a name?"

"Yeah, Ishman Oneko."

"Ishman," Cade said. "It's not a common name, is it?"

"Why?"

"I just heard it over dinner as part of a story about a mine nobody can find."

"Seriously?"

"I'll let you know what I find. Like I said, I'm planning to make it back in time for the hearing, and hopefully in time to review your speech for the event."

"And if you're not."

"I will, but if something happens you should get in touch with McGown's chief of staff, Rachel. She's got her finger on the pulse of everything."

Cade hung up and stared. The mountains had been calling him for two days, but first they needed to find a graveyard somewhere around Jarbidge.

TWENTY-EIGHT

CADE EMERGED FROM THE OFFICE into a house perfumed with soap suds. He found Fey in the kitchen arranging silverware in a drawer.

"Is there a graveyard around here?"

"Just north of town on the far side of the river. We passed it twice today. Why?"

"Just another coincidence to check out. I'd like to see if there's a grave marker for a man named Ishman—like that legend you just told me."

"I've never been to the cemetery," she said. "My dad wanted his ashes scattered across the Diamond D, so that's what I did. We can stop on our way to the mountain if you want."

"Thanks, yeah, I'd like that."

"You ready for bed?"

"I'm dead tired."

She motioned for him to follow, and they went out the front door beneath the heavy canopy of cottonwood trees. It had stopped raining, but water dripped from little heart-shaped leaves and spattered in the dirt. She went to the road and open air of the corral beyond. Cade followed her to the fence, his arms crossed to keep warm. Water spattered in the after-storm cool, a soothing pitter-patter that stood out against the desert's stark silence.

"Thought you were showing me the guest room?" he said.

"I wanted to talk first."

She leaned on the fence and surveyed the corral where the filly browsed on some grass. A soft desert perfume filled him with verve he hardly remembered and completely craved.

"You mentioned your wife out in the desert yesterday," she said.

He leaned on the fence and matched her gaze, staring into the quiet.

"I did?"

"When I asked how you feel about the land you said you feel about it the same as you feel about your wife."

He closed his eyes and welcomed lungs full of sweet-smelling sage. It was his past rushing back to fill him up.

"I guess I did," he said.

"Where is she?"

"That's the funny thing about it. I guess I haven't seen her in a couple years."

"A couple years," she repeated.

"Or maybe three or four. I stopped counting."

"Since?"

"Since the crash. You could say my wife left 'cause I couldn't be me anymore. I was mad at her for a while, but I think I get it. It changes you, trying to get past something like that."

"You wanna tell me more about it?"

Cade sighed. He did and he didn't.

"You were only partly right when you said it was the same thing as your son dying," he said. "My daughter died, too, but so did a whole airplane full of firefighters. She was strong like them and soft in other ways. I hated the idea, but she wanted to be like her old man. She wanted to be outside and feel the thrill of life going a million miles an hour. She wanted to be a smokejumper."

He let the silence rush back, tears welling at the corners of his eyes.

"I was the pilot, Fey. They all died because of me. My little girl is dead because of me."

His tears transformed into a sob, which he choked back. Fey didn't respond for a long time.

"I imagine it was hard for your wife, too."

Cade nodded in the dark.

"But instead of one tragedy you lost everything."

He recoiled. He wouldn't have chosen to lose his entire family. Nobody would.

"I'm not sure I'd put it like that," he said.

"Course you wouldn't."

The darkness was almost absolute, and he heard her pivot and felt her looking at him.

"When are you going to get back to yourself?"

"What do you mean?"

"When we were talking this morning it all came kind of clear. I reckon you haven't let anyone in for a while, try to do everything alone. Locked yourself in the city away from everyone you ever cared about, then let the kid out here to die without even lifting a finger to look for him."

"People looked for him." Cade felt his pulse quicken.

"But you didn't. Don't get me wrong, I don't think you're responsible, but I've watched you these past two days. You're a little soft, but you're not out of sorts in the wilderness. You get it out here. You could have helped, and I'd guess on some level you wanted to. Seems to me you were probably pretty damn capable once upon a time. You don't belong in that city—or any city."

"Don't know if I belong on a ranch, either." Instead of upset he was beginning to feel simply exposed.

"Maybe not, but I'm not backing off my point. You locked yourself away from it all."

Cade kept his eyes aimed into the depth of the desert dark, but he felt her looking at him. He resisted turning toward her. He hated that she saw him so plain.

Gradually, grudgingly, he turned, her silhouette framing shadowy features: high cheekbones, soft curls, determined eyes. Over the previous year he'd built Fey up to almost mythic proportions: his arch nemesis who'd undermine his work at any opportunity. But through all of the political duels he never imagined she'd be able to punch him where it hurt most.

"I let you in," he said sheepishly. He was glad it was dark because he was sure his cheeks reddened like a boy's.

"No, you didn't," she laughed, "and maybe you won't. That's okay. Doesn't have to be me."

He turned back toward the silence of the desert. It was time to go to bed, time to go back to the city. But she had him cornered. Anything he did would be a turn away from the truth he hated and needed at the same time.

"Have you found a way to let people get close?" he asked.

He felt that she still looked at him. On a level he barely acknowledged and didn't want to admit he wanted that kind of focused attention.

"It's never the same as it was," she said. "There's always a push and pull, some vicious tug-of-war at the middle of your soul. Any time you let someone in you realize about the same time it's too late. I mean, you know what it feels like to have your guts ripped out, and every time you meet someone it's a fresh chance to feel your evisceration all over again."

"I try not to think about it."

"You can protect your heart, man. You might even succeed. But if that's what you want it's gonna change. Maybe already has. If you lock your heart up in a coffin it'll do more than stay protected. It'll just rot. That's death of your own choosing."

"That's my work, Fey. I live in that house because I work there."

"Sure, maybe. But I think it's more complicated than that."

"And you're here to save me."

"You've got to save yourself."

She reached her hand out, and he didn't back away. She pushed her palm onto his neck, her fingers curling toward his spine. He was surprised he didn't recoil. Instead, he felt the anger and disgust and fear and sadness fall away. He was entirely present, just he and his unexpected host on the plateau, he a man working to protect the land, she a woman born of it.

He was so enthralled with his first human touch in years that he didn't even see it coming. She leaned across the dark and pushed her lips to his. It was a soft, caring kiss, not unromantic, but not wholly charged with passion, either. The pressure of her lips lasted a minute, long enough to share a few breaths, then began to wane just as he felt the gravity of her body drawing him across the darkness. He was losing himself to the quiet calm of her and then felt the sudden pressure of her palm against his chest.

He took a step back and blinked.

"You feel better?" she asked.

He didn't understand what it was or what it meant, and he definitely didn't know how to put it in words, but he'd momentarily let everything go.

"The guest house over there has a bed in the loft. Clean sheets. Glasses for water in the cupboard."

"Fey," he started.

"Let it go. I just hope you got a glimpse of yourself again. If so, you're welcome."

Cade nodded. He understood and didn't understand at the same time. Fey went into the corral to put the filly in for the night as he made his way across the Diamond D toward the guest house cabin she'd pointed to.

His thoughts weren't clear at all, but on a level he was barely conscious of he wished she would join him.

The cabin was roomy for a one-room structure, its decor warm and welcoming. Standing just inside the front door there was a coat rack to his left, a small kitchen straight ahead and a cast-iron wood stove atop a stone hearth and fireplace across the room. Near the top of the chimney was an elk mount, its antlers almost touching the ceiling. A timber staircase climbed along the wall to a second-floor loft directly over his head.

He felt strangely at ease, relaxed in a way he hadn't been in years. He drank a glass of mountain-clear water and looked out the window toward the main house where the porch light flicked to life, filling the grounds with a warm glow. He felt the comfort of the place and didn't linger or explore. He climbed to the loft where he found a mattress and comforter on a plywood frame positioned against a window. He turned the lights off, threw the window open and lay a pillow across the sill, listening to the silence, which consumed the place absolute. There was a stillness to the place like it was under a spell: the crickets silenced, the dumb and dirty sounds of the cows subdued. The canyon was the essence of quiet. There was nothing but the present moment. And for the moment, Cade felt in his bones that the moment was everything.

His head touched the pillow, and the canyon's damp sagebrush perfume and eerie-still silence took him quick.

— PART III —

*"The mountains hinge on a geologic fulcrum that pries at my
understanding of how things are supposed to be."*

—Miles Fourney's journal

TWENTY-NINE

THE GROAN OF A WORKING-HOT TRUCK ENGINE pried Cade's eyelids apart. He rolled onto his stomach and looked out the window. It was difficult to tell what direction the vehicle came from—sounds had a way of bouncing off canyon walls in the desert—but the engine grew steadily louder.

His back creaked as he sat upright, and it wasn't just his back. Everything hurt. His hands were blistered from climbing the cliff, his back ached from sleeping in the dirt, his legs were sore from hiking for the first time in years. He needed more than a day's rest to heal his aching bones.

Cade peered into the heavy darkness, and the gold glow from a vehicle's headlights curved across the cliffs above the ranch. It had arrived from the west, and there wasn't much out that way except desert silt and sagebrush. Something was out of place.

The engine's groan grew louder, then stopped. Cade looked out the window and saw a pair of just-turned-off headlights fade into the night. The truck had stopped atop a ledge right above the ranch.

Cade wiped the sleep from his eyes and gathered his things. It might be nothing, but after the previous day's chaos he wanted to be prepared. He dressed and went to the cabin's first floor where he hung Miles' orange pack from a peg in the closet. He stood on his tiptoes to see through a small front-door window. Caked with neglect it obscured his view, so he opened it and stepped into the cool.

The roads were damp, the scent of sagebrush hanging thick among the cliffs. There were no stars—no lights—nothing. The sky was draped in a quilt of clouds that continued its suffocating march. The house and barn lights were out, the ranch hands he'd seen bustling around the property having gone to sleep hours before to prepare for the work that awaited before sunup. A chill bit through Cade's borrowed shirt.

From across the stillness he heard the bold clunk of a vehicle door closing. It reverberated throughout the canyon. Someone had arrived from across the desert. Someone was coming. Someone didn't care if anybody knew about their arrival.

Cade was determined not to be hunted like he had the night before. He scrambled into some bushes beside Fey's house, crouched low and waited. Only a few minutes later, the sound of boots squishing through wet dirt arrived on the road, followed by a silhouette that moved in and among the houses. It looked like a man in a cowboy hat. He went from house to house, either confident that everyone slept or completely unconcerned if they saw him coming. He walked past the bushes where Cade hid, climbed onto the porch and entered the main house through the front door.

Cade didn't know how things worked on the ranch—who came around, who left, or when—but the man's middle-of-the-night arrival seemed mysterious. He crept around the side of the house and peered in a window, which gave him a clear view of the living room. The man stood by the bookshelf where Fey kept her family pictures. He picked one up, looked at it for a moment and put it back down. He next went to the table where the letter from the Department of the Interior lay unopened. He picked it up and carried it into the kitchen.

Cade went along the side of the house to the next window. The kitchen light flashed alive, and a white beam shone out the window, lighting a patch of Earth like a spotlight. Cade stepped away, his nerves firing. He heard a soft noise that sounded like a chair dragging across hard wood. He stuck his head back into the light and found the man sitting at the kitchen table, his hat cast aside and his head in his hands. He stayed like that for a while, then held his head up so that his face was plain. Four-day stubble peppered his chin. He had deep brown eyes and a full head of brown hair creased by a sweaty hat-ring. Most surprising, the man's eyes were wet. He'd been crying.

He picked up the envelope and drew a finger across the top, then pulled out a single page of typed white paper. As his eyes scanned back and forth his hands shook slightly. Cade had studied the same envelope when he'd first arrived on the ranch. It had been addressed to Paul and Fey Dunham. The man reading the letter must be Paul.

He watched as the man clenched his shaking hands into fists and started tapping them on the table as he read. His lips were tight and pencil-thin. He continued to read and then wadded up the envelope and threw it. He looked to the brick staircase that spiraled to the second floor where Fey slept. He looked back at the letter. Then he grabbed the document, stood and went for the stairs.

Cade was unsure what to do. He was the stranger. He was the one who didn't belong. This was their business, not his, but if Cade was right it was the same man who'd shot bullets at them earlier that day. Cade's body tingled with indecision. He had to act.

He went to the screen door where he and Fey had entered when they first got to the ranch.

"Hey you," he said through the door, and the man spun with surprise. If Cade had been closer he's pretty sure the man would have knocked him flat.

Cade pulled the door open and went into the kitchen.

"Where do you think you're going?" he asked.

The man looked with his mouth open, brow furled, eyes wide.

"This is my house," he growled. "What are you doing wearing my clothes, spending time with my wife? She's a fool to trust you."

"So, you're Paul Dunham. I can't let you go up there."

The man let loose a raspy, ungrounded laugh.

"This was my house more than ten years. You can't tell me what can and can't be done in my house."

Cade knew before he'd acted this was a dumb thing to do. Now he felt that truth in his gut.

"All I know is you don't live here anymore and you shot at us, both of us. That's attempted murder where I come from."

The man paused as if to consider the weight or repercussions of Cade's words. He broke eye contact, looked out the kitchen window and, to Cade's surprise, changed the subject.

"Where's the backpack?" he said in a harnessed tone. Cade was surprised he hadn't yet seriously considered that the man in front of him knew anything about Miles Fourney or what happened to him.

"What do you care?"

"Where is it?"

Cade supposed it had been obvious all along. Paul had thrown the pack in the river to cover up his involvement in the kid's disappearance.

"Did you kill him?" Cade pressed.

"I didn't kill nobody."

"Why'd you kill him?"

"I'll get my hands on that pack one way or another. I've got half a mind to beat its location out of you, but at this point I'd rather watch Fey do it."

The man turned to go up the stairs, but Cade reached out and grabbed him by the shoulder as he arrived at the second step. The man's body tensed, and Cade pulled back, easily yanking him off balance. The house shook as he hit the floor, the letter flying from his hand. Momentarily dazed but uninjured, the man crawled to his knees, then stood with fire in his eyes.

"Just remember this was your choice," he said.

Cade turned and ran out the screen door, hoping to draw the big man into the open where maybe he could run circles long enough to tire him out. Paul followed, and Cade jumped onto his back, wrapping an arm around his neck. Paul didn't go down, instead staggering forward and clawing at Cade's arm. The man was an ox.

Paul spun in a circle, but Cade hung on firm. Then Paul backed toward the cottonwood tree, slamming Cade into its trunk. Cade gasped as he felt his ribs bruise, but didn't loosen his grip.

The man pulsed with raw strength. Cade had gotten a jump on him, but it was only a matter of time until he was overcome. Little by little, the man's fingers worked between Cade's arm and his neck, and Cade knew he'd soon be defeated. Paul easily pried the arm away and threw him to the ground, coughing.

Cade rolled and stared up at the man, whose sheer physical presence seemed all there was. Paul stepped confidently forward, cleared his throat and spat as Cade stood and backed toward the road. Then the screen door slammed, followed by a hot-white glare that lit the yard like a theater.

"Hold it right there!" He heard Fey's voice before he saw her. "Paul, you'd better have a damn good reason for being here. Cade, get your ass out of the way. This is between me and him."

Cade turned momentarily to see that Fey held a rifle, but he shouldn't have looked away at all.

"Paul, no!" he heard, and there was a fast flash of splitting pain, and the sudden metallic taste of blood. Cade slumped toward the dirt and lost consciousness before he hit the ground.

Some time later—he had no idea how much—his eyes half-opened into the hot glare from the porch light where moths and flies flitted in and out of the beam. He heard voices—a man talking—a woman. There was the sound of shuffling boots in the dirt. He tried to focus on what they said, but his surroundings were a haze.

He felt detached, like he was present in the world and far away at the same time. It was like he saw the ranch in third person. He felt the morning coming but was stuck in the cool quiet of the night. He saw the desert like a bird, the quiet undulations of the hills, the canyon's sheer cliff walls, the hoodoos that stood tall against the forces of wind, weather and time.

Once again he felt a longing for a piece of himself he'd locked away, and then just as quickly he was himself again: brow-beaten, bloodied, swollen and sore. None of that's what bothered him, though, because most of all he was untended and alone. The cold quiet of the desert swallowed him up, and he closed his eyes tight, unable or unwilling to move.

THIRTY

ANDY JIM THE THIRD SQUINTED into the cottonwood trees where heavy boughs kneaded shadows into derelict forms. In the heart of darkness, the river flowed like ink. Andy inched his way along the path, back the way he'd come, crouched in some riverside willows and waited.

He wasn't the kind of man to deal in politics, but the guy in the pin-stripe suit and wire-rim glasses had gotten his attention. If Andy helped distribute pocket constitutions and turn the crowd against the new park, the man would help solve riddles that had haunted Andy for twenty years or more. It was a no-brainer for Andy, a cause he could get behind and a possible end to his search for a treasure nobody believed existed.

What he hadn't seen coming was the young police officer who started figuring things out. When she'd asked about Heben Nuk being something other than a place, he realized how hard she was thinking about his family inheritance, and he had no intention of letting her get to it first.

He'd followed her and sat in the dark outside the condos by the river for more than an hour. When she'd emerged on the porch talking on the phone he couldn't believe his luck. She'd said it plain as day. Heben Nuk meant "I am here" and Ishman was buried in the Jarbidge Cemetery.

Now he had everything he needed save for one, the damn book he dropped on the Basque Block in the middle of the night. He needed the coordinates he'd written in that book, and then he could forget about everything else: the dead kid, the man in the suit, the police woman, the long months of numb nothing he'd experienced at the hands of the doctors. It was time to turn the page, for Andy Jim the third to prove all the doubters wrong.

After squatting in the bushes for another half-hour, he heard a door open and close in the darkness. His ankles popped as he shifted to get the blood flowing.

The night was so deep that he heard her breaths before he saw her. Short and fast, they were rasps that cut the midnight calm. As she drew closer, he also heard her shoes padding soft on the path. Her shadowy form came into view, but he couldn't tell if she still had her black briefcase. She passed so close he could smell her, a mix of women's deodorant and sleep-in-your-clothes sweat that hovered like mist in the dark.

He stood slow, then moved like a shadow, his gait awkward but quiet—a product of his long-ago military training. He fell in behind her and followed a hundred yards until she turned toward the parking lot where she'd left her car. She stepped into the shine of a streetlight, and he saw the briefcase slung over her shoulder. He stepped behind a tree and watched her put the bag on the hood of the car while fumbling in her pockets, probably looking for keys.

He'd been prepared to take the bag by force if he had to, but maybe fortune was smiling on them both. He found a small rock at the base of the tree and with all the strength he could summon from his sixty-seven-year-old tendons hurled it at the Ram Restaurant and Brewery. It struck with a silence-splitting thud before bouncing onto the concrete patio and clanging into some furniture.

The woman startled, her spine stiff, her head up, her right elbow in the air as her hand instinctively went toward the grip of her holstered weapon. She went around the front of the car toward the noise, and he waited.

Ten feet.

Twenty.

Thirty.

Andy stepped from behind the tree and hurried to the front of the car. He entertained the idea of smashing the windows to get his box of pocket Constitutions back, but he'd be better off if she never knew he was there. He flipped two buckles on her bag, opened it and reached in, feeling a small stack of paper and a single cardboard folder. He probed the folder, frantically feeling for his booklet.

He looked up. She was across the lot, poking her head into the bushes near the restaurant. She'd turn around any second.

His pulse hammered as he dug and finally felt it. He dislodged the stack of paper as he yanked the booklet out, and one of the pages fluttered to the asphalt near the car's front tire. He had what he needed and was out of time. He flipped the briefcase closed and skulked into the shadows just as she turned back.

He crouched near the river and watched. She walked to the car, the key already in her hand, snatched the briefcase from the hood, and then paused. Andy's teeth gnashed as she squatted and picked up the page he'd dropped.

She stood slow with the paper in her hand and looked into the shadows. She seemed to look right at him, but if she actually saw the silhouette of his hat or shine of his eyes her body language didn't betray her. She drew her fingers across the top of the page, appearing to contemplate the chances that she'd dropped it herself or weighing the threat that might lurk in the dark.

Then she opened the car door and got in.

Andy breathed a sigh of relief when the car's engine snuffed out the riverside quiet. She backed out of her parking stall and pulled away, her lights receding into the silence.

He looked down at the document in his hands, the glow from the lot's soft-orange security lights revealing it plain, and smiled. It was a pocket-size copy of the United States Constitution, the exact booklet he'd had with him for years, and now the only place he knew that contained all the information he needed to recover what was rightfully his.

FOUR HOURS LATER, ANDY JIM THE THIRD welcomed the warm sun that slanted across the upper Owyhee Plateau. His eyes were sore from squinting at the highway all night, but daylight gave him a renewed sense of excitement and fresh dose of purpose.

He aimed his old beige pickup through a notch in the desert's volcanic crust and motored among the Jarbidge River canyon's sheer rock walls.

It was only another thirty minutes before he'd be back in the heart of Jarbidge country where the legend was alive and the promise of undiscovered treasure still called.

THIRTY-ONE

THE WARM, WET TONGUE OF A border collie worked across Cade's forehead, out onto his temple and above his left ear. Cade felt his head pulse with each beat of his heart, and when the dog's tongue worked to the side of his head he felt a sudden sharp flash of pain.

He swung his arm to shoo the dog away and opened his eyes slow, lifting a hand to the part of his head the dog had just licked, above his left ear. The swelling was obvious, a golf ball-sized lump that was sticky and wet. He brought his palm down to his eyes. It glistened red.

The border collie—was his name Sherman?—sat with its eyes locked on him, cocked its head sideways and whimpered. The sun wasn't up, but the land was coming alive with the soft, diffused gray of twilight. He lay on his back in the dirt, unsure why he'd been left outside all night.

He looked down, his clothes caked in mud from yet another desert ordeal. He sat up slow, feeling the creaks in his joints from two days' trials in the wild. He rolled onto his hands and knees and uncurled slow into a standing position, wavering and dizzy. He turned toward the guest house and then stiffened at the sound of a slamming screen door. He moved without looking, but Fey's voice stopped him.

"You son of a bitch!" she shouted. "I oughta tie you up and drag you through town behind my truck. I know you saw the letter on my table yesterday, and you just pretended it wasn't there at all."

All he wanted was a change of clothes and an aspirin. He made another step toward the guest house.

"No, you don't. Stop right there. You're gonna own this here and now."

He felt a trickle of blood drip down the side of his head and across his cheek. He turned to face her as a cow across the canyon welcomed the morning with a protracted moo. The border collie turned with him, his ears perky and alert at Fey's early-morning ire. She was dressed in the same clothes she'd worn the day before and waved a fist full of paper.

"Damn you Cade Rigens," she spat, now within arm's length. "I don't know who you think you are, but you won't take my ranch now or when I'm cold and dead. Not now or ever. Damn you."

She spat again by his boots, and he looked at her with confused eyes. "I don't . . ."

"You do," she shot back. "It's right here in black and white."

She thrust the papers at him. He took them, struggling to focus through the pain that split his temples, and read. He assumed it was the same letter he'd watched her ex-husband read the night before. It was typed on Department of the Interior letterhead.

> Dear Occupant:
>
> You are advised that it has been determined necessary to the interests of the United States Department of the Interior that private properties held by the Diamond D Ranch be acquired to uphold resource preservation and national security.
>
> Pursuant to existing law and the Fifth Amendment of the United States Constitution, a condemnation proceeding will be instituted in the United States District Courts for the Districts of Nevada and Idaho to acquire all of the ranch's lands, buildings and holdings, together with all personal property owned by the ranch and used in connection with its operation. Although acquisition is of the utmost importance, it has been determined that it will not be necessary for you to surrender complete possession of the premises until March 31, 2016. It is felt that this procedure will enable you to conclude seasonal operations and make all arrangements necessary to vacate.
>
> You are further advised that all records pertaining to the aforesaid condemnation proceeding will be sealed, by order of the Courts, and public inspection of such records will be

prohibited. Accordingly, it is requested that you refrain from
making the reasons for the closing of the ranch known to the
public at large.

Sincerely yours,
U.S. Secretary of the Interior
Cc. Gov. James McGown, Chief of Staff Rachel Simplex

Cade was confused—and pissed off. A move like this could ignite a full-fledged revolt. The land beneath their feet was the birthplace of the Sagebrush Rebellion. Condemnation proceedings could help that smoldering fringe movement grow into a full-fledged conflagration of angry farmers, ranchers and citizen militias hell-bent on finding something to fight about. It would ignite the exact threat they'd been preparing to avoid.

"This isn't me," Cade said.

"Bullshit."

"Seriously, this is reckless." He held the heel of his palm to his throbbing temple. "It's not even necessary. Your ranch was officially deemed a low priority for acquisition."

She waved the letter in front of him, her eyes stones.

"You'll stop talking or I'll send you hiking one-way into the Diamond Desert, and there's nothing out there except coyotes that'll gnaw at your shins and ravens to pick at your bones. This letter arrived yesterday morning before we got back here. If I'd have opened it then instead of driving your sorry ass to town it would have saved us both a big old chunk of time. That's the end of this conversation."

Fey waved the letter in front of him while she talked, and he reached out and snatched it. The name was plain as day and might as well have been the only text on the page: Rachel Simplex. His eyes widened, and his mouth fell open. This is what she'd done with the list he'd given her. It was amazing she'd executed the orders so swiftly, and he wondered how many others there were. He was shocked, but not bewildered anymore. He'd been right that she was up to something that went beyond designation of a national park. He knew condemnation for the plateau's private properties was possible, but he'd pushed back on the idea and instead had organized sensitive negotiations with land owners. Fey's ranch had been on the list, but she'd never even been contacted. Hers had been deemed a low-priority acquisition.

Cade realized he'd been left out of the loop in the chain of command of people making the real determinations about private properties—and perhaps other aspects of the park as well. The National Park Service wasn't just a federal agency. It was 23,000 people spread out across the entire country, and the fact was, some of them were assholes. A lot of the assholes—people who'd barely stepped foot on the land—were people who'd climbed into positions of power. Cade fought with them all the time. Trying to explain all that to Fey wouldn't even start to get into the politics of answering to Congressional committees that controlled the agency's budget and rules.

"Fey I can't do this without you."

"You've been doing everything on your own for a long time. Now get to it, ranger man. I regret knowing you. One of my ranch hands is leaving for Twin Falls in an hour. You'd better be in the truck, or you'll be the first man I ever shot."

She turned and strode back toward the house, leaving Cade bloodied and alone in the early morning chill.

The border collie followed him to the guest house, where he went into the bathroom to wash his fresh wound. The dog watched as he blotted the side of his head with a wet washcloth and thought about his predicament. He'd made it this far only to feel further away than when he started. The warm comfort of his Boise apartment might have been insulated from the truth, but it was safe. It's where he wanted to be.

After taking a shower, Cade pried his way back into the same clothes Fey loaned him the day before and went to the cabin's loft. He sat on the edge of the bed and ruminated. Fey had helped him this far, but he didn't need her to keep going. His guilt over Miles had grown, but it was rapidly being replaced by resolve.

He took out the map and looked close at the small symbols in the corner. The backpack and maps were the only links he had in a broken chain, and he was determined to put it back together again.

He heard a truck door slam and went to the second-story window to find Paul climbing out of Fey's light-blue Scout. He unloaded a half dozen common spades and a rifle from the back and lay them on the side of the road before heading for the main house, leaving the Scout where he'd parked.

For an estranged ex-husband who'd fired bullets at his wife the day before, Paul sure was at home on the ranch. Cade couldn't understand why she'd welcomed him back so easily.

He thought back to the advice she gave him the day before and pulled the handkerchief from his pocket. "Finish what you start," it said. "Know where to draw the line. Do what has to be done."

THIRTY-TWO

PAUL DUNHAM SPAT OFF THE SIDE OF FEY'S FRONT PORCH and wiped his chew-stained cheek with the back of his hand. He'd just finished gathering shovels they could use at the protest in Boise and then helped Fey tend to the horses. He loved the feel of the Diamond D's dirt under his boots and the valley's morning chill on his spine.

Fey sat with her legs dangling over the porch edge, her arms folded across her chest. They'd done their time, and he could read her pretty well. When she was mad she attacked. This quiet simmer was different. It seemed less predictable and maybe more potent.

The rain had stopped before sunup and the clouds were now tattered and torn. A soft orange crept across the high-desert. He gazed past the canyon rim where heavy cumulous clouds still crowned the upper peaks. It was a view he'd admired thousands of times, perhaps tens of thousands of times. He knew it in the soft glow of early morning and the hot late light of afternoon, how it changed from one season to the next. He knew the smell of budding willows in the spring and blowing sagebrush pollen in the fall. He knew the sounds the cows made when they were afraid and how they acted when they weren't. The ranch was Fey's, but it had been an easy place to call home. He and his brother grew up in Elko, but Paul had never found his home until he arrived at the Diamond D.

"How long you been on the ranch?" she asked without looking, her eyes focused on the same scene unfolding off the front porch. Before he could answer, she continued. "You've got balls bigger than your brains, Paul. Running around the desert like a gunslinger's gonna get you killed— or at least thrown in jail. They think I burned the government truck yesterday, and that ranger's presumed missing. For the time being, they think I made him disappear. I don't aim to take a fall for you."

Paul heard her, but his thoughts were elsewhere. He thought back to the days before Tanner died, when they'd sit on the porch like this for too long pondering their luck at landing together in such a beautiful oasis. He thought about how awful the place was for him now. It was the same ranch, a place full of the best memories a man could hope for—except the one. There was no getting past that. Their boy had died in the waters of the Three Creek Valley, and there was no way he could stay.

Paul stayed quiet, his mind working things over. He wanted to share everything with Fey but didn't totally trust her. If he kept his cool, he might be able to find out what she knew about the kid's backpack and make sure his secrets stayed lost in the desert. He needed to sort it out before the ranger left, and one of the ranch hands was supposed to drag him to town within twenty or thirty minutes.

"Where'd you and that man sleep out in the canyon?" Paul asked. "Did he touch you?"

There was a delay before she answered with a question.

"Would you have really shot either of us? You're a lot of things I don't like, but a killer's not one of 'em."

"You mean you'd like me better if I was a killer?"

"I'd like you a lot less. Since I don't like you already, you better just watch your back."

He scratched his head, not following what she'd just said, then pushed a little harder.

"Did you sleep with him?"

"Who I've been sleeping with is none of your goddamn business. You imply that I'm easy again and you'll speak your last word."

He leaned away with a hand in the air, which seemed to satisfy her. They fell into a comfortable quiet as they pondered the land they'd cultivated together. Her eyes began to glisten as she stared.

"You ever wonder if you messed everything up too bad to fix?" she asked. "I'm gonna lose the ranch, Paul. I'm gonna lose it. The damn government's gonna take it."

Tears dripped down her cheeks and puddled on the porch's peeling paint.

Fey had treated Paul with contempt for so long the opportunity to console her wasn't what he expected. He went to her, though, and put his arm around her. She leaned into him like she used to, her head buried in his shoulder, her arm around his back, and for a minute Paul felt like everything was the way it should be: the two of them, the land, the cows—before the promise of new life was ripped away like a willow plucked from a raging stream. He felt his body tense, and she felt it too. She pulled away as seamlessly as she'd leaned in. He felt the stab of the emotions at once: pain, jealousy, alone-ness—three familiar friends rushing back.

"We're going to stop them from taking your ranch," he said.

"This thing's bigger than you or me. The government will do what the government will do."

"That doesn't sound like the woman I married."

"Maybe the woman you married has been beat down too many times. Maybe she can't get up."

Paul looked at the ribbons of water coursing the valley and slopes of sagebrush angling up to the black basalt cliffs. It was strange how a piece of land could become so familiar it was like an extension of yourself. You breathed in, and it was part of you. You breathed out, and you were a part of it.

"The government's declared war on you," Paul said. "This land is rightfully yours. You should stand up and defend it by whatever means it takes."

"Maybe I'll have my lawyer look into it."

"Lawyer, pfft. You need to make a statement too big to fail. The people—We the People—can make that happen. We've got God-given rights granted in the Constitution. You just need enough Americans—enough patriots!—to notice what's going on out here."

"You sound like your brother. You're better than him. I'll fight my battle; you fight yours."

He nodded. He'd back off for now, but he knew the unfolding war over the ranch was one he would fight with or without Fey's help or blessing.

He returned to the task at hand. Maybe he'd been going about it the wrong way. Maybe the most obvious way was staring him in the face. Maybe he simply needed to ask.

"Fey, this might seem like an off-the-wall question, but do you know anything about a backpack from Sheep Creek canyon?"

Her body language didn't show him anything. If he'd struck a nerve she didn't show it. If she'd seen the pack, she might not have put it together. She shrugged.

"I haven't seen that backpack since the ranger took it with him last night."

His spine stiffened. It was right there. A stone's throw away.

"I'm gonna need that pack," he said.

She looked at him with a new expression. Her curiosity seemed plain, but there was something more in her eyes. It might have been fear.

"Why, Paul? What do you know about that missing kid?"

He saw that her mind spun. Paul didn't understand it all, either, but he had a head start. The kid had been on to something. It just took everyone else some time to catch up. If the backpack hadn't turned up, the mystery might have stayed lost in the riverbed forever.

"I know enough to know it's good for all of us if I have that pack."

"Paul," she said and stared into space. "Did you . . ."

"No."

"What do you know about it?"

"It'll be easier if you just get me the pack."

"I'm not sure that's possible. At this point three or four people have seen what's in there. Nobody knows what it means, but just about all of them are trying to figure it out."

Paul wrung his hands. This wasn't how it was supposed to go. The kid's pack was supposed to be lost in the desert forever.

"How about the papers your dad gave you? The ones that show how the ranch came into existence?"

"Now's not the time."

"Maybe it is. What if that's your key to keeping the government off your back, stop 'em from taking this place?"

She didn't respond, just looked at him with hopeful eyes.

"Trust me. Let's get those papers, and maybe I'll be able to show you."

The attic wasn't a place Fey went often. Nobody did. Spiderwebs collected in the corners, and boxes were covered in a coat of dust that layered thicker with each season of cattle drives and dirt road traffic. The stairs spun steeply upward, and Paul followed close behind his ex-wife.

The space was dark, and there wasn't any light aside from what filtered through small windows beneath the home's roofline gables. Fey went to a corner where she kept a file cabinet alongside a few boxes full of keepsakes.

Paul knowingly lifted the lid off one and withdrew a ribbon of white silk.

"You've still got it," he said.

"Not the kind of thing a girl lets go of."

"You know," he began, but she cut him off.

"Not now, Paul. Maybe not ever. Besides, you're looking in the wrong box."

She went to a box labeled FAMILY. She opened it and out came a flood of memories and stories she'd heard from her mom and dad, roots she didn't dwell on and usually pretended not to have.

The box contained clothes her Basque ancestors had supposedly worn on the boat across the Atlantic. There were papers from their visit to Ellis Island and the first dollar her great-great-grandfather made in America selling pretzels at a New York City street stand. The story went that he'd hopped the Union Pacific railroad and made it to Salt Lake City where he met another fellow from the Basque country. Then they started walking. They walked four weeks until they arrived in the Jarbidge country and found jobs with a local sheep operation.

She dug deep in the box and produced a stack of folders near the bottom. She made a mess as she pulled the papers to the surface and handed them to her ex-husband.

"I've got an idea," Paul said. "The boys have been talking about property rights and stuff. Didn't this place come from the Homestead Act? Your grandpa or great grandpa or something was a farmer, right? That's how this place came to be, right?"

Paul opened one of the folders, scanned the pages, folded it and cast it aside. He continued until he found a folder titled "Kuhl family ranch."

"Here it is," he said and scooted to one of the small windows where there was enough light to read. He flipped through the file and located an envelope labeled Deed. He opened it and felt his heart sink.

"What is it?" Fey asked.

He turned the page, so she could read it: a hand-written note scrawled in messy blue ink. The note said "IOU" at the top. It amounted to an apology for taking the deed, but promised to return it. The note was signed, Uncle Andy.

"Oh Andy," she said.

"Oh Andy, is that all?"

Paul rifled through the remaining files, hoping it was a mistake, but when he looked back at his ex-wife, she wasn't paying any attention to the box, files or him, instead crouched low and staring out the window.

"What is it?" he asked, but she didn't answer.

He stuffed the files back in the box and moved to the window, following her gaze through the cottonwood branches where he saw someone walking around Fey's Scout, right where he'd parked it. Whoever it was paused before jumping into the driver's seat. Paul was surprised when the truck's engine fired to life, backed into the road and lurched toward town with a quick skid of tires.

"What's going on?" she said, the unfolding events not yet registering. "Everyone here knows my truck's off limits."

"That's not one of the ranch hands," Paul said as the ranger came into view.

"That self-righteous son of a bitch." Fey's hands were fists, and she stood so abruptly the floorboards shifted.

"He's still got it, doesn't he?" Paul said.

Fey looked at him incredulous.

"Can't you let it go?" she asked while he shook his head no.

"I'm such an idiot. I shoulda burned it."

"What did you do, Paul?"

He continued shaking his head as he moved for the attic stairs, Fey following close behind.

"What are you going to do, Paul?"

He looked briefly back.

"I'll get that backpack by whatever means it takes."

THIRTY-THREE

I F THERE'S ONE THING CADE RIGENS KNEW in the marrow of his bones
it's that he was better off alone. He was stronger, faster and smarter without people weighing him down.

He glanced over his shoulder as he crested the canyon rim and saw into
the heart of the ranch where the logs were piled in plain sight. Nobody
seemed to notice his departure, or maybe nobody cared.

He turned back to the road—toward that part of himself he might be
able to save—and drove fast. Whatever it was that happened to the kid, it
was now his singular purpose to find out. He had to look in the cemetery
for a Basque man's grave before embarking on what now seemed like
an inevitable trip into the mountains to explore this mysterious place
marked Haben Nuk.

When he arrived along the Jarbidge River, Cade slammed the truck
into second gear and sped through the refreshing scent of summer willows
toward town. He scanned for the small road Fey described would lead to
the cemetery. She'd said it was on the north side of town on a small side
road that turned toward the creek.

When he found a two-track that fit the description he followed it to a
small bridge crowded by willows and the smell of rushing water. His tires dug
into the hillside's after-rain soil and bounced up to a broad, flat bench cleaved
from the edge of the vertical-walled canyon like a stair-step built for giants.

An iron gate and old wood fence came into view as he crested the step.
Welded with rusted steel were letters declaring he'd arrived at the Jarbidge

Cemetery. Cade nosed the Scout close to the gate and powered it down. It was tough to see the graves among high grasses and scattered sagebrush. The tombstones were small, some of them simple wood crosses, others plain and unmarked. The Scout's hot engine block ticked in the cool damp of the after-rain morning. It was an intermittent staccato among a chorus of crickets, and otherwise the place was eerie-still. To the south he saw the tailings piles along the mountains' lower flank confirming he wasn't far from town and the heart of the Jarbidge gold belt.

The iron gate easily creaked aside, and he went through to walk among the dead. None of the markers were large or made of marble like he expected. There were small wooden crosses with barely-legible names and dates, some small chunks of rough-hewn stone propped upright with names chiseled into their iron-oxide skins. A few of the more ornate gravestones were made from larger rocks topped with bolted metal plaques, but none was more than a foot or two tall. Cade assumed most were from the town's mining heyday, and there was nothing at all that seemed Basque or displayed the name Ishman.

He wondered how much time he had before Fey or Paul tracked him down. Nobody seemed to notice his departure, but he knew they'd pursue. He paced fast among the graves, but was interrupted by the roar of an approaching engine. The sound slowed as the vehicle hit the steepest part of the hill and growled closer. Cade considered hiding, but at this point was more interested in confronting things head-on. He squared up and waited.

When the vehicle appeared, he was surprised to see a Ford pickup with faded beige paint, nothing like any of the trucks he'd seen on Fey's ranch. When it stopped, he half expected Fey to get out, but another familiar figure emerged, someone easily recognizable but far removed from the place they'd met: the old man he'd spoken with on the Basque Block in Boise, the man with a big mole beneath his left ear, handlebar mustache and Drum tobacco in his shirt pocket . . . Andy Jim the third.

The man went through the cemetery gate and ambled with a weak stutter-step across the graves toward the far end of the bench where he sat with his back against the soft bark of an aspen tree trunk. Cade was bewildered. The man acted as if Cade was a ghost—or at least as if they'd never met before. He decided to approach.

Andy Jim sat on the ground, his soiled hat tipped low, his boots extending toward the cemetery, his back against the tree. Cade watched him take a slow pull from his cigarette. The smoke swirled around his head and vanished in the morning sun. Cade stood nearby, but it was as if he wasn't there at all. After some minutes Cade broke the silence.

"Mind if I sit down?"

Andy Jim didn't hesitate. He responded naturally, without surprise or concern, the stutter Cade remembered gone.

"This here's a free country, and you can sit on it the same as I can."

Cade marveled at his calm disinterest. He breathed slow and easy. Cade sat, and the man turned to look. His light blue eyes shone like liquid from their weathered sockets, his handlebar mustache curled slightly at the corners of his mouth.

"Haven't we met before?" Cade asked. "Didn't we meet in the city a few days ago?"

"That could be."

"You're not sure? You're one of the reasons I'm here. You were crouched in an archaeology site in Boise and said the missing kid interviewed you about things. That's one of the reasons I came out here."

"That wasn't anywhere near here."

Cade sighed. The man was still only half there.

"Why are you in Jarbidge?" Cade asked.

The man didn't answer.

"Come on."

"Why you want to know about my story? I'm just a man trying to figure himself out."

He snuffed his cigarette in the dirt, then pulled the package of tobacco from his shirt pocket. He produced a rolling paper and spun it into a tidy cigarette. The dexterity with which he rolled belied his haphazard gait and delirious speech. He stuck the cigarette below one of his curled handlebars without lighting it.

"Maybe I can help," Cade said.

"How's a guy like you gonna help?"

Cade had learned a lot the past couple days, but he still had more questions than answers. He wasn't even sure what the cowboy was after.

"Why were you poking around the archaeological dig the other day?"

"I went to look for the bullion. It's all gone. I can't find it."

Cade had a fast flashback to the weird conversation they'd had. Cade wasn't sure he believed any of what the man said except he'd obviously been right that Miles had been up to something. Maybe he wasn't entirely off his rocker.

"And now you think this missing gold could be out here in Jarbidge?"

"You know they don't leave the mining with the states anymore."

"I know a bit about mining," Cade said. "I work for the government. I know people who keep the records, and I know how to look for information."

"Could be," Andy Jim said. His hat didn't move; his eyes trailed across the cemetery into the canyon beyond.

They sat with their backs against two aspen trees at an impasse, Andy Jim peering from beneath the brim of his hat, Cade feeling the tug of the passing minutes. The old man lit a match and held it to the cigarette. A swirl of blue smoke wound around his hat and vanished in the calm.

"My grandpappy used to tell a story about the mountains."

A raven landed on one of the aspen tree branches in the grove where they talked.

"Is that your grandfather who owned the mine?" Cade asked.

"I'm trying to tell you a story."

The silence resumed. Andy Jim looked at the canyon, his head tilted down, and he took another drag from his cigarette. Cade looked at the raven, which watched the unlikely pair with inquisitive eyes. Another minute passed.

"My grandpappy used to tell a story about the mountains."

He paused, Cade assumed, to see if Cade would interrupt. He didn't.

"My grandpappy said the mountains were like time capsules for your life. In the winter all your loves and pains and joys and tears got frozen in the mountains. In the winter the pieces of your life were hard to get at unless you wanted to spend a bunch of time digging in the snow like an idiot. But when the thaw comes all you've got to do is go sit in the mountains, and whatever it was you looked for will come back. Sometimes I don't like coming out here. There's lots of things I'd just as soon forget. But sometimes you have to look. I was traumatized. I was traumatized real good. Life dealt me a few tough blows, but I came up here to see what happened."

Andy Jim fell silent again. Cade let the silence settle for a minute and pondered the man's words. He'd been avoiding the mountains for years. In a sense, he'd buried a part of himself out there, too.

"Can I ask another question?" Cade said, trying to respect the man's space and pace but mindful he was out of time.

"You can ask, but some of this stuff's pretty confidential. I got in a lot of trouble down there."

"Down where?"

The brim of his hat lifted, his eyes flicking to life.

"They strapped me down and stuck needles in me. I've been traumatized real good. I've been through some bad stuff. They strapped me down and stuck needles in me. That ain't right. They stuck needles in me."

His hands moved to the open collar of his shirt, Cade assumed, to show that he'd been stuck with needles in the chest.

"I'm in a lot of trouble," Andy Jim said. "The sheriff's looking for me."

"Why are they looking for you?"

He saw it crawl onto the man's tongue and recede.

"I'm in a lot of trouble," he said.

It was time to change the subject.

"So, it's your grandfather who gave you the mining company?"

"My grandfather was a man named Ben Kuhl. He lived most his life in prison. They say he was the last man to rob a stage in the old West, happened just down the hill over here back in—oh, 1915 or 1916 or something. Was the first man ever convicted using a fingerprint, too."

"What happened to the mine?"

"I'm not the businessman type."

Cade had a sudden realization and felt foolish for not putting it together sooner.

"Your name's Andy. Like Uncle Andy?"

"Some call me that."

"Were you in Korea?"

"I served."

Cade wasn't sure if he should tell Andy that he knew his niece or not. From the sounds of it they hadn't seen each other for years.

"Why are you in the cemetery?"

Cade had his suspicions now. Something connected, but he didn't know what. He got the map out of the kid's backpack and showed it to the cowboy.

"Have you ever seen this before?" Cade pointed to the small drawing of a Basque Lauburu with an eye at its center.

The cowboy looked at Cade like Cade was the crazy one.

"Course I have. Why do you think I'm here?"

Andy stood and walked with a haphazard gait into the grove of aspen trees, pushing the branches aside and entering a kind of inner sanctuary of fluttering leaves that danced in the morning sun. He waved for Cade to follow and went to one of the trees.

Cade followed his liquid-blue eyes to the side of the tree where the bark was carved in the shape of a Lauburu with an eye in the middle.

"What's this?" Cade said. "Is someone buried here?"

He scraped his boot across the ground and felt a hard stone covered in decades of decaying leaves and grass. He scraped them aside and uncovered a round stone, once again with the image of an eye at the center of a Basque Lauburu. The name I. Oneko was carved in the stone, but that's all that was there.

"Not even a date?" Cade asked, glancing at their trucks by the cemetery's arched gate. "I was expecting some kind of explanation about what the Lauburu and eye mean."

"Heben nuk means "I'm here," the cowboy said.

"Andy, I think you and me are looking for the same thing."

"You're looking for the bullion?"

"I'm looking for the kid who was looking for the bullion. Those mountains have been calling my name for three days. It's time I heeded their call."

"Maybe I could help."

Cade studied the old man, broken too many ways to count.

"How are you going to help?"

"You know where you're going?"

Cade wanted to move without the cumbersome weight of companions, but he knew he could use some local knowledge. He grunted and turned the map over in his hand.

"I'll ride with you," Andy smiled.

They walked among the tombstones and went out through the arched iron gate. Cade climbed behind the Scout's steering wheel and put it in gear as Andy Jim the third got in beside him.

"To the mountains," Andy said.

To Heben Nuk, Cade thought. "To the mountains."

THIRTY-FOUR

THE USUAL ORGANIZATION OF FEY'S BEDROOM CLOSET had given way to her crazed summer schedule, and she threw clothes over her shoulder looking for the combination of layers that would see her through a day in the mountains. Paul paced impatiently by the bedroom door. She knew his fresh air of determination could be trouble, but she didn't have the energy to hold him at bay, and she wasn't going to let him go without her.

She stuffed a jacket into the top of her pack, shouldered her way past him and descended the brick stairs into the kitchen where she filled a plastic bottle full of water.

"Come on," Paul said, his arm holding open the screen door. "He's got a huge head start. Your house would burn down if you threw water on it at the same pace you're packing."

She ignored his frustration, but followed him outside and threw her pack into the bed of his pickup while he threw the pile of shovels and rifle in alongside it.

With Fey in the passenger seat, the truck rumbled out of Three Creek Valley, across the plateau and down Elk Creek Grade into the bottom of the canyon by the Jarbidge River. Paul drove fast, his knuckles white with a tight wrap around the wheel, his eyes keen on the road ahead.

Fey wanted her truck back, but she didn't share Paul's urgency. She was angry with Cade and simultaneously uncomfortable with the reversal that took place in the middle of the night. She'd promised to help Cade in the mountains. His purpose had seemed genuine. Hell, he hadn't wanted to come to the desert at all. His confusion at seeing the letter seemed real, too. He was either a good actor or maybe—was it possible?—he'd told her the truth. Maybe he hadn't known about the letter to begin with.

Paul ran through the gears as his truck came up to speed, and gravel sprayed into the bushes as he rounded sharp corners. He was quiet, his eyes focused, his lips tight. What could be in the pack that was driving him so crazy? What was he trying to hide?

When they arrived in town, Paul parked in front of a small cabin near the river and jumped out.

"I'll be a minute," he said, and she sighed. The day was already out of hand, but it was about to get more complicated. Paul disappeared around the cabin and returned a few minutes later with his brother, still wearing his Band of Indians ball cap and snap-up cowboy shirt with blue piping around the collar. The brothers had the same build: tall, broad and thick, but Morgan's beard made him look the part of a mountain man. Fey knew the two of them together were dumber than they were apart.

"Where's your new buddy?" Morgan shot at Fey.

She didn't answer.

"Paul tells me you helped dig the kid's backpack out of the desert. Paul's an idiot. We need to get that thing back."

Fey felt dizzy. They knew something they weren't sharing.

"Did you, Morgan? Did you do something to that kid?"

"Nothing he didn't deserve," Morgan said. "But no, I didn't do anything. That kid did himself in."

Fey felt her temples pulse.

"Will one of you tell me what happened? I just spent two days of my life looking for him."

Morgan looked at his brother.

"Are you gonna tell her or should I?"

THIRTY-FIVE

A PAPER-CUP COFFEE IN HAND, Amaia Ibarra let the door slam behind her and went into her garage studio in Boise's North End, where old trees towered over hundred-year-old bungalows.

The neighborhood was a mix of old and new, and its residents matched. They ranged from hazy-eyed hippies with mountain-town flair to expat Californians who brought with them an admiration of yoga pants, aviator sunglasses and black SUVs. The neighborhood was diverse, but gentrifying fast.

Amaia took a deep breath. The place smelled like cat. No matter how diligent she was at buying scented litter and keeping it clean, the studio was too small to keep the smell at bay. Izie was an affectionate calico who sat in the sun of the apartment's south-side window most days. She'd been with Amaia a couple years, but was grumpy about their recent move across town. At the last apartment, she'd had a back yard and neighborhood to prowl. In the North End, where they lived close to foothills filled with foxes and coyotes, Izie stayed safely inside.

Izie jumped from her window and rubbed back and forth on Amaia's legs, purring loud enough to fill the room.

"Missed you too, girl." Amaia stroked the cat's soft back.

She went to the apartment's kitchenette and filled a bowl with dry cat food and put it on the floor next to a pile of dirty clothes.

"All right bud, mom's gotta work."

She'd returned from her Dad's well after midnight, stripped and passed out on the couch before waking rickety and grumpy. It was Friday, and she was scheduled for an afternoon shift, but certain things couldn't wait. She'd thought hard about it when she went for coffee that morning and now that she'd decided felt some urgency to come clean about her activity the previous twenty-four hours.

She unbuckled her briefcase and reached inside, probing for the small copy of the United States Constitution she'd been carrying. Unable to find it, she dumped the contents onto her coffee table and wasn't surprised to discover it missing.

She'd seen the cowboy hunkered in the willows and had decided not to "corner a wild animal," to use the words of her police academy instructor. Besides, she'd already gotten what she needed. She knew the old codger was looking for the same thing as Miles Fourney, which meant he was looking for the same thing as Cade. It was time to call it all in.

She picked up her cell phone and dialed her boss, Sergeant Gustafson.

"You're off this morning, right?" Gustafson asked. "What's up?"

She hesitated. She knew he wouldn't be happy.

"Remember that pocket Constitution I showed you the other day? I have reason to believe that document—it's owner, actually—played a role in the Miles Fourney disappearance."

"We talked about this, Amaia. That case is closed, and you were supposed to move on two months ago."

"The Park Service ranger went out there a couple days ago and found the kid's backpack. There's a map that leads to a specific location in the Jarbidge Mountains. What's more, that document was stolen from me last night by a crazy old man who's been following me since yesterday morning."

Silence.

"Jim?"

"Okay Amaia, I'm not sure where to start. First of all, you are not supposed to be working on that case. We talked about that a long time ago. Second, why the hell is this the first time I've heard about it if you've had a mysterious man following you and stealing evidence? What the fuck, Amaia?"

She knew this was how it would go. She resisted the urge to explain that his response was the exact reason she hadn't said anything.

"There's one more thing." She heard him sigh. "The Owyhee County Sheriff called yesterday. He found the ranger's truck pretty severely vandalized. The ranger called me a couple times to ask for help, so I know he's okay. Well, I knew he was okay."

More silence.

"Okay, Amaia, I need you to come in here and file a report. First, though, get in touch with the governor's office and tell them you will not be MC'ing the public hearing on Saturday, or participating in that hearing or its security detail in any way. Furthermore, I don't want to hear about you volunteering with the Basque cultural stuff anymore. You need to focus on your actual job. Do that for a few months and we can talk about the possibility of volunteer work."

Amaia felt a pit forming in her stomach.

"But," she said, and he cut her off.

"Call the governor's chief of staff and tell her she has to find someone else. End of discussion."

Amaia put the phone down soft. She knew Jim would be upset, but the conversation had gone worse than she imagined—missing the chance to do her culture and her father proud—not attending the public hearing at all?

She picked up her phone and dialed Governor McGown's office, asking for Rachel Simplex.

A superficially cheery voice arrived on the line. "Simplex," it said.

Again, Amaia paused before proceeding. She wouldn't be able to reverse course once she defied her boss' direct order.

"Rachel, hi. This is Officer Amaia Ibarra with BPD. I've been helping Cade Rigens with security for this weekend. Also, because of my Basque heritage and some volunteer work I've done with Cade, he asked if I'd MC on Saturday. I'm worried, though. He left town a few days ago, and there's no indication he's going to make it back."

"Cade and I had a deal," Simplex said. "He didn't follow through, and there's still a lot to get done. Do you still want to help?"

There was something about Rachel's response that caught Amaia off guard. She seemed unnaturally calm.

"Well, that's why I called. I felt like you needed to know he wasn't back, but he also promised to help prepare and review my speech. I'm new to this political stuff and want to make sure I do it right."

"Can you come to my office downtown? I'm happy to help with your remarks, but I need to pin down a twenty-four-hour timetable to get things in order. Assuming you have the time, you might be able to help."

"When are you thinking?" Amaia asked.

"Five minutes ago would be great."

"On my way."

THIRTY-SIX

CADE SQUINTED INTO THE NARROWING CANYON as he drove the light-blue Scout across the old mining town's southern border and began clawing into the mountains. The road was carved from granite ledges fifty or a hundred feet above the river, which gorged up tight and rushed in a storm-fed froth. Slate-colored clouds collected over the peaks, and trees began to sway with the shifting weather.

Where the main road turned in a bight to ascend the west canyon wall, Andy motioned for Cade to turn onto a small road that continued along the river. They crossed a small bridge after a mile and stopped in a clearing where four jeep roads converged, one of them little more than a pile of rocks that went steeply up.

"Time to lock the hubs," Andy said.

They got out and rotated the knob at the center of each wheel to put the truck in four-wheel-drive, then Cade returned to the steering wheel and fired the truck back to life, ramming the shifter into four-low. They lurched and began inching onto the incline, too narrow to pass another vehicle and too steep to turn around. They were committed to a path that had been cleaved from a near-vertical mountainside.

The Scout cleared the road's embedded boulders and loose rocks, but the sulphury smell of gnashing gears and firing pistons filled the air as it strained against the grade.

Detritus from the Jarbidge gold rush was scattered across the mountain's lower folds. Rust-colored tailings stained the Earth burgundy-orange, but there was other debris, too. They passed ore cart tracks still embedded in the earth, scattered timbers and worn cables strewn about like fishing line on a riverbank. At one steep switchback Cade recognized a rusted steam boiler riveted together in the same fashion old railroad steam engines were built. It would have been used to winch carts of ore up and out of the mines and down the mountainside for processing.

Nothing about gold mining in Jarbidge could have been easy. Cade knew he was tough, that in his day he could spend weeks in the mountains and emerge stronger than when he left, but that was with state-of-the-art gear that wasn't even invented until the 1980s. He tried to imagine showing up in Jarbidge in 1910 with little more than a wool coat, leather work gloves and canvas backpack with a blanket and canteen. The men who mined the Jarbidge Mountains were tough on a level today's mountain men couldn't fathom.

Cade and Andy encountered more mining equipment and an even larger pile of rust-colored tailings, then after two more switchbacks the road straightened and traversed the steep lower mountainside.

Cade pulled to the side of the road to let the truck rest, but he also wanted to look back the way they'd come. He stepped to the edge of the road, which may as well have been the edge of the Earth. The wind from the advancing weather whipped his hair as he peered a thousand feet to the valley floor where they'd stopped to lock the hubs. It was shocking how much they'd climbed, or that a road had been built there at all.

To the northwest he made out the long slant of the Earth as it tumbled toward Fey's ranch and the canyon country beyond. It was hard to see through the building clouds, but he knew the dark slash of Sheep Creek was out there. He'd come a long way since he left the asphalt behind three days before.

The groan of another straining engine dragged his gaze back to the mountainside below. Six or seven switchbacks down, near the bottom of the grade, a big white pickup had begun to climb.

"Took long enough," he whispered.

The wind whipped harder, and a few raindrops spattered his cheeks, the mountainside growing darker as the thunderhead built. Driving an old convertible, they'd need shelter soon.

He returned to the Scout, popped it back into gear, and continued following the road as it traversed at a consistent elevation. They crossed a creek bed and crept onto a treeless ridge when the storm lashed out. Trees whipped in the wind, and visibility dropped to a hundred feet or less.

Cade drove slow to avoid steering off the road, and Andy raised his arm to point when they arrived at the old workings of the Bluster Mine. Cade pulled to the side of the road by the portal. Boulders had fallen from above and covered most of the ore cart tracks that ran parallel from the adit and curved toward the mountain's edge. A steel-bar gate was locked across the tunnel entrance, but one of the bars had been bent and broken. Andy crawled through, and Cade followed. They went about twenty feet to the place where dark and light mingled, and the fury of the wind dissipated. They sat opposite each other, their backs against stone walls, and took a few breaths.

The gate was silhouetted against the wild white crush of the storm. The world outside lit with a dramatic flash followed by a fast crack of thunder that rolled from one side of the canyon to the other, echoing through the white noise of the downpour and rolling into the desert beyond.

THIRTY-SEVEN

PAUL'S TRUCK LABORED AGAINST THE HARSH GRADE as they climbed the lower shoulder of Jarbidge Peak. Fey sat shotgun, Morgan in the back seat. When the road smoothed in between switchbacks, Fey pulled out the ash tray. Out came a small photograph of the family with baby Tanner, smiling and toothless.

"He had your eyes," she said.

"We're not doing this," Paul said.

"Christ, Fey," Morgan shot from the back. "Can't you let the man mourn on his own time, in his own way."

"Some things are too big to be shoved under a rug."

Paul snatched the picture from her hands and returned it to the ash tray. She'd seen it just then. Tanner had definitely had his eyes.

"So, what's in the backpack?" she asked.

"Can you be satisfied that we didn't kill him?" Paul said.

"There are a bunch of people wrapped up in this. Now I'm wrapped up in it, too."

"We've been trying not to tell you," Paul said, "because you're going to be happier if you don't know."

"Tell me now," she said.

"Have it your way," Morgan said. "The kid was on to something."

Paul put his finger in the air to encourage his older brother to pause, but Morgan shrugged the motion away.

"The kid was on to something," Morgan continued. "As you know, he was out here tracking down old claims so they could be closed or bought out. That obviously got the hackles up on a lot of locals.

"At one point he asked Paul here for help. As you can probably guess, Paul didn't help him much, but he was curious about what the kid found. I'm speeding the story up, but the kid had a bead on your ranch, Fey. He uncovered some kind of history that showed there's a gold vein on your property. The reason nobody will tell you what's going on is because Paul's been trying to cover it all up. He's been trying to make sure things stay the same. I don't know why the hell we're heading into the high peaks, because this whole damn thing's about your ranch."

"That's impossible," she said. "I was given that ranch from my dad, and from his dad. Hell, Paul and I were just looking for the papers this morning."

"Was your grandfather a man named Ben Kuhl?"

She nodded. "Great-grandfather, actually."

"Well you know the story. He was the last man to rob a mail stage in the old West. It looks like he stole the deed to your property. Your great-grand-father killed the mail driver, stole the deed, and passed the ranch down to his son. Paul tried to bury it all in the desert to protect your ranch, to protect you. That's the whole damn point. Fey, you're not the rightful owner of the ranch. Your great-grandfather stole it."

"Damn it, I've been trying to do this slow," Paul said.

"She asked. She damn-near insisted."

Paul picked up where Morgan left off.

"Fey, do you remember the old legend your uncle keeps going on about?"

She nodded.

"The kid found an old letter that amounts to a treasure map that he thought showed the Lost Sheepherder Mine was homesteaded to cover up existence of the mine. He said the letter leads to your ranch."

They looked at her for a reaction, but her awareness of the world faded. Morgan and Paul kept discussing details of what they knew, didn't know and when, but she barely heard them. Time sped up and the rain fell in sheets as they wound up the steep switchbacks that climbed the formidable shoulder of Jarbidge Peak toward the abandoned workings of the Bluster Mine.

"So, you killed him?" Fey finally managed. "You killed the kid to protect me and my ranch, your son's resting place and a piece of land you love more than life itself?"

"I didn't kill nobody," Paul grunted.

"I'm not sure I believe you," she returned, her voice soft and resigned, almost meek. "What do you intend to do to the ranger when we catch him?"

"We'll deal with him any way we have to," Morgan said. "He's the one heading for the kid's grave, and that's something he brought onto himself."

THIRTY-EIGHT

BEDRAGGLED AND SHIVERING, CADE AND ANDY had nowhere to go without returning to the raging whims of the storm. They sat across from each another, their backs between piers that supported huge timbers that held the mountain at bay. The filtered blue light and white noise of the outside world leaked into the mine's entryway where dirt and gravel dug uncomfortably into their backsides.

Arms folded across his chest to keep warm, Cade peered into the tunnel. He couldn't see very far, maybe fifty or sixty feet. That's where darkness swallowed daylight and the ore cart tracks ran parallel into the abyss.

There was something about being beneath an entire mountain of rock that let the imagination work unchecked. He fancied it the perfect place for a long-necked toothy creature to live, waiting long years to attack a wayward traveler. He felt like he should have left that part of his imagination under his childhood bed, but it wasn't just him. When Andy spoke, he revealed similar thoughts.

"Ever hear of Tommyknockers?" he asked.

Cade shook his head.

"Supposed to be spirits of dead miners that knock on a mine wall before it caves in. A miner who hears a Tommyknocker probably heard his last sound."

"Folklore."

"Hell, yeah it's lore, but the stories happen because these things cave in. They say miners used to leave parts of their lunch behind to keep Tommyknockers happy."

"If we had any food, I think I'd eat it."

"Hope they didn't hear you say that."

Cade kept a steady eye on the darkness, the gravity of his journey pressing down like the gravity tugging at the rocks over their heads. Both seemed unpredictable, dark and too big to control.

Andy turned his head toward the soft light filtering through the gate. His weathered features glowed, his eyes watery and alive. Cade appreciated the man's help, but he needed to tell him about their pursuers, that his niece was among them.

"There's something I need to tell you."

Andy's eyes pivoted across the tunnel.

"We're gonna have a problem soon—a few minutes, really. There are people following us."

"What do you mean, following us?"

"I borrowed the truck we drove up here. The people I borrowed it from aren't happy about it. They're looking for the same thing we are, I guess."

They sat still, soaking in the underground cool. Andy Jim didn't respond, so Cade continued.

"Andy, I think you know at least one of the people."

He looked at the cavern's ceiling, then back at Cade with a squint.

"I thought I recognized your truck. Not many like it anymore."

"I have a newfound respect for your niece, but she's mad as hell at me. I'd love to explain, but we're out of time—I'm out of time, anyway. I don't expect you to keep helping me at this point."

Cade heard the whump-whump of closing car doors. Andy took a deep breath and sighed. The rain's white noise filled the space between them. It was the kind of sound people in the city paid for and played through wireless speakers to help them sleep at night. In the mountains it meant flash floods and landslides. In the mountains it meant life or death.

Cade reached into the backpack and took out the Ziplock with Miles' maps. Like other nearby mines that were part of the historical record, there was an x in their location at the Bluster Mine. The hand-drawn map showed Heben Nuk higher on the mountain and a little farther south.

"What if Heben Nuk isn't on the surface?" he asked. "What if it's actually in here?"

"Aren't those GPS coordinates? You can't log coordinates from under a mountain."

"We're out of time, Andy. The only direction we can go is into the tunnel. Either the search ends here or it continues inside the mountain."

"There's nothing in these tunnels but dynamite boxes and pick-axes. There's seventeen miles of tunnels in here, and I might have walked 'em all except, damnit, I hate it underground."

They heard footsteps in the rocks outside the gate. Circumstance was about to decide for them.

Cade looked at the map to consider their orientation to the hand-written coordinates high on the west ridge. They'd be restricted by the tunnels, but it was possible they'd lead to an area roughly beneath where the coordinates were on the map, and at this point he was pretty sure they were looking for some kind of old mine.

He fumbled through Miles' pack and took out a compass, using it to orient. Satisfied he had at least a rough grasp, he shone his light into the dark.

"We're out of time, Andy. You can stay here, but I need to go."

The old man nodded.

"I've been looking for the Lost Sheepherder Mine for twenty years and never seemed to get any closer," he said. "I'm with you for now."

Cade wasn't sure where Andy's allegiances lay, but he was relieved he wouldn't have to face the darkness alone. He shouldered Miles' pack, and they went single file, step by step, into the deep.

THE LIGHT FADED FAST AS THEY LEFT the smell of still-falling rain behind. The timbers that supported loose rock walls and a caved-in ceiling near the entrance gave way to solid rock scraped and shaped by working picks, shovels and dynamite. It seemed sturdy until after a few hundred feet when they encountered a pile of rubble blocking the way forward. The rocks overhead had given out.

Cade scrambled up the rocks and peered through a small gap near the tunnel's ceiling. The darkness on the other side continued. He turned and shone the light so Andy could follow, but quickly realized his mistake.

"Hey there!" he heard from the tunnel entrance. "Give us the pack and you can go free!"

Cade saw three figures silhouetted in the portal, hands cupped around the edges of their eyes. The flash of Cade's headlamp had given them away.

"Time to go," he said and held his hand out to Andy, who hesitated only a moment before taking it.

"Can't believe I'm going underground with a damned park ranger."

"You sound like your niece."

Cade pulled the old man up, then helped push him through the small opening.

"Don't make us come in there," came a man's voice.

Cade heard the gate clank. He bellycrawled through the narrow opening and tumbled down a slope of jagged boulders to the floor. Now on the other side of the cave-in, the darkness was absolute. The soft orange light from Cade's headlamp was all they had and hardly enough to illuminate the walls. There were shadows and blind spots in every direction. After a few hundred feet, Cade asked Andy to pause. They stood motionless and strained their ears until they heard what Cade hoped they wouldn't—more footsteps in the darkness behind them.

"This here's what they call an adit, built to access the mine," the cowboy said. "They've got vertical shafts for air and ore chutes used to pass rock down level to level. You don't want to step in a hole. Follow me."

They followed the mine's parallel-running ore-cart tracks, but the path was littered with splintered dynamite boxes, fallen timbers and left-behind equipment. Judging by the age of the gear, the mine had been active late into the region's gold rush. The tunnel was bigger and longer, the equipment more sophisticated than the primitive mines that had been dug out entirely by hand.

By Cade's estimation, they'd gone one to two-thousand feet, maybe as much as a quarter mile, when they arrived at a Y-shaped junction. He looked at his compass. The right-hand drift led southeast, the left more to the north.

"Did your search and rescue crews ever look for the kid in these tunnels?" Andy asked in a low voice.

"I wasn't here, but they didn't go very far in if they did at all. If he got lost in one of these systems it's a needle in a haystack."

Cade pulled the compass from his pocket and held the light to it, then pointed to the right-side tunnel, waving for Andy to go that direction.

After a short distance the mine's silence gave way to a faint, far-off dripping, which became sharper and more distinct with each step. After another hundred feet, the noise became a steady splatter, and then they arrived at the edge of a rough-hewn rock precipice. The horizontal tunnel they'd been walking intersected with a large vertical shaft that went up toward the mountain's surface and down to some untold depth.

Cade looked up and blinked as water sprayed his face. He took off his headlamp and handed it to Andy to keep it dry, then shook his head free and squinted into the shadows of the vertical shaft again.

"Can you hold the light in there?" he asked.

Andy poked his arm into the space and away from the spattering water. Cade looked up and was surprised to see the smallest pinprick of light jabbing through the darkness. The rain seemed to collect and drip into the vertical shaft more than a hundred feet above. Andy shone the light across the tunnel over Cade's shoulder. It glowed orange on the walls of a completely vertical shaft, about ten feet in diameter. On the wall, within reach from his perch, was a metal ladder bolted to the rock. It went up and down into darkness. He looked back at Andy who seemed to understand. The man's expression immediately said no.

"Uh uh," he said. "No way. I ain't climbing in there."

The old man stepped to the edge and kicked a rock. They listened as it clicked against the stone walls and clanged against the ladder and continued clicking until they couldn't hear it anymore.

"That goes right into the pit of Hell," he said.

"What if I go," Cade said, his voice elevated to compete with the falling water. "We've only got one lamp, but I'll come back as fast as I can, and you won't have to climb."

"Uh uh," he said, pulling the light close to his chest. "What if you get lost?"

"Then you're gonna climb with me," he said. "At least far enough to . . ."

It was difficult to tell because the sound of falling water filled the mine and they were caught up in the logistics of continuing their exploration, but Cade thought he noticed a sound from the darkness behind the cowboy.

"What is it?" Andy asked, but the imposing mass of Fey's ex-husband came into view over the cowboy's shoulder, and Cade knew they'd deliberated too long. A hand appeared from the shadows and fell on Andy Jim's shoulder. The old man spun, but he had nowhere to go.

Cade reached into the vertical shaft and grabbed firm to the ladder, swinging into the cold spray. It stung his eyes and dripped down his face, but he climbed one rusty rung at a time, testing each before committing his weight to it. He climbed about thirty feet into the darkness and paused, clinging tight to wet metal, the leather soles of his cowboy boots slipping on the rusty wet rungs. He looked down to the adit where Andy had been caught between their pursuers and the open shaft. He saw the jerky-jerky glow of their lights, but they were gone from view.

"Keep yer hands off me," he heard Andy snap.

"Don't I know you?" came another voice, and then Fey's voice was clear among the confusion. It was surreal in the cool of the underground, but Cade clung to the ladder shivering wet in the dark, and listened as Fey and her Uncle Andy reunited for the first time in years.

"Andy?" she questioned. "Why aren't you at the hospital?"

"It ain't for me, that place. I came up here with the park ranger."

"Are you still looking for that old mine?" she returned.

"And getting closer, too."

Cade clenched his fingers and felt his forearms begin to burn. He wouldn't be able to hang there forever.

"Uncle Andy, I don't think it's here. We need to get you someplace safe. Tell us where the ranger is so we can get out of here."

"Where is he, Andy?" Paul interrupted. "Do you know where he's going? Does he know where he's going?"

It was a fair question. Cade had no idea where he was going, but he had no intention of stopping, either. Both Fey and her uncle had been helpful. In their own ways they were the only reasons he'd embarked on this journey or made it this far, but he could finish on his own.

"I have his flashlight," the cowboy said. "He has no light."

There was a pause, then Paul spoke again, louder this time.

"Fey, help us convince your friend to come out."

She didn't answer, and Cade was sure she didn't know what to do—or maybe she didn't care.

"What are you going to do to him?" she asked.

"It'll be over quick, and then you're coming to Boise with us."

Morgan joined his brother. "You're coming with us whether you want to or not. You started this fight, and you'll see it through."

"This is all wrong," she said. "There's got to be another way."

"Do you want to keep your ranch or not? Help us or get out of the way."

"Don't talk to her like that."

"You get out of the way, too, old man."

"It's my ranch," she said. "These are my decisions."

"Paul, can you remove your wife from the situation? She's fighting against her own best interests."

"Get off me!"

Fey's protests were followed by scuffling and grunts, then the old man's shouting. Fey's objections transformed into frantic screams and more commotion with heavy breaths and scuffling boots. Then it was silent.

About forty feet below, Cade saw a flashlight poke into the shaft. It shone in a semicircle, then up and down the ladder. He was far enough away that he might not be visible. He held his breath and closed his eyes. If they saw him, they didn't act on it. The light withdrew and went back into the side tunnel.

Cade's heart raced, and his mind spun. He didn't want to be left in the mine without a light, but even more than that he didn't want Fey and Andy Jim to be stuck with two half-hinged men whose intentions weren't entirely clear. His teeth ground as he over-gripped the ladder and felt the strain in his forearms and back.

"Stop!" he yelled. "Stop!" His voice reverberated up and down the tunnel, vanishing in the void.

A light appeared again at the portal forty feet below and shone up to where he clung. His fingers shimmered burgundy-orange with rubbed-off rust and water.

"I thought you'd want to see daylight again," the voice called.

The light went away, and Cade heard voices again. Then two lights appeared and encouraged him to climb down. He scrunched his face, drew in a deep breath and held it while clenching his stomach firm. There just wasn't anything more he could do. He exhaled hard and slumped against the ladder, his strength and determination spent. One slow step at a time, he went down, his hands glistening with wet rust, the soles of his boots slipping from one rung to the next. He descended to the level of the adit where the odd quorum of rural westerners waited. As he prepared to step back onto solid ground, an arm reached out and grasped at the backpack still strapped to his shoulders.

"Can you wait a minute?" he called and jerked his torso away in protest, but his shifting weight caused the smooth leather soles of his boots to slip. His knuckles instinctively cinched the rungs, but his blisters dug into the rusty metal as his boots swung into the open air. He clung precariously and didn't have much time. A feminine silhouette appeared behind one of the big men and shoved the man away. Fey came into clear view and leaned toward him. Face to face, she clawed at his forearm.

"Don't. Let. Go."

Her eyes were steely, and her hands grasped at his arms, but the spattering water made a slippery sheen that coated everything.

It was all just a little too late.

The grains of rust ground into the open sores on his palms as, one by one, his fingers released and he seemed tethered to the present by the slightest strand.

It was the kind of moment he'd only experienced in dreams, when life was on the cusp of some great upheaval that would forever send him a new direction. He expected to wake and discover he was buried beneath piles of pillows and blankets at his West Yellowstone home with his wife and daughter on a happy autumn day.

But he didn't wake. His fingertips lost whatever was left of their purchase and uncurled from the rusty rung. He took a soft breath and slipped silently into the abyss.

THIRTY-NINE

THE ELEVATOR RAN SMOOTH TOWARD THE TENTH FLOOR of the historic Hoff Building, eleven-stories of glass and steel built in the Art Deco style of the Roaring Twenties.

Amaia Ibarra watched through glass windows as the city fell away. Her palms were sweaty and clenched, and a knot pulled tight in her stomach. She'd already told Simplex that Cade wouldn't be back, but this in-person meeting seemed to have finality that she hadn't necessarily intended.

Establishing a clear plan for the public hearing in lieu of Cade's involvement would have repercussions for Cade's career. At the same time, she knew her own professional trajectory would be impacted as well.

The elevator chime dinged with its arrival at the tenth floor. Amaia went down a hallway and into a spartan lobby where a single chair was positioned across from a chest-high countertop.

"You Amaia?" asked a woman at the counter, and Amaia nodded. "Go on back. She's expecting you."

Amaia went through an arched doorway and turned left to find herself in a spacious office with big glass windows looking out on the Idaho State Capitol. Simplex sat in a high-backed chair with her chin resting on her hands, looking at the view. Amaia cleared her throat, and Simplex turned.

"Amaia, come in. Can I get you coffee, water, tea?"

"I'm fine."

"Well come in; sit down."

Amaia sat at one of two well-worn chairs positioned across from the desk and noticed they seemed shorter than Simplex's own chair.

"Thanks for getting in touch earlier," Simplex started. "We have a lot to sort out in a short amount of time. First, though, I need to understand what you know about Cade. Just hit the high points."

Amaia backed up two days to the meeting they'd had at the Basque Block market and Cade's concerns about mounting tensions before the hearing. She shared that Cade had called from Nevada a couple times and had sent a fax depicting an old Basque dialect in relation to the country around Jarbidge. She shared that he suspected Miles Fourney had gone missing, following that map.

"I warned him he was running out of time, but he just kept telling me he'd make it back. Sorry if calling you was the wrong thing to do."

"He's lucky to have someone like you watching his back," Simplex said. "You should have told me or someone at the Park Service sooner, though. When's the last time you talked with him?"

"Late last night."

"Do you know where he was or where he was going?"

"I did some research about the words and symbols and passed that along to him. He didn't say what his plan was."

She turned and looked out the window as if considering something she hadn't thought of before, then turned back to Amaia.

"What did the words mean?" she asked.

"What do you mean?"

"I want to know what you figured out."

Amaia considered her for a minute. She didn't even know what the words were, much less have any context for what they might mean. She went on anyway, explaining the meaning of the words Heben Nuk and their use in the legend of the Tartaro.

"Did Cade figure out what Miles Fourney was looking for?"

"I don't think so, but if he did he was a step ahead of me."

Simplex looked away for another moment and Amaia saw she was about to change the subject. She looked around Rachel's office. There were no pictures of family, no plants in the windows, just two book-cases full of three-ring binders and a desk piled in orderly stacks of paper. Against the wall was a cardboard box with its top slightly open, the words Hardrock Holdings on its side. It was filled with pocket-size

Constitutions like the ones the cowboy had been distributing on the Basque Block the day before.

Simplex took a deep breath before continuing.

"Amaia, I need you to keep this to yourself until tomorrow, but the park's a done deal. If it hasn't happened already, Congress is passing it today as part of an emergency omnibus spending bill. It'll be on the president's desk Monday morning. We expect he'll sign it."

Amaia recoiled like she'd been slapped.

"You heard me right."

"Then why bother with a public hearing?"

"We're going to use the hearing to announce the park's designation. It's just fortuitous timing, really. The hearing was scheduled before we pulled the votes together, but at this point we're confident we'll be able to announce a new national park to a mostly-friendly crowd tomorrow."

"And you're sure the president will sign it?"

"Unless he wants a government shut-down."

"Did Cade know about this?"

"He helped organize it."

"What did he think?"

"He supported it, of course. I'm telling you because in order to pull off tomorrow's event, the key organizer—that's now you if you're willing—needs to know."

Amaia took a deep breath. This was definitely not what her boss had in mind when he'd told her to stop volunteering, but the opportunity went beyond her personal goals and dreams of doing something that would celebrate her cultural roots. Her mind went to her father and the chance to make him proud while his life still hung in the balance.

"What do you need me to do, exactly?" Amaia asked, and Rachel smiled.

"I think you're going to have a prosperous career," she said.

FORTY

CADE OPENED HIS EYES AND FELT THE COOL SERENITY of the afterlife. A kaleidoscope of twinkling lights drifted across his field of vision. It was an apparition that hovered and pulsed before fading and twinkling back into existence again.

He blinked. The lights were gone, and the darkness absolute. He waved an arm in front of his face. There was nothing, just black. He let his hand drop and ran it along the ground. It was rough, firm, damp—not just firm: stone-hard. He was in no afterlife.

He lay on his back, his right leg straight, his left crossed underneath. His left arm extended across the ground, his right folded across his chest. He lifted each arm. They seemed to work. He reached his hands to his head and ran his fingers over his face, around the back of his neck. He was covered in liquid and found a swollen knot where his head touched the ground. He wiped the liquid from his forehead and put his fingers in his mouth. It had the metallic taste of blood and the cold consistency of water.

How far had he fallen? When his fingers came unwrapped from the ladder, he was sure he'd plunge to his death, and maybe that would have been better. He remembered the rock they'd kicked into the shaft. They'd never heard it hit bottom.

Cade was as confused as he was scared, and as he worked to calm his erratic breaths he noticed something different about the smell. The omnipresent scent of earth, rock and water he'd gotten used to was joined by a sour smell, like clothes worn for weeks without washing.

Without moving his body, he swirled his hands in small circles like he was making a small snow angel. There seemed to be an arm's width of ground around him. He dragged his hands to his hips and pushed toward a sitting position, but felt his equilibrium tip unexpectedly forward. He lay back down.

What had just happened?

He took stock again, this time gently rocking to test the floor's integrity and moving his arms to feel that he was in an area big enough to sit. Then he kicked his extended leg and realized it wasn't extended at all, but dangling into space.

Panic rose up. He must have fallen onto a ledge, but in the absence of light he had no way of knowing how big it was or if the precipice dropped three or three-hundred feet. He was afraid to move, but if he didn't he might as well be buried alive. He'd have to move blind.

He used his hands to push backward until the top of his head knocked into a stone wall. He winced but continued to push, curling his head forward and shoving his torso until he slithered upright with his back supported and both legs resting on solid ground. His heart pounded, and his breaths were short. He was freaked out, but he was no longer worried he'd blindly fall into the depths of the Jarbidge Mountains.

He probed the space to his left and right to get more bearings. To his right his hand found a texture he couldn't place; stiff, but not rock; pliable, but not fabric—a burlap sack, perhaps, or old clothes discarded by miners decades ago.

He ran his hands up and down his legs, then across his stomach and chest and stopped at the two padded backpack straps wrapped around his shoulders. He'd forgotten. The cowboy'd had his headlamp, but he still had Miles Fourney's orange backpack.

He didn't know how far he fell, but landing on his back had been lucky. The pack's internal frame probably absorbed some of the impact.

He removed it in slow, deliberate movements and lay it in his lap, opening the main compartment. He pushed a hand inside and held on firm with the other. He felt Miles' extra sweater, which he'd used to stay warm in the desert and the zip-lock bag full of maps. He felt the water bottles and broken GPS unit. He pushed deeper and felt a small pang of relief when his fingers closed on a cloth satchel pulled tight with a drawstring. He fumbled in the darkness until he opened the bag and felt the items he'd first seen in the dry creek bed two days before: the glossy-smooth finish of a folded emergency blanket, the spongy softness of a roll of toilet paper, a wound-tight coil of cord and, finally, a hard plastic cylinder about three inches long and an inch in diameter. He'd given the cowboy his headlamp, but he still had Miles' emergency supply of matches. Cade unscrewed the lid, tipped it on its side and tapped it with his finger until he felt a couple of matches and a striking pad fall into his palm. He set one match on his thigh and held the other against the striking pad, then flicked his wrist.

The fast flash of burning sulfur forced him to look away, but as the initial flare passed and his surroundings came into focus he jumped with shock. The soft orange glow revealed a prone form on the ledge beside him. His hand hadn't touched fabric a minute before, but skin that had decayed and wrapped tightly around bone.

His heartbeat quickened. It's like he'd found a secret entry into his soul. It's the entire reason he hadn't helped search for Miles the summer before. He didn't want the answers and now found himself paralyzed by the prospect of actually getting them.

His fingers singed as the match burned the whole way down. He shook his hand, and flicked the match into the darkness, which rushed back fast. He needed to be smart. He had fewer than ten matches and a long way to get to the surface.

He struck a second match, this time trying to ignore the figure beside him. He was on a ledge not five feet wide. Beyond the edge, the darkness rushed up from an untold depth. He looked up. The adit where he'd climbed onto the ladder—assuming it was the same one and that he hadn't fallen farther—was about thirty feet up. It wasn't too far, but far enough to have been seriously hurt. Beyond that, once he craned his neck, he made out the pinprick of light at the top of the shaft. It was still daylight. He hadn't been there long at all. The ladder where he fell descended to his level, but it was on the far side of the shaft, about ten feet across where water continued to spatter.

The second match singed his fingertips, and he flicked it into the darkness. With limited supplies, it was time to be strategic. He set the matches to his right, memorizing their location in relation to his seated hips, and reached into the backpack, this time fumbling until he found the kid's camp stove and fuel canister. He lit another match and set it on the stone, then quickly worked to set up the stove, a procedure he'd practiced in the dark for times when he arrived in camp after sunset. The match expired, but he finished by memory, priming the fuel line and turning the knob to allow some white gas to settle in a small pan below the element. For the fourth time, he struck a match. This time the stakes were high. If the stove didn't light, he'd be four matches closer to permanent darkness. He held his breath and positioned the match next to the stove's element. It flicked to life with a soft orange flame. He wouldn't know if it worked until the element was hot. He watched the flame, motionless in the mine's calm, and felt its life-giving warmth. When it began to dwindle, he turned the fuel canister regulator knob, and the stove came to life with a soft white-gas roar.

He smiled. He had light that would last at least a while. He was in a hurry, but maybe not in a panic anymore.

He looked over his left shoulder to see how much room he had to work with and found the ledge wasn't isolated, but at the end of another tunnel similar to the one they'd followed into the mountain. Cade checked his compass. The tunnel went east, the wrong direction if survival was his goal, but he didn't want to stay on the ledge with a dead body any longer than he had to. He used two hands to pick up the camp stove and fuel canister and went into the tunnel, holding it close to the rocks.

He willed himself forward, the heavy beats of his heart audible in the dark, and left the dripping moisture of the vertical shaft behind. He followed the tunnel about fifty feet to a small, dry, weirdly clean chamber. The light cast by the camp stove followed him in a circle as he tapped the fuel canister against the rock, making a light clicking sound like he was knocking on a door. It echoed into the tunnels beyond.

"Hello?" he called softly. The sound of his voice seemed foreign and out-of-place. Silence came back.

He walked in a semicircle, discovering a dead end. There was nothing to explore. The only way out was to go back the way he'd come. He had to return to the ledge. His senses tingled. He felt the answers coming.

Cade returned to the pile of clothes, which, while dirty, looked like fairly contemporary hiking clothes someone would buy at an REI or Patagonia outlet. The figure was stone-still and looked not-quite human. It was as if someone had positioned the clothes alone to look like a body.

Cade regarded the figure for a minute, then slumped against the wall about two feet away. His eyes straight ahead, he avoided the truth sprawled in front of him. The whole cavern wreaked of it, but he couldn't bring himself to look.

"Finish what you start, live with courage, do what has to be done."

He reached out with the toe of his boot to nudge the pile where the shoulders should have been. Whatever it was that held the clothes up crumbled at his touch. He moved the toe of his boot to another spot where the hips should have been and felt a hollow cavity beneath. The clothes were suspended by little more than decayed flesh suspended over a slender rack of bones.

Resigned to his task, Cade moved closer and studied the clothing. Something protruded from the back pocket. He pulled at it and discovered a small leather-bound journal. His heart skipped a beat as he read the initials on its cover: M.R.F.

Miles Richard Fourney.

He leaned against the wall, put his hands over his face and exhaled. Miles was dead after all. After all the time that passed he realized he'd still held out hope that the kid had just fled to Baja for a season of surfing and would show up one day with bright eyes and a dark tan.

The journal's spine cracked as it opened, and Cade scanned pages that chronicled a summer's worth of work in the mountains. Each page was dated, but aside from that there seemed to be little continuity. One page of poetry or odd drawings led to another tabulating hours he'd worked in the field or a journal entry detailing ethereal thoughts. Cade leafed to the second-to-last page, the final entry, and read:

> *May 11, 2015, summit of Jarbidge Peak*
> *There are beginnings and endings in the mountains*
> *where folds layer one upon another, concealing mysteries*
> *tucked inside. Each crease is a beginning, and each crease*
> *is an end. They're dawns and dusks, and they're folds within*
> *us as much as without, places where questions and answers*
> *mingle as one.*

Cade looked at the pile of clothes. Had he really written that the same day he vanished?

"I'm sorry kid," he sighed as tears blurred his vision.

He moved to put the journal down, and a small square of paper fell from inside. He unfolded it and found two brittle pages. The first was a blank U.S. Postal Service ledger labeled Star Route 70333. In the corner was a small yellow post-it note labeling it part of the "Ben Kuhl Collection." Cade flipped the document over and discovered a letter written in a faint-but-legible hand. It was dated December 5, 1916 and was signed by a man named Ishman Oneko, who called himself "The Last Sheepherder."

Cade sat among the shadows and read:

> *Dear Marko,*
>
> *I don't expect you to forgive me for leaving you and your mom, but I hope you've found the courage to live large and full. Please trust I did what I had to.*
>
> *Contained in these words is the reason I never came back. Handle this with care and don't tell anyone unless you've ensured the safety of yourself and those you hold dear. The gold in these mountains makes men do wild things.*
>
> *With this letter are legal papers filed under the Homestead Act for ownership of a ranch ten miles outside Jarbidge. It's a good piece of land with enough water to farm and plenty of space for cattle and horses, but it also has riches difficult to describe. When they found gold in Jarbidge in 1909, I knew it was only a matter of time until they found my strike, too. Instead of filling a mining claim, I went to the land office, filed the ten-dollar fee and went to work building a cabin and growing food. That was five years ago, and I've only just finished what they call "Proving Up" the land. Enclosed is the deed, which I left blank so you could file it under your name.*
>
> *Trust when I say that the location of The Lost Sheepherder Mine is not lost at all. Also trust that you are now the sole owner of that land. You'll find further information about how to locate the riches from the mine at the Basque boarding house on Grove Street in Boise. Just remember your Basque roots and consider the legend of the Tartaro like I used to tell you. Heben nuk!*
>
> *I'm sorry I wasn't there for you, but I'll die a little easier*

knowing you, your grandchildren and their grandchildren
may live with comforts I was never able to afford.

Mait Zaitute, your father,
Ishman Oneko
"The Lost Sheepherder"

The second document was a copy of a property deed signed by President Woodrow Wilson in 1916. It included coordinates laid out using Township, Range and Section survey descriptions, which could be used to describe properties anywhere west of Ohio. The numbers weren't all legible, but they looked like 4—N 58E—. Cade couldn't be sure, but they might be the exact numbers he'd seen in the ragged old Constitution on the Basque Block days before. It looked like a real, unadulterated deed by which an original homestead had been decreed.

Cade leaned back, put his hands over his face and exhaled. His stomach was twisted into a complicated knot. Miles had died looking for a mine after all. He'd died doing the job Cade sent him to complete. And, like Fey had said, there was no treasure because it was already mined.

He sat in the quiet with his thoughts, and all the guilt he'd accumulated over six years of running away flooded back. It had all started with a clear-blue sky. Then came the shifting wind, a blinding belch of smoke, the engine's seizure, the emergency buzzer, the fear in their eyes, and the final terrible moments as they plowed into a wall of lodgepole pine by the Firehole River.

He sat alone in the dark belly of the Earth and felt it consume him. His eyes filled with the truth of it. His little girl, who'd wanted to be like her old man, wasn't coming back. None of them were, and he'd been at the controls. The whole damned plane had gone down because of him.

The dominoes of his failures were lined up in his mind. He thought about how his marriage had then fallen apart when he couldn't let go of what he'd done, how he'd abandoned his love of wild places in exchange for a job that might compromise them. Next was Fey, who'd helped him only to feel betrayed before being hauled off by her in-laws. Now, finally, here was Miles, another victim of Cade's carelessness.

His cheeks grew damp as the tears flowed. He felt scared and alone, but they weren't tears of fear or loneliness. The harder he tried to cast the feelings aside, the more the guilt and shame flooded back. He couldn't control it anymore. It was in the marrow of who he was.

He'd ignored it for years, thinking the more he looked away the easier it would be. Instead, he'd ignored everything he was and everyone he'd ever loved. Now he sat next to Miles Fourney's decomposing bones and embraced the core rot that ate him from the inside.

It was time, he thought. It was time to give it all back to the mountain. It was time to join Miles the way he should have joined his little girl and the rest of the team six years before.

The decision came without deliberation or ceremony. He reached out and turned the small red knob on the stove's fuel canister and watched its feeble final flickers wobble and vanish in the pitch.

The emptiness rushed back as Cade leaned against the stone belly of the Earth and welcomed it. The dark was all there was, and he felt like he'd finally found the rest he craved and peace he deserved. Through the darkness he heard the faint whispers of his childhood calling, a call-and-response hymn he knew by heart from so many Sundays in his Grandfather's western Pennsylvania church:

It is well (it is well),
With my soul (with my soul),
It is well, it is well with my soul.

FORTY-ONE

FEY HAD BEEN IN A LOT OF CIRCUMSTANCES that made her blood boil, but being held hostage by her ex-husband was now at the top of the list.

They were parked outside Morgan's cabin in Jarbidge, and for the time being it was just she and Paul sitting in the front of Paul's truck. Morgan had gone around back to gather things they'd need in Boise where the brothers planned a statement too big to fail.

"Where do you get off telling me what to do, or when?" Fey spat.

"I'm sorry," Paul shrugged.

"Don't apologize to me. Fight your own damn battles and stay the hell out of mine."

It had only been an hour since they left Cade for dead and Uncle Andy on the side of the mountain looking for his lost inheritance.

"We hoped you'd join us," Paul said. "You've been the leader of the opposition. You built the movement that's coming together to fight back. You just didn't take it far enough, so that's where we come in."

Morgan appeared at the side of the house carrying a cardboard box with black lettering on the side. As he drew close she was able to read it. "Hardrock Holdings," it said on the box. He put in the back seat behind Fey and stuck his head in the cab.

"She behaving?"

"For now."

"I'll be a few more trips. We'll roll soon."

When he disappeared around the cabin, Fey reached into the back seat and flipped open the box he'd stashed. It was full of small booklets with pictures of George Washington on their covers: a hundred or more copies of the United States Constitution.

"Where does he get these things?"

"From a lady in Boise who works for the governor. I'm not sure where she gets 'em."

"Isn't the Governor advancing the park? Why would someone from his office spread the gospel of federal overreach?"

"You'd have to ask Morgan."

"You know, I agree with you about the land, Paul, but your methods are wrong."

Paul lifted his head, encouraging her to continue.

"Remember how it was with the South Canyon Road and the original Shovel Brigade?"

He nodded.

"I've thought a lot about that, and I think it was the wrong fight. There's no sense fighting over a road that doesn't go anywhere. We've got real fights to bloody our fists over: maybe starting with roads that actually lead someplace, but grazing, mining, water, our way of life."

"That's why we're going to Boise." His voice was filled with enthusiasm. "That's why you're coming with us!"

"Here's my rub with the whole shovel brigade thing."

His body slumped, his excitement gone as fast as it arrived.

"Wrong fight, wrong time or whatever—those are tough judgements. You could just as easily argue that you've got to dig your heels in somewhere, so they might as well have done it here in Jarbidge. Anyway, here's the rub: not many of those Shovel Brigade boys were from here. Hell, most of them weren't. So, if you're going to be mad about some ranger from Boise, Elko, Twin Falls or wherever in here trying to decide how things should work, then I've got to be pissed off at those boys, too. That shovel brigade was about way more than a road; it's a movement, and it's a hell of a lot bigger than Jarbidge. Most of those boys want to fight, and they want to fight the biggest bully they can find. For better or worse, that's the federal government, and it's going to get you in trouble."

Morgan appeared from the side of the cabin again, this time carrying an armload of ordinary, rust-covered shovels. He threw them in the back of the truck alongside the shovels Paul had loaded at the ranch, then poked his head into the cab.

"Care to give me a hand?" he said. "Just one more load."

Paul tugged at Fey's elbow, and the three of them went around the cabin to a back deck, which hovered over the river. He reached under the deck and dragged out four or five more common spades, then reached in again and dragged out a few more.

"Water's on the porch if you wouldn't mind grabbing a few," he said with a nod at Fey, and she grabbed three bottles of Dasani glistening with condensation in the heat. Beside the water was a machine that looked like an ice fishing drill, but larger and covered with dirt and dust.

"What's that?" she called to the brothers, their arms full of shovels.

"Core driller on loan," Morgan said. "Been doing some rock hounding."

"For what?"

"It's a gold belt, after all," he winked.

The three of them returned to the truck. With Paul in the driver's seat and Fey in between the brothers, the truck's V8 rumbled to life, and they returned to the network of roads that wound north toward Boise.

"I'll start calling the troops as soon as we get cell service," Morgan said. "Who's on the list? I've got the neighborhood ranchers, a few farmers from the plain, the patriot groups—basically all the folks Fey's been organizing against the park."

"Put it on social media, too," Paul said. "Facebook, Twitter and every-place else. We've got ourselves a shovel brigade to build."

Fey slouched, her arms folded, defeated and dark. She was about to lose her ranch, held hostage by a man she'd loved and had become part of a hair-brained protest that had the potential to introduce violence into the tinderbox of conflict on the plateau—conflict she'd eagerly fanned to pursue her own anti-park campaign.

Paul reached over and put his hand on her arm.

"Don't touch me," she snapped.

She looked out the window and watched the land she'd known her whole life pass by: the hoodoos, cliffs, winding river and sweet-smelling sage. She felt the change coming, and she felt helpless to stop it.

— PART IV —

"Love, give, forgive, settle differences and live. Choose life."

—Miles Fourney's journal

FORTY-TWO

Howooooooo.

The silence was all-consuming, but there it was again, something far away and distinct.

Howooooooo. It was a long, semi-high-pitched sound like a howl or protracted low whistle.

Cade's eyes opened slow on absolute black. His head was foggy. He had no idea how long he'd been in the underground or, at first, why. And then he heard it again, a voice or sound so far off he couldn't make out what it said.

Howooooooo.

It could have been the wind from high on the mountain, but that seemed unlikely. He was too far down, too far in. His mind was cloudy, but it crept through all the possibilities of what the sound might be: a way-ward bird, wind or water working through cracks, old timbers bending or bowing in the dark.

He heard it again.

Howooooooo.

He didn't know if he'd been asleep a night, a day or a week and felt silly at his lack of conviction. If he'd actually intended to let himself expire he could have done better than falling asleep underground. Hell, he should have flung himself off the ledge into the depths. He felt like he had some small understanding of the commitment people possessed when they stepped off a building or pulled the trigger of a gun. He'd been trying to achieve Miles' fate, but Miles had fallen or been flung into the dark. Cade had light if he chose to use it.

Howoooooo, he heard again.

Instead of closing his eyes and waiting for the darkness to retake him, he allowed his mind to pace backward. He remembered how he'd detested Fey's arrival at his office and how they'd forged some kind of understanding fleeing bullets in the night. She'd helped him without asking for anything in return. He remembered the soft touch of her lips. For just a moment he allowed himself to reach into the darkness to understand the sense of betrayal she must have felt when she read the letter promising condemnation of her ranch. Even after that, when Cade had been about to fall from the rusty mine-shaft ladder, it was Fey who'd reached out and tried to help.

Now, when she'd been taken by the brothers against her will, he'd simply laid down to die, still showering in the loss that had splashed all over his life.

He sat suddenly upright and fumbled in his pockets, locating the final remaining matches. He struck one and located the stove. Like he had when his survival instinct first kicked in, he went through the steps it took to light it and watched it hum to life, casting a blue-orange hue across the cavern.

Cade felt courage begin to well up inside him. It was small at first, just a kernel he supposed had already been there, but it quickly swirled into something that filled more of his stomach, and then the empty cavity of his chest.

It was warm sun that spread like a growing rumor across the snow-covered topography of his soul. For the first time in years he didn't feel the tug of his past, but the open road of a journey about to unfold.

He was so enthralled with his sudden desire to help Fey and make sure Miles hadn't died for nothing that he didn't even recognize that he'd found his feet and stood, the courage to live resulting in a body that was ready to leave before he knew he'd made the choice.

The steady hum of the stove on the cavern floor faltered, and Cade's pulse quickened. His time in the mountain was limited unless he truly wanted to stay in darkness.

He heard the sound again, still far away but unmistakably similar every time.

Howooooooo, it said.

"Howooooo!" he shouted, the sound echoing through the labyrinth of darkness.

"Howooooo!" he yelled again.

He put the journal in his pack. He looked to what was left of Miles on the cavern floor.

"Thanks, Miles, for the backpack, the maps, the matches, the stove. Weird as it is, thanks—I guess—for the advice. I'm sorry I wasn't there for you, but I think I get it. I can still be there for other people."

Cade picked up the stove and fuel canister and paced the ledge. He set the stove near the edge and adjusted the flow of gas so the flame turned from hot blue to a cooler, brighter orange, a light that would shine up toward the small pinprick of light he'd seen. He clipped the backpack's chest strap, backed up a few steps, and ran, flinging himself into the darkness toward the uncertain security of the ladder. For a moment he felt the emptiness rush up, and then he hit hard, his forehead smacking one of the ladder's rungs. His blistered fingers grasped for purchase.

When he regained his balance, he clung with all the strength his fingers could manage. His legs crimped tight, his core muscles clenched, his forearms throbbing from over-gripping the wet metal rungs and his head fuzzy with the sudden exertion. His body shook with an electric current that, little by little, dissipated as he relaxed. When his breathing finally slowed and his focus restored, he willed himself upward. As he climbed he left the lapping orange flame of the stove behind and passed the spot where he'd fallen, where Fey had tried to help him. He passed the point where he'd waited in the dark. He climbed far beyond that, and as he climbed with machine-like purpose the orange glow of the camp stove completely vanished below. He couldn't see but climbed on with trust at his core, and as he climbed found himself increasingly splashed by cold water that matted his hair and stung his eyes. He climbed through the discomfort, determination and faith his only guides.

Cade didn't count but guessed he passed a couple hundred ladder rungs ascending an equal number of vertical feet. His fingers fought against gravity and his blisters were open sores. He was in absolute darkness, but as he neared the top, an almost imperceptible gray light from a small vent filtered in. The ladder topped out near a ceiling made of wood two-by-sixes cross-braced with two-by-fours. In the center was a body-size hole. A short section of rope was secured to the top rung and went out through the hole. Cade couldn't tell how securely it was tied or what it was fastened to, but unless he wanted to climb down and try to get out the way they'd come in the rope was the only way.

He looked into the depth of the mountain beneath his feet. He imagined he saw the camp stove burning on the ledge, flickering in vigil to the empty promise of a life cut short, but the truth was that it was too far down and had probably already gone out. Whatever happened to Miles in the mine would stay there.

Cade reached back and held firm to the rope, allowing his weight to settle and then pulled hand-over-hand up the final few feet toward daylight, his feet dangling into the depths and treading the open air. He reached over the lip and pulled himself up, propping his elbows on damp wood. With all the strength he could summon, he pushed himself into a cool mountain drizzle and saw the deep blue minutes of twilight behind a quilt of clouds.

He looked to see who'd made the sound that pulled him out of his inner-earth repose. Nobody was there, just rocks, pines and thin mountain air scented with rain, a small stream that spattered the rocks and disappeared along the edges of the wood. Maybe it had been the wind after all. He wasn't surprised to see the spot marked with a torn piece of black webbing that matched the torn shoulder strap of Miles' backpack. Now he knew it was just another milestone on a journey that led somewhere else.

He smiled. He finally had answers and wanted to pursue instead of hide. He felt a pang of joy and panic—and with those feelings some measure of resolve. He had to get to Fey and finish what Miles had started. He had to, time willing, travel to Boise to make sure things were okay before the Dunham brothers got their protest under way.

For just a moment, though, all of that could wait. He rolled onto his back and lay in the rocks and let the rain wash all the dirt and dust from the mine's deep innards back into the mountain. The rain was cold, but it washed him clean, and he felt like he was born anew.

FORTY-THREE

IN THE MINE CADE HAD BEEN BLIND, but now he made out the subtle silhouettes of trees and rough contours of the ground. The charcoal gray was enough to hike by, even if he occasionally lost his footing. He noticed the fresh scent of pine, the way the rocks moved under his feet, and how the blue-black clouds rolled across the sky. His senses were sharp, and he felt alive.

It was hard to see, but he realized he'd mistaken morning for evening when he arrived at the surface in the rain. He'd been asleep in the mountain overnight and had returned to the world just before dawn. His feet were sore, but he willed them with fresh purpose and resolve.

The light grew stronger, and the rain eased and stopped. He descended a few hundred feet and pushed his way over a reef of loose rock and through a clump of damp bushes. The silhouette of a road cut came into view. He stumbled down an embankment and turned on the road, heading north toward the area where they'd gone into the mine a day before.

He found the Scout parked in the same place they left it, the hubs locked, the keys dangling in the ignition, the upholstery soaked from the overnight storm.

He heard a shuffling behind him and turned to see Andy Jim the third emerge from the mine shaft.

"I hate it down there," he said.

"What are you doing?"

"Looking for you."

"Why didn't you go with them?"

"They left me. I never did like that Paul Dunham much."

"So, it was you?"

"Me what?"

"Yelling in the mine."

"I didn't yell anything. Didn't really have much hope, actually."

"You know," Cade began, but Andy cut him off with a wave of his hand.

"That's between you and the mountain. They took my niece against her will. Those boys are headed for trouble."

"We're wasting time," Cade agreed.

The rainwater soaked the seat of his pants as Cade sat behind the steering wheel. Andy climbed into the passenger seat, and Cade turned the key. The engine roared to life.

Clumps of mud flung from the Scout's tires as they careened down the switchbacks toward Jarbidge, where a low mist draped across the valley floor. They dropped into the fog and accelerated into the unseen.

With a whole night's head start, there was no way they'd catch the caravan of protesters heading for Boise. There was only one way to get there in time, and Cade didn't like it. He cast the idea from his mind. He'd face that demon when he had to, but he knew it was coming.

The road was rocky and rough on the mountain, but the switchbacks led to the smooth dirt that paralleled the Jarbidge River and ran north into town.

Jarbidge had barely begun to wake when they sped through without slowing or stopping. The engine's roar echoed from one canyon wall to the other in the morning stillness. A "No LBNP" picket sign flipped in the wake of the fast-moving truck. Andy waved to a small group of men drinking coffee on the front porch at The Outdoor Inn. One of the men waved back, but by the time his hand was in the air the Scout was already across the bridge and speeding into the canyon. They passed the stone hoodoos that helped give rise to the legend of Tsawhabitts, then turned left past a ROAD CLOSED sign onto the Deer Creek Grade. The Scout's tires dug into the mud, and its engine raced as they climbed and crested the plateau, then slid sideways toward Three Creek Valley and the Diamond D Ranch.

Cade skidded to a stop between the suspended fuel drum and gray sheet metal in the cliff wall where he'd helped Fey garage the plane two days before. The ranch was desolate, its half-dozen workers either asleep or away. Cade went to the double sliding doors held firm with a padlock and jiggled the lock, producing a clanging that split the morning silence. He looked frantically for a solution.

"Could shoot it," Andy said.

"No, not shooting it," Cade answered. "That'd spray us with shrapnel and damage the plane. You think she keeps a key in the truck?"

"Maybe she has a bump key."

"A what?"

"A bump key for picking locks. Looks like a normal key except the teeth are all filed down."

Cade looked back with a blank expression.

"I'll go look in the truck for a spare," he said.

"See if you can find a beer can."

Again, Cade looked at him with a blank stare.

"Could use it to shim the lock."

Cade rummaged through the glove box while Andy searched beside the building for an aluminum can. Cade found a few old food wrappers and a couple quarts of motor oil but no keys. They could search the house, but that would take all day.

Andy returned with a weathered Genesee beer can.

"No keys?" he asked, and Cade sighed no.

The old man slipped a knife from his front pocket and unfolded the blade.

"I hate to dull my steel on aluminum," he said and braced the can against the ground. He cut it into two even halves, then sliced one into a rectangle. He trimmed two small triangles out of the bottom edge, and folded the top down on itself. In this way he built a narrow strip of aluminum attached to something that looked like a handle.

He took his contraption to the Masterlock and slid it along the outside of the shackle. With steady and practiced purpose that belied his usual jitters, he worked the shim for a minute and seemed about to curse when there was an unmistakable click, and the lock popped open.

Andy Jim stepped aside, smiling.

"I'm not asking how you learned that," Cade said and removed the shackle from the latch. Then he pushed hard on the two doors, which slid aside to reveal the cavern where Fey's plane was parked.

He surveyed the rock overhang with new curiosity. He knew it was weird the first time he saw it, but now he wanted a better understanding about why it was there. For centuries people had built man-made structures beneath rock overhangs. Places like Mesa Verde and other Southwest cliff dwellings were premier examples, but this was different. The overhang was rough-hewn and man-made. It was large, too, big enough to cram in another plane if it was parked creatively.

The odd cylinder of rock he'd seen the first time he was there still lay on the ground near the plane's wing. He picked it up and studied it, starting to confirm a suspicion that had taken root on the mountain. The cliffs that wound in shadowy ribbons around the Three Creek Valley were chocolate-brown basalt, the result of old lava flows that formed most of the plateau. The rock of Fey's airplane hangar was granite, the same stuff that made the Jarbidge Mountains and the central Jarbidge gold belt.

He smashed the cylinder against the wall until he knocked a chunk of speckled gray granite loose, then stuffed it in his pocket and returned to the plane.

They were in a hurry, but time seemed suddenly still.

Cade stood by the plane with his feet and shoulders squared, his hands open at his sides, the posture of a man about to jump into a fight. He approached cautiously and held out his palm as if meeting an unpredictable dog. A shiver shot down the back of his neck when his hand touched the cool metal. He walked along its side, dragging his fingers and feeling the demons of his past well up.

He muttered aloud to nobody and everybody, the morning breeze and Andy Jim his only witnesses. He walked around the plane as he mumbled, his mind slipping into places he usually only went when he slept

He had a fast flash of a smiling little girl, a skinned knee at the playground, a birthday cake shaped like a Rubik's Cube. He relived her quiet determination leading to first steps at fifty-four weeks. He smiled at her report card full of Cs, her first soccer goal and those God-awful awkward conversations about puberty. He thought about the whole team of smoke jumpers who got on his plane that day, how his little girl fit right in, how proud he was of her ability to see her goals through. There were four in all; four souls lost to the raging winds of an out-of-control fire along the Firehole River. Why he'd been the only survivor was beyond his comprehension. It's like two and two didn't make four.

Andy Jim stood near the hangar's sliding double doors. Cade didn't ask, and Andy didn't say, but the old man seemed to understand that Cade needed space.

"Sometimes all you've got to do is go sit in the mountains, and whatever it was you were looking for will come back," Cade said. "Sometimes it was right there all along."

The plane had gone down with him at the controls, so blaming himself had been as natural as breathing. The fact was, there wasn't a pilot alive or dead who could have predicted the sudden shift of wind and smoky whiteout that resulted. The forces of nature, once the North Star that helped him make sense of the world, had turned against him. The shifting wind wasn't his fault. The tragic loss of life was immense, but it wasn't his fault.

It wasn't his fault.

He repeated the words to himself over and again before returning to the front of the plane where Andy leaned against the prop. In the short time they'd known each other they'd achieved an understanding. They were both crazy in their own ways and seemed to respect each other for it.

"Demons can be tough to put to rest," Andy said.

Cade smiled. His new frame of reference didn't erase the tragedy, but it brought him back to himself.

They went to work.

The two men pushed the sliding doors the whole way open and removed the chocks from the wheels. Cade climbed onto the wing, extending a hand to his new friend, and climbed into the cockpit where he eased into the pilot's seat. He reached around his neck and removed the gold chain with a small pendant of a Pulaski. He wrapped it around the controls and spoke aloud.

"Another flight for old time's sake?"

It was fleeting, but there was a moment of connection where he felt like she was with him again, her goofy adolescent smile shining like the sun.

He turned to his new friend.

"All right, Andy, pull that door shut and lock it. There should be a checklist around here somewhere, so see if you can find it and read it off."

Andy looked back with a blank expression.

"A checklist?"

"We're doing it right, or we're not doing it at all. Now let's get to Boise and fix this thing."

Cade found his headset on the floor, put it on and fired the plane's engine to life, then, for the first time in more than six years, pushed the controls of an airplane to taxi for takeoff.

FORTY-FOUR

FEY LOOKED TO HER LEFT AND right and considered the level of preparedness and seat-of-the-pants ineptitude of her captors. During the drive Paul had called ranchers and farmers who planned to join the public hearing takeover. He sent emails and posted social media messages to militia members he knew were sympathetic to the cause. They wanted to make a spectacle in front of a crowd and to send a message to the federal government. Their plan had grown from a common grassroots protest into something more sinister. It had evolved into a takeover of federal property like they were planning a Sunday afternoon grouse hunt.

She looked out the windshield and saw Basque flags strung up on light poles and families wandering the streets with ice cream cones. The smell of sausage, cheese and fried bread wafted through the open side window; the far-off sound of folk music rose up and fell away.

They passed a crosswalk filled with people wearing red and green, the colors of the Basque homeland. On the other side of the street was a long line of television news trucks parked single file. Outside one was a man with a microphone in his hand talking to a camera on another man's shoulder.

The brothers knew the public hearing had been scheduled during the Basque festival to boost visibility and support, and now they planned to use that attention to advance their own cause.

Morgan turned the truck into an underground parking garage and wound in big circles into the cool depths where there would be ample shadows and fewer prying eyes.

Fey knew that if you asked the brothers or their friends, their answers would vary, but most simply wanted to be heard. Like she was, they were angry about the park, but they were too eager to follow any leader willing to wage that war. More than angry, she knew they felt powerless. Charging into federal property would give them a feeling of control, but Fey had little patience for their perspective. They were lost in their far-right interpretations of the Constitution, and she was pissed at their arrogance. She was on their side, but they acted like they had some birthright to the land superseding anyone else's. She was against the park, but she believed in the processes established to protest it. Hell, she might even believe in the process established to designate it—even if she didn't want that to happen.

The most hard-nosed—or perhaps mislead—of the protesters she'd worked with also wanted to disrupt federal employees working on the new park and to transfer ownership of federal land to citizens, states, or local governments. An armed takeover of federal property was, to them, some form of civil disobedience like when the anti-abortion crowd showed up with picket signs on the capitol steps.

Fey was disgruntled about a lot of things, but she was mad as hell that she was now being used as a pawn in their game. She didn't feel threatened by them, but she knew she was their captive, held against her will to leverage another goal. She tried to think of a different word, but there wasn't much else you could call it. She was her ex-husband's hostage.

They pulled into a parking garage about a block from the Basque festival and the new national park's would-be headquarters. Morgan told Fey to stay put while Paul gave her a raised-brow look, as if to apologize. She held up a middle finger.

"It doesn't have to be like this," he said and closed the truck's door.

The two men huddled with a couple dozen others at the back of the pickup and talked in hushed tones. There was an assortment of shovels and spades they'd tossed in the back alongside a couple of hunting rifles. Whatever they had planned, it seemed like a risky urban version of the Jarbidge shovel brigade from 2000.

Fey talked herself through a set of contingencies she'd employ if things got ugly. If the men became distracted by any kind of drama, civil or violent, she'd use it to duck for cover. If police arrived it would be more complicated; she'd look like one of the militants. If possible, she'd hold her hands high to make sure she wasn't targeted and jump clear of her captors.

If they made it into the park headquarters, she'd find an opportunity to use the bathroom and make use of a window or another escape route. Above all, she needed to separate herself. Of all the plateau's ranchers, she'd been the park's most visibly vocal opponent. For all she knew, authorities would assume she was the leader of this ragtag militia. She had no allies. She was completely alone.

It was only after talking herself through the contingencies that she remembered Paul had stashed his gun in the truck's glove compartment. She looked over her shoulder to see if they were watching. The men were gathered near the tailgate, huddled over a notebook they filled with black and blue ink. Paul looked in her direction every thirty or forty seconds, and the others looked around nervously in every direction every minute or two. She knew her window was short.

As Paul looked away, she reached for the glove compartment knob but found it stuck or locked. She hit the knob with the heel of her hand and realized she'd made the whole truck wobble. She looked over her shoulder to find the whole group looking up from their papers to see what caused the jostling. She tucked her hands in her lap as Morgan walked to the car door, opened it and leaned inside.

"Kicking and punching isn't gonna help, sister. We'll be a few more minutes, so sit the fuck still."

He closed the door hard, and they refocused on the notebook. She'd only get one more chance.

She reached across and tried again to turn the knob. It was still stuck. This time, instead of striking it, she picked a nickel out of the ash tray and used it to pry at the lock. The knob grudgingly turned, and the box flipped open with a clunk.

She sat abruptly upright and turned to see if any of the men had looked. Nothing changed. Paul glanced up at her, then looked back at the notebook.

She took out Paul's revolver, a Ruger Blackhawk 357 she'd given him on their second wedding anniversary to shoot rattlesnakes and coyotes at the ranch. She flipped the cylinder open and dumped the bullets into her palm, then quickly returned the weapon to its stash. Knowing Paul was shooting blanks—and, more important, that he didn't know—might give her an opportunity to flee. If he tried to use it, and she hoped to God he didn't, she might save him from murder or worse. With a little luck it might create enough confusion for her to slip away.

It wasn't the best plan she'd ever conceived, but it made use of the resources she had. She slipped the bullets into her shirt pocket as the men returned and opened the doors on either side.

"Time to go," Morgan said and reached for her elbow, which she pulled back as she got out of the truck.

"I don't need your help," she said.

Paul took the Ruger out of the glove box and tucked it into the waist of his pants, then covered it with his untucked shirt tails. Each of the men grabbed a shovel from the back of the truck and shouldered it with its spade high. In this fashion, they formed into a single-file brigade and marched military-like toward the Basque Block and the public hearing.

FORTY-FIVE

THE DRIVE FROM THE RANCH TO the road that doubled as a backcountry airstrip was about a mile of dirt. After two days of rain, it had become a sticky mud mess, and Cade had to gas the plane to get it to move. Even then it slid sideways like a car on a backwoods race track.

With enough throttle, the plane crawled up the grade, and Cade felt the familiar nerves begin twisting in his midsection. He swore he'd never fly again, but here he was on a rainy morning about to attempt a takeoff from a muddy road in canyon country he'd never flown before. It defied any kind of logic he could think except that he had to fix things, and in order to do that they had to get to Boise as soon as possible.

They taxied on a north-south running road, which was the same surface they'd use to take off. The wind was out of the west, which meant a cross-wind that would further complicate things. That only left the question of north or south, and it didn't make sense to take off toward the mountains. Cade doubted anyone did that, even when the weather was calm.

It took ten minutes navigating the mud before they arrived near the top of Deer Creek Grade. Cade turned the plane 180 degrees to face north, maintaining high RPMs to keep it from bogging down in the mud.

Most backcountry airstrips had an orange windsock that could be used to estimate wind direction and speed, but there was nothing like that along the road. Cade spotted a tree near the canyon rim and guessed the wind was blowing twenty to twenty-five knots by watching its branches. Light raindrops spattered the windshield, and the clouds were only a few hundred feet above the ground. They'd be flying blind less than thirty seconds after taking off. Complicating things even more, the straight part of the road was short, probably less than a thousand feet. On a clear, dry day it wouldn't be a problem. In the rain on a muddy surface in poor visibility, just about anything could go wrong.

Cade gave the gauges a final check and lowered his flaps to accommodate for the mud. Everything looked good. He pushed on the brakes and throttled the engine to full power, then let the brakes go with the RPMs screaming.

Muscle memory from years of training kicked in, and he pulled back on the controls to relieve pressure on the landing gear. Raindrops drifted on the windshield and then peeled across the glass as the plane powered into the morning. He felt the drag of the mud on the tires as they approached forty knots, but that wasn't enough. They needed to get over sixty to generate lift. While he knew adding flaps would help, the drag of the mud on their landing gear slowed them more than he'd guessed. He summoned all of the plane's power, but the road began its soft curve to the left out ahead. His knuckles were white as the plane went over fifty knots, about fifty-seven miles per hour. It still wasn't enough, but it sure as hell was too fast to make a corner on a muddy dirt road.

He scanned the dashboard for anything he might have missed and realized he hadn't set the fuel mixture properly, something you always adjusted before taking off from a high-altitude airstrip. He tugged on the red mixture control knob to lean out the fuel and felt the engine surge with renewed life. It was as if someone had released a thoroughbred that had been held back from expending its pent-up energy, and Cade lifted the plane into the air. He knew they were getting extra lift from being close to the ground, so he pushed the nose down and hugged the contours of the plateau until they reached eighty-five knots, then he raised the nose and began to climb, slowly taking out the flaps. His grip stayed tight, but he exhaled hard. The takeoff had gone worse than he'd have guessed. Now they were in the air, which came with an entire suite of new challenges.

He kept the horizon in the windshield to avoid climbing too fast. The ride was immediately turbulent as they rose into the clouds and lost visibility. They were at about nine-hundred feet and climbing when the engine coughed and then sputtered to a stop. The sound of rain on the windshield and rushing-by wind was all there was.

Superb description on flying a small plane. Very accurate.

A dashboard light shone red and a stall buzzer blared. Cade immediately pushed the nose forward to keep the plane from dropping to the ground, then frantically scanned the panel to see what he might have missed. The prop sat idle as he thought through a mental checklist of contingencies he hadn't considered in half a decade.

Turning back to the road where they took off was the first and most natural thing that came to mind, but under a thousand feet that maneuver was something pilots called The Impossible Turn. Trying to turn that sharp could cause the plane to stall and spin, a death sentence so low to the ground.

The rule of thumb was that you had about thirty degrees to the left or right. He looked desperately through the windshield, but clouds hid the canyon country from view. There were roads in the bottoms of those canyons, but they didn't run straight. The only option he could think was to make the airstrip he'd passed with Fey two days before during their approach to the ranch.

The unnerving quiet of wind on wings rattled his fragile composure. They were losing altitude fast.

"We're in trouble, buddy," he said and glanced at Andy, who was stoic and quiet. "I'm gonna try to put it down at an airstrip I saw a few days ago, but if we can't make it we might have to land in the canyon. That won't be pretty."

It was only about ten miles to the airstrip, but they had no power and the air was too thin for good gliding. The plane dropped, and as they fell through the cloud ceiling and were finally able to see again, they were only a hundred feet above the canyon rim with almost no time to react. Cade positioned the plane over the Jarbidge River to give them another couple minutes. They were losing altitude at a rate of about three-hundred feet a minute. They weren't going to make the airstrip. Whatever happened, it would happen in the canyon, and it would happen in less than a hundred and twenty seconds.

Cade looked out the side window and watched the canyon walls drift by. The land was so big and timeless, beautiful and hard, delicate and persevering. It didn't care whether a few people lived or died, or whether their interpretations of justice played out or not. The land had its own form of justice dictated by gravity, wind, erosion and the passing of time. The drama of life sometimes seemed so big, but in the end it didn't really matter. The land would keep going with or without the people, towns or cities and the highways built to connect it all. The land would keep going without all the fights about how to take from it, use it, protect it or enjoy it.

Cade scoured the unfolding canyon walls for any kind of opportunity. They were stalwart and unrelenting and continued parallel into Idaho. He used the controls to guide the plane left and right to follow the canyon's contours, buying them as much time as he could.

Then he saw it.

From around one of the corners appeared a chink in the canyon's basalt armor where a creek joined from the west and eroded a giant gap. With a strong west weather system, the valley would funnel wind into the canyon there.

"Hang on, Andy. If this works it's gonna be a ride."

"If it doesn't?"

Cade knew he didn't need to answer.

He scanned the panel a final time looking for anything he might have missed, and this time it jumped out at him like an exclamation point he'd been reading right past: the fuel tank selector valve. He switched the value to the left tank, then guided the plane toward the canyon wall, positioning his wing just feet from the rock, preparing to take advantage of the wind.

As he turned to the west, the propeller started windmilling in the headwind, and after a few seconds the engine coughed back to life. He throttled the plane and pulled back on the controls, the plane skimming off riverside treetops.

He leveled the plane and set the prop angle to climb steadily back above the canyon, the sweat on his face hot and thick. He didn't know what had happened with the right fuel tank, but with all the rain it might have been as simple as water having worked its way in.

"That was almost it," Andy said in his understated way.

"That was almost it."

FORTY-SIX

THE FLATBED TRAILER IN FRONT OF BOISE'S GUERNICA OAK was draped in Basque and American flags. Amaia paced back and forth beneath the tree's deep shade, her forehead beaded with sweat. She wore a pair of chino slacks and a white button-up blouse, an outfit she chose to regulate heat while maintaining a professional air.

She wiped her forehead with the back of her hand and scanned the street for a glimpse of her boss, the one person who might stop her from taking the stage in a few minutes. She didn't see him, but the look up and down the block gave her a minute to appreciate how it had been transformed. Amaia had worked with Rachel that morning to organize teams of volunteers who'd erected a podium atop the flatbed, organized grids of folding chairs that filled the street and positioned pop-up tents where non-profit groups were set up to distribute interpretive materials about the park. With grids of flags and twinkly lights hanging overhead, it looked official, but still had Jaialdi's festival atmosphere.

She looked down at the notes Rachel helped her prepare. She'd start by talking about language and use that to transition to Basque history and the more recent story of Basques in Idaho. Then she'd introduce a traditional Basque dance before inviting the Interior Secretary to talk about the Park Service's legacy and, finally, the Governor to make the announcement that the park had actually just passed and simply needed the President's signature to become reality.

She looked to the sidewalk in front of the museum where the speakers were assembled in a patch of shade. The Governor and Interior Secretary were there, as well as representatives from the organizations that participated in the collaborative process that built the park proposal. Amaia wondered if they all knew about the pending announcement. If they didn't, how would they take it? How would the crowd take it?

Chairs began to fill at about quarter till noon. Amaia surveyed the building crowd. With Jaialdi well underway, her Basque brothers and sisters were well represented, but she recognized a lot of people from the state's conservation community, too. She recognized several dozen Indians who'd probably driven up from the Duck Valley Reservation, which would sit on the park's south border. There were dozens of people dressed in traditional Western dress, so she pegged them for ranchers or farmers. There was also a large proportion of bureaucrats and business types in starched white shirts and ties; also, hillbillies, cowboys, Indians, rich, poor, and mostly white. It was, she estimated, a pretty accurate cross section of the people who lived, loved, made a living on, and fought about, the land they were about to discuss.

Amaia glanced at her watch. It was noon; time to start.

She took a final look around and made eye contact with Rachel, who stood among the dignitaries in front of the museum. Rachel cocked her head toward the stage, encouraging Amaia to start. She wiped her hand across her cheek to clear away the sweat one more time, walked onto the stage and took her place behind the podium.

"Kaixo eta ongi etorri," she said into the microphone. "In the native Basque language that means hello and welcome."

The seating was full, and people overflowed onto sidewalks. The adrenaline of the moment cleared her nerves. Amaia felt the command she held over the crowd and stood tall.

"It's been a long road working to get to the point where we're actually considering Legends of the Basques National Park. Amidst all the debate about what a park will do for the land, to the economy and for our traditional ways of life, some of the cultural significance seems to have been lost."

She reached to her back pocket and took out a quartered piece of paper, which she folded flat on the podium. Then she held the crowd's attention with a steady gaze.

"Language," she began, "matters. It's the cornerstone of our ability to get along and resolve differences. It conveys love, pain, pleasure and sorrow. It's a pillar of civil society. It establishes laws and repeals them, can exploit our lands and waters or protect them. With language we can solve our differences and build a national park that matters for the people and natural resources of Idaho and Nevada. By using language to enact a law that creates a new national park, we can declare to the nation and the world that this part of the Earth matters."

A light round of applause rippled across the crowd.

"Language is also one of the central foundations of Basque culture, which is my culture. Our language, called Euskara, which I used to greet you here today, is the only language of its kind in the world. We call ourselves Euskaldunak, which literally means 'we are the people who speak Euskara.' The Basque people are very proud of this. Our culture literally means, 'We are the people who speak that language,' and we are humbled that this national park will, in name, bear the significance of Basque heritage in the Intermountain West."

Another round of applause rippled across the crowd, this time stronger and more supportive.

Amaia proceeded to identify additional groups that deserved to be honored with naming of the park—notably the Shoshone-Paiute people who'd called the region home for thousands of years. She pointed to the Governor and Idaho's senior Senator. These great people, she said, had made the park possible. She then began a brief history about the Basque people's ancient roots, about their arrival in Idaho and Nevada to work as sheep herders and miners, and how they found a sense of community in the boarding houses of the region, places like the historic property where they were now assembled.

"A Basque family bought this house," she said with a wave toward the bricks and mortar over her shoulder, "as a place for people to come together. I think they'd be proud that we've come together today to take the next steps toward preserving our beautiful wild country and honoring their culture."

Amaia continued into her speech, which she hoped would set a tone of reverence and respect for everyone assembled. People collected to the north and filled the street as far as its east and west intersections. At the edges of the crowd, standing in staggered formation, were a dozen or so Boise police officers in the positions they'd practiced. Amaia scanned for her boss again but didn't see him.

"So, before we move to our esteemed speakers who will talk about eco-
logical, historical and political considerations, I want to share with you
some of what we're working so hard to keep alive here in Boise. This dance
is called the Agurra, which is performed as a show of respect and greeting
to visitors. We think that's fitting today. Please give a warm welcome to
Boise's world-renowned Oinkari Basque Dancers!"

Two women and a man wearing red and white Basque folk costumes
walked onto the stage and stood behind the microphone. The man carried
an accordion. One of the women held a tambourine and the other a small
traditional flute called a txistu.

The woman raised the txistu to her lips and made two sharp, high-
pitched notes that silenced the crowd's light chatter. About thirty men
and women wearing red and white folk costumes filed into the street and
bowed toward the visiting dignitaries and then to the assembled crowd.

Then all three musicians started an upbeat melody while the dancers
moved their feet in intricate, mesmerizing steps, kicking high and turning
to the music.

Amaia had seen the performance a dozen times, but found herself tapping her feet in time with the music. That's when she caught a glimpse
of something that made her look twice. It was so out of place she wasn't
sure what it was at first. Above the sea of people was a row of black shapes
suspended on sticks. The shapes began to move and entered the center
isle toward the stage. Amaia looked around to see who'd noticed, but the
crowd's attention was fixed on the dancers. The black shapes on sticks
moved closer, and Amaia finally understood what it was.

Walking single file toward the flatbed trailer, was a line of men with
shovels on their shoulders like they were carrying muskets into battle.
Nearby television cameras, which had been focused on the dancers, began
to shift toward the men with shouldered shovels. The eyes of the crowd
did, too.

As they arrived at the flatbed, the music stuttered, and then stopped
altogether. The men, about two-dozen in all, marched purposefully onto
the stage and lined up facing the crowd as the dancers filtered toward
sidewalks. Amaia jumped onto the trailer as if to stop them, but the man
in the center beat her back with a hard glare. She looked across at Rachel,
who waved Amaia back. She looked to see how her peers from the
department were responding, but they stood down as well, apparently

content to see the events through. Amaia stepped slowly backward to the sidewalk beside the trailer.

The man who'd glared at Amaia went to the microphone.

"My name is Morgan, and I'm with a group called Common Sense," he said. "Thanks for your time; I'll only be a few minutes."

The man's name got Amaia's attention. It's the same name Cade had asked her to run through NCIC. If she had a radio she'd tell the other cops, but she wasn't even supposed to be there and didn't have any of her police equipment.

"The oppression and tyranny that's taken place here in Idaho and across the United States—We the People need to take a stand," the man started and held his shovel in the air.

Cheers and whistles rose from the crowd. With so many people who disagreed about the park, Amaia knew the balance was delicate. The wrong move would be a lit match near tinder.

"Fifteen years ago, the people of Jarbidge, Nevada, took up arms in a shovel brigade to reopen a road the United States government no longer wanted to maintain. That's when I took an oath, like my brothers up here, to fight back."

He took a mini Constitution from his shirt pocket and held it above his head.

"The people of the Owyhee Plateau are good people, and this tyrannical government, which has no jurisdiction—it's local land; Owyhee and Elko County's land!—has come in to take over. It's shameful."

He paused to allow people of like mind to cheer.

"As defenders of the Constitution, we've sworn an oath, and it's not just to protect against all enemies foreign and domestic when it's convenient. That's not how our independence was won. Our very own Declaration of Independence says it's our right and duty to cast out despots to provide security for our nation. And I quote: 'whenever any form of government becomes destructive of these ends, it is the right of the people to alter or to abolish it, and to institute new government, laying its foundation on such principles and organizing its powers in such form, as to them shall seem most likely to affect their safety and happiness.' Folks, that's the enlightened vision of our founding fathers.

"I'd rather be fishing today, but if we don't take a stand this tyrannical government will continue to grow more powerful and oppress We the

People. If we unite, though, if we take a stand, if we come together and act as one, there's no stopping We the People."

He said he and his friends had filed a "petition for redress" to stop or slow the park. Those papers had been dismissed or ignored.

"We've carried out the official avenues of reproach. We executed our First Amendment right and filed an address of grievances and a petition with more than a thousand signatures. All of that was summarily cast aside. What choice do we have? I've had to think hard about this, and I'm with good Americans who've done that, too. We're willing to die to fight this oppression. That doesn't mean we want war, but, as Thomas Payne said: 'I prefer peace, but if trouble must come, let it come in my time, so that my children can live in peace.'

"Southwest Idaho and northern Nevada used to be a land of abundance. There was ranching, mining, farming—and the federal government came in and changed all that. Now the BLM and the Park Service or the Forest Service or the Bureau of Indian Affairs, they come in and tell ranchers—people with actual dirt under their fingernails—they're telling them how many head of cattle they can have, where they can and can't go, where they can and can't drink water. On their own damn land!"

A series of whistles flew up from the crowd.

"Friends, that's tyranny!"

Another whistle and then cheers.

"The success of our nation depends on us coming together. We need real men here, real men and women. We need tried and true red, white and blue Americans. We need men and women who have the backbones to take a stand and say enough!"

Cheers.

"We need to unite!"

Cheers.

"Today is the day we're taking back what is ours, and we're starting right here in this city where we're biting the head off the snake."

What happened next gave Amaia chills despite the day's heat.

The men on stage each pulled a weapon from under his shirt, returned his shovel to his shoulder, and filed off stage toward the historic property that included the Park Service office. The assembled elected officials were rushed by nearby police in the opposite direction.

Amaia didn't think before she acted. She moved only from instinct and

Amon Bundy attitude.

an interest in preserving the treasure trove of culturally-sensitive memorabilia she'd spent hundreds of hours reading and organizing in the office. She ran after them and charged into the carriage house, running headlong into the group of men, some holding shovels, a few with their fingers still wrapped around the triggers of their guns.

"I just want to grab some files," she said in a pant, quickly realizing her mistake. She had some training, but there was no way she was equipped to deal with armed insurgents by herself.

"What files are those?" one of the men shot back. "These right here?"

The man grabbed a stack of folders from a nearby shelf and threw them on the floor, then unzipped his fly.

"No," she gasped.

The man chuckled as the room filled with a spattering sound and the sour scent of deep-yellow urine. Amaia lunged, but was held back by the strong arm of someone behind her. She turned to see the arm was attached to a woman in a cowboy hat.

"Don't be stupid," the lady said. "It's just paper."

"That's a lot more than paper."

"And a lot less than your life."

The man with his penis in his hand finished wetting the floor and offered an exaggerated satisfied groan.

"Let's get something straight," he said to Amaia and walked toward her until his breath was hot on her face. "This property no longer belongs to the federal government. We've taken adverse possession, and we're going to convene a citizen grand jury. So here we are—lucky you. It looks like you're going to be the first to stand trial for your crimes against We the People and the sanctity of the Constitution of the United States of America."

FORTY-SEVEN

THE PIPER'S ENGINE BUZZED CONFIDENTLY out of the storm into a desert-sun glare. Cade's death grip on the controls let up, and his shoulders relaxed, but neither he nor Andy Jim the third spoke.

He didn't think he'd ever fly again, but he imagined if he did it would have been on a crystal-clear morning with no wind, weather or deadlines in sight.

Andy was calm and quiet, his light-blue eyes steady on the horizon. If their ordeal had rattled him, he didn't let on. Cade let the man sit in silence. They'd achieved a comfortable quiet. Had it really only been four days since they'd met in the courtyard outside the office? Now here they were, flying 150 miles an hour to intervene in a situation that, if he'd simply stayed in Boise, might not have been possible to begin with.

As they drew close to Boise, the desert's shades of beige and brown gave way to an irrigated geometry of green circles and squares where farmers coaxed crops from parched land on the outskirts of town. Interstate 84, a highway that connected isolated Boise with Salt Lake City, Portland and Seattle came into view, and they followed it toward the city.

The expansive campus of Micron Electronics came into view, then a grid of white and beige warehouses, trucks and trailers. Farther north, Cade saw the industrial area fold into miles of tree-lined residential neighborhoods that tumbled gently toward the thick green stripe of the Boise River, which split the city down its middle. Beyond that was the city's modest urban skyline itself and foothills that folded upward for five-thousand feet toward Idaho's high mountains and central wild core.

Cade flicked the radio button, and it crackled to life.

"Boise tower, Warrior 2711 Foxtrot is ten miles south along the highway, requesting landing.

"Warrior 2711 Foxtrot, Boise Tower. Runway twenty-nine cleared to land. Winds are three-hundred at eleven. Boise altimeter 3,011. We have reports of bird activity south of the airport."

"Thanks for the heads up, 2711 Foxtrot."

The runway came into view and Cade set up for a straight-in approach. He touched down gently as if he hadn't missed any flying time at all.

Safely on the ground, Cade's focus shifted to the question of what was happening in the city's downtown core. He didn't want to wait until they got there to find out.

"Boise tower, this is Warrior 2711 Foxtrot. Do you have time for a question?"

"Warrior 2711 Foxtrot, sure, what's up?"

"There's a big event downtown today. I'm involved and have pretty good reason to believe there's trouble. Have you heard any news? Local authorities may need to be alerted, 2711 Foxtrot."

There was a long silence on the other end of the radio, enough time for Cade to doubt the wisdom of asking. The radio crackled back to life.

"Warrior 2711 Foxtrot, actually, sir, you're right. Radio traffic indicates armed protestors took over a public hearing about half an hour ago and holed up in offices managed by the National Park Service. According to radio traffic, it sounds like a hostage situation, and it's escalating."

Cade looked at Andy, whose light-blue eyes had lost their calm.

"Thanks for your help, 2711 Foxtrot out."

FORTY-EIGHT

CADE'S PALMS WERE WET, HIS BROW furled. He watched through the cab's side window as urban strip malls, tree-lined side streets and weed-filled lots went by. He noticed a sensation he hadn't experienced in a long time, a sense of being out of place, or out of the right place, like a tree growing in the middle of an asphalt parking lot.

The first time he'd experienced it was after a childhood backpacking trip. He'd spent five days on the Appalachian Trail and was surprised when he returned that the city and his home felt dirty. It was the irony that he'd made that discovery after spending five days sleeping in the dirt that struck him. He guessed it was a simple trick of reframing one's perspective, but he took it as a lesson about where he felt most at peace. There was something distinct about human-made filth compared with the dirt borne of natural processes. Now, after just a few days in the desert, he felt that truth again.

It was about three miles from the airport to the capital city's downtown core where his National Park Service office was under siege.

They arrived in the area's periphery a little after one o'clock, a full hour after the hearing was scheduled to begin. Cade handed the cab driver a twenty, which was five bucks short. He fished through his pocket and was surprised to find another ten. Money had been so irrelevant the past few days.

"Keep the change," he said, and the cab was swallowed by the flow of traffic. He turned and looked east toward the Basque Block, which was cordoned off with yellow CAUTION tape. Four police officers wearing riot gear and armed with semiautomatic rifles were positioned near the tape.

"Can you tell me what's going on?" Cade asked. "My office is in there. I need to know if my people are okay."

"You can watch the news like everyone else," the officer said. "This is a Department of Homeland Security situation. Step back, please."

Cade ignored the request.

"I heard there's a group of men in the Park Service offices. Is anyone in danger?"

"This is the last time I'll tell you. Step off."

Cade grunted and turned to scan the crowd for anyone who might help. He spotted a man with a curly ponytail, a local news reporter he'd worked with on a few stories about the park. The reporter talked with a cop on the other side of the street.

Cade nudged Uncle Andy and nodded in the reporter's direction. The reporter thanked the cop and tucked his notebook in his back pocket.

"I guess that answers that question," the reporter said, looking at Cade.

"What question?"

"The police said someone was taken hostage. They wouldn't say, but it looks like it wasn't you."

"I just got back to town. What else did they tell you?"

"So, you weren't here for the hearing? Weren't you in charge?"

"I'll give you an exclusive about that later if you tell me what's going on. What else did they tell you?"

"Not much. They're playing this close to the vest. Based on what I gathered, it sounds like a group of armed militants—carrying shovels on their shoulders, mind you—took over the public hearing, made some declarations about state's rights, the Constitution and Declaration of Independence and stuff, then charged into the house where you keep your offices."

"Did they have a woman with them?"

"Didn't say."

"Did the police talk about the office? I don't think it's very defensible space."

"Not at all, and they said that. That's not the issue. First, they don't want a single bullet to fly. Second, and maybe more important, they don't want any of the hostages to get hurt."

"Did the police say how long they'll wait?"

"As long as it takes. They're giving these guys a chance to slip up. There's not a whole lot they can do. They told me on background, but one idea is to cut power and water. It'll get pretty hot without air conditioning. It could be days, or I guess even weeks. It seems like media attention is what they want, and they've got that pretty well secured at this point."

Cade thanked the reporter and looked across the street to the yellow caution tape and line of police determined to keep people off the block. In the middle of the street were hundreds of empty chairs in front of a flatbed trailer where the public hearing had been. Some of the chairs were overturned and askew. American and Basque flags flapped in the breeze.

"We've got to get in there," he said to himself as much as anyone else, but Andy heard him and turned his head slow and confident.

"Why didn't you say so?" he said.

Andy motioned for Cade to follow and went west, away from the unfolding drama on the Basque Block. In a couple minutes' brisk walk, they arrived at a central square where the foundation for a large building was under construction. It was a half-block completely walled off from nearby sidewalks and streets. Andy went to a sheet of plywood and pulled hard to produce a gap barely big enough for a person to fit through.

"Go on," he said. "Don't fall in; it's a deep hole."

Cade ducked through and pushed his way onto a narrow ledge atop a forty-foot wall. He stood with his back to the plywood, unsure where to turn. He heard a short high-pitched whistle and realized he'd left Andy outside. He turned to see the cowboy's hat being held through the gap. Cade took the hat and pushed on the plywood as Andy crawled through and joined him on the ledge.

Cade handed the man his hat. He put it back on his head in a smooth, unconscious motion the way a politician buttons or unbuttons his blazer.

"You don't need a front door to get into that museum," he said. "Look down there."

He pointed to a platform midway along the wall below and to their right. A scaffold held the platform aloft, and a ladder connected it to the ledge where they stood.

"Like I told you," Andy said. "I've been looking for the bullion a long time. I've learned a lot along the way. This city's full of tunnels."

Cade took stock. They were in a huge open pit in broad daylight, easily within view of any security guards.

"Well hurry up," he said. "Let's at least get out of the daylight."

They went to the ladder and descended to the platform, which was in line with a chain-link gate that covered an opening in the side of the pit.

"How'd you know this was here?" Cade asked.

"I knew this was here when it was a door in a basement," he said. "It might be out in the open now, but finding it like this was a good deal harder. This damn city's growing up too fast."

FORTY-NINE

FEY SAT ON THE FLOOR NEAR what she assumed was Cade Rigens' desk. It was the back room of the historic property's carriage house, and maps of the would-be national park hung from the walls. Among them was a map detailing the Diamond D Ranch, complete with legal boundary descriptions. The word "condemnation" wasn't there, but it may as well have been in flashing neon lights. She was disgusted with herself for letting her guard down around Cade.

The young woman who'd charged in the front door—she'd learned her name was Amaia—sat next to her. Her brother-in-law sat at Cade's desk and fiddled with the drawers and files, tossing papers willy nilly on the floor. There were twenty-two men in total who'd taken over the property. They wore an eclectic mix of army fatigues, ranch clothes and police riot gear and were stationed at various windows and rooftops to defend the building from authorities.

When he was done fiddling with the drawers, Morgan put his gun on the desk and looked in Fey's direction.

"This place disgusts me," he said. "Does it disgust you like it does me?"

Fey didn't answer, and Morgan continued.

"You two know what a grand jury is?"

They looked blankly back.

"Let me help you understand." He stood and walked along the row of maps and surveyed them as he made slow, deliberate steps. "We the People are going to convene a grand jury and charge you with crimes suitable

The exact number who took over MNWR in Oregon.

to the nature of your infractions. The citizen grand jury comes from the Fifth Amendment. This one probably interests you, Fey, because the Fifth Amendment also says private property can't be taken for public use."

He paused next to the map of the Diamond D Ranch and leveled her with a hard stare. She remained expressionless.

"But that's not the point of why we're here today. The Fifth Amendment also holds that 'no person shall be held to answer for a capital, or otherwise infamous crime, unless on presentment or indictment of a Grand Jury.'"

Fey glanced at Amaia, who looked like she was ready to speak her mind. She turned her glance into a hard stare, hoping her eyes admonished the young lady to stay quiet. Her message either didn't get across, or the kid didn't care.

"What do you think you're going to charge us with?" she said.

Morgan took a deep breath and blew his hot wind across the room. A sour smell carried, and Fey's nose curled.

"You, young lady, are in big trouble. I don't want to presuppose the inclinations of our grand jury, which we'll convene shortly, but among other crimes you're going to be charged with treason for your work to subvert the preeminent law of the land, the United States Constitution. We haven't figured out what to charge her with yet, but obstruction of justice might be a good start."

Fey rolled her eyes at the absurdity of it all.

"Spending hundreds of hours in internet chat rooms doesn't qualify you as a lawyer, and you're not the least bit qualified to pretend," she said.

The young woman joined in.

"You can't be a grand jury," she said. "You've self-selected to reinforce each others' beliefs and biases. Juries represent diverse communities of people."

Morgan stood and walked over to her. He swung at her cheek, which split and swelled puffy and red, blood dripping across her lips.

"Only one of us in here is making the rules right now," he said. "We'll convene a grand jury as we deem necessary, and I'm the judge."

FIFTY

ONCE AGAIN CADE AND ANDY STOOD AT A PORTAL leading to the underground. This time they didn't hesitate. Cade pushed the fence aside and went in, discovering he'd entered a man-made cavern something like the mine he'd been in less than eight hours before.

A thicket of cobwebs ensnared Andy's head and wrapped his formidable hat in a cottony cocoon. Cade reached out and cleared some of the cobwebs away.

They stood in the tunnel entryway where the stale air was cool but blended with a hot wind that puffed through the chain link gate.

They peered into the tunnel. Darkness peered back.

"Any idea how we're going to see?"

Andy took about ten steps into the fading light, knelt near a cinderblock and produced two flashlights that were balanced on end beside five or six others.

"Construction crews," he said. "They've been putting up walls where there weren't any, working to seal things off."

"How many times have you been in here?"

"Enough."

They each grabbed a flashlight and shone it into the tunnel where Cade found a threshold of vertical timbers suspending a massive overhead beam. They descended a flight of timber steps, and the sounds, smells and diffused blue light faded behind them.

The floor was dust, and timbers along the walls propped up horizontal supports cottoned over with cobwebs. Above those was a mass of loose rock and the city above. In every way Cade could think, it resembled an old mine's horizontal adit. They worked cautiously forward into a stew of intermingling smells: mildew and rust, rat scat and dust.

By Cade's calculations they were at least a couple blocks from his office.

"Any idea who built these?" he asked.

"By most accounts it was Chinese miners holed up in opium dens. Some say the Basques, but maybe it was the folks running liquor during prohibition. Sure as shit they're here, though."

Cade heard rodents scamper across the floor ahead of them, and the tunnel nosed tight, forming a passageway about three feet wide and five feet high. They crouched and scooted forward.

After walking another hundred and fifty feet, far enough to go under one of the city's main streets, the passageway arrived at the first of several intersections. The cowboy led, and they went left and right, right and left, straight at one intersection, and arrived at a T. Cade was pretty sure he could find his way back, but they'd made enough turns he wasn't sure. What's more, their meandering network had intersected a larger tunnel with a pair of ore cart tracks positioned in the middle. To the left, it was open. To the right it was blocked by a partially-built cinderblock wall.

"What are the tracks about?"

"Somebody used to move stuff around down here," Andy replied.

Cade rolled his eyes at his own stupid question and the old man's willingness to answer it.

"Do you know where they lead?"

"To the Capitol. That wall's new, though. When I was here before it was just barely started. They've been doing this all over town, trying to keep people out."

They stepped around the wall, which filled three quarters of the passage. On the other side, they followed the passage, which bent left, a soft enough corner so that the tracks positioned in the tunnel's center were still underfoot.

"We're arriving under the Basque Block now," the cowboy said. "There's three passageways that come off the tunnel here, all on the right. The first is the old handball court, the second's your office, the third's the Basque Cultural Complex where they have all the events. The line dead-ends after that."

They passed the first tunnel and arrived at the second. A set of timber stairs rose toward the surface. Cade followed Andy to a small metal panel about three feet high. Andy extended his palms and pushed it aside, waving for Cade to go through. Cade was amazed to find himself among the cardboard boxes and draped-over furniture in the basement of the front house, the main museum. The cowboy crawled through behind him and pushed the metal panel closed. Cade turned and stared. Unless you studied the spot, you'd never notice it at all. He opened and closed it a few times, marveling at how it was hidden in plain sight.

"That's not all," Andy said.

Cade left the hidden door ajar, and followed the cowboy across the basement to the furnace. He went into the tight space behind it and knelt again, this time pushing another small panel aside.

"This one goes almost the whole way through, but it was sealed with cinder blocks at some point. If we can get through those, we can get into your office."

Cade crawled about forty feet and arrived at another cinderblock wall, this time fully built.

"How are we getting through that wall?"

"I've been working on that," Andy said. "The chinking's loose on the sides, and I've been cutting at it little by little."

"Why's everyone want to break into my office?"

"What do you mean?"

"Just show me. You think this goes into the basement?"

He nodded.

"We can't make any noise."

He nodded again and went to the cinderblocks, wrapping his fingertips around the edges and pushing. As he did, the whole wall of blocks moved. It was a section of four or five blocks that, if gone, would make enough space to crawl through. As the wall began to move, Cade wondered what it looked like from the other side. The fact was, they didn't know how high off the ground the blocks were or if anyone was in the adjoining basement.

"Is there a way to keep those blocks from making any noise?"

"I thought about that."

He took off his belt and attached the big buckle's clip to the top of the blocks, then continued to push until they broke loose. Cade wasn't sure what the belt buckle did because the blocks fell into the basement with a crash that vibrated the foundation. He braced for an inevitable rush of activity, but the calm persisted. He and the cowboy sat for a couple minutes, but the longer they did the clearer it was that nobody had heard the crash.

Cade pushed his head into the basement. A soft light filtered down from a closed door at the top of a rickety set of wood steps, but otherwise the space was empty and dark.

"It's clear. Can you fit through?"

"I'm skinnier than you."

Cade pushed his hands through like he was diving into a pool of water. His shoulders and torso were tight, and one of the buttons popped off his shirt as he dragged himself over the ragged edge. Once inside, he turned and helped Andy, pulling on his hands so he wouldn't scrape his chest. On his feet again, the old man brushed dirt off his pants and looked at Cade.

"I got us here, but I sure as hell don't know what to do next. You're the one with a hard-on for this. You damn well better have a plan."

"Of course I have a plan," Cade said, looking quickly away. Getting that far had taken all his focus and determination, and he was as surprised as anyone they'd made it. Now in a position to actually do something, he was at a loss.

"Give me a minute. I'll need to refine things a bit before we move."

FIFTY-ONE

WITH MORE THAN A HALF HOUR TO SIT AND THINK, Fey began to simmer. Every goddamned man she knew had been maneuvering in some way to get his hands on the ranch her dad gave her. It was land she'd proudly worked and reworked, not as a way to make money but as a way of life. The operation had to be profitable, sure, but she loved the smell of the range and wind in her hair, the way hard work gave her life meaning and purpose—and kept her strong, too.

She thought back through the persistent offers Morgan had made to buy the place. He didn't want to be a rancher any more than she wanted to sell used American pickups. The fact that the brothers had known something about the property gave those offers new perspective.

She looked to her right where Amaia held her head on her hand. The welt on her cheek was plain, and blood dripped across her lips.

From time to time the men in the house traded places, and the wood floors and steps creaked with their movement. She heard one of them climb to the second floor, but in addition to that familiar noise came a thud that didn't fit. She looked to see if anyone else heard it, but it didn't seem like they had.

There were two doors in the direction she'd heard the noise, both five-panel relics surrounded by Victorian-style casing that had been painted a dozen times. One led to the bathroom where the men came and went every twenty minutes. The other was a mystery. She was pretty sure nobody had gone through it, and she puzzled about what might have made the noise.

She nudged her elbow into Amaia's ribs.

"Did you hear that?"

"Hear what?"

"Where's that door lead?" The woman followed Fey's gaze.

"I think it's a basement. I haven't been, but I think it's just junk."

That was fine, but Fey knew something was down there, even if it was just a stray cat. And if that was the case, there was also a way in or out of the house.

She looked at their captors again. Morgan sat with his boots propped on the desk. Paul paced along the opposite wall studying the array of maps on display. Others were positioned at windows throughout the house, guarding the place like it was Fort Knox. None of them paid any attention to the basement door.

Fey decided to explore.

"Mind if I use the bathroom?"

Paul turned to answer the question, but his brother talked over him.

"Only if he goes with you," Morgan said with a nod at Paul.

"Where's your sense of decency?" she replied.

"Like he never saw you naked."

"It's okay," Paul said. "I don't need to go."

"I'm telling you that you do."

"We're divorced, you asshole," Fey said.

"Don't make me hit you, too," Morgan said.

"Fine, he can watch if it makes him happy," she shrugged.

"It doesn't," Paul said.

She didn't really care if Paul watched her piss, but she wasn't sure how she'd manage to get in the basement with him close behind or beside her. Her plan had been to open the wrong door. If they noticed, she'd simply say, "oops," and turn for the bathroom. If they didn't notice, she'd have a few minutes to look around, but it wouldn't work if Paul went with her.

She went to the two doors, which were beside each other in a small hallway set apart from the rest of the rooms. She turned to Paul. They were eye-to-eye, mouth-to-mouth, and had just a moment before she had to commit to one of the doors.

"You're more of a man than he'll ever be," she said. "You don't have to let him treat you like that."

He puffed up.

"Be quick," he said and turned around.

"You pussy," he heard Morgan yell.

Paul didn't say anything back, and she enjoyed a smug moment of appreciation for the man she'd married.

She grabbed the doorknob for the basement stairs, pulled it open and went in, pushing the door closed as fast as she could.

It took a few minutes for her eyes to adjust, but as they did a set of old wood steps came into focus. They went down to a small platform near the corner of a stone foundation. She descended carefully, making sure none of the steps creaked, and as she did the whole basement came into view.

It was small, maybe twenty by twenty feet, and a lot of things became clear at once. First, she saw what had made the noise. Beneath a red pipe protruding from the wall were four or five cinderblocks that had been removed from the foundation. More shocking, though, she was suddenly face to face with her Uncle Andy and Cade fucking Rigens. She almost shouted with surprise and anger, but was conscious that her time was being monitored.

"What the god damn are you two doing here?" she whispered. "How did you get in here? What are you doing together? These assholes are serious. They've got guns and shit. Do not go parading up there to save the day."

"Nice to see you, too," said Uncle Andy. He leaned over and kissed her forehead.

"Look guys, I don't have time for this. They think I'm in the ladies' room. I came down here because I heard those freaking cinderblocks fall. Cinderblocks! You're lucky it was me."

Cade elbowed the old man. "I told you somebody would hear that."

"Jesus," said Fey, "You're like a teenager. Now listen, you two are going straight back out the way you came in."

Cade shook his head no.

"They don't know we're here. We can surprise them."

"You said it on the plateau when you met Morgan. He's a man looking for a cause. He wants to fight. More than just about anyone, you're the person he wants to fight."

"We heard there are hostages. Anyone aside from you?"

"Some kid named Amaia. He pistol whipped her, but I'm pretty sure he'd do a lot more to you."

"Is she okay?"

"A little beat up, but yeah she's fine. She's a tough kid."

"She's a cop," Fey. "He hit a freaking cop."

"Well she'd better keep that to herself because he's looking to thumb his nose at any kind of authority he can find. Look, I'm out of time here. As far as they know I'm taking the world's longest piss."

"Hold on," Cade said, his eyes rolled up under his lids. He held a finger in the air to encourage her to wait. "Why don't you get Amaia to come down here? Actually, both of you. Tell them you need to take her to the bathroom to clean or dress her wounds. You can slip down the stairs, and we'll get out of here."

She rolled her eyes. "I thought you were dead, Cade."

His mouth moved like he was trying to answer but no words came out.

"I'm glad you're alright," she added. "I've got to go."

"You can both slip down," Cade repeated as she turned her back, went up the stairs and out the door.

When she got to the landing by the two doors, Paul still had his back to her, and nobody paid her any attention.

She tapped Paul on the shoulder, and he moved aside.

Then she went into the room, sat on the floor and waited.

FIFTY-TWO

CADE PACED NEAR THE OLD WOOD STEPS unsure whether Fey would participate in his ad hoc plan. He knew she was upset, but he also knew she didn't support the protest unfolding upstairs. Andy Jim shuffled around on the other side of the basement not ten feet away.

"What are you doing?" Cade whispered, but he didn't respond. He was engrossed in something at the edge of the crawl space, a concrete slab roughly chest high and ten feet across. Cade went to see.

"What is it?" he repeated but knew before he saw. He'd become so focused on helping Amaia and Fey that he forgot about the riddle Miles Fourney had been trying to solve, that he himself had now been following for four days, that Andy had been trying to unravel for two decades or more.

Andy was hunched over the slab, which extended into the shadows under the house. It was stacked with old wood and smelled like dust. He pushed the wood aside and fanned the dust with his palm.

An embossed message quickly came into view: the now-familiar combination of eight letters that, before the week started, Cade had never seen or heard before: Heben Nuk.

He was dumbfounded. It was more or less directly beneath his desk, a place he'd been sitting for two years. He pulled out the letter he'd found in Miles Fourney's journal and scanned it, arriving at the pertinent lines:

*You'll find further information about how to locate the riches
of the Lost Sheepherder Mine at the Basque boarding house*

*on Grove Street in Boise. Just remember your Basque roots
and consider the legend of the Tartaro like I used to tell you.
Heben nuk!*

Whoever wrote the letter didn't say that Heben Nuk would lead to the
Lost Sheepherder Mine, just that it would help "locate the riches."

Andy put the heels of his hands on the edge of the slab and leaned into it
with whatever scant weight he had. It made a small chirp but didn't move.
Cade joined him, and they leaned into it together, producing a small gap
above a shadowy cavity. Andy reached in and pulled out a dust-covered
leather sack cinched tight with a knotted cord. He untied the knot and
pulled it open to reveal a block of shiny metal. He held his light close, and
its gold hue shimmered.

"What is it?" Cade asked, and Andy beamed. He rotated the block, and
an engraving became clear: a Basque Lauburu with an eye at its center.
Below that were numbers that had been chiseled into the metal's skin:
"14.7 oz."

"Tell me there's more of that in there."

The cowboy shone his light in the hole and nodded. "Quite a bit," he
said. "Concrete's just a shell."

"That's impossible. It's four feet tall and—what?—ten feet wide. That
would be millions of dollars. Hundreds of millions of dollars."

"I told you I've been looking for the bullion."

Cade pushed him aside and stuck his head in the gap. They took turns
like that, peering in and wondering just how deep or wide it went. They
speculated about the trail of clues leading there and why. They become so
engrossed in it they completely forgot about what had been happening just
ten minutes before.

Then Cade heard a noise that sounded like a clearing throat.

"What was that?" he asked.

"What was what?"

Cade turned and saw right away the mistake they'd made. Fey and
Amaia stood in a beam of light halfway down the steps. Right beside them
was Fey's brother-in-law, Morgan.

"Never mind how you're alive or got in here," Morgan said, "but what
are you guys looking at over there?"

"Ain't nothing," said Andy Jim.

"I can see that's definitely not the case," he said and waved his handgun to show them who was in charge. "Why don't you join these two women upstairs."

"You weren't paying attention," Fey snapped.

Cade didn't answer. He didn't have an excuse. He hadn't traveled so far that day to unravel the mystery of the Lost Sheepherder Mine, but he'd been momentarily all-consumed by it. After all that time, he'd been distracted the same way Miles and Andy had.

They did as they were told and climbed the stairs into Cade's office where they joined Fey and Amaia with their butts on the floor and backs against the wall.

FIFTY-THREE

IN THE FOUR DAYS SINCE HE'D BEEN THERE, Cade's office had been turned upside down. Documents were scattered as if a gale had blown through, and the place smelled like urine. He sat on the floor's worn pine boards, a completely new perspective. The floor had a slight hump in the middle, and the baseboards hadn't been dusted in months, or maybe years. The underside of his desk wasn't stained and showed wear from thousands of passing knees or feet.

To his left were Amaia and Fey. Andy sat to his right. Fey's ex-husband stood near the desk rummaging through the orange backpack until he pulled out Miles' journal, then tossed the pack aside. Another man with an assault rifle slung over his shoulder stood near the front door where a dozen shovels had been propped in the corner.

Reunited for the first time in days, Cade summoned enough grit to look Amaia in the eyes. His concern was genuine, but his guilt just as real.

"You okay?"

"You couldn't leave the police work to the police?"

"Sorry," he shrugged.

"I'm not sure sorry cuts it."

He understood her cross tone on some level. He'd taken over her case, and now she was a hostage with a swollen cheek and bloody lip.

"Seriously, are you okay? That looks like it hurts."

"It does hurt; I'll be fine."

"That hit should have been mine, Amaia. I should have been here."

She leaned toward him, eyes glistening near the bridge of her nose. He draped an arm around her.

"This sucks," she said, and they didn't speak for a few minutes. The only sounds were their captors' soft syllables drifting from corners of the building.

Cade allowed her some time, but needed to know what was going on.

"What do you know about these guys? Have you picked anything up about their plan?"

She leaned away from him, pulled her hair behind her shoulders and brushed her shirt as if wiping fallen tears away.

"The lead guy—I think his name's Morgan—he wants to avenge some kind of federal action on a ranch. They call it the Ace of Diamonds or something."

"You mean the Diamond D. We call it Property F. There's a map on the wall over there. Fey, who you've already met, she owns the ranch."

Fey lifted a dismissive hand as if to say, yeah great.

"The governor's office pulled strings to set federal condemnation proceedings in motion. Its—well, it's definitely ruffled feathers."

The sound of boot soles on wood steps emerged from the basement, and Morgan appeared carrying one of the rough-edged squares of shimmering metal. He went to Cade's desk and placed it on a stack of manila folders like a paperweight.

"All these years, and old Andy Jim wasn't crazy after all. This changes a lot of things. If we can figure out how to get it out of here we can fund a proper resistance instead of that scrappy little effort Fey put together."

Cade tried to read Fey's emotions. He knew she sympathized with her brother-in-law on some level. More money might seem promising given the challenges they'd faced fighting off the national park, but if she thought anything of the possibility her expression didn't show it.

"Okay everyone, listen up!" Morgan sat upright, placed his palms on the desk and cleared his throat.

"The number of alleged criminals among us has doubled, and it's time to fulfill your rights to due process. It's time to convene our grand jury. Paul, go get a half dozen of the boys, and we'll get things underway."

Paul left and returned after a few minutes with a half-dozen armed men. Morgan motioned for Andy, Fey, Amaia and Cade to scoot closer to the desk while keeping their backs to the wall. Their captors stood single-file on the other side of the room and faced the defendants. Morgan pulled the pocket Constitution from his chest pocket.

"Under the Fifth Amendment of the United States Constitution, I hereby convene this citizen grand jury on the first day of August, 2015. The Fifth Amendment holds, and I quote: 'No person shall be held to answer for a capital, or otherwise infamous crime, unless on a presentment or indictment of a Grand Jury . . .' For those of you who are still learning, that means today is your day in court."

Cade scrunched his nose and looked left and right to see what his fellow defendants thought of their predicament. Their expressions were flat, eyes ahead, apparently resigned to whatever fate Morgan intended to doll out. Cade couldn't bite his tongue.

"You're no court. You're a bunch of felons who've taken over federal property."

"You're right about one thing," Morgan returned. "This isn't a court in the traditional sense. It's a citizen grand jury, one of the oldest and most sacred rights afforded We the People of this great nation. We're not gonna determine your guilt or innocence, but if our jury finds the evidence merits, we'll restrain you and hand you over to the authorities for trial."

"That's funny, I sorta had the same idea," Cade snorted.

Morgan motioned to one of the militiamen who crossed the room and kicked Cade in the stomach. He doubled over coughing.

"Let's get these proceedings underway," Morgan said. "I promised the young lady over here she'd go first, but I think we need to start with the person at the center of this fiasco. If you're done nursing your wounds I'd like the Park Service ranger with the big-ass mouth to stand up."

Cade looked to see Morgan glaring at him. He'd obviously already decided Cade was guilty. It was all pomp and circumstance.

"I'm not participating in any kangaroo court," Cade said.

"You don't have a choice." Morgan waved to the man who'd kicked Cade in the ribs.

Cade got the meaning and held a palm up in submission. "Give me a minute to collect my thoughts."

He took a breath and stood slow. Despite the tenuous nature of their situation he felt confident. He didn't know how things would go, but his fear was replaced with something more potent. The unfolding events were a mystery, but he was confident he could handle the ordeal. Morgan looked twitchy, and Cade wondered if this was what Fey had tried to explain when they sat on the bridge in Jarbidge a few days earlier. Sensing the dynamics, Cade took control.

"Are you keeping a transcript?"

"Grand jury proceedings are kept in strict confidence."

"I'll participate on condition we build a record. If you've got a good case, that should be appealing. There's a digital recorder in the top left drawer."

The older brother didn't respond. He surveyed the dozen people crammed into the office and then quietly pulled the drawer open and took out a small digital voice recorder. He fumbled with it a moment until he found a button that made a small red light come to life. He put it on the desk and initiated the proceeding by reciting the Fifth Amendment as he had before, then continued with a small speech.

"The labors of a few have always protected the freedoms of the many, and the many continue expecting liberty when they deserve serfdom."

He cleared his throat.

"And then we have people like some of our defendants today, who work to actively suppress life, liberty and the pursuit of happiness by indoctrinating our land using a Marxist model. Turning private property into public land—folks, that's the first plank of the Communist Manifesto.

"The founding fathers of this great nation paid a high price to set up a system that allows Americans to preserve their freedoms, and we must pay a price to maintain them now.

"It has never been easy, but for those who survive the coming battles, peace without the stench of tyranny will be sweet. Throughout history, no matter how dire the circumstances, the patriots—with God's help—have always prevailed."

He looked at Cade and pointed to an area beside the desk. "Stand over here."

Cade moved as instructed and stood beside the desk as if behind a witness stand. Morgan sat at Cade's desk like a judge.

"State your full name, age and occupation for the record."

"Cade Anthony Rigens, 52, Acting Chief Ranger for the United States Park Service's Boise unit."

"Where are you from?"

"Born and raised in Hollsopple, Pennsylvania where my family's been working as coal miners, steel workers, farmers and ministers for at least three generations. My dad's the first in the family to go to college."

Cade saw subtle surprise crawl onto Morgan's face. Imagining Cade as a small-town son of miners and ministers couldn't have been what Morgan expected.

"When did you start working for the National Park Service?"

"I came on as a smoke jumper in 1985 and based out of West Yellowstone. It's hard work, and my body couldn't take it forever, so I trained to become a pilot and flew about fifteen years. I quit six years ago and landed an office job with the Park Service. One thing led to another and here I am being interrogated about pushing pencils for the government."

"You do a lot more than push pencils. What's your job involve?"

"I'm sort of a liaison between on-the-ground work and the political process. First and foremost—and I want to make sure this is clear—I am not here to advocate for a new national park, but to manage this historic property and provide support to the people who are actually deliberating the park."

"You don't advocate for the park?"

"Look, my job clearly depends on the existence of national parks and the National Park Service, but no, I don't really care if this park succeeds or fails. It's been my job to provide staff support to the people making those decisions."

"Do you think the public land in question merits national park status?"

"Absolutely. The canyons of the Bruneau, Jarbidge and Owyhee rivers are remote, stunning and practically unheard of. The region has a unique history that ties the story of Native Americans and European settlement—including Basque immigration—together. It's an unparalleled opportunity for designation and protection."

"But you're not an advocate?"

"I know that may be tough for you to understand. I have incentives that come from the bureaucratic and political processes, but I am not an advocate for the sake of advocacy—or, to use your vernacular, for the sake of locking up the land. I would agree that the whole country can't be tied up as a national park or wilderness area. At the same time, the whole country shouldn't be available for oil, gas and mineral exploration, or to run cattle or sheep. There's got to be balance."

"Whose job is it to strike balance? Is that your job?"

"No, that's the job of the people. In theory, it should be all people of the United States because the land belongs to all of them. In this case, though, it's six NGO groups representing diverse interests. It's far from perfect, but this collaborative approach has proved successful in other places."

"You mean six groups will decide what to do with land that rightfully belongs to the states?"

"I didn't say the system's perfect. There's no way six lone groups can represent all of America's interests. But I'd also disagree with you that our lands belong to the states. That's been established by legal scholars smarter than you and me many times."

Morgan thumbed his lip, apparently satisfied he was making headway with his argument.

"Is it part of your job as acting chief ranger in Boise to examine potential property acquisitions for the new park?"

"It is."

"When did you become interested in federal acquisition of the Diamond D Ranch?"

He saw Fey lean into the pregnant pause that followed.

"The Diamond D Ranch was officially determined a low priority acquisition."

Fey let out an audible gasp. Others in the room looked surprised, too.

"That's not true, though, is it?" Morgan pressed.

"If you're asking why a condemnation notice showed up a few days ago, I'm afraid I only have suspicions."

"You mean to tell me you're in charge and don't know where the notice came from?"

"I might know where it came from. As of this morning I might also know why. Just to be clear, though, I'd be speculating."

"We already know why; it's to put ranchers out of businesses and add their land to the federal register to make way for the park."

"Maybe not."

Those gathered in the room showed expressions that ranged from surprise to disbelief.

"Explain yourself," Morgan said.

"About a year ago the federal government reprioritized a list of what it calls 'strategic minerals.' They're basically minerals deemed high priorities for military or economic reasons—sometimes both. We've been working within the framework of that shift because we've been cataloguing old mines that fall within the park's boundaries. We wouldn't be allowed to close any mines containing strategic minerals, and that's the work I hired the young man, Miles Fourney, to do. In our surveys we didn't come up with any strategic minerals—or so I thought. Miles might have stumbled onto something he never told me about."

"Why would he do that?"

"I don't know, but I think I know someone who does."

"Don't shift blame."

"Who in this room knows or has talked with the governor's chief of staff, Rachel Simplex?" Cade asked.

He now had full control. Nobody moved, apparently nervous about Morgan's reaction, but Morgan proved curious as well and rolled his arm to encourage their answers. About half of the militiamen raised their hands, as did Andy Jim and Amaia.

"I think Miles Fourney knew her, too," Cade whispered.

There was an awkward, inward pause as everyone appeared to think back through their interactions with the woman.

"So, some of us know Ms. Simplex," Morgan said. "What does any of this have to do with strategic minerals?"

"It's about antimony, a mineral frequently found alongside gold ore. Everyone knows Jarbidge was rich in gold, but it looks like there's anti-mony, too, especially in the Lost Sheepherder Mine, which we now know is on Fey's ranch."

A wave of chatter rolled across the room, Fey's voice rising above it all.

"What the hell are you talking about?" she shouted. "There's no mine on my property. Everything we found pointed to the high peaks and the old tunnels."

The chatter continued. Paul lifted a hand to his temple. Amaia shrugged in confusion. Andy Jim looked thoughtful.

"I knew it was weird, but I didn't know why until this morning when Andy and I went in there to get the plane. Fey, that rock outcrop where you park your plane is the Lost Sheepherder Mine, already stripped of its gold generations ago."

FIFTY-FOUR

Rachel Simplex pinched the lapels of her blouse and fluffed the white fabric, passing a little air in an attempt to dry her sweat-damp skin. When the guys from the plateau went into the federal offices with shovels on their shoulders like they were marching into war, Rachel had been dragged by the elbow to a building where the governor and other dignitaries were being kept from harm's way. After half an hour of persuading the governor's security detail, she made her way back to the street where she found herself stuck in a sweaty mass of bodies under a full glare of sun about a block from the Park Service offices.

She muscled into the shade of a nearby tree and paused to marvel at how well it had all gone. She hadn't told them what to do, but the actions of the ranchers and militiamen were sure to draw attention from around the world. She pulled a cell phone from her briefcase and checked the social media feeds of several prominent newspapers. "Specter of Federal Land Takeover Triggers Citizen Revolt," "Shovel Brigade Turns Tide in National Park Dispute," "Domestic Terrorists Take Over Federal Offices."

They weren't all perfect headlines, but the issue was trending, and that would achieve the intended goal. Legends of the Basques National Park would be a figment of anyone's imagination soon enough, and Hardrock Holdings would assume comfortable control of a strategic mineral deposit that nobody knew existed.

Rachel felt a bubble of pride swell in her chest. It wasn't just the right thing to do; it was god damned patriotic. She was watching out for national security. She was watching out for corporate health. It was her job to make sure the nation stayed strong and that people served whatever higher purpose they were meant for. That sometimes included using her boss and the power of his office to get what she knew was right.

The patriots from the plateau did their jobs well, and while they had pure intentions, they didn't always see the big picture. They fought for individual liberty while failing to see that maintaining it required overlords to defend it. They fought against taxes without acknowledging that government spending propped up every damn business in the nation. Rachel wanted them engaged, but distracted. She needed them at the voting booth and at pertinent meetings—and sometimes visible to the media—and then she needed them to go back to their internet chat rooms.

She dialed a number and put the phone to her ear.

"Nice job, Corporal," she said. "The park should die an abrupt death and the land transfer should slip through. Can you get out of there?"

She frowned as she listened.

"Look, you can't get arrested. You'll compromise our progress and blow my cover. Your work is done. There's an old tunnel linking the Basque Block with other parts of the city. Find it, move and meet in my office at the statehouse as soon as you can.'"

She listened again.

"Fine, but don't take too long."

FIFTY-FIVE

THE CITIZEN GRAND JURY PROCEEDINGS ground to a stop while Morgan held a cell phone to his ear and talked in a clipped tone. Cade listened to Morgan's side of the conversation with mounting interest.

"I'm not leaving. I've got indictments to deliver. Sergeant, why aren't you coming here?"

Cade held his breath. Had Morgan just called someone sergeant? He was clearly talking with a person who had helped orchestrate the day's events.

Morgan nodded, his face turning red.

"I need at least thirty minutes, probably closer to an hour."

He nodded again.

"Okay. Yeah. Right."

He hung up, and Paul stepped forward.

"You're leaving?" Paul asked.

"I'm not going anywhere."

"Who was that?"

"Nobody important."

Morgan looked around the room to see who was listening. They all were.

"Let's get things back on track," Morgan said, ignoring his brother. "Where were we?"

"You were wondering about antimony," Cade said.

"Right, what the hell is antimony?" Morgan growled, grabbing the ingot from the desk and examining it as if answers would appear printed on its side. He seemed less tethered by the moment.

Cade reached into his pocket and produced the rock he'd collected next to the airplane that morning.

"Fey, someone's been digging core samples on your property. One punched through the ceiling of your hangar. I broke this off the rocks there this morning."

He extended the rock so everyone could see, then handed it to Fey.

"That gray stuff is stibnite, which is about seventy percent antimony. It's a mineral that wasn't as valuable a hundred years ago. It's used for a bunch of things—batteries, suppressing fires, hardening other minerals like bullets and shrapnel, for example. The global supply mostly comes from China, a country that limits its export, so it doesn't take a rocket scientist to see why it'd been labeled a 'strategic mineral.'"

A few of the men in the room nodded, and Cade knew he had their attention a little longer.

"That also makes it more valuable."

They nodded again.

"The point is, I think the governor's office has been using the national park as cover for acquisition of the Diamond D, which appears to be rich in antimony. Either that or they discovered antimony while compiling the park proposal and are now blowing it all up to facilitate further exploration."

Cade studied the older brother, whose red face had begun to sweat. He stood from the desk and paced the wall. The grand jury clearly hadn't gone as he envisioned. The digital recorder's red light pierced the room.

"The government doesn't run mines," Fey blurted.

"But Hardrock Holdings does," Cade said.

"I saw that name on the side of a box of Constitutions just this morning."

"It's the United States Constitution for God's sake," Morgan said. "I should damn well hope our corporations are run by God-fearing Americans."

"I don't think they're distributing them to initiate a wave of patriotism," Cade said.

"That's right," Amaia joined. "My boss told me about these particular Constitutions a few days ago. They're annotated with footnotes that skew the document's meaning."

"They're being used to sow seeds of division and create a distraction, this very distraction," Cade said, "while the mining company makes a play to acquire private property."

"So what if Hardrock Holdings wants the ranch?" Fey blurted. "Morgan and Paul told me it might never have belonged to my family to begin with."

Cade reached into his pocket and produced the documents he'd found with Miles' body.

"Thanks to the brothers here, I found what was left of Miles Fourney in the mountains last night. He had a letter and deed from 1916 in his back pocket. According to the letter, the original owner homesteaded the Diamond D Ranch instead of filing a mineral claim under the Mining Act like he should have. He says the point was to cover up existence of the Lost Sheepherder Mine. This man, Ishman Oneko, signed the letter 'The Lost Sheepherder.'"

"Where'd you get that," Fey shot.

"I think the question is: Where did Miles Fourney get it? He had the letter and deed with him when he died."

Paul lifted both hands to his forehead while Cade extended the letter to Fey. She scanned the lines and shook her head. She read aloud the words of a man attempting to relay a gold mine to his son.

She looked at Andy Jim.

"Does this make sense to you? The ranch was passed down from grandma's side of the family, but Marko is our flesh and blood, too. Is it possible that one of our ancestors stole it from the other? That it's both stolen and rightfully ours?"

Andy and Fey leaned against the wall together, Andy twirling his mustache while Fey exhaled long and steady.

"It's possible," she continued. "But, shit, I mean, shit. What's it matter? The damned government's gonna take it."

Amaia had mostly watched the proceedings with an expression of passive disinterest, her cheek still swollen and lips smeared with dried blood, but something in Fey's remark lifted her from her contemplative silence.

"You mean the government took it," she said.

The whole room rotated toward her. Cade hurried toward Fey to soften the blow.

"It already happened," Amaia went on. "Cade, you know that, right? She was planning to finish the park this weekend and set it all in stone. For all we know, that already happened. Federal acquisition of your ranch might be a reality at this point."

"What did you say?" Fey's hands trembled.

Cade sat next to her and put a hand on her arm.

"The park might already be done," Amaia said.

"Probably not," Cade joined.

"But maybe," Amaia said.

"Possibly," Cade said.

"Were you going to tell any of us about that?" Fey nearly shouted.

"It all happened pretty fast."

"When did you know?"

Cade paused.

"When?"

"The morning after you showed up here at the office. For what it's worth, I was against it."

Fey's body trembled. Her fists were clenched into little balls and tears dripped down her cheeks. Her agitation plain from across the room, Paul approached with a handgun he'd pulled from the waistline of his pants.

"Leave her alone," he said, looking at Cade. "You've put her through enough."

Fey suddenly became very sober.

"Paul, put that thing away. You're better than him. I'm sorry for what we've been through, but he's leading you down the wrong path."

Morgan stepped into the middle of the room.

"Better than who?" he asked, his voice elevated. "Than me? You're saying Paul is better than me? That I'm misguided?" His voice rose as his questions turned into shouts. "You think I'm misguided?"

Morgan walked toward her and raised an arm, but Paul's voice caught him short.

"No, you don't."

The gun had pivoted away from Cade and toward his brother, whose arm was still raised, ready to strike.

"Paul, no," Fey said again, her eyes big white circles. "You're better than him. Just put the gun down."

With those words, Morgan's fist fell hard across her forehead, but there was hardly any time to respond. In the next instant Cade heard the empty blunt click of Paul's gun. He'd pulled the trigger aimed at his older brother, but the gun hadn't fired. He pulled the trigger again, and again it clicked on an empty chamber.

The following seconds unfolded in slow motion. Morgan turned with fire in his eyes, leveled his weapon at his brother's chest and fired. The impact threw Paul backward. He slid down the wall leaving a red streak against the map of Property F, the Diamond D Ranch, the place he'd worked so hard to protect, the one place he'd ever felt truly at home.

Fey shrieked in surprise and confusion and rushed to his crumbling figure. She took his head in her lap and used her fingers to comb the hair across his forehead. Paul coughed, his breaths gurgling, his lungs drowning in the pooling of his blood.

"I'm sorry, Paul," she said. "I'm sorry about Tanner. I'm sorry about us. I love you. I still love you. It was just too hard."

"I didn't kill that boy," Paul gurgled.

His breathing was labored, his body clenched in a fit of coughs and spasms.

"I didn't kill that boy in the mountains. Just wanted to protect the ranch."

Cade watched the man's eyes glaze, his inner stew of jealousy and sincerity evaporating into an atmosphere of hate and confusion.

The life faded and flickered, and then his eyes were empty.

FIFTY-SIX

THE HOT-WHITE FLARE OF EMOTION PASSED, and Morgan Dunham wiped the back of his hand across his beard. Cade's jaw was agape. Here were brothers killing each other over land neither of them owned and a woman neither was involved with.

"Everyone sit still!" Morgan shouted waving his gun at nobody and everybody. "Do not move! I need to think!"

Fey sat with Paul's head in her lap. Andy had his arms around her. Amaia huddled near the door to the basement. They heard a rush of footsteps outside the windows. An onslaught of police and National Guard troops would stream into the office any minute, but Morgan appeared even less tethered. He staggered side to side, fire burning in his eyes. He went to the desk, grabbed the gold block and leather-bound journal, stuffed them in Miles Fourney's orange backpack and went to the basement steps where he tugged Amaia by her shirt collar.

"Stand up," he said and waved his gun around the room. "Come on! Stand up! Stand up!"

Amaia did as she was told, and Morgan shoved her into the stairway leading to the underground.

"I'll kill this woman if any of you follow," he said and tugged the backpack over his shoulders before turning into the basement.

Another young person Cade had mentored was now in harm's way. Things were different, though. Inaction wasn't a choice. He grabbed Paul's gun from the floor and opened the chamber to find it empty.

"Here," he heard. Fey extended a palm full of bullets. "You'll need these if that gun's gonna do you any good." She choked back a sob.

Cade loaded the bullets into the revolver, and snapped the barrel shut. He grabbed the digital recorder from the desk and went for the basement steps.

He wasn't surprised to find the basement empty. He went to the cinder-block opening where he'd arrived with the cowboy, and found both flashlights missing. Undeterred, he crawled into the darkness and scuffled into the adjacent building's basement. The space was lit from cracks in the floorboards but nobody was there. Morgan had continued farther into the tunnels.

Cade found the other hidden door ajar and went through to the ore cart tracks at the bottom of the steps. He heard footsteps ebbing into the darkness where the tracks curved north. He followed quietly, feeling more than seeing and moving slow as a result. When he arrived at the cinder-block wall he and the cowboy had passed, he crouched to listen and look. A faint light ebbed in the dark.

He followed and entered an unfamiliar part of the labyrinth, continuing even when the flashlights vanished. After a few hundred yards the tunnel dead-ended, and some light sprinkled in from above. Cade found a large door in the west wall. He pushed, and it creaked open on oversized hinges. He went into a softly-lit room built from huge, stacked stones. A ladder climbed twenty feet to another wood panel. He went up and drove his shoulder into it until it rotated against a wall.

He poked his head through and discovered a dust pan and broom next to a yellow plastic bucket and a mop. It was a rather ordinary-looking custodian's closet. He pushed himself up, stepped over the bucket and opened the door. He'd arrived in a hall with marbled floors and ceilings, a place he immediately recognized—the Garden Level of the state's power center, the state Capitol itself. Footsteps echoed among polished surfaces, and he tracked them to a staircase across the room. He followed and crossed a mural showing a miner on the right and a woman holding scales on the left. The miner represented the state's chief industry of the day, the woman with scales represented justice.

Cade went up the stairs to the Capitol's ground level where a compass rose was inlaid in the marble floor at the building's center. Above the rose was a circular balcony and the open air of the capitol rotunda two-hundred feet above where the American and Idaho state flags were draped.

It was outside normal business hours, but the capitol was open to tourists. If the doors were unlocked, Morgan might easily escape and be lost to the city. Cade went to the center of the compass rose and looked up, his ears alert for the sound of hurried feet. He heard them going up another level. A sense of desperation welled up inside him. He ran.

At the top of the stairs, he arrived in the main visitors' lobby. He hurried to the three sets of double doors at the main entrance and looked out. Some kids on the front sidewalk pushed a replica of the Liberty Bell until it dinged, the ringing clearly audible in the vaulted stone halls where he stood. He turned to the marbled central dome where eight Corinthian columns circled the rosette. Hallways led east and west to executive branch offices and more white marble stairs ascended to legislative chambers and the room where he'd had a private meeting with Rachel Simplex a few days before. Morgan and Amaia were out of sight, and Cade didn't know which way to turn. He went toward the center of the building so he could see and hear as far in every direction as he could. He took a deep breath and slowed his pulse. The building smelled clean and polished. Sounds, even small, like the flushing of a far-off toilet were easy to hear. He strained his ears, and then a clatter grabbed his attention. He looked up to the third-floor balcony and saw Morgan near a stone banister, his gun aimed down. Cade lunged behind one of the marble columns as a crack filled the hall and echoed through its chambers.

"I told you I'd kill this woman if you follow," Morgan said. "Don't test me further."

Cade closed his eyes, feeling once again like he was at the controls, flying blind through the smoke, unable to command the outcome. For six years he'd learned to look away and pretend it hadn't happened. Something in him had changed, though.

"Go ahead and kill her," he called from behind the column and immediately began to move.

"This is a government of the people, by the people, for the people," Morgan said. "Jefferson and Adams wrote that states can rebel when the federal government surpasses its constitutional grounds . . ."

While Morgan talked, Cade went to the staircase and inched his way to the next level. When he arrived, he was behind Morgan and saw that he held Amaia behind the neck with one hand and aimed his gun down to where Cade had been moments before. Morgan's speech had concealed the noise of Cade's movement.

"The federal government thinks it can come in here and tell us what to do, how to do it," Morgan continued. "We know this land. We have God-given rights to the land. We're restoring balance."

Cade interrupted, the pistol in both hands. Morgan didn't move, and Cade said. "If anyone has a right to the land out there it's people like Fey and her uncle who've been working on it for generations. I love this country and its laws. It's not perfect, but it's the best system of self-governance in the world. You're twisting the meaning of those laws to serve yourself."

Morgan turned, his big hand still on the back of Amaia's neck.

"You betrayed your sister-in-law over the dirt under her boots and murdered your brother because he loved a strong-headed woman. They trusted you, Morgan. We might disagree about how to interpret our nation's laws, but you've broken the most basic laws of humanity. You cast love aside, betrayed your family and murdered an innocent kid."

Morgan kept turning, his torment plain on his wrinkled forehead.

"Stop," Cade said. "Don't move another inch."

But Morgan knew Cade would be uncomfortable with a gun and turned until they were face to face. It was like their first meeting along the Jarbidge River, only this time they were armed and Amaia was caught in the balance.

Morgan was right to call his bluff, but with a little luck he might be able to take Amaia out of the equation.

"Sorry kid," he said and squeezed the trigger. Amaia crumbled to the floor, and Morgan ran sideways, firing three times. Cade ducked behind a marble railing as slivers of stone rained down the back of his neck, and then he heard the gun's mechanics click on an empty chamber. He heard it again and knew Morgan was out of ammunition. He peered from behind the railing. Morgan heaved the gun, which hit the wall and clattered down the stairs. Then Morgan ran toward the upper staircase, which led to the House and Senate galleries and the building's fourth floor.

Cade scrambled to Amaia.

"You shot me," she yelled, her eyes furious.

"I saved you," Cade said. He bent to look at her thigh where her chino slacks were soaked with blood. "I tried to knick you."

The bullet had gone through the fleshiest part of her thigh, but it didn't look like it had hit an artery. Cade heard glass smash on the fourth floor above and scrambling feet on the ground floor below. The gunshots had already drawn attention from security crews and police.

"I think you'll be okay. Use some direct pressure. I need to stay on top of this guy." Cade handed the pistol to Amaia. "If he comes back, defend yourself."

Once again, Cade followed Morgan up a flight of stairs and this time arrived at the top floor. He looked high into the capitol dome where eight huge columns circled the upper balcony. He passed two sculptures on the south side of the building and went into Statuary Hall where he and Rachel had their private meeting four days before. There was a shattered window next to the door with an electric keypad lock and a sign declaring "AUTHORIZED PERSONNEL ONLY."

Cade reached through the broken glass and turned the doorknob, then entered a part of the Capitol few people ever saw. He went up another marble staircase, arriving in a room lit only by a circular window to the west. The walls were unfinished brick with crumbled chinking. They were scrawled with hundreds of names and dates, some of the dates going back a hundred years. On the far wall was another glass-paned door and two large windows that revealed another set of stairs. Cade continued his pursuit up the stairs and found himself in a tight, brick-lined corridor that wound in a circle around the dome's base. He ran the circumference, becoming frantic that he might lose Morgan in the dizzying array of ladders, stairs and corridors. Then he noticed an open door at the top of another staircase, this one made of unrefined metal. He felt hot wind puff from the door and continued into daylight.

He was on a small walkway behind the columns that ringed the outside of the upper dome. Not many of Boise's buildings were as tall as the Capitol, and he easily peered into the streets where police cruisers closed in, their lights flicking and sirens blaring.

He ran along the outside of the dome and found still another metal staircase. He grabbed the railing and hurled himself toward the sky, arriving at a door that went back into the building, back into the dome's high vaulted ceiling. He entered and looked around. He was on the spiral staircase that wound in a tight knot, the same set of stairs that captured his imagination earlier that week before his coalition meeting about the park.

He wound upward into the dome's vaulted ceiling and found Morgan panting at the top, his chest heaving with the effort of his climb. He was hunched over, his hands on two metal railings, Miles Fourney's orange backpack still on his shoulders.

Cade looked around. The upper reaches of the dome were made entirely of metal girders and walkways. There was a large blue disk painted with gold stars suspended from the ceiling. Below it was the capitol dome's oculus, an opening about twenty feet in diameter, and it hovered over two-hundred feet of open air.

"I don't know how you didn't die in the mine," Morgan said. "But your luck has run out."

They were the words of a man with nothing else to lose.

Morgan lunged, and Cade pivoted onto the catwalk.

Morgan continued his advance.

Cade retreated until he felt the railing on the small of his back. With nowhere else to go, he attacked.

Morgan blocked, parried and grabbed Cade by his shirt, easily lifting him in the air.

Cade tasted blood in his mouth and felt the fabric of his shirt ripping around the chest and armpits, then felt his weight swing like a pendulum toward the railing and open air of the oculus. He grasped at the only thing he could think, and that was the orange backpack straps still fastened around Morgan's shoulders.

He pulled backward, and the big man lost his balance, dropping Cade to the catwalk as their momentum swung.

Cade kicked, and Morgan fell backward. He shook off the impact, charged, and Cade's world tipped over. He grasped at the railing to arrest himself, but it broke from its base. The railing bent and swung. Cade's feet dangled into the open air. His fingers still open sores, he was barely conscious of anything except the gravity that tugged at his legs. If he fell this time, there would be no ledge to catch him, no matches to light, no ladder to climb.

He looked up at the catwalk, where Morgan paced left and right, talking as much to himself as to Cade.

"These are the times that try men's souls," he said. "Those who expect to reap the blessings of freedom must, like men, undergo the fatigue of supporting it."

He seemed to be thinking aloud, rationalizing, uncertain and untethered at the same time. Morgan bent and picked up a scrap of metal that had broken from the handrail, leaned over and swung at Cade's fingers. Cade felt some of his bones break and cried out in pain, but held as firm as he could. Morgan repositioned in an attempt to swing the pipe at Cade's other hand. This was it, Cade thought. He was out of time. He closed his eyes and searched himself for inner calm. As his pulse slowed, the words came back.

"Live each day with courage, take pride in your work, finish what you start, do what has to be done."

Morgan had repositioned himself poorly, so Cade had a whisker of time in which to move. He inched his hands toward an intact part of the broken railing. Morgan moved closer and swung again. Cade let go with one hand. Morgan missed, and Cade grasped at the pipe.

"Be tough but fair, keep your promises, talk less and say more."

Morgan crouched low and pushed his head and shoulders through the opening where Cade clung. He reached out to pry at Cade's fingers one by one.

"Remember some things aren't for sale, ride for the brand, know where to draw the line."

Cade knew the man was tired. He knew that, suspended over hundreds of feet of open air, he would have the upper hand. With Morgan still in a crouch, Cade reached up and grabbed one of the orange backpack straps.

Morgan lost his footing, flipped into the oculus and caught himself on the broken railing, hanging from the same bar. Without the menace of his attacker above, Cade clawed back onto the catwalk and reached down to help the big man who'd killed his brother a half hour before. Morgan's eyes had gone dark.

"You'll never know what happened to that kid in the mountain," he said and let go.

He was there, and then he wasn't. He fell face up through the open air of the capitol dome until he became ensnared by the wire that suspended the huge American flag. It flipped him upside down and yanked him sideways into the Idaho colors. Then the wires holding both flags broke, and Morgan flapped like a streamer in a mishmash of navy blue, red, white and blue through the open air of the Idaho State Capitol.

The wires whistled through the dome as Morgan fell, but before he hit the floor they snapped taught with a twang. The big man groaned and looked up, the disgust plain in his eyes, as he dangled like a marionette, the flags falling in a gentle pile on the floor behind him.

"I don't need to know," Cade said to everyone and no-one, his syllables echoing in the emptiness of the dome.

He looked down through the open air to see a pair of familiar eyeballs beside an enormous Corinthian column on the capitol's fourth-floor balcony. It was Rachel Simplex. Sergeant Rachel Simplex. For how long she'd been watching, Cade could only guess.

For thirty seconds or more Cade looked back. Then without a word, wave or discernible expression of any kind Simplex turned and went toward the marble stairs.

FIFTY-SEVEN

CADE RETRACED HIS PATH THROUGH the capitol dome to the main level where he found paramedics tending to Amaia, and Morgan Dunham being untangled from the Idaho and American flags and taken into police custody. Cade went to Amaia and knelt.

"Have you ever shot a gun before?" she asked.

"Not since I was a kid."

"You could have killed me."

Cade looked at the paramedic wrapping Amaia's leg in gauze and an ACE bandage.

"Is she good to go?" he asked.

"She's been hit by a bullet; she needs to go to the hospital."

Cade turned to her.

"I need help, Amaia. You heard me in the office. Morgan Dunham didn't organize this himself."

She sighed and propped onto her elbows. "What do you need?"

"Everything just unraveled for Rachel Simplex. She'll try to cover her tracks."

"Help me up; I'll do what I can."

"Ma'am," the paramedic said, but Amaia waved him off and extended her hand toward Cade, who pulled her to her feet.

"a loopie."

CADE PEERED THROUGH A GLASS WINDOW and found the reception area of

format / printing error.

the Idaho governor's office empty. The door should have been locked, but it opened silent on heavy, well-greased hinges, and he went in.

From the main lobby, he heard the soft electrical buzz of a machine working somewhere within the suite's network of offices and meeting rooms. He went slow toward the noise.

He passed the room with the spider plant where he'd had the meeting with collaborative participants earlier that week, past the governor's office, and into the open doorway where the noise originated.

Two figures were hunched over a desk. Simplex stared at a monitor and clicked the buttons of a mouse, and a man in wire-rim glasses plunged pages through a humming paper shredder. Neither noticed Cade.

"Stan Hubbard, right? Hardrock Holdings," Cade started. "I should have known this would be a long week when you showed up at the collaborative meeting on Wednesday."

Both figures turned and looked at him.

"Was the collaborative ever real?" Cade asked. "Or was bringing everyone together to sing kumbaya just a distraction?"

Rachel took a breath, her eyes scanning the room for options.

"How long have you been setting the park up to fail, Rachel?"

"It's about national security," Simplex spat. "You wouldn't understand."

"Try me."

She looked toward the door and back at Hubbard.

"Stan, you should probably go," she said, but Cade blocked the way.

"Morgan Dunham gave me a United States history lesson before he fell into the capitol dome. He feels like he's fighting a noble cause and seemed to want to die rather than be taken into custody. Those annotated Constitutions he's been passing around are skewing what it means to love your country, and they're sowing seeds of division among neighbors. They're being distributed by Hardrock Holdings, so I think Stan should stay."

Simplex took another deep breath.

"Morgan isn't too different from a lot of Americans," Cade continued. "People want to do good by their country, and they're looking for leadership about how to do that. You led Morgan astray."

"Morgan was a good soldier. Not the sharpest tool in the shed, though. He took things too far."

"So, you didn't think it was a good idea for a militia to take over federal property?"

She didn't answer, and Cade understood her quiet to represent complicity.

"There's someone else who got tangled in your web, and he's dead. Miles Fourney asked questions that got him killed. Questions you told him to ask. Questions that made your own political operatives target him with anti-government rage."

"Miles Fourney's disappearance was tragic," she said, "but I didn't know him."

Cade measured her for the slightest indication she was lying but found her composure mannequin-like.

"I think you did," he said.

He reached into the orange backpack and pulled out Miles' leather-bound journal, flipping the pages and pausing for effect when he found what he sought.

"Miles was a prolific writer," Cade continued. "He wrote poetry, drew pictures, made notes about his work. I found Miles' remains in a mine last night, and he still had his journal with him. It says here you approached him about the Lost Sheepherder Mine and asked him to report only to you about what he found. Those are the questions that got him killed."

"I don't have to listen to this," she said and looked again toward the door.

Cade filled the opening with his shoulders.

"What are you two doing in here, anyway?" he asked. "Deleting files? Shredding documents? Don't you have anything better to do on a Saturday afternoon?"

He reached to the stack of paper Stan Hubbard was working to shred and pulled a page off the top. It was a copy of an email communication between Simplex and executives at Hardrock Holdings and laid out, in part, her plan to undermine the park and facilitate federal condemnation proceedings.

"I never liked the idea of a new national park," Rachel began, "but I was willing to do my job. Right up to the point when we found strategic minerals out there. Yeah, Miles Fourney helped me locate antimony at the Diamond D Ranch, but you sent him out there to begin with. That kid's blood is on your hands."

"You stoked the fire on the plateau," Cade countered. "You pitted neighbors against each other and made them question one another's ideas about what it means to be an American. That's a lot more than politics. People died."

"What would you know about duty?"

Cade heard a throat clear over his shoulder. He glanced into the hall-way and saw Amaia.

"We're ready," she said and limped through the open door leading to the conference room.

Cade turned back to Simplex and Hubbard.

"I might not have served in the military like you and Morgan, but I went to war in our woods for thirty years to defend the West's people and communities from wildfires. I also know that when it comes to hard con-versations, the people of this nation have a duty to come together and talk. That's the cornerstone of the collaborative process where you listen, find consensus and forge shared paths. That's how our democracy operates and what it means to be American. It's about building community, not tearing it apart. It's about uniting, not dividing. One nation. Indivisible. Liberty and justice for all. That's our duty as Americans."

Cade took a breath and motioned toward the door. "There's something I'd like to show the two of you."

With nowhere to go, Simplex scooped up the pile of paper beside the shredder and put it in a briefcase, then followed Cade down the hall into the conference room. Simplex and Hubbard stopped short with surprise when they saw the crowd that had assembled. Seated at the table was Governor McGown accompanied by the diverse participants of the national park collaborative. They represented farmers, native Americans, environmen-talists, miners, ranchers, Basques and government—the group that had met once a month for two years to find and build consensus that would be taken to Congress and ratified as law. Amaia and a police officer in a navy-blue uniform leaned against the wall.

Simplex took a step backward, but once again Cade blocked her path. A voice came from the table.

"I hear you've been busy, Rachel. Why don't you take a load off and tell us about how you sat in this room with these good people and encouraged them to find common ground while you circumvented the whole process," the Governor said.

Caught in the headlights of her own undoing, it was the first time Cade had ever seen Rachel shrink back or at a loss for words. Her lower lip moved, but no words emerged.

"I think I can help," Cade said. He stepped forward, placed the digital recorder at the center of the table and pressed the play button.

α This doesent comport — after what happened at Basque Center.

For the next hour the group sat and listened as the device recounted Morgan Dunham's citizen grand jury proceeding, the frantic chase into the capitol dome and then Rachel Simplex's incriminating conversation with Cade.

The collaborative participants didn't say what they were thinking, but they didn't have to. They leaned forward with curiosity while they heard Cade's explanation about discovery of the Lost Sheepherder Mine and antimony. They squirmed at the sound of gunshots that culminated the citizen grand jury proceeding. Their foreheads crinkled with concern when Simplex admitted to stoking conflict on the plateau to undermine the national park and usher strategic minerals into a mining company's portfolio.

Having heard enough, Governor McGown didn't wait for the recording to end and leaned forward, raising his voice.

"You always impressed me, Rachel: your military background, work for the mining industry, quick wit, tough demeanor. You're just about everything a governor could hope for—except honest or ethical. I'm not sure if the charges will stick, but I'm asking these officers to take you into custody as an accessory to murder. Even if they don't stick, you've worked in politics for the last time."

A vein pulsed across his temple as the governor turned to Stand Hubbard.

"And you'd better get out of here before I lose my temper."

McGown leaned back as the officer in blues placed Simplex under arrest and nudged her through the door. Stan Hubbard followed as the recording arrived at its conclusion: words Cade had spoken to Simplex just an hour before.

"One nation. Indivisible. Liberty and justice for all. That's our duty as Americans."

FIFTY-EIGHT

AMAIA IBARRA FELT THE MUSIC BEFORE SHE SAW IT, a familiar melody that resonated at the core of who she was. She limped around a corner and went into the surging scrum that had converged on Boise to celebrate ten-thousand-year-old roots and the course Basques had charted in the American West.

It was twilight, a day after insurgents had taken over the culturally-rich block, since Cade had shot her in the leg. For the people celebrating, though, it was business as usual. Money, politics and career ladders were distant. Beer and wine flowed. The crowd moved as one, dancing to music with thousand-year-old roots.

Amaia stopped at a vendor's tent and ordered a kalimotxo, a half-and-half mixture of red wine and cola popular among Basques. Unlike the lore that had become her focus that week, the kalimotxo was invented by contemporary Basques sometime in the 1970s. She downed it in three big gulps, then continued around the flat-bed trailer where the band belted out a rock-n-roll version of a Basque folk song she'd known almost all her life.

She went through the white picket fence and limped beneath the Guernica oak toward the Park Service offices in the back. When she arrived in the courtyard, she found Cade and the old man named Andy Jim hunched over the archaeological dig. One of Cade's hands was heavily taped. Neither of them noticed Amaia at first. She moved close enough to hear.

"If he was buried in the Jarbidge Cemetery, what does this stone mark?" Cade asked.

"I don't think this was a grave at all," the old man said. "It looks like a gravestone, but I think it just marks the tunnels."

Amaia peeked into the pit. Andy Jim straddled a slab shaped and etched almost exactly like the one Cade had looked for in the desert, a lone eye in the center of a Lauburu, the eye, presumably of the Tartaro, the cyclops—what they now knew was a pseudonym for the Lost Sheepherder.

Amaia interjected.

"Any idea about the ore cart tracks? Why this part of town is connected underground with the Capitol?"

Both men turned.

"Maybe that's how all that gold was stored in the basement without anybody knowing," Andy Jim volunteered.

"It seems like gold would have arrived here and gone to the Capitol, not the other way around. Water flows downhill, and money flows toward politicians," Amaia said.

"I reckon that's true," Andy said, standing and brushing the dust from the thighs of his Wranglers.

"What's happening to the gold?" Amaia asked. "You may have been searching for it a long time, but it's on Park Service property."

Cade climbed out of the pit.

"Ishman, the Lost Sheepherder, he never mined it legally to begin with and then stored it on someone else's property—in a different state. The actual gold was hauled to a federal vault yesterday afternoon, but I think the answer about who owns it's gonna get caught in the courts."

Amaia put her hands on her hips and thought. Hadn't Morgan Dunham put one of the gold ingots in the backpack before fleeing to the Capitol? Hadn't Cade ended up with that backpack? She decided not to ask in front of Andy Jim.

"There's something else eating at me," she continued. "It's that phrase from the story of the Tartaro, Heben Nuk. Why'd it lead to the high peaks? What did you find up there?"

"I found a lot, and I found nothing," Cade said. "The coordinates from the deed to the ranch are worn, so if you fill it in wrong they point to the peaks. All I can figure is that Miles created his own sort of treasure map that pointed to his final resting place and not much else."

The whine of the accordion stopped, and the crowd out front cheered.

"You have a minute to talk in private?" Amaia asked Cade as the cheering subsided.

Andy Jim excused himself and went toward the street while Cade motioned for her to sit with him on the porch.

"Glad to see you can walk without crutches," he said. "Sorry about that. At the time it seemed ..."

"You could have done that differently, but I'm not here for an apology," she said.

He nodded.

"You know what's happening with Morgan Dunham or Simplex?" he asked.

"Morgan's scheduled for arraignment tomorrow. The prosecutor hasn't announced charges, but I suspect he'll stand trial for murder with the other charges being dismissed. Rachel already posted bail, and it's still not clear if the charges against her will stick. Just so you know, though, I'll no longer be an insider on police matters."

"Come again."

"I'm resigning. Things got squirrelly this week. My boss told me to stop volunteering for the park, and that was a day before I went on stage to introduce the public hearing. You know how it went from there."

"Sorry Amaia."

"Well, you know, my heart's elsewhere. Besides, I might have an offer."

He looked up. "Grad school?"

"Actually, the governor offered some help. He pulled me aside yesterday after all the mayhem at the Capitol to say thanks. He's pulling strings at the State Historical Society. That should look good on my PhD application."

Cade patted her on the shoulder. "Maybe we'll get to keep working together, you and me."

"I'd like that," she returned and patted him on the shoulder in return. "See you around, Cade."

She stood, limped around the house and went into the unfolding celebration to raise her glass high.

FIFTY-NINE

Andy Jim the third eased behind the wheel of his beige-painted pickup, gave his mustache a twirl and aimed for the Boise city limits and open road beyond.

He felt a pang of guilt at leaving without saying goodbye, but at this point also felt an intense thirst for wide-open skies and land that wasn't built-up solid with steel and concrete. A day in the city was as much as any man could take and, besides, a new adventure was about to unfold.

At the south edge of town, Andy stopped at a T intersection and considered his options. East went into the state's rugged interior, west across an ocean of sagebrush toward the coast.

He turned toward the mountains and after a few miles left the asphalt behind as he rumbled along a dirt road beside the sinewy meanders of an ice-cold stream. The sun slunk below piled-up ridges behind him, and he reached into the passenger seat and flipped his cowboy hat over to reveal an object wrapped in fresh newsprint. He tore the paper away, then felt the cool weight in his palm. He glanced down to see the engraving of a Basque Lauburu with an eye at its center and "14.7 oz." chiseled into its skin. Cade had invited him to Park Service property to talk about the archaeological dig. They'd discussed that a bit, but Cade had also passed him the news-wrapped ingot while they crouched in the pit and talked.

It wasn't the vast fortune he'd hoped for, but it was worth about six-thousand bucks and was enough to live on for a few months if he cared to sell it—but he wasn't sure he did. After so many years of searching, it felt more important to keep the actual gold instead of turning it into cold-hard cash.

He pulled to the side of the road and turned the engine off, listening to the stream trickle over its stony riverbed and a chorus of crickets pulse from the sage across the canyon.

He rewrapped the cool metal in the newsprint and buried it in the glove compartment of his truck, then pulled out a notebook and began to sketch. He drew a rectangle at the top and bottom of the page and connected them with two parallel-running lines, then labeled the rectangles: "Capitol" and "Basque Block."

Then he put a big question mark in the middle of the page.

A man was nothing if he wasn't true to himself, and Andy Jim the third had learned he was the best version of himself when he was searching. He was still a man who put family and country first, but when those bases were covered it was still a good mystery that called him the loudest.

He turned his old beige pickup south, crossed a one-lane bridge and began threading the mountains toward the southern plains and the town of Gooding, named for one of Idaho's early governors.

It was only another couple hours before he'd be returned to the Snake River Plain where the legend was alive and the promise of undiscovered treasure still called.

SIXTY

IT WAS A PERFECT FALL DAY in the high desert of far-south Idaho. The sky was blue, the riverside willows gold, a dusting of snow icing the high peaks of the central Jarbidge Mountains.

Cade Rigens rumbled up the road along the Jarbidge River behind the wheel of his Toyota pickup, windows down and the wind blowing freely across the cab. He turned onto an intersecting dirt road that climbed as the canyon narrowed. There was no sign marking the state line, but after a few miles he crossed into Nevada. A few miles later the canyon opened up on Three Creek Valley and the Diamond D Ranch.

Cade pulled in front of the main house where he found Fey Dunham sitting on her porch steps. She looked up as he parked. He stuck his arm out the window and waved. She offered a feeble wave in return.

He wore normal street clothes: a pair of worn blue jeans and an old flannel. He stepped onto the dirt where he was greeted by her border collie, Sherman, then walked across the yard beneath an autumn-gold cottonwood tree. He sat next to her and inhaled deep the scent of sagebrush and livestock.

"There's not going to be any national park," he said.

She stared out at the view stoic and silent.

"I thought that would make you happy."

"I guess it does," she said. "What happened?"

"The stunt Paul and Morgan pulled worked, I guess. Paul's death drew enormous media attention, most of it sympathetic to his cause. They pulled

a shirt

the bill and all the supporting legislation that went with it—like the land transfers, for example."

She looked at him. "You seem sort of unconcerned," she said.

"I was never really in favor of the park," he said. "I wasn't really against it, either, but coming out here with you helped me see things a little different."

He took a deep breath and measured her before continuing.

"I quit the agency last week."

She looked up a second time.

"You'd probably do more good there than most."

He'd thought a lot about it, and every time he did came back to the notion that he couldn't stand the politics any more. He'd climbed the bureaucracy's professional ladder as far as he could.

"Early retirement might suit me," he said.

"I doubt that."

He looked around and noticed the doors of her airplane hangar were gone, a giant rock overhang in their place.

"What are you doing with the Lost Sheepherder Mine?"

"I filed paperwork under the Mining Act to keep digging legally. I'll harvest antimony in a way that preserves the status quo out here, keeps the cows happy and water clean. Might make a couple bucks in the process."

Cade took a deep breath and noticed how quiet the ranch was.

"Where is everybody?" he asked.

They're off today. Things are winding down, so I sent 'em to town for some fun. Besides, it's kind of nice enjoying the quiet up here."

"It is quiet."

They stopped talking. A chorus of fall crickets surged against the basalt cliffs. The valley's creeks trickled.

"I'm sorry how things went, Fey. I'm sorry you and Paul got caught up in all that."

"There's things that can't be undone," she said. "We all choose our paths."

She said she'd spread Paul's ashes around the banks of Sanovia Creek where their son Tanner had died.

"I hope he finds peace there," she said. "He deserves it. He had a hard life."

Cade reached into the chest pocket of his flannel and pulled out the handkerchief Fey gave him in August.

"I had a friend teach me about a certain way of looking at the world. She told me it's about hard work, courage and pride. But there's part of what she taught me that I had to figure out on my own, sort of the culmination of all the different lessons. It's about faith, I think, faith that you can trust even when you can't see, faith that it all matters somehow."

She looked up at him.

"I want to give it back, kind of a reminder you don't have to do this alone."

She took the cloth and held it in her hands, nodding as she choked back mist from her eyes. Cade put a soft hand on her shoulder and looked across the road where a pile of logs was in need of splitting and stacking before winter set in.

He stood and went to the logs, picked up an axe, then turned back to see what she'd do.

She just watched for a minute, then stood and walked across the road to join him.

He bent and picked up a pair of worn leather gloves and handed them to her, grabbed another set and pulled them tight over his fingers. Then, together, they lifted their axes high and let them fall.

ACKNOWLEDGMENTS

THE HISTORIC BOISE BOARDING HOUSE USED as a United States Park Service office in this book is, in fact, owned and managed by the Basque Museum & Cultural Center, a top-notch nonprofit that celebrates Basque culture and history in Boise and throughout the region. As portrayed in this book, Basques moved to the Intermountain West around the turn of the twentieth Century and helped shape the cultural identity of the region. For continuity's sake, the Spanish spelling of Guernica was used in this book for the city, Picasso painting and tree, but I want to make mention of the preferred Basque spelling: Gernika. Thanks to the museum's Community History Project Director Patty Miller and intern Ane Uribetxebarria Azpiroz, who helped vet the legend of the Tartaro and wrangle the probable meaning and origin of the phrase, Heben Nuk. Special thanks to Miller, who taught me about the history of the old boarding house in Boise. She's a warm, gracious and deeply knowledgeable woman who I got to know during the time I rented an apartment from the museum. Also, special thanks to retired teacher Megan Overgaard who shared her knowledge and expertise about Basque culture, in particular contributing to portions of this book dealing with Basque language and dance. For more about Basque history, culture and identity in Idaho and the West, visit grstahl.com.

The public land collaborative process dramatized in this novel is based on real processes that have been used to resolve public land disputes throughout the United States. In southwest Idaho where this book is set, legislation called the Owyhee Initiative was passed by Congress in 2009 following an eight-year collaborative process. The Owyhee Initiative did not create a national park, but it implemented innovative strategies that continue to shape public land management in southwest Idaho. Thanks to all of the Owyhee Initiative's participants, who illustrated that challenges among diverse people can be overcome by building consensus and working together. For more about collaborative processes on public lands, visit grstahl.com.

Most historic events underlying this work of fiction are factual. The Legend of the Lost Sheepherder Mine is genuine folklore from the Jarbidge region, but there's nothing to indicate the story is of Basque origin or featured Basque characters. In fact, the name Ishman is most likely of Middle Eastern origin. Ben Kuhl was the first man ever convicted using a fingerprint and the last man to rob a mail stage in the old West. There is no known connection, however, between the Lost Sheepherder Mine and Kuhl's robbery. The Legend of the Tartaro is widely known in Basque and Celtic folklore. The version cited here, which uses the phrase Heben Nuk!, comes from "Basque Legends," compiled by the Rev. Wentworth Webster, M.A. and published by Griffith and Farran in London in 1879. For more about these old legends, visit grstahl.com.

Thanks also to the following people who helped make this project possible:

My wife, Wendy Jones: Thanks for believing in me, but thanks most of all for believing in us. I love you.

My parents, Jennifer and Richard Stahl: You made me read, write and go for hikes, and I'm a better man for it. Thanks for the foundation of faith, love and hard work that makes me who I am.

Chris and Larry Jones. You were two of my most valuable advocates and readers. Thanks for your love and support.

Andrea Gregg. Success is made of networks. Thanks for hooking me up.

Jennifer McCord at Coffeetown Books. Your keen eye for story made this story better.

The following people helped in ways big and small: Michael Ames, Jon Duval, Carey Arthur, Gabe Millar read drafts and gave feedback that made a clear difference. Ethan Lynn offered invaluable expertise about flying small planes. Deena Merrill-Reagle is a naming whiz.

Finally, I wouldn't be who I am as a writer without my journalism mentors and colleagues over the years. Thanks in particular to my excellent editors: Greg Moore, Greg Foley, Ken Retallic, Adam Tanous, Jennifer Pattison Tuohy and the late Ron Soble. You taught me how to report and write, and showed me how to love your work.

G.R. STAHL HAS BEEN WRITING ABOUT public land issues in the western United States for twenty-five years. His journalism has been recognized with more than fifty state, regional and national awards, and his guidebook to rafting and kayaking in Idaho is the most thorough book on the subject in publication today. A Ted Scripps Fellow in Environmental Journalism at the University of Colorado at Boulder, Stahl has studied water law, public land law, natural resources law and has a particular interest in the ways people shape and are shaped by the land and water around them. In addition to journalism, Stahl works as a marketing copywriter, policy advocate and sometimes-carpenter and tile setter. In his spare time, he kayaks, skis, mountain bikes, hikes and climbs around the Western U.S. Deception at the Diamond D Ranch is his first novel.